...tricia,

T

C000001129

enjo~ best wish~,

Best wish

C♯ xx

Element Tree

THE RECURRING MANUSCRIPTS VOLUME I

Catherine McCulloch

WILDCARD PUBLISHING
RUTLAND

*Mum, I am dedicating this book to you,
for all the love, support and inspiration you have given me.*

Chapter One

December 2009, London

It was snowing in December. London is a beautiful place, especially when there is a blanket of fresh white snow on the ground. Rik Stevenson had gone into The Coultard to view an exhibition, and although he had only been in the art gallery about an hour, there was already an inch of snow on the ground when he came out again. He stood beneath one of the huge stone arches that made up the front façade of the historic building, adjusted his scarf and buttoned up his dark grey trench coat. In this part of the city, at the end of Fleet Street, there were not many signs of the festive period. Businessmen and women rushed for the tube stations, as the streets were becoming grid-locked. People panicked to get home, as it would not be the first time the snow had caused the train service to come to a standstill. The deep snow meant long queues outside the underground station, no taxis or buses and a strong possibility once the passengers reached the mainline stations that many of the trains would not be running. Rik could see most of these people checking into hotels for the night.

As huge snowflakes fell, delicately collecting on the icy pavement, Rik put on his grey beanie hat and strode out into the dark, early afternoon. There was an unusual light, which often accompanies a heavy, snow-filled sky. The low clouds were a sepia colour, as the bright streetlights of London reflected off them. There was also an eerie subdued sound, as the falling snow muffled all noise, and with the reduced visibility as snowflakes melted on his warm cheeks, Rik imagined it would be easy to feel isolated, despite being surrounded by chaos. Whilst everyone around him rushed, desperate to get home before they got stranded, Rik sauntered towards Trafalgar Square. He was in no hurry, as the meeting was not until four, so he had time to walk up The Haymarket to Piccadilly Circus, and then up Regent Street. The huge department stores would have all their festive windows decorated, and Hamleys was a must-see experience, even though Christmas made him sick to the stomach. However, the look of excitement and amusement on children's faces as they became enchanted by the moving figures in the toy shop windows was uplifting, and reminded him of when his children were smaller. Christmas had a meaning back then, and to these poor souls, there was no reason for them to think that this might be one of their last Christmases.

Predominantly red and black stationary traffic, spewing diesel fumes poisoned a marvel of nature; small, crystal snowflakes, which themselves could cause so much mayhem. Tempers were flaring, with taxi and bus horns regularly showing signs of impatience and aggression, but there was nowhere to go, as the city festered in the building traffic fumes. Rik was warm and dry, despite the conditions. He walked past the National Gallery, and considered calling in to view the Impressionist wing, which he had visited many times before. However, even though he had plenty of time, he had to allow for a delay due to the traffic problems, so getting to Richmond might take longer than usual. He had made this trip 11 times, in the last 25 years, and things had changed. In the last quarter century not only was the increase in traffic obvious, but people's attitudes had changed too. Everyone was in such a hurry. Working, buying, sleeping. Working, buying, sleeping, day in, day out. Nobody seemed to have time to just stop. Stop and think, or stop and look around them. As he got to the top of The Haymarket and entered Piccadilly Circus, he stopped and looked up. On top of the building on the corner, 1 Jermyn Street, he smiled as he saw The Three Graces. Many tourists stood to have their photograph taken with the Horses of Helios, rearing out of the fountain built into the corner of the building at street level, but not many people ever bothered to look up. Here, they would have seen The Daughters of Helios, though the people who knew of their existence called them 'The Three Graces'. The three, gold-plated diving women, suspended from the top of the building were elegant and beautiful. Rik liked to look at them as he knew they were a secret part of London. *If only people would stop and think and look,* thought Rik, as he turned to walk past Eros.

Piccadilly Circus was its usual, hectic, jammed self, with Regent Street, Piccadilly and Shaftsbury Avenue all leading off from it. The bright lights of the illuminated billboards reflected through the falling snowflakes, turning them into a multitude of colours. One side of Piccadilly was owned by the Crown where advertising was not permitted. The regal buildings unadorned with gaudy advertising were far more appealing than the ones decorated with electronic signs. Rik squinted from the snow as he looked up at the signs, with the Sanyo sign being the longest running since the 1980s. *Gordon's Gin was the first in 1923,* thought Rik, with a certain amount of anger, *buy, this, buy that!* He stopped and pondered for a moment, watching homeless people mixing with businessmen and women, tourists and schoolchildren. Only the tourists seemed to not mind the weather, everyone else was either marching, or being frog-marched back to whatever forms of transport would take them home. Huge crowds had formed around the entrance to the tube stations, and Rik noticed station staff calmly pulling across concertina metal gates, closing the station for safety. He smiled to himself, thinking how all those people would be stressed and worried. He cared for those desperate to get home to their children, elderly relatives, or to care for the sick, but in general, he knew that if these people put a little thought into their lives, they would not be herded like sheep, as they all followed each other. They could break free from the flock, if only they would think for themselves.

It took him a while to get through the crowds by instead opting to walk up the road, as the traffic was going nowhere. The nearer to Oxford Circus he got, the people around him changed. The business folk were now predominantly tourists and shoppers, enjoying the festive snow, in stark contrast to the businessmen who were losing vast amounts of investment as industry around the country closed for the day. *Some make it all day, some spend it all day, but they all have one thing in common: money!* thought Rik. *Money, greed, consumerism. Not how Christmas was meant to be at all.* He enjoyed the bright coloured lights that were strung across the street, and the highly decorated shop windows. The fresh snow and cold temperatures meant the snow had not yet turned into a brown, dirty sludge, though once the traffic started moving, it would not be long. Street vendors sold roasted chestnuts from little heated carts, and the sweet, nutty smell was too much of a temptation. Rik's wife would not approve, *but let's face it, there are more important things to think about,* he thought, as he peeled the shell off a hot nut as he walked along.

He thought of his wife and his twin boys, at the homestead in Dorset. He had acquired the large plot of land 24 years ago, and was virtually self-sufficient. He had a massive vegetable patch and fruit trees, and a barn where his free range chickens lived luxurious lives. His barn was full of hay and straw for his animals, and sets of onions hung from the low rafters ready for use. Long shelving units ran on one side, full of jars for pickling and preserving the excess fruit and vegetables from the last harvest. The homemade labels identifying the product and the date it had been made had been hand painted, showing images rather than writing as to what the jar contained. There was also a cellar to the barn, reached via a trap door. Here, freezers also stored bags of frozen veg, which his wife had laboriously prepared, so there was no need to buy any vegetables for the winter. He thought about his two boys. At 15 years old, the homestead was an isolated, remote place, but as they had been born and grown up on the farm, the contrasting life of living in a city was alien to them. All of their needs had been met, and important values had been instilled in them from an early age. They had horses, housed in stables built at the end of the barn, and even at their young age they had mastered all of the requirements of the animals. Rik knew that by this time of day, the animals would be fed and secured into their houses, and the boys would be brushing their horses, and rugging them up for a potentially cold night, *no doubt with some rock band, Muse, maybe the Foo Fighters, blasting out!* he thought. His wife would be checking on the slow cooker, making sure the homemade stew was coming along well. He thought how idyllic it all sounded, but it was a culmination of 24 years of hard work and planning, where everything was run like a military style operation. If anything was not put back in place, or something was done at the wrong time, it could prove disastrous, especially as now the time was getting closer. Rik was confident his family would cope, and he knew he had covered every eventuality. It was just a matter of when.

To most people, Christmas is an exciting time; overeating, drinking to excess and buying useless gifts for people you hardly ever see. Of course, it is an important time for families, with young children unable to contain themselves, persuaded to be good by the threat that Santa may not come. However, the true meaning of Christmas had been long forgotten, with corporate greed becoming a priority. Every year in the news, it was all about how much money was spent in the shops. Even the true meaning of Christmas varies from person to person. To Rik, it was not a religious festival, as although he celebrated Christmas for the sake of the children, he insisted they also celebrated the Winter Solstice too. A few days before Christmas, the house was decorated with home crafted decorations. There were little wooden carvings made by the boys, ceramic ornaments made by himself, and fabric decorations made by his wife. The whole house would be decorated, with the sweet scent of pine, homemade mulled wine and cinnamon and orange decorations. Berries and branches from holly and ivy, grown in the nearby hedgerows decorated doorways and the banister rails, and hundreds of homemade tealight holders illuminated the rooms, with only the kitchen having the proper light on. There were lights in all the rooms, but Rik insisted that the celebrations should be as natural as possible. The family were already used to living their lives by the limits of nature and the weather. They got up when the sun did, and used the natural light to get things done that would be awkward by candlelight. All his hard work had paid off, and his family did not suffer the usual trappings of sibling rivalry, jealousy or neediness. They all seemed content in the world he had created. *Shame there isn't more contentment in the world* he thought, as he waited for the taxi bike he had pre-ordered.

Half an hour later, Rik was walking through Kew Gardens, just south of the River Thames. He had made this trip 11 times, and always tried to put time aside to call in at The Orangery before the meetings. Originally built in 1761, it had been poorly designed to be a hothouse to grow citrus trees, which had proved unsuccessful because of the building's low light. It was now an elegant café. Over the years, the classically styled building designed by Sir William Chambers had had various uses, from a galleried museum to a timber store. The white building, with its high walls, had ground to roof windows and was lovingly maintained. Rik loved the cakes served there, and would always have a pot of tea, and sit beside one of the windows. He could look out over the gardens, and think about what would be discussed at the meetings. They were all top secret; not even his family knew what was discussed. After each one, he found it harder and harder to restrain himself, but he knew that talking about the agenda could prove fatal. His last visit had been just six months ago in the summer, when the colour combinations then were vibrant and hot, compared to the olives, blues and purples of winter. The gardens looked very different today, as the heavy, grey sky continued to dump its snow vigorously. He sat in the warmth admiring the old horticultural studies hanging on the walls. Being an art lecturer, specialising in ceramics, he admired all forms of art, and had often thought about purchasing a poster or two of the paintings to hang at home. There was virtually no one else in the café. The winter hours were different to the summer ones, but with his staff pass he was able to access the gardens when the public were not permitted. All five of the leading members of the MBHK had one of these passes, as there might be a time when an emergency meeting was called, when the gardens were closed, and so they would have to swipe themselves in through an undocumented staff entrance, reserved for officials, royalty and important beneficiaries.

It was time for the meeting. Rik was never sure how to feel about them. There was always the possibility that what had already been put in place could be cancelled, or even that proceedings needed to be escalated. On this particular occasion, there was a feeling of anticipation, as it had only been five months since the last meeting. It could go one of two ways, either things had heated up, or the danger had passed. He was sure the other members would be feeling the same, except for the member who had organised the meeting. Uncle Sam, as he was known, was a 70-year-old American. He had the looks of Father Christmas, which was appropriate for the time of year. He had a long, white beard, wizard-like long silver hair and sparkling eyes. All that was missing was a red suit and a reindeer. *Uncle Sam must have some new information,* Rik thought as he took his tea tray to the server, and walked back out into the snow. There were already a few inches on the ground, and he was grateful that there was always accommodation available at Kew, should the members need it. It was basic, but warm and comfortable. He realised that he had no chance of getting back to Dorset tonight, and so knew he would be at Kew for the night.

The Palm House was the site of all of the meetings so far. Built in the 1840s by Richard Turner, it was the greatest example of Victorian glass and iron architecture. It had been built to Decimus Burton's design, to house unobstructed, tall palms. As the Grade I listed building came into view, Rik walked under the naked branches of mature trees, and passed empty flower beds and terraces. The antique lighting shining out from the Palm House was warming, illuminating the snowy ground around it to a golden, yellow glow. Although the landscape was barren, the various genres of trees and shrubs still put on a full range of colour. Rik loved this building, and felt especially privileged that he was able to visit it when it was closed to the public. The white framework clearly stood out despite the snow, due to the vast array of luscious green plants growing in its tropical climate, with condensation covering the lower windows. Rik walked into the hothouse, and marvelled at how well all the plants looked. Every time he came to Kew, it highlighted just how sick and poor the countryside looked. He had noticed over the years, how England's green and pleasant lands were turning a dirty, browny green colour; how hedgerows were not as vibrant, and the trees' growing seasons seemed to be producing a poorer quality fruit. *People should look, they would see for themselves that things were not right!* he thought, as he walked along the central corridor of the hothouse, towards a white, wrought iron spiral staircase that led to a galleried walkway up in the treetop canopy. He had taken off his coat and hat, and left them on a bench beside a small pond, with lily pads on it. He passed pitcher and hibiscus plants at the feet of tall banana and coconut palms, stopping to take in the beauty that these plants offered. It was a whole new experience visiting the greenhouses when the public were not about, and as he was not distracted, the smells, colours and humidity seemed to be stronger and more apparent.

As Rik climbed the spiral staircase, he could hear muffled voices quietly talking, and smiled. Although these meetings were of vast importance, he did enjoy meeting up with the other members. They had been through a lot together, secretly, unable to discuss what was said with anyone, other than with each other. They were not even allowed to discuss anything over the phone, by email or post. It was all done in face-to-face meetings, which he liked. The members had been picked for various reasons, but none of them were quite sure how they all got involved in the MBHK. They had all entered a competition, unlike any other competition. They'd had to write papers on a chosen subject, analyse the news through alternative news sources, study natural disasters and produce a 50-year plan on how to form and run a new community from scratch, based on their findings. The prize had been a plot of land each that could be made into a self-sufficient small-holding, which is how Rik got his home in Dorset. One of the members had written about geoengineering, another on music genres and the people they attract and another had written about the doomsday theories. Whilst Rik's paper had been on the history of ceramics, Uncle Sam's had been on the American slave trade. All of the papers had been about a wide selection of subjects, but the one thing that had bonded them together was the fact that they all discussed in depth the effect the chosen subject had had on the population and the past, present and future effects of the people. As part of winning the prize, the entrants had to maintain their research, and to inform the other members whenever a change or event occurred that might affect the MBHK.

The atmosphere got lighter, as Rik ascended into the top reaches of the Palm House rising above the heavy humidity of the lower levels. The damp, warm smell of the sodden peat and foliage had gone, as had the condensation on the windows. As he climbed, Rik could see the skyscrapers of London and The City with its financial district, housing The Bank of England. Only a mile square, The City of London was comprised of historical old buildings, of various architectural styles. Not many people knew that there was a city within a city, just like Vatican City is within Rome. The snow had settled thickly on the arched greenhouse roof, and Rik imagined it was similar to an igloo, if not for the moist heat. Once at the top of the steps, he walked along a narrow gantry, which was not for the faint-hearted, across the top of the palms. He looked down, and thought *jungle*, then looked up and thought *arctic*. He smiled at his private childlike thoughts and joined his friends.

As Rik left the meeting, there was nothing to laugh about. The day had come which he, and the other four members were dreading. It was hard to believe that everything they had planned in the last 25 years was, after all, going to be tested. They had been worthy winners of the competition, and due to their dedication, and the need to maintain their homesteads, their studies were accurate, up-to-date, and all confirmed what the others had discovered. Part of the winning agreement was that they had to maintain their studies, or the land they had each won could be taken away from them. There were other conditions too, but this was the one that kept the members arduously working on their chosen subjects, even though there was no evidence that their research would ever be needed. They prayed their research would never be needed, but tonight, their prayers were going to go unanswered. There were going to be some very busy weeks coming up, with a lot of things to organise. Although all preliminary decisions rested with the five key members, there was a team of highly qualified staff available to them, should they need it.

The MBHK organisation had been funded and run by several private millionaires, who had all made their money through environmentally friendly pursuits, such as offshore wind farms, organic food producers and green fuel promoters. Some of the beneficiaries were self-made millionaires, starting off with a simple idea which brought them fame and fortune for the future. How the MBHK had been formed was top secret, but the founding family's lineage could be traced back to the sixteenth and seventeenth centuries, when ancient civilizations were being discovered in South America, Peru and Egypt. It was rarely discussed by lower ranking members of the MBHK, but it was widely explained and understood that something had been found, that had started the ball rolling four centuries ago, and all members' energies were to be totally focused on what needed to be done to save the future of humanity, and not to waste time pondering on the past. All staff members had been handpicked, with considerations being taken into account that went into great depth, such as parentage, nationality and ethical beliefs. Members of staff included telecommunications specialists, logistics technicians, historians and scientists, and in total there were nearly 100 members of staff. The five members had top security clearance, should they need to investigate or verify anything, but they were not permitted to discuss what they needed the information for. During the meeting, the five had been unanimous, after hearing what Uncle Sam had said. Ed Lizard had also informed the members what the findings meant. Silence had followed his statement, until Uncle Sam had spoken.

'Okay, are you sure, Ed?' he had asked, raising his white, bushy eyebrows as he scanned the concerned faces of the other four members. 'We have to know the date is correct, it's the most important thing in all of this. If the date's wrong, we're seriously up shit creek without a paddle!'

'I know. I've been checking the information since the last meeting, and with what you found, Sam, we are definite. I've had the idea for several years, and having concluded my research, I know I am right. It's been checked by Oxford and Cambridge. Some kid is doing a paper on the research, though obviously doesn't know its significance. He's a bright guy, but not a critical thinker. For an educated chap, he watches a lot of shit on the television!' Ed replied. 'Besides, once I investigated and questioned it, the horticultural guys confirmed what I asked them. It's starting, and it's sooner than you all think.'

Chapter Two

May 2011, Lincolnshire

The only sounds were a rhythmical buzz of a nearby honey bee, the gentle rustle of the warm breeze through a discarded magazine and the blood pumping intro to Rammstein's *Sonne* hammering out from the house. Coco lazily sipped on a cold cider, from the bottle naturally, and took a long drag on a home grown. One might consider this scene only associated with the unemployed youths often seen swigging beer on town centre benches, but it was as far from that as could be possible. Coco was at the start of a successful career as an illustrator, and on a warm May afternoon was swinging in a hammock bound between two of her apple trees. The pastel coloured hammock creaked gently as it swayed absentmindedly, whist Coco planned what to do for the rest of the day. She loved Tuesdays, as she knew it was the worst day of the week for other folk. The memories of the previous weekend would be fading, and the next weekend was days away. This is how she used to view the week, like many other people, but things were different now every day was a weekend.

The honey bee was joined by a few friends, and they busily collected the pollen off the spring blossoms. The orchard was fabulous this time of year, as not only were there 30 different apple trees, some monitored by the National Apple Society as they were rare, but there were plum, cherry and pear trees. The blossoms were a vast array of every shade from white to the deepest cotton candy pink, and with the soft breeze, the petals that had made a bid for freedom fluttered to the ground. The little orchard sat behind a small railway cottage, which had had a few extensions through its 100-year life. The old railway that used to run beside the house, taking brick and coal trucks up to the quarry were long gone, but you could still see the scar through the countryside where the track had once laid. The gaps in the forestry made it possible to see the next few railway cottages, whose residents' job was to manually control the gates across the isolated lanes. Coco's orchard had been planted 50 years ago, by the previous tenant, but when he died, the priority for the family was that the new tenants should have the same passion for the landscape, and would have to be prepared to look after the fruit trees. Around the edge of the orchard on three sides were other fruit bushes, mainly blackberry, redcurrant, gooseberry and raspberry. They were mature, having been lovingly tended all of their lives, being given the perfect environment to live and thrive in. They were also protected by tall walnut trees, interspersed with hazelnut and almond.

Taking on the smallholding was a huge responsibility, but Coco and her partner, Art, had taken on the task with boundless energies, ideas and plans. They wanted to continue what the old man had started, if not for their own rewards, but also for the family who'd had the pleasure of being brought up in such an idyllic location. The previous tenants had been firm family friends of Art. As soon as the house became vacant, the family decided they would rather someone they knew took it on, so they might still be able to visit. The house never went on the market, though it had been several months before a mortgage had been raised to purchase it. That had been a test in itself, not only between Coco and Art, but also with the banks. The economic climate was extremely unstable, and the banks had been told not to invest or lend to anyone. Even though Art had a completely clean credit history, the banks refused to lend as there was 'insufficient evidence that your client can repay the funds', Art's solicitor had been told. The rows with the banks had been taxing, but Coco and Art survived their first true test, and as a couple moved into the house a year previously.

On the forth side of the orchard, on its western side, were ancient woods and trees. It was not a massive expanse of forestry, (the nearest neighbour was just the other side of it about a mile away), but it held a little secret. A small path led from the orchard, through a tall, arched, wrought iron gate, down a gentle slope through the mature trees. This was an undisturbed place, and had been left to its own devices for hundreds of years. The canopy overhead was really luscious, and so the wooded floor was sparse, with fern growing in a few spots where the sun managed to reach the ground. The path was soft, from generations of autumn leaves falling to build an enriched top soil. Brambles fought amongst the stinging nettles. The pathway gradually widened, until a real gem became visible… a big, natural lake, full of uncaught fish, surrounded by overgrown and overhanging trees and bushes. Every shade of green and blue reflected in and around the water, with ripples distorting the greens of the foliage and blue of the sky's reflection.

The lake was not part of the land that came with the house, it was just a perfect accessory as far as Art was concerned. Privately owned and valued at about one million pounds, it was the property of an elderly gentleman. He was a grouchy, miserable old man, though he did have some good principles. He was saving the woodland and lake for his daughters for when he died, and no matter how many arguments the family had, he refused to sell it. The rows got worse as the family pestered and nagged continually. They wanted new cars, expensive holidays and designer clothes. The old man had grown up in a different time, so this modern world was alien to him. Technology had totally passed him by and there was a complete misunderstanding about what an iPad did, or what a Facebook was. He had been to a bookshop in Nottingham, asking for a copy of *Face Book*, but the surly shop assistant had made him feel like he was batting out of his depth, and so he left the shop grumbling about the state of today's youth.

The arguments about the lake had reached a crescendo when he received a letter in the post. It was not often letters came through the post these days. His daughters dealt with all his bills and requirements, and it always seemed to be a mystery to him how his daughters could order his weekly shopping whilst on a phone sat in an airport departure lounge, and within a few hours the supermarket would deliver it. Nor could he understand why the local street market had been reduced to just a few tatty stalls. Where were all the fruit and vegetable growers, the bulb and flower sellers? This was Lincolnshire, there were miles upon miles of rich, fertile soil growing all manner of crops, specifically green-leaved vegetables and fresh bulb flowers. The modern world did not really agree with the old man, and as so rare these days, his faced beamed when he read Art's letter.

Art had explained how he'd purchased the cottage near the lake, and had planned to maintain the natural development of the plot. The house and landscape would be refurbished with Coco's sculptures and craft ideas from recycled materials, and he was planning on having honey bee hives put in the professionally managed orchard. Art had gone on to detail the self-sufficient means of power he would use, involving a domestic wind turbine and solar panels. Did he 'mind the wind turbine; it wouldn't spoil the landscape?' This young man sounded the exact opposite to his family. They were all fake tans, fake nails, fake hair and fake people, prioritising money and glamour over natural beauty and creativity. And yet here was someone passionate about being part of the land, preserving it, tending to it, in the hope he might reap the rewards it gave back in abundance. Art asked if he could become a bailiff for the lake, watching over it, ensuring its beauty was preserved and that no one trespassed on the land. In return, Art would like to be able to fish the lake, and make a catalogue of the fish stocked in it. He planned to write a book about the refurbishment of the plot, and would like to include the lake. The old man loved the idea, and by return post offered to visit Art at the cottage to discuss the idea.

Coco had walked down to the lake edge, and sat on the dusty floor. There was a small heat haze shimmering above the water, as a sudden flash of turquoise nipped across one of the little bays. There were a few kingfishers here. Art had befriended one, as it had taken a liking to sitting on his fishing rods in the evenings. He had not handled it, or even approached it, but it came most evenings, but would not stay for long. It would dart off, and then come back before disappearing until the next day, its orange flash and bright blue plumage easily distinguished as the lake darkened at sunset. It was such a beautiful place. Untarnished, no trace of human existence, just nature at its best. The day's weather had been a one-off, as the spring had been very wet and cold so far. Coco reminisced of the day she came home and could not find Art. He had laid a message out on the front doorstep, using twigs and stones. It was technically the back door, in fact the only door, as the front door overlooking the road had been boarded up years ago. Coco and Art had unblocked the brick space where the front door had been, and instead of a door had fitted a floor-to-ceiling arched window. The top half opened, allowing the delicate smelling jasmine and sweet pea scents to drift into the lounge, with the southern aspect ensuring the sun warmed and lit the otherwise quite gloomy room. Art's twig message read 'LAKE', and so she had gone to the lake and found him fishing. Art explained that the old man loved the ideas for the house and land, and detested his own family's neediness for possessions, more technology and wardrobes full of expensive clothes. The cottage reminded him of a simpler time, when the weather and seasons dictated what needed to be done. People had to think more for themselves, rather than have the television telling them what to buy, where to go, what to eat. He was tired, an old man who lived by a different ideal, and felt that Art and Coco deserved to have the lake. He knew they would love it as it was; that it would not be made into a get-rich-quick scheme. His family knew it had a great potential to bring in a decent income from fishermen willing to buy a season ticket for it, but in turn, this would ruin the ecosystem of the wood and lake.

Art had proceeded to tell Coco that the lake was now theirs, but there were some conditions that went with it. The old man had given them the lake, on the understanding it was never sold and that Art was the only one allowed to fish it. He could have friends over, but the natural balance of the lake and its contents were not to be compromised. The old man's only regret was that he would not see his daughters' faces when they found out it had been sold before he had died, *What's the worse they could do to me, kill me again?* He had also assured Art that the paperwork would all be in order, so the decision could not be contested after his departure. Art and the old man had wandered around the orchard, and had a cider together, sort of like a gentlemen's agreement. It was also discussed that the old man from time to time would come and fish Art's lake, and from that day, a great bond had been formed. It was a dream come true for Art, a truly unbelievable dream. The only problem with dreams coming true is that it also opens the gates for nightmares to become real. No matter how good things can be, it can just as easily be really that bad.

The Manor House, Lincolnshire Sands

'But Daddy, my phone is rubbish, I need a new one. Today. Can I have the money? I need the money today!' shouted Lena. 'This house is like prison. Daddy, you're dripping with money, but are too tight to give me five hundred for the new smartphone I want!'

'Honey, I got you that phone just a few months ago. Is it broken?' replied Drayton, looking up at his demanding daughter, as she stormed back up the wide, sweeping staircase. BANG! A distant bedroom door was violently slammed, followed by a dance CD being turned right up. The music reverberated around the solid stone house. *I must soundproof her room!* Drayton thought. He had made his money in the building industry, having started it from nothing, and built the business up on reputation alone. He was on his second wife, Lynnie, with his first being Lena's mother. He was in his mid-fifties, mild-mannered, with a good sense of humour and would go out of his way to help people who were in need of it.

He did not support any charities, there was no way to know if the donations he made got to the people in need. Instead he had refurbished a big Victorian house which he then opened as a women's refuge. He had paid close attention to detail, getting in an advisor to assist with the features that would turn a normal house into a home for woman in desperate need for somewhere safe. He had a room allocated as a play room, where painting and crafts were encouraged for both the children and mothers. There was a comfortable family TV room, with satellite television, a selection of DVDs and CDs. Another of the ground floor rooms was just for the adults, somewhere the mothers could go for total relaxation. Reclining chairs with MP3s in them allowed for headphones to be plugged in. The grounds had various play areas for children with cushioned flooring, brightly coloured wooden playground rides, and planted flowerbeds to create a true retreat. It was funded by the government, but Drayton would donate several thousand a year, and insisted on doing any repairs himself. Despite its remote location, overlooking the North Sea on the Lincolnshire/Norfolk border, it was always full. The women showed a lot of respect for Drayton, and would often talk to him about their problems. He was a good man, well-liked, unlike his horrendous daughter, who 'surely had to be sired by the milkman,' some of the refuge woman would gossip. None of them liked Lena.

The music went silent, followed by some heavy footsteps, as the bedroom door was flung open. Lena walked down the wood panelled stairs, to find her father feeding kittens in the kitchen.

'Do you have to do that in here? They probably have fleas and it's not hygienic to feed them in here,' retorted Lena, dressed in designer, fashion riding clothes that were a little too tight for her fuller frame. She did not own a horse or indeed ride; it was just the latest fashion. She had applied a heavy layer of make-up, and tied her dyed blond hair back. 'You're disgusting. Can I have that cash now? I'm going out for a while, with Trish. She's picking me up. We'll do lunch and get the new phone at the same time in town.'

'I don't have the cash on me, Princess,' replied Drayton, getting his wallet from his back pocket to show her its contents.

'It would be full if one of your sluts asked you for some!' she screamed, 'Perhaps I should move in at The Lodge?'

'If you like, Princess, I'll build an extension and furnish it for you. Just for you and help you...'

'Daddy, how stupid can you be? I'm not leaving the Manor House to live with whores,' Lena said softly, her change in tone causing Drayton to look up from the little, defenceless kitten he was holding. It was too small to get to the saucer of kitten milk, so he was setting another shallower plate for it to drink from, 'I have a better idea,' she continued in the same quiet tone, 'why don't you go and live with them. You could be all their daddies then, leave me here. Take Lynnie with you. Take these filthy things with you as well!' she said, throwing the other three kittens from the work surface towards Drayton, who comically and deftly caught each kitten, in an apron he was wearing, using it like a fireman's blanket. 'Oh god, you piss me right off!' and with that, she stormed through the back door, causing the runt kitten to cower in fear of the loud noise. Tyres kicked up stones on the gravel drive as a vehicle accelerated away, Drayton let out a long sigh. The house almost heaved a sign of relief too as did the four kittens, who went on to finish their treats in peace.

'Drayton, hiya,' said Adele, the housekeeper at The Lodge, 'I'll buzz you in. Tea in the pot if you want it?' He drove through the gates and parked his van down the side of the house. Although he had a good gardener come in twice a month, the plants and flowers looked drab. The spring had been the coldest and wettest on record, and even though there had been the odd short spell of warm days, the gardens looked tired and withered. Normally fully grown rose bushes would be fresh green, with coloured buds starting to open. Instead, the old bushes near the massive bay window hardly had any buds coming, with leaves looking grey and lifeless making the whole bush look sick. Drayton walked to the utility room door which led onto the kitchen, passing equally sick looking bushes and small trees. He placed the pet basket he was carrying on the table, and sat down at a farmhouse-sized solid wooden table.

'Would we be able to have these here?' he asked.

'What you got there, love,' Adele replied, going over to the basket after handing Drayton a big mug of tea. Their relationship was strictly professional; there was no attraction between them, and just a mutual respect for what they both did for the women at The Lodge. Adele had been a care worker with the NHS, but had given it up to run the refuge. She was very clued up with youth culture and attitudes, and took time to understand the different lives of the people under her care. She was well loved, and many of the woman considered her a mother, teacher, nurse and friend. 'Oh my Lord, how cute are these? They are divine. I'm sure we could home them here. They'll be good for the kiddies, and I dare say some of the younger mummies will love them too. We should ask them all really, make them feel part of the decision, part of the running of the house.'

By the evening, the kittens had been named, bought collars, feeding bowls and beds. They lived in the utility room at night, but had the run of the downstairs rooms by day. It was a new excitement not felt at The Lodge before, as everyone seemed to bond and care for the kittens. Despite the severity by which many of the women ended up at the refuge, the simplest of things could lift spirits, and bring smiles to sunken, unhappy faces. Drayton could not get the image of his garden out of his mind. He got back to the Manor House, relieved that Lena was still out. He switched on the computer, and started to research, to see if it was just Lincolnshire Sands that looked poorly, or if the problem was more widespread. He was totally astonished with what he found. When Lena came home at two in the morning, banging and crashing her hefty frame around the house, Drayton was still researching on the computer. *So, I need to look at the skies, study the clouds. Sounds daft, but so many people seem to know what they are talking about,* he thought, *Spraying the skies with chemicals, and as they were saying on the net, if the governments were spraying something good up there, 'they' would be shouting about 'the good' they were doing.* Drayton's research had uncovered a whole world of alternative news reports, covering all manner of realist and bizarre topics. There was a lot of information on chemtrails, which were long vapour clouds sprayed by military planes. The chemicals would be dispersed by the wind, spreading the vapour throughout the atmosphere.

'Well, it would explain the sick countryside,' he said under his breath, as he made his way to bed. Lynnie had left him to it, and would be asleep by now. He would speak to her tomorrow about what they should do about Lena. *Shame the chemtrails don't seem to stop Lena growing,* he thought, regretting his malicious thoughts instantly. No matter what she was, she was still his daughter, 'I think!' he whispered to himself.

A squat, Nottingham City Centre

The stench on the concrete stairwell was burning the hairs in Rev's nose, as he swayed his way to the middle floors of the high-rise. The carrier bag in his hand had four more Special Brew, and some cheap strong cider in it, bought with the last of his benefit money. He carried on climbing, stopping to catch his breath. He had never smoked, but the damp conditions he had been living in had caused a serious chest infection. He did not eat well, never enjoyed fresh air, as the inner city derelict block of flats stood next to an unused, stagnant canal. It was either traffic fumes, the ammonia in the flats or the stench from the canal. Plus the damp from glassless windows and no heating were not helping. Rev got to the seventh floor, and pushed open a door to the place he was living. He lived here with his friend John. They had been friends from school, and for the last 15 years had slowly become what some might consider, the dregs of society. An inaccurate analysis, once their circumstances were realised. Bad luck, unfortunate situations and deviant associates had caused the situation they were in, and it was the drugs and alcohol that kept dark, forbidding memories away.

They had chosen this flat for several reasons. In the first instance, it was high enough up in the block not to be easily found, and secondly, it had all of its windows, except for a small corner missing from one, was fully carpeted, and there was some furniture in it. Rev and John had a bed in a room each, with shabby, dirty secondhand bedding. They had an old leather sofa sat in the main room, facing a curtain-less window, with a magnificent view. It faced due west, and many a good sunset had been witnessed. 'Better than any TV show, Bro,' Rev would slur each time he saw it. It would be a very rare occurrence if by nighttime he had not been drinking. On the few occasions he had been sober his addiction would kick in, causing his cravings for alcohol. The restfulness and shakes would demand attention. Sweats would follow, and a fruitless search through the bin to find a few drops in an empty can. His tensions and cravings would build, until his mind was full of the sickening images which he tried to block out by drinking. He would remember how he came home from work, and found his girlfriend, who was pregnant, dead with a broken neck at the bottom of the stairs. He had not gone back to work, he couldn't face it. His ruthless parents-in-law blamed Rev for not being there for their daughter, 'But I was working to buy her new things for the baby!' he had explained. Grief has strange effects on people, and just when he needed them most, the only physical reminder of his beloved Jess, her family had kicked him out as he 'did not deserve to have memories of her'.

So, here he was with his friend John, a victim of an equally disturbing circumstance. There had been no help for them, no one really cared. To start with the council had told him to find a warm park bench. He had to be escorted out of the building after this comment. He knew there was a hostel for homeless people just down the road from the council. The woman there had said he was not eligible, as he was not vulnerable, nor a danger to society and did not have a criminal record. However, if he *had* a criminal record, they would have housed him. Friends put them up on their sofas, but without working, money was in short supply. Eventually they had found themselves on the streets more times than on a sofa, and decided to find somewhere that was at least dry and safe. There are different levels of safe; some think of big fierce dogs with security gates, others like Rev and John consider anywhere that was not on the street to be 'safe'. Being vulnerable to police arrest, taunting youths drunk after a night out and tutting, disapproving people hurrying past them on their way to their semis in suburbia, were all safety issues. Rev was used to being a book judged by his cover, but John had more difficulties with accepting his situation. He used hard drugs, and had nearly died twice. He could never work out why he had survived, after all, 'I have nothing to live fa, so why am I still 'ere?' he would say, 'I died, I should be dead.' John's esteem was a lot lower than Rev's. He had been framed at work, used as a scapegoat. Although there had been evidence to put John in the clear, it would have implicated one of the top bosses, who had a lot of money and very good barristers. Therefore, John got sentenced, lost his home, and his girlfriend left him for the son of the top boss, as they had met during his court case. Whilst serving his sentence, his parents had been killed in a car crash, on their way home from visiting him in prison. It was doubtful John would ever get over the guilt he felt for the loss of his parents. Psychiatrists had studied him, and counsellors had spent hours of compassionate time trying to help him get over it. As if it was not bad enough that his parents had been killed, he should not have been in prison in the first place. When he was released he had nothing.

Nothing!

Luckily, the first person he saw when he left prison was Rev and their high school friendship was rekindled.

'You 'ere?' asked John, as he staggered into the flat, with bags and bags of shopping, 'Rev... REV?'

'Bro, it's a two-bed flat, not Buck Palace. You okay, Bro, what you got?' asked Rev, with a new street-slang accent he was trying out, losing his slur lightly as he engaged his brain. He moved quickly to help John with the bags, 'Bloody hell, these are awkward. You been pinching again?'

'Well, yeah, na. Yeah. Na!' John replied in an excited tone, 'Look what I got! I got the best thing ever. It's the absolute best, you won't believe what I got. Guess, guess what I got!'

Rev had not seen John so happy in a long, long time. There was a youthful look in his eye, as John snatched the bags back from Rev, insisting he guessed what the great haul was.

'Did you nick it?'

'Yes, but never mind that. Guess what it is, not how I got it!'

'Is it expensive?'

'Um, na, but it is priceless!'

'Can we sell it, you know, is it hot?'

'No, we can sell *them!*' he said, smiling, small dimples Rev had never noticed appearing on both cheeks, adding to the childlike expression on his pale, blemished skin.

'Cool, we can sell them. Okay, how big are they?'

'As a whole, or individually?' asked John, sitting on the sofa with all his bags around him. They were from various local supermarkets.

'Um, dude, you done over the supermarkets all in one day?' Rev knew when he started the game that it would be a long game. They had managed to spend many a night entertaining themselves, just by one of them thinking of something good, or nice, and the other had to guess. There was a certain amount of honesty involved, but as they had no reason to lie or fib, the game became popular. It meant they spent some time thinking of enjoyable things, rather than the reality that surrounded them.

'No, I came home earlier and collected some plastic bags I had found on the streets. I need to empty these and go get the rest. There's about the same again!'

'What is it?' Rev continued, hoping the urgency in John's voice meant he would give in with his game.

'I've got hundreds of 'em. The rest are hidden behind the skips!'

'You've been skipping again? You'll get nicked, you have a record!'

'Thanks for the kick in the bollocks,' said John softly. He knew his friend was right, and that he was only looking out for him, but just for once, he was a gnats-cock happier than usual, and Rev had just knocked him right back down again, 'Here, I know you love these, so I got the lot. There's nowt wrong with them.' He left the room, having tipped out all of his bags, and left Rev staring at the bootie, with his mouth and eyes wide open. There, on their carpet, were Rev's favourite Easter eggs, the ones with little packets of buttons on the inside of the shell.

'John… mate… John!' called Rev, rushing in a haphazard fashion, tripping over eggs, jogging out to the top of the stairwell, 'JOHN, mate!'

'Fuck you!' was the very short and to the point reply John gave, letting Rev know exactly how he felt.

Rev went back into the flat, and started picking up the eggs, and stacked them in a corner of the front room. He changed his mind, and decided to make a fort front, so when John came back, it might cheer him up again. Due to his dependence on alcohol, his balance sometimes caused him to drop or knock things, so building the fort took some time. He even made paper hats out of an old newspaper. Once his fort was made, he sat down and waited for John's return, starting on his cans of beer. He worried about John when he went rummaging through the skips behind the supermarkets, though there had been times when he'd come away with some worthy loot. It was by no means a great way to live. Dangerous, dirty and morally it can bring a man to his knees. But John seemed to be lucky, if being homeless and destitute can be ever classed as 'lucky'. Over the years he'd found a thousand pounds' worth of packaged meat, a freezer's worth of bread and packets of bed linen. Using the products to swap for other goods and services, they could live with a certain amount of dignity, despite not having any running water or electricity.

Just as the skies were changing to a golden yellow, and the sun started to sink behind the office blocks in the distance, Rev could hear someone coming up the stairs, banging bags on the metal banister rails, and swearing when it sounded like someone had tripped. A few moments later, John appeared with his bags, double what he had brought in the first trip. His load was so wide, he couldn't fit through the door.

'John, I'm sorry. Made y'a fort,' Rev said, popping up from behind a chocolate egg wall, proudly spreading out his arms in welcome, with a beer can in each hand.

'Yeah, I can see. Good innit? Must 'ave took you hours!'

'Na, about two!' they both laughed, 'made y'a hat too!'

'Wicked. Mate, Rev, mate, I'm not going to do the skips anymore. Ya right, if I get nicked. It's not worth it!'

'Okay dude, good call, Bro!'

'Quit this "Bro" bullshit will you, you're *white* homey!'

For the rest of the night, they drank, took speed, ate chocolate eggs and John smoked weed. The mountain of purple egg foil and little boxes that formed in a pile on each end of the sofa would have made any chocoholic jealous, but it's easy to get sick of chocolate, when that's all there is to eat for weeks on end.

The Apricot Mews, Chelsea

Victoria drove her Audi slowly over the cobbled stones and waited for her electric garage door to open. It automatically closed behind her once she was parked. The Audi was brand new, a treat for herself, as way of a reward after her promotion. She was home earlier than usual, as she had booked the afternoon off from the museum, to go to the travel agent. The little mews house, painted a soft apricot colour, with pots of white geraniums which stood around the front door was in a long, narrow courtyard, surrounded by big, lavish houses. As with most of the mews in Chelsea, it looked classy, was expensive and was well sought after, which was a far cry from what the buildings had originally been designed as. The garages were formally carriage houses, each with a stable next to it and living quarters above. The terraced houses, some still with their original, carriage house wooden doors, others having had conversions, were all painted pastel colours and had pot plants, hanging baskets and troughs planted with bedding plants that had not started to flower yet. There were many of the original features, with original stone water troughs, now filled with flowers. Some of the doors were replica stable doors and the cobbles near the security gate had narrow grooves in them, where the carriages had passed through onto the street. Modern features included the security lights and gates, satellite dishes and discrete CCTV cameras. At the top of the street, huge, black wrought iron gates, controlled by the residents each having security fobs, kept them safe in the knowledge that despite being in the heart of London, their properties were secure.

Victoria walked through to the kitchen, at the back of the house. There was no backyard, as the mews were surrounded by the garden walls belonging to the surrounding three-storey townhouses. They had specifically fallen in love with the cottage, as it was open-plan, had huge skylights, but still had some original features. Iron rings still stuck out of the wall and there were still cobbles on the floor, with bare beams supporting the ceiling. It was tastefully decorated, with a modern Shaker style kitchen, of slatted wooden units, painted white, with very healthy houseplants trailing and climbing from their lofty locations on top of the cupboards. The green of the plants, fed by the all-day sun from the skylights and the clean, white furniture, was refreshing and Victoria had added splashes of lemon and tangerine orange, to give a Mediterranean feel. She checked if the plants needed any water and made herself a green tea; switching on the iPod dock before sitting at a little round table, with a big, glass bowl of citrus fruit in the centre. She looked at the holiday schedule she had just booked for herself and Flynn.

African tribal music softly played through speakers throughout the house as she thought how fabulous the trip would be. She had booked three weeks in South America, including trips to the Nazca Lines on the plains of the Andes Mountains, the Mayan city of Machu Picchu in the Peruvian Andes and the final week was for relaxing in Mexico, on the exotic beaches of Rio, including a trip to the impressive Aztec Pyramids of Teotihuacan. It was a dream trip, something they had talked about for months. She looked at the clock on the wall and grew excited at the thought of telling her husband when he got home. It was strange being home so early in the day and she wondered how to fill the afternoon till Flynn got back. She went up the open staircase and changed out of her work suit, into fleecy lounge pants and one of Flynn's old Chelsea football shirts. She had decided later, she would run a bath, using Champneys bubble bath and light some scented candles. She had planned for them to bathe together, which is when she had planned to tell Flynn.

They had been together three years and had met one Christmas, on a party boat on the Thames. Victoria had been on her works do and Flynn had been someone's plus-one. It had later turned out that he was out with his wife, a pretty woman who worked in the Textiles Rooms at the museum. With Victoria working in another department, the Ancient Britons Rooms, they had never met and so she had no idea who Flynn was with. There had been a second's moment of eye contact between them and from that moment on, they seemed to bump into each other for the duration of the boat trip. As the months had passed, Victoria thought about the handsome archaeologist from the Christmas party and would often fantasise about the good-looking 'Indiana'. They eventually got together six months later. Flynn had started to visit the museum to see his wife but one day decided to wander around the Ancient Briton Rooms. As their friendship developed and the obvious mutual attraction developed, Flynn started to talk about his troubled marriage and how he thought his wife was cheating on him. Victoria had very strong principles, and despite really falling for Flynn, she would never do anything that might hurt his partner.

Quickly after becoming a couple, they bought the little house in the mews and a year later got married on a butterfly farm. Victoria was blissfully happy; she was young, had a beautiful home and partner *and* a dream job with a good wage. She missed Flynn when he was away giving lectures and seminars around Europe and sometimes America, but her own job gave her plenty to do. She would use the time he was away to work overtime, which was one of the factors that brought about her promotion. Flynn was a loving man. He would organise little surprises for her, such as horse riding in Hyde Park, hot air balloon rides in the Chilterns and weekends away to his parents' holiday cottage in Clovelly, on the Devon coast. He was tidy, undemanding and kind. He would occasionally remind her that he had a strong belief that a woman should be cared for, loved and treated with the ultimate respect. There had been a few bumpy months when he had first split up from his wife, but Victoria just had to accept there would be loose ends to tie up. She felt sorry for him having to deal with it all, no doubt with many unanswered questions about why his ex had cheated on him. Every time he had to see his wife, whether at the solicitors or at the home they had shared, he aways bought Victoria flowers and she in return would make sure she gave him some space to clear his head.

As she passed the upstairs window, she saw a familiar powerful, black motorbike waiting for the security gates to open. Flynn was home early too, what a great surprise! How did he know? He was never home early with so much work on. She skipped down the stairs, adjusting her hair and checking her appearance in the lounge mirror and busied herself in the kitchen. Then, she thought it would be fun to be waiting for him in bed, with the holiday schedule on his pillow, so she ran upstairs and slipped into bed, just as she heard a key in the front door. The white Egyptian cotton sheets, with bluebell coloured fitted sheet and pillows were cool and a small shiver ran down Victoria's spine, partly from being cold, but also with the excitement of telling Flynn about the holiday. The bedroom was situated above the garage, which had been the carriage house, and the open ceiling left oak beams visible, making the room seem bigger than it actually was. It was a minimalist room, with just a big wooden sleigh bed and a table with a flat screen television mounted above it. They had used the second bedroom as a walk-in wardrobe and a little office, where their computers sat side by side on a long glass table, under the window.

She heard Flynn put his bike helmet on the table and giggled silently to herself as downstairs went silent. She was about to call out to him, as he had obviously not seen the tea cup in the kitchen, nor gone into the garage, so he would have no idea she was at home. Then she heard him on his mobile. He must have been in the kitchen, as his voice was muffled. Occasionally his voice rose and it sounded like he was warning someone not to do something. He was a tough person to work with, ruthless about deadlines and protocol. She did not want any distractions when telling him of her surprise, so she decided to wait until he came off the phone. The next thing she heard was the front door opening as Flynn went back outside, got on his bike and sped off through the still open gates. Victoria watched as he nearly knocked over a pregnant woman who was about to step off the pavement and Victoria wondered what had upset him so. He could lose his temper easily if someone at the university made a careless mistake, but she knew he took road safety quite seriously and would not usually speed in such a built-up area. She walked back down the stairs and got her book to read. She switched the iPod back on as the next album started, which was Gregorian Monks chanting. Victoria knew it was not everyone's sort of music, but it had a primitive quality, haunting and spiritual. She would never listen to it when she was feeling unhappy, and so recently played it a lot. The album had such a sorrowful echo to it, she would always end up crying. She always marvelled how music could change her mood and that her collection was so varied. She had a wide selection of music from different cultures, all of which had an effect on her thoughts. She also enjoyed modern music, such as Biffy Clyro and

The Arctic Monkeys, but her favourite driving CD was Alternative '80s, which was a compilation of all the alternative music she had grown up with, her favourite being The Damned.

She had not really been into the music that her school friends had been into. She knew it had something to do with her upbringing. Her father was one of the top record producers of the early 1980s, and it would be quite normal for her to come downstairs in the mornings, to find numerous members of the music industry still up drinking from the night before. She would come down in her school uniform, to find a bass player snorting coke in the hallway, or a selection of people sat at the huge kitchen table smoking weed, with the air as thick with smoke as when the chimney had got blocked by a dead pigeon. She was rarely academically challenged and found most of her studies quite easy, so her unconventional home life rarely reflected on her grades. The only time she did not like the eccentric home life, was when her father would drop her at school in a brand new Bentley, or when he got one of the more sober, less wasted house guests to drop her off. Her close school friends knew about her home life, but she did not want the whole school to know. She liked her friends liking her for who she was, not for the concert tickets or autographs she could get. There were also the jealous types that could make her life hell. She had been taunted at school for years, with every name from druggy, crack-whore and rich bitch, to dyke and swot. There was even a rumour at one point, that she paid someone do her homework for her, which was how she was always at the top of the class. She knew it was just the ugly head of jealousy rearing up and that anyone at that school would want her lifestyle, but the fact her studies came easy to her was a massive advantage. She kept herself to herself, listened carefully, did as she was told and eventually left sixth form with four 'A' grade A Levels.

At weekends she would stay up, enjoying the company of so many diverse people, sneaking sips of their drinks and having a go on a joint. As the house was an 'open house', with all manner of people calling by at any hour, she did not feel the need to overindulge in alcohol or experiment with drugs and never considered any hard drugs. They were around her all of the time and with no secrecy about them and their effects; she did not develop a curiosity for them. The music industry was just getting over the short and sweet punk scene, adjusting to a new expressionism, where men wore make-up and women wore pin-striped suits. Victoria particularly enjoyed chatting with the transvestites who would sometimes stay all weekend, stimulated with coke and speed. Their flamboyant, colourful clothes and exquisite make-up really fascinated her. Some of the men looked better than most of the woman. She also enjoyed talking to the gay musicians, as they bitched and gossiped, with exaggerated hand movements, comparing who had slept with who, and who was the rudest or 'biggest'. Admittedly an unusual upbringing for a young woman, but it was the only lifestyle she knew. She stayed focused on the world around her and enjoyed the thought that some of those people at school would sell their own grandma to be where she was. It turned out however, that the people who visited were aware there was a young woman in the house, so the understanding was there were to be no hard drugs injected, no sexual urges to be carried out and most of all, Victoria's father insisted that there was to be total respect shown to his daughter. Anyone he caught not doing so, would be physically thrown out of the house, possibly with an air rifle up their backside!

Victoria turned up the Gregorian chanting, closing her eyes she felt the music. She turned it up even more, knowing her neighbours were out and let the male voices swim through her mind, thinking of nothing except ancient remote monasteries and a simple, idyllic lifestyle on an uninhabited island. Suddenly, in-between two songs, she jumped as the doorbell rang. Looking through the window, she could see it was the pregnant woman who had been stood outside the gates. She went and opened the door, thinking the lady was going to make a complaint.

'Hello, I'm sorry about my husband,' Victoria stated, making sure she got the first word in as a genuine apology.

'Your husband?'

'Yes, the daredevil on the black bike… I saw him nearly knock you over!' carried on Victoria, gently placing one hand on the woman's arm. 'Not that it's an excuse, but I think he had just had some bad news on the phone, so was driving a little too fast!'

'Oh. Um, yes. The bike's your husband?' said the woman, 'I think I'm at the wrong house.'

'Well, the bike isn't my husband, just the guy on it! Are you okay? Do you want to sit down?'

'Um, yes, please. Um, no, I'm looking for Vic actually. He's my partner's housemate, and I'm sure this was his address.'

'There's no one living here by that name, just me and Evel Knievel.'

'Do you know any of your neighbours? Or do you know which house two guys might live at, Vic and Flynn?'

'Pardon?'

'I'm sorry, I am wasting your ti–'

'Did you say Flynn? Flynn lives here. And you want to see Flynn?'

'Are you Flynn's sister?'

'No, I'm Victoria, Flynn's wife!'

Half an hour later, the pregnant woman was sat on the sofa opposite Victoria. The atmosphere was one that neither woman had ever known and neither knew what emotions they were feeling. After a moment's silence on the doorstep, when both woman realised what was happening, Victoria had invited Elizabeth into the house, as she had felt a tight pinching in her stomach. Being a compassionate person, even though her whole world had just fallen apart, she could not turn the woman away, as her life was now equally in tatters. It had become apparent that Flynn was not who they both thought he was. Elizabeth was pregnant with his baby and had been seeing him for 18 months. She lived in a small, remote village in-between Durham and Newcastle and had met Flynn when she was working in a country pub. He had called in whilst visiting Hadrian's Wall. She knew he travelled a lot, but was prepared to see him whenever he got the time. The two women had compared their mental diaries and it became apparent how easy it had been for Flynn to lead a double life. When she had fallen pregnant, Flynn had lost all interest, saying his housemate Vic had just been diagnosed with a life-threatening illness which meant he had to spend more time in London. Elizabeth finished her story, explaining how she found Flynn's address on the internet.

It had turned out that the reason Flynn had come home, was to intercept the post. Elizabeth had sent him a letter asking him to decide if he wanted to be part of their child's life or not, but obviously Flynn did not want Victoria to find it. Elizabeth had sat waiting at a café across the road to the mews entrance, having to resort to extreme measures in order to try and talk to Flynn, or even to speak to the nonexistent Vic, whom they quickly realised was short for Victoria. Elizabeth had sat waiting and couldn't believe her luck when she saw Flynn pull up at the gates to the mews. She rang him, to say she was across the road, would he pop over just for a quick chat, she needed to know what to do?

'That must have been the phone call I heard him take in the kitchen. He didn't know I was here, and then he left quickly, which is when I saw him nearly knock you down,' Victoria said.

Elizabeth nodded as she carried on with the story, explaining how she was thinking about stepping through the security gates, when Flynn came out of the house again. He had totally ignored her, speeding off on his bike without giving her a second look. She then decided on plan B, to talk to Vic. She had stepped through the gates and by the time she had got to the cottage door, she wasn't sure what she would say. Then the gates had closed, so she had no choice but to knock. As the music had been so loud, she had waited till there was a gap in the songs.

The two sat in the pretty little mews, the lilac walls changing colour to grey and back to lilac, as the sun moved around the room. A huge, very thick purple rug lay between the sofas, with polished cobbles around the edge of it. They sat in silence. They both had just been delivered a bomb shell. Victoria had not had a clue that the man she thought worshipped her, as she did him, could possibly do such a thing. Elizabeth on the other hand, also had concluded she would now definitely have to be a single parent. They sat looking at each other, wanting to hate the woman who had ruined their lives, but they could not blame each other. How could they get angry with one another, when it was Flynn who should be the one suffering, not having his cake and eating it. They could not decide how they should tell Flynn, who should tell him, or if indeed, they might not tell him at all. Instead, they chose to set him up and humiliate him in the worst possible way. Neither of them knew how they might do that, but both liked the idea of playing him at his own game. They came up with a plan, that would utilise Flynn's scheming, cheating mind to its full and knew that revenge was definitely a dish best served cold.

Chapter Three

May 2011, Lincolnshire

'Brought you a cold one, dude,' said Pod, 'figured you'd be down here when I saw your hammock was empty. First time you've left it in a week, isn't it?'

'Cheeky feck! I'll have you know that as I haven't mastered the art of she-peeing off the damn thing yet, I do have to get up for the loo! You know what it's like, once you break the seal? Plus I soaked my fag papers with cider yesterday, so had to go to the kitchen for some more!'

'Ha, you should design a hammock companion, so you can keep all your stuff just at arm's length, but out of 'arm's way... get it, 'arm's way?'

Coco and Pod had been close friends since they were sixteen, twenty-six years ago when they had enrolled as art and design students. It is true what they say about students, eating curry for breakfast, cereal for tea and living off £36 for a term because they have blown their student loans on weed and cider in the first month. With the exception of drama students, art students are probably the most renowned for hellraising and partying their way through college. Some do not consider art to be a real subject to study, but there was a lot more to it than people might imagine. Researching was the key to success, experimentation with different materials, and exploring and stretching the boundaries of the mind. Long lunchtime sessions in the pub were frequent, with five friends sharing a burger and fries, and being kicked out at three in the afternoon when the pub closed. There were some fun afternoons, where the usual rabble would play Sardines. Coco remembered the toilet incident.

'D'ya remember when we all got stuck in that little disused toilet at college? None of us realised the door opened into the room, we all eventually piled in, then discovered we couldn't get out! How many of us were in there, seven, eight?'

'Can't remember mate… can't remember much about those days!' Pod replied, with a sheepish look on her face.

'No, me neither. I do remember telling the old dears in the college office we had no bus fare every night, they would lend us it, and we'd use it for chocolate on the bus ride home!' Coco replied laughing, 'then every morning we would repay them, and borrow again that night!'

'Bless them, yeah, we weren't exactly bad 'uns, just a little wayward,' said Pod.

'A little wayward isn't what I'd call it! Locking the staff room door shut with the college principle still inside!' Laughing, Coco got up and brushed woodland debris off her backside, 'Anyway, we didn't get caught, and I don't remember much hellraising after that. Did it scare us into doing some work rather than fooling around?'

'No,' Pod replied, 'it was about two weeks before we left, so I think we can class that particular incident as the grand finale!'

'Wicked, what little shits we were! The amount of times you and I got hauled up for not getting the work done! Surprised we even saw the end of the course, never mind actually pass it!'

The two girls walked back up the path to the orchard. It was late afternoon and although the day had been warm, the surrounding trees at the cottage caused the temperature to dip once the sun started to set behind the wood. The weather so far had been the coldest, wettest spring on record, so the warmth of the day had come as a surprise. Considering how cold it had been, the trees and plants were growing rather vigorously. Midges danced in the rays of sunlight as the coolness of the shadows grew deeper and darker. On leaving the orchard through an arch of honeysuckle that formed a broken hedge with raspberry bushes, the path turned into a mosaic of tree trunk slices. These were laid close together, with smaller trunk discs filling in the larger gaps. The discs had been placed and fixed, a framework had been put around the edges, and the middle filled with a resin to seal it all, so the path became smooth but see-through. As it had set, Coco had pushed little gravel pebbles to frame each tree disc, to act as a grip when the path was wet. This was a new design idea Pod and Coco were trying, and so far, it had performed perfectly. The tree trunks had maintained their colour, and all the rings could still be visible under a thin layer of resin. The pebbles formed circular patterns raised as a fail-safe, non-slip feature. It was a recycled natural crazy paving path, which ran perfectly straight and parallel between the double length garage and protecting Leylandii tree hedge, with raised beds on either side. They were made of railway sleepers, probably from when the track had passed right beside the house, and allowed good drainage for growing vegetables. Canes at the back were in ready for peas to climb up, and various parts of the fertile soil were in different stages of readiness for the next crop.

Although Coco and Art had lived here just over a year, the refurbishment had been slow to begin with. Money had never been of much interest to the two of them, but all of a sudden it had dawned on them how much work they wanted to do on the place. They had known from the beginning that it was going to be a very long, slow arduous test of stamina and emotion to finish the house, and neither had really considered the full extent of how much it was going to cost. When they had first moved in, the little cottage was perfectly habitable, and in truth, there were not many things that needed doing. The only door into the house faced a small paved area, where Coco chose to have herbs growing in terracotta pots and a rock garden like no other. An area big enough for four cars to park lay between the house and a wooden potting shed and next to that was the double length garage. The whole area had needed landscaping, as it was just bare ground, but a year on, most of the hard work had been done. Whenever Coco or Art saw a rock plant or herb that they liked, it would be brought home and ceremoniously planted. Care was taken with this; the plant would be placed in several locations, till its ideal home was found. A hole would be dug, homemade fertilizer put in the hole, followed by the plant. Once secure in the ground, it had a good watering. All the plants had had this amount of care, and the dedication they had received was displayed with thanks in a multitude of different coloured and shaped leaves. Due to their location, the rock garden and herbs were well tended, as anyone arriving at the door was encouraged to weed, deadhead or prune as they passed.

The back door of the house was original, and had been stripped back to its natural finish and varnished. It was furnished with a brass knocker shaped like a pine cone, with each layer of the cone spinning on a central axis. Its natural feel and movement were the first indications that it was calling to attention a house designed to be at one with the nature surrounding it, and free from the trappings of modern life.

Coco and Art had worked on the house together, although each had different skills. Coco had her Masters in the Renaissance, having done a total of eleven years studying at various points in her life. Whilst Coco had her artist eye, Art was strong and practical and could build anything. Art's father was also hands-on, and was always available to help out. It was a perfect example of opposites attracting. The only thing was, with Coco and Art, whilst academically they were total opposites, they were identical in most other aspects of their lives. They met at work, supported the same football team, both loved festivals, cider, tattoos and loud, fast music. Art was into his Metal, and Coco into her Punk. Although the genres are different, they were equally similar, and so their music tastes had developed as they shared each other's favourite bands. Even before they had met, they had the same banks, even accounts as each other, they both had several pairs of Vans trainers and both drove cars previously owned by their mothers.

People can say 'I love his style of clothes' or 'I love her taste in music', but words can be adapted to suit, and said to fit into a particular situation. With Coco and Art it was as if they'd had parallel lives with too many coincidences. Each family had nurtured a proper family home, and so Coco and Art's upbringings had both been secure and solid. With all parents in their sixties, they were still working in their professional chosen careers, looking forward to retirement after forty years contributing to their industries. Anyone who saw Coco and Art knew they were a genuinely happy pair.

Pod and Coco went through the back door and into a slate floored open plan dining area. Originally a small kitchen, the previous tenants had extended, with two rooms and a kitchen running off a corridor. Art had knocked through, so there was a big open space for a round dining table, with a galley kitchen, guest bedroom, art studio and fishing room leading from it. The spare downstairs bedroom had been massive, but Art had put a false wall in, creating a light, smaller bedroom, and a dark, five foot by twelve foot space, he hoped, he could turn into an art studio. Before the downstairs could have the structural work done, the guest bedroom was the main room they lived in. It had been added as an extension to the house when the elderly couple could not climb the stairs, which subsequently meant that the upstairs had not been lived in for twenty years. The three small double bedrooms were the first rooms to be decorated, and over a cold February, Art and his father had knocked down some walls, added a support pillar or two, and created one big bedroom, and a room-size walk-in wardrobe. It was a beautiful living space. Coco had been looking on Free-cycle for months, and had collected a vast array of fabrics.

Their bedroom was decorated in autumn berry colours, purples and reds, with the walls painted a ripe wheat colour. All of the walls were the same colour throughout the house, accented with different colours all representing the nature of the surrounding countryside. The bedroom had been lovingly laid out, with the bed facing an easterly window, which if left without a curtain would be the perfect morning alarm clock. In the corner, a silver birch tree trunk stood, acting as a pillar. It was the middle part of the tree, so it had some strong branches that had been trimmed to fit the room. The effect made the tree look like it was growing through the house, growing through the floor, ceiling and walls. It had seemed a shame to break the fallen silver birch for firewood, so it had been cleaned up and used in the house.

The walk-in wardrobe was originally the bedroom at the front of the house. It had its original fireplace, which Coco insisted should be cleaned up. It was a simple design but beautiful. She replaced the hearth with Victorian tiles, and stood one of her sculptures on it. All around the walls there were purpose-built shelves, rails, drawers and hooks for all Coco and Art's clothes, linens and towels. It had been a very long six months getting the upstairs done, but it meant Coco and Art could finally move out of the guest room. It was mid August, just as the berries were ripening that the room was finished. Sea-grass flooring had been laid, and once the antique pine furniture and soft furnishings were put in their place, the room looked homely, cosy and beautiful. They had chosen the luxury of the sea-grass flooring, as despite being made into a heavy duty, natural matting, there was still a grassy, sea salt odour, which made the room smell woody and warming. Coloured woollen rugs scattered the floor, as although natural, beautiful and hard wearing, sea-grass is hardly the softest of carpeting. A soft, twinkling glow from the coloured tealight holders finished the room off perfectly, looking like little fireflies dancing around the tree branches.

Once the upstairs of the house was complete, it gave way to free up the space downstairs. The narrow twisting stairs were also painted the same wheat colour, golden, rich buttermilk, and the same sea-grass flooring covered the stairs. This part of the house would not see much traffic, as it only led to the main bedroom from the lounge, as the bathroom was on the ground floor. Coco had hung lots of different sized and shaped framed pictures of their favourite rock idols. Slash and Johnny Rotten rubbed shoulders with Dimebag Darrell and Dave Grohl. It was like a mini hall of fame, with Guns and Roses gold discs and signed band merchandise hanging on the walls and around the window halfway up the stairs.

Art always felt it was good to remember who you are and where you come from, and so by walking past his heroes every day, he was reminded of who he was, and how close friends and family help you become the greatest you can be. These heroes must have had the same treatment, as they were each the greatest at what they did. Family is important, whether they are blood-related family, or the 'family' you are part of through your individual interests. At the bottom of the stairs was an antique pine, latched door which led into the lounge.

Pod went through to the studio, whilst Coco got two more ciders out of the fridge, and the rolling tin. Coming out of the long, narrow kitchen, which overlooked the herb garden, she turned left directly into the studio. There had been a wall and a door into the downstairs bedroom, but Art had removed those. Instead, he built a false wall across the bedroom, leaving a double bedroom with windows on one side, and a space ideal as a studio on the other. This room also made the dining area appear larger, as in effect the wall had been removed to the downstairs bedroom, leaving the art studio open-plan along with the dining area and galley kitchen. The next problem had been lighting, and they jointly decided to use a long, arched window, two thirds of the size of the one in the lounge, to naturally light the little art studio. It had been slightly extravagant, but as it was the drawings that had paid for the window, it seemed sensible to properly light the studio. A wide desk ran the narrow width of the room under the window, with a drawing board and adjustable top. It had sliding shelves for computer keyboards, racking underneath for the towers and flatscreens mounted on movable arms. A large black leather chair, claimed free from a skip when a local factory had a refurb a few months ago, was stationed at the desk. Coco stepped over Pod, who was lounging on a squishy cream sofa, with her feet on a book shelf. With the space being long and narrow, it had been planned for an ideal drawing point of view, not entertaining, so the maximum capacity the studio could take was two, if one was laying on the sofa, or three if the first person did not need to get out in a hurry!

There was work to discuss. There were a few small exhibitions coming up, and some competitions abroad to research. As Coco had a commission to complete, Pod agreed to look into things. When Pod left college she became a web designer, but once Coco had started to have success with the illustrating, she concentrated on helping Coco, and only did the web design jobs she liked the sound of. She helped Coco manage things, leaving more time for the drawings. Pod would do promotions, and book galleries or exhibitions. It was all quite small to start with, but six months since she had won an art competition, Coco had been inundated with requests and interviews. Nothing major, nothing like the front cover of *Hello* or featured in *The Sunday Times* supplement, but enough interest that her work and ideas were being thought about.

Spinning the leather chair back to face the window and drawing board, Coco critically analysed what needed to be done on the drawing. Pod got out her phone and started browse the internet. 'Are you still set on not having internet out here?' she asked, waiting for the connection signal. 'If things take off, you'll need to be on the net!'

'Na, not happening, don't think. I really believe that we all got on just fine without the net, and how are all you boffins going to cope when the plug gets pulled on it?' Coco replied, not looking up from her drawing. She switched a reading lamp on, that projected bright light onto her drawing board, without casting a shadow.

'So how are you going to get discovered by the bigger fish, if you won't jump into the big, worldwide ocean?' asked Pod.

'I'll let people over here find me, as they are starting to, then let *them* use their internet to tell the Yanks and Chinese, or whoever is interested. I like the old fashioned way, sending out brochures, arranging meetings, rather than just sitting at a computer all day. Bloody hell, you could even order tea off the computer, it's getting to the point where you don't have to lift an arse cheek to do anything. Besides, phone calls and the postal system may take longer, but it's personal, I like that!' Coco went on, 'The internet and computers are killing everything. High street shops, the national football... it's all going tits up because people can't be away from their computers, or computer games or Facebook for more than half an hour. Why walk in the rain to a muddy footie pitch out the back of beyond, when you can sit at home in the warm, with your mama bringing you warm milk and cookies every half hour, whilst you can pretend to be scoring for Barcelona in the Champions League!'

'Not this one again, Coco, bless you, that one still niggles you, doesn't it?'

'Not as bad as it used to!' admitted Coco, leaning back in the old chair to look at the last bit of drawing from a distance. Pod got up and had a look.

'Wow, nice one. We need to start thinking about what you want to do with all these drawings. You must have 20 big ones, A1 size, plus all the smaller ones. You've got the money, get them all framed and we'll get a decent exhibition going, somewhere nearer London.'

'Cool, yeah, do that. I'll have a think about what to frame, not doing them all. Besides, I'm exhibiting my artwork, not the bloody frames. I might not have any framed, just hang them as they are. If I frame them, people will only see them as I present them. If they buy them naked as it were, and then frame them how they would like to see them, they will all be different, with the individuals' characters framing them in different ways!'

'Certainly save on some cash!'

'Yes, that is what we shall do, savi?' said Coco, turning the chair to face Pod and the sofa. They talked and smoked some home-grown, talked and drank some cider. Some early eighties punk music acted as background noise, and the shadows outside the window grew longer. As the violets and dark blues that signify nighttime ensued, the girls thought about a pasta tea.

Chapter Four

May 2011, Italy

Ten days in Italy backpacking sounds a long time, but the trip could have been longer. There was so much to see. May was the best time to visit Italy as it was warm enough for short sleeves, especially in the southern part of the country, but the main attractions were not overrun with tourists. Sophie and Miriam had already spent a day in Rome, having landed there on a budget flight. They had bought sightseeing tickets for the tourist open-topped bus, and had hopped on and off all day at the major sights. The Colosseum had been as spectacular as they had imagined it to be, and they had even found a reasonable tour for just 20 euros. The guide talked in English, pointing out all the important features of the imposing building. It was difficult to get a true feeling of the spirit of the place as it was so crowded, even though it was out of season. At the height of the summer the heat and crowds were unbearable, but although it was busy, the chaos went unnoticed with such grand surroundings. Once the guide had finished his tour, he answered a few questions and gradually his audience drifted away.

Miriam and Sophie found a few steps high up in the middle class seating area to sit on, and admired the interior of the sports arena. Just behind them was a metal barrier prohibiting people from wandering too high into the stands. With 2,000 years of outdoor erosion and general wear and tear, the building was in need of some love and attention. The fumes and pollution of the city were not helping its aging process, with modern fast roads passing close by on two of the Colosseum's sides. The remains of ancient Imperial Rome lay in ruins on the other two sides. Walking out of the Colosseum, they passed the Arch of Constantine, and walked up the Via Sacra, Sacred Way, towards what was the seat of Imperial Rome. Huge white columns and archways, statues of Roman citizens and the basic layout of the city were still visible, and to a creative eye, it would be possible to envisage the buildings all intact. This was the high society end of Ancient Rome, where the senate would meet, and rich citizens would have grand homes with armies of slaves to cater for their every wish. After leaving the Colosseum, the girls walked through the ruins, looking for somewhere to sit down and have a quiet break. They found a little flight of stairs leading to a marbled balcony, though the rest of the building was missing. They sat on some fallen stone, and took in their surroundings.

'Remember when eight of us came here a few years back? That was a good trip!' said Miriam.

'I remember pushing someone around in a bloody wheelchair for the first few days, up and down these wretched hills over cobbled stones!' replied Sophie, 'and the best thing was, that by the end of the trip, her partner had done his back in pushing her around so they swapped and she pushed him. Turned out she didn't really need the chair after all!'

'Well, I'm not complaining. We didn't have to queue to get on the aeroplane. Was that the trip you and Shifty wanted to carry on drinking after the bars had shut, so you got a load of take-out and rode the lift all night? By the morning you were both slaughtered, and Shifty had even started filling the bottles back up because you couldn't remember which floor your rooms were on, to go to the loo!'

'I remember!' laughed Sophie, 'we did 12 bottles of Breezer each in that lift. No idea how many miles we must have travelled in it! We'd never have got away with that in another country. I think the building we were in was part privately owned and part hotel. We couldn't remember which floor we lived on... till you came out and told us to shut up!'

'All we could hear from the room was the whirring of the lift mechanism, and you two giggling getting louder and quieter as you rode the lift. Gradually you got quieter, but every now and again you both laughed hysterically.'

'I think that was probably when Shifty realised he needed more room in his pee bottle, and was quickly running out of time for decision-making. I was nearly wetting myself because I was laughing so much'

'No wonder us Brits get such a bad name from alcohol-related incidents. Disgraceful when you think about it,' said Miriam. 'Luckily that was our last night, and you two had stonking hangovers.'

'We were still drinking at four in the morning, and we had to leave the hotel at seven. I guess with every good there comes bad!'

It was the middle of the afternoon and warm enough to wear just shirts. Tourists of all nationalities marvelled at the ancient ruins, whilst busy Italians hurried about their daily business, with total disregard for the history around them. Cyprus trees stood on the ridge above the remains of Ancient Rome, and a strong smell of pine drifted on a spring breeze. Some small birds were causing a commotion in a nearby bush, squabbling over some yellow berries. There was so much going on around, and yet the site of the ruins seemed quite tranquil; an ideal place to have a think, if it were not for all the tourists. From their elevated position, they could look down on the Forum Romanum, with the three remaining marble columns of the Temple of Caster, the foundations of the Basilica Lulia, and in the distance the Arch of Septimus Severus, with the Curia, the meeting hall of the senate besides it.

There was a short walk to pick up the bus, with the next planned stop being St Peter's, the home to the Pope and head of the Roman Catholic Church. As the girls were not returning to their Rome hotel, they had their backpacks with them. They had specifically planned to travel light, knowing they would have to carry all of their belongings at times. St Peter's had been fantastic, because they had managed to see the *Pieta* by Michelangelo. It was a stunning masterpiece. The two girls continued their argument as to which Mary the artist had portrayed in the sculpture. They had been having this discussion for years, as to whether it was the Virgin Mary, Jesus' mother, or Mary Magdalene, Jesus' partner.

As they queued at the metal detectors of their last sight-seeing spot, they planned the following day. They had left their bags at a nearby luggage store which was a nice relief. After St Peter's, they would take the early evening fast train to Naples, then get the Cirumvesuviana, a slow, local train that ran past Pompeii, and on to a small fishing town called Sorrento on the Amalfi Coast. They planned to have a relaxing evening, a good night's rest, and then take the local train back to Pompeii in the morning. The whole day had been allocated for Pompeii, after which they would go straight from Naples to Florence, several hundred miles north of Rome. The queue moved quickly, but there was no real hurry. The weather was fine and dry, with a watery blue sky stretching as far as the eye could see. The magnificent foreground to St Peter's has a centrepiece obelisk, which had originally been taken from Egypt by Emperor Caligula and placed in Nero's circus nearby. A rounded colonnade swept round to enclose the square, topped by 140 statues of saints. It was such a grandiose setting, the girls became lost in their own thoughts. This was the finest example of Renaissance architecture by greats such as Michelangelo, Bernini and Bramante. Pigeons flew around the highest points of St Peter's, putting into perspective just how big the dome was.

Once Sophie and Miriam were inside the basilica, they went straight over to the Pieta, situated on the right as you entered the church. It was a lot smaller in real life, approximately five feet square, but the detail was so intricate. How Michelangelo had managed to carve such detail out of very hard Carrara marble was astonishing.

'She has to be Mary Magdalene!' exclaimed Sophie, looking into the beautiful sorrowful face of the young woman with Jesus lying across her lap. 'She looks younger than Him, so how can she be his mother?'

'But she can't be Mary Magdalene, she must be the Virgin Mary!' Miriam replied. 'The church would never allow Jesus to be seen with his girlfriend, partner, wife or whatever she was.'

'You know my opinion on religion, "my imaginary friend is better than your imaginary friend" kind of thing,' whispered Sophie, deciding that this particular point in time, at this particular location, was probably not the best time to discuss religion. 'Jesus, you know how it winds me up. Take this statue, why don't they sell it and feed a few hundred, thousand kiddies in Africa?'

'Shhh, don't take the Lord's name in vain,' Miriam replied, looking over her shoulder at a security lady looking in their direction, 'particularly not in here, anyway!'

'Don't start me off on blasphemy, Miriam!'

'I know, don't tell me, 'there's no such thing as blasphemy until the name taken in vain is proven to exist!' Miriam quoted, having spent many a drunken night with Sophie discussing such things. They both had such different views on religion, though Miriam was not a practising churchgoer, she had some faith. 'Come on, let's have a look around.'

'And another thing,' Sophie piped up, causing Miriam to take her by the arm and usher her away from a suspicious security lady, 'besides, the church is still pissed that science came along and started to disprove a lot of what they had been preaching for the last god-knows-how many years!'

'Soph, less of the *god* word in here, please mate, though I must say, your sense of timing is impeccable, but I had thought you'd got over that one by now?'

'Mirry...' Sophie took her arm to get her to stop and look at her. 'Just look around you. Vatican City is one of the richest countries in the world, and yet the majority of its followers live in poverty. Why should that be right?'

'Sophie, I don't know, I can't answer that. Power can do strange things to people. It makes them see things differently I guess.'

'But some Popes, Mirry, they're no better than Nazis!' Suddenly Sophie turned around and briskly walked out of the church.

Miriam was left in stunned silence, that out of all the places in the world to hear that, Sophie had chosen St Peter's. 'Totally unbelievable, you couldn't write this stuff,' muttered Miriam, walking slowly in Sophie's footsteps. She was in no hurry, as she knew Soph would be sat on the steps outside, having a cigarette. Slowly taking in all the different marbles that St Peter's interior was made from, she headed out into the warmth of blinding, bright sunshine. Sure enough, sat on a shallow, wide step was Sophie, lying back with her face turned up to the sun, leaning on her elbows. Her skinny black jeans were stretched out in front of her, tipped with bright red suede Doctor Martins, with red tartan shoe laces.

Miriam walked over towards her, *a free spirit who doesn't give a shit!* she thought.

'Come on then, let's go get this train!' said Miriam, not slowing down as she walked past Sophie.

'Hang on then,' replied Sophie, scrabbling up off the ground, cigarette hanging from her mouth, as she collected her tobacco tin, lighter and jumper. 'I was just saying mate, what does the church actually do? It has all this money...' she dropped her jumper, and by the time she had picked it up, Miriam was already a few paces ahead. 'Miriam, tell me...' Sophie trotted on to catch up. 'Dude, hang on, I'm dropping all my things.' Miriam stopped and they organised themselves. Once again, Sophie took Miriam's arm and said 'Mate, what *is* it that they *do*? The Church, Mirry, what do they do? As I see it, it's just clever men cashing in on sun worship! Why did they discredit science? Because they knew science could prove the church to be a crock of horse shit!'

They went to collect their bags and walked to the bus stop for their final ride through Rome to the central station. Sophie continued with her one-sided discussion. Miriam put across her opinion every now and again, and continued to monitor who could understand what she was saying, by the raised eyebrows and tuts. 'It's just as well most of them haven't got a clue what she's banging on about,' thought Miriam, 'there'd be an international incident!' Sophie eventually wore herself out, with the last five minutes of the bus journey passing in silence. There were all types on the bus, lots of tourists and even two nuns sat bolt upright in the front row of the upper deck, chattering away at one another. They both had their hands in their laps, and looked so similar they might have been twins.

'Look at those two!' Sophie started up again, nodding her head in the direct of the front of the bus.

'Oh, no, Soph, surely you're not going to have a go about those two lovely, happy old dears? Probably the nicest people you'll ever meet, little tiny old ladies who've served God all their lives!'

'I was going to say, ah, look at those two, aren't they cute-ums but then remembered the stories my mate used to tell me, about life in a school run by nuns. Those women are brutal, man, I mean, proper tough from what I heard!'

'Yes, but knowing some of your friends, I imagine a bit of toughness would do them some good!' Miriam said, enjoying the day's banter.

'My friends... *my* friends!' said Sophie. 'That's rich, Miss Shinier-Than-Yow, you've had your run-ins. You may be 20 years older than me, but you told me what you used to get up to... Punk!'

'Yes, alright, you got me, enough said,' replied Miriam.

'You punks set the benchmark for what was to follow. Set it rather high too!'

'And now look at me, babysitting you around Rome, spouting off how crap religion is. It should be the other way around!'

The bus pulled up at the Termini station and a few tourists got off. As with most cities, the area surrounding the main station was never the most desirable of areas. Although Rome had all its magnificent architecture a stone's throw away from the station, it was not the most aesthetic of places. The massive station, with its Euro-star connections to all the major destinations in Italy and Europe, was as busy as ever. The bus terminal in front of the station was a deathtrap to negotiate, especially adding on the Italian aggressive way of driving. Stylish Alfa Romeo taxis appeared from nowhere, with optional indicating! Crossing to the main building was a test of nerves. Every nationality was represented in the people using the station. Various groups of students stood waiting for instructions, amidst Romans going about their daily businesses. For a nation synonymous for its high fashion and designers, the locals certainly represented their fellow kinsmen. Graceful, slim women briskly walked with a confidence that success and fine clothes can bring. Their olive, flawless skin and stylish haircuts complimenting expensive sunglasses pushed back onto their foreheads, and perfectly cut dresses floated about smooth, shapely legs. Confident young men with tailored fitted shirts in bright complimentary colours erratically talked on their mobile phones, with exaggerated hand gestures.

Every type of eatery was represented on the station concourse. From fast food outlets, to coffee shops, sandwich bars and paper stands. There were long queues at the ticket office, where non-Italian speaking tourists were trying to buy train tickets. Patient and polite as the ticket staff were, it was written all over their faces that just for once, it would be nice if these foreigners would at least make an effort to learn the language. After all, they were expected to understand English, German and Japanese! The station was a hub of activity, with the sweet smells of fresh coffee and bread mixing with the heady smell of diesel.

It had become quite muggy, with thunderous rain clouds forming at an alarming rate. The train journey to Naples would be a few hours, and so the girls bought fresh paninis, beers and bottled water for the trip. They had decided to get a fast food take-away when they arrived in Naples, as they would be arriving in Sorrento quite late, with the possibility of missing dinner at the hotel.

'What platform do we need?' said Sophie. 'There's like 10,000 to choose from!'

'The information board will tell us. Here we are, platform six!'

'I'm looking forward to the trip "dahn sowf",' Sophie replied, putting on a fake cockney accent. 'Pompeii is going to be wicked. I can't imagine how it's going to feel... you know, what with all those people dying there when the volcano blew its stack. It looks amazing what they have already uncovered from the site, and I'm hoping it's not going to be busy.'

'May is usually the lull before the storm as far as tourists are concerned. We should be able to get away from the throng of it. I can't wait too, shame we don't have time to go up Mount Vesuvius!'

'We can do it another time. Maybe fly into Naples and explore Southern Italy?'

As they showed their tickets and walked along the platform, trains came and went at an alarming rate.

'Isn't Mussolini responsible for the clockwork running of the Italian rail network? Sophie remarked as she got on the train. 'If it's scheduled to leave at 11 minutes past, it does!'

'No, I think that's a myth about Mussolini. But if they are as reliable as people say, we should be leaving in...' Miriam checked the station clock. '... about twelve minutes' time!'

Twelve minutes after getting onto the train, a whistle blew, and the train carriages gave a small jerk, and glided into life. They rattled and clattered over the hundreds of railway track junctions; a complicated mass of parallel tracks criss-crossing over one another. There were miles of overhead cables running above the tracks, with signal boxes and lights showing different instructions and colours. Gradually, as the lines merged, the ride became smoother, until the train was able to pick up speed, as it settled onto its set of tracks. Passing through highrise flats and suburbs of Rome, the train accelerated, developing a rhythmical motion and sound. The track occasionally crossed over gated roads, where lines of Alfa Romeos and Fiats sat patiently; a rarity when considering Italian driving. The concrete urban jungle gave way to more greenery, until the train was speeding through the spring Italian countryside.

Luscious fields of sunflowers not yet fully in bloom flashed by, with the occasional field of grapevines. Olive and fig trees flourished in the development of summer, gradually shrouding ancient farm buildings and barns with their foliage. Beautiful country residences of dusky pink, with green shutters, or creamy yellows with grey shutters were dotted about as the train headed south. The rural Italian architecture had a very distinctive look, with impressive square buildings holding up shallow, pyramid roofs, each featuring weather-eroded masonry.

Looking out of the window, Sophie said, 'There's something about buildings in Italy. It's especially so in Venice... the more weathered they are, the nicer they look. I mean, Venice has its fabulous palaces along the Grand Canal, but then when you get into the northern part, the ghetto, the old and uncared-for buildings look just as good!'

'I think that too. The buildings that need a lick of paint actually look better than the ones that are maintained. I guess the climate over here, with it being warmer and drier erodes differently to the damp, cold of home!'

'Don't remind me about the cold and damp of home. Had a text from a friend who said the weather is crap, the coldest and wettest on record or something!'

'Looks like we are in for a sprinkling too! Look at those clouds ahead of us!'

'Bloody hell, looks like Armageddon. It's different abroad isn't it, I mean, if we had those massive black clouds at home, you know it's rain, and that it's gonna rain, and worse case scenario is... you'll get wet. Out here though, not having grown up with this weather, how do we know if those clouds are bringing severe doom and gloom, or are they just full of rain!' Sophie said, looking around the train carriage. There was no one else in their compartment. A long corridor ran the length of the carriage, with sliding doors on one side leading to a pair of long benches, facing each other. She got up to slide the door open. All was calm. 'No mass hysteria out there, so I think it's safe to say that it's just going to be one huge, fuck off thunderstorm!'

'It'll have passed by the time we have to get out at Naples. We don't have to be exposed to the outside world now, till about nine tonight when we get off the Cirumvesuviana in Sorrento.'

'It's only half five now. How long is the ride on the little train going to take. Are we going to have enough time to get everything done?'

'Yeah, plenty of time. We can see Sorrento tonight and if we're lucky, have a snack somewhere nice. Tomorrow we'll get up early for the ride back to Pompeii, and if we leave there by three, we'll be getting off the Eurostar in Florence for about eight!'

'D'ya think we've tried to fit too much in? All sounds a bit package-holidayish, rushing around and stuff?'

'It's only these first few days. If we hadn't have wanted to see Pompeii there would have been more time, but as we both agreed that the travelling is part of the trip, and neither of us mind the train rides, Sorrento and Pompeii is do-able.'

'Yeah, it looks so beautiful. If we're in that neck of the woods, we might as well I guess. Be great to have some seafood by the Med though.'

'Thought you wanted fast food at Naples station?'

'I've been thinking about that one, and think tea in Sorrento, especially as it's only going to be nine-ish. We've got enough here to keep us going till tomorrow, so, what d'ya say, tea by the sea?'

Miriam was used to Sophie's indecisive nature, having raised two children with the same traits. They had met a few years ago, at college, where Sophie was straight out of sixth form and Miriam had returned to education as a mature student. They studied together on a Design Crafts course, and were highly talented. They both got top grades in all of their modules, and had decided to take a tour round Italy as a well deserved break. Maybe not the intended purpose of their student loans, but it was better than most, who spent theirs on cider and weed. They were fortunate enough that the course they were on was in their home town, and so although they were entitled to, and claimed their student loans, it was not ear-marked for rent and living expenses. Sophie worked part-time in a little bakery on the high street, and Miriam had the loving support of her husband, himself a talented musician. The use of recycled materials was strongly supported by the tutors, which made stretching the loans a little easier.

They had been on the train for just over an hour, when it was noticed that it was slowing down. It came to a gentle halt and silence ensued. Children could be heard laughing and playing, whilst a slim buffet cart banged off the narrow walls of the corridor. Ten minutes later, a tall young man pushing the trolley stopped outside the compartment Sophie and Miriam were in. They watched, as he ducked down to look out of the window running the length of the corridor. He muttered something in Italian whilst using his right hand, to cross himself.

'Well that doesn't look too bloody hopeful, does it!' exclaimed Sophie, with genuine concern in her voice. 'Jeez, when the natives are praying to Him upstairs, you know it's going to be bad!' She sprang off her seat, and slid the door open. Looking up and down the carriage, people were doing the same thing, each noticing the ominous spectacle ahead on the horizon. As Sophie turned to look in the same direction, at first she thought there was a blind to pull up.

'What's going on, mate!'

'Oh my fucking God!' came the answer, as Sophie stood with her nose squashed against the thick glass. 'Um, think you might want to see this!'

Miriam joined Sophie at the window and could not believe what she was seeing. The clouds were the blackest she had ever seen. Lightning flashed sporadically, creating spotlights that lit the countryside. There were early signs of residential areas, the beginnings of Naples's suburbs. Over in the very distance, the Bay of Naples could be seen, where the Mediterranean Sea joined the mainland. If the view had been clear, a distant Mount Vesuvius would have been visible on the other side of the bay.

'Fuck me!' whispered Miriam.

Sophie turned slowly to look at her best friend, one she rarely heard swear. 'Excuse me. Do you mind, potty mouth!'

'Fuck me!' Miriam repeated, 'That is one serious motherfucker of a rain storm. Do you think that's why the train has stopped?'

'Dunno, trains can go through rain, can't they?'

'Yes, but it's an electric train, powered by cables overhead, and with that being one massive electrical storm...'

'Oh!'

Miriam craned her neck at the window, looking in the direction that the train had just come. There was a purple line where the rain cloud ended, and the deep, blue sky of spring started. She stepped back into the compartment, and looked at the skies on the other side. She could work out that the heart of the storm was over the Bay of Naples, and the skies on the other side of the train were not as menacing. 'It's worse your side than this!' Miriam called out to Sophie, 'think it's centred towards the bay!'

'My eyesight has gone all funny. I could see things in the distance, now my line of vision seems to be getting shorter and short... SHIT!' screamed Sophie, jumping back from the window.

Pandemonium struck the train, along with lashings of rain. It was as if car wash bristles were battering the outside, whilst supernatural forces threw massive buckets of water at the windows. The carriages rocked, their heftiness not a match for the torrent of nature attacking the flimsy metal of the train. The rain against the windows reduced the visibility to zero, as the rocking motion increased. Bags started jumping around in the overhead compartments, and people had trouble keeping their balance. They could be seen with arms outstretched holding onto both sides of the corridor. The noise was phenomenal, with people shouting, children crying, the creaking of the train and the thunderous torrents of rain blasting the windows and roof. People were running to gather screaming and sobbing children, the elderly sat huddled in their seats, quite clearly praying. Sophie and Miriam looked at each other and simultaneously mouthed 'SHIT!'

Then, there was blackness. The lights flickered back on briefly and then went off altogether. A chilling moment of silence inside the train was emphasised by the noise outside. With the exception of the moaning carriages, the occupants of the train were struck dumb by fear, followed by hysteria. Sophie and Miriam both rushed towards their sliding door and dived into the compartment, sitting in the seats furthest from the window. The other travellers were shouting, women were crying, and strong male voices could be heard above the commotion. Although the attack continued outside, the panic on the train subsided a little. Miriam looked up the corridor from her seat, and saw a man and woman dressed in the livery of the train company walking down the length of the carriage, poking their heads into each compartment. They spoke in calm Italian, their immaculately tailored suits looking as fresh as the first day they were worn. The more they spoke, the quieter the train became, the passengers obviously understanding what they were being told.

The train staff came to Sophie and Miriam's part of the train, having to steady themselves with the rocking carriages and started speaking in Italian. They quickly realised the girls did not understand them, and so the male attendant spoke in broken English, 'Ladies, my English no good to speak. Be calm. Is safe here,' he said in a confident manner, 'the train, has many rain outside, but here is safe.'

'Cor, he's a handsome guy,' said Sophie quite openly, 'I bet he would indeed keep us safe!'

'Miss, my English speak a little, but my English understand very good. You are... how you say... very petty!' he smiled at Sophie, then Miriam, and then at his co-worker.

'Shit, Soph, he understood you and now you've pissed him off. Don't go upsetting him, 'cause in case you haven't noticed, the train is still stationary and he could throw us off!'

'Petty, what the fuck did I say that was petty! Cheeky fucker,' Sophie turned to stare at the attendant, whose smile quickly vanished as he succumbed to a barrage from the feisty English lady, which was heard over the downpour pelting the roof and windows. His colleague led him away to the next section of the train, whilst Miriam tried to calm Sophie down. 'Don't worry about it. Main thing he says we are safe, and whatever the reason he was able to tell the other passengers, they trust him, so should we.' The rain could still be heard and the rocking of the carriage had not abated. Suddenly, the male attendant came rushing back down the corridor, and handed Sophie a slip of paper.

'Oh no, he's going to throw us off the train!' Miriam said, her mouth suddenly very dry.

The handsome man took Sophie's right hand and instead of leading her out of the compartment, he kissed it. He held it for a little while longer, muttering softly in Italian, then turned to Miriam, smiled and winked before leaving the carriage. 'What the f...' said Sophie, as she unfolded the piece of paper he had left in her hand. 'It's only his phone number *and* email address!'

'What? Are you joking?' replied Miriam, nearly falling over as she stood up to sit next to Sophie, just as the train did a massive jolt, 'let's see!'

'I'll be blown!'

'Think that's what he's hoping!' laughed Sophie, 'back in a minute.'

'Oh no you don't, you're not leaving me here on my own. Besides, he just called you "petty" for complimenting him, which he quite clearly understood!'

They then both looked at each other and said 'Pretty!' and laughed.

'We really ought to try and learn the language you know,' said Miriam chuckling to herself. A different attendant opened the sliding door. 'You English ladies?' he asked, as the girls nodded, 'the weather is bad, so train stop for safety. All is good. We go soon, delay only a little,' he said, smiled and disappeared again. The train was still being battered by the rain, and the rocking motion had become an accepted part of life. Little emergency lights had come on, casting an old fashioned yellow light through the carriage, when suddenly there was a sharp jolt, accompanied by little shrill screams from the rest of the carriage. The rocking had subsided, and the second jolt led to the train to start on its way. The rain continued as heavy as it had been, but the rocking could no longer be felt.

'Why are we starting off again if it's still crap out there?' asked Sophie.

'I dunno mate, the rocking has stopped, so maybe it was the wind that was the threat, not the rain.'

'I guess. How long till we're in Naples. It's nearly seven now!'

'Not long, we're on the outskirts of the suburbs.'

'Wicked. I think a beer is in order before we get the next train, and you never know, Handsome Train Man might be finishing here too. Is this train going on?'

'No, think it's terminating here!'

'Wicked' smiled Sophie.

'Yeah, great,' replied Miriam, sarcastically, 'I know one thing though, we need to check if the Cirumvesuviana is running, as it's only like a local train, slow and rickety. Plus it runs along the coast sometimes crossing ravines on viaducts. Be buggered if I want to get stuck on that out there!'

An hour later, the girls were drinking Peroni out of the bottle, sat in a little bar at Naples station. The rest of the journey had been uneventful, thankfully, and when they got off the train, more than a handful of passengers 'crossed' themselves as they touched down on terra firma. Naples station was as big as the Termini at Rome, but it had a certain scruffiness, older and disrespected, dirty in places. The beer had been expensive, but very much needed. A television was on, hung from a wonky bracket above the bar. It was showing some weather report. Miriam got up and walked closer to the screen, trying to pick out the few words of Italian she knew. It was still raining heavily outside, as people were coming into the bar drenched. Even those with umbrellas had wet shoes and legs. The news showed a map of Italy, zooming in on the Bay of Naples. The reporter was talking too fast for her, and she could not work it out. Her faced contorted as she tried in vain to understand what was being said, as she was sure it had something to do with what had happened on the train earlier.

'Waterspout!' said a voice she recognised. How could she recognise a voice, she had only been in Naples a short time? Miriam turned to look at the voice, and saw Sophie mouthing in the distance, 'Told you'. It was the train attendant who had just finished his shift, who she had heard and recognised.

After a second bottle of beer, the decision had been made to move on with the journey. The three of them had chatted about the basic facts of their lives. *He obviously likes Sophie,* thought Miriam, as she watched her friend's body language, and the way the stranger was responding to her. *He's got a gorgeous smile,* she continued to think, as he leaned in towards Sophie, while she sat on the tall bar stool, with one leg tucked underneath her. In the background, the old television on the wall was running a news report on the waterspout that had been so powerful; it had travelled ten miles inland.

'We better get going,' Sophie unexpectedly said, jumping up off her stool. She hitched her bag onto her back, and picked up Miriam's bag to help her put it on. The attendant's smile had faded, but then beamed again, as Sophie gave him a kiss on the lips. It was a little longer than perhaps necessary, but it's not as though she was going to see him again. They left the bar, and headed for the Cirumvesuviana, Sophie smiling to herself at her handling of the Italian.

'Why the sudden haste to leave?' asked Miriam, as they walked through the station's many corridors for their next connection. 'Things were going so well!'

'They were, till he mentioned his wife or girlfriend or someone!'

'You dick, he was talking about his mother,' replied Miriam.

'You have to be kidding me!' screamed Sophie, causing passers-by to look at her.

Chapter Five

The Apricot Mews, Chelsea

Over the next few days, Victoria and Elizabeth primed their mark. Flynn had absolutely no idea what he was heading for, as the women had hatched a truly master plan. They were very careful to cover their tracks, and ensured they never left any records of texts, phone numbers or messages on their phones or computers. It had taken a few days to formulate, but due to their determination to get the ultimate revenge, they played their parts perfectly.

Victoria started to tell Flynn she had been having erotic dreams, about trying a little girl-on-girl action. They had always been able to talk about anything, and so it was not an unusual conversation. As Victoria was planting the seed, Elizabeth fed it a little. She sent Flynn a text to say sorry, and that she would not be bothering him again. She said she had no malice towards him, as at the end of the day, eventually their child may want to know who its father was and so for the sake of the child, Elizabeth would not create a scene, as it was clear 'for some reason' he did not want to be involved. Therefore she was happy to raise the child by herself. She had a wealthy family who owned five hotels in the surrounding villages and so money would not be an issue. She even thanked him. Flynn was not driven by money, but his opinion of fatherhood suddenly changed when he realised he would not have to support the child. Victoria would never need to know, as there would never be a discrepancy in the bank account. He could carry on as he had been, throughout all of his marriage to Victoria. She was a lovely girl, perfect... he just could not resist a temptation, especially when he knew his wife would never find out. 'Victoria never knew about Emily, doesn't know about Elizabeth and certainly won't ever find out about Baby Flynn,' he thought to himself, after thinking about his previous affairs and Elizabeth's text.

Victoria's next task was to borrow a girly porn film off Phil, her drag queen friend from her childhood. He was the oldest and biggest queen in town, with his six-foot-four frame dressed in lavish costumes and four-inch heels, playing at Madam Jojos every Saturday night in Soho, to a packed audience. He still had the quickest tongue in the trade and was always up for revenge. The plan continued and although the bait was set, it was now down to the crucial moment, when Victoria would drop the bombshell. It had to be subtle, but with just enough of the worm dangling, so they were sure Flynn would get hooked. Victoria suggested how nice it would be to go to Cumbria, for a long weekend like they used to. She had even found a hotel, that was part of a little chain of family-run old inns and Flynn could show her the best bits of Hadrian's Wall. The women knew that at this point, if Flynn had not smelt a rat, then it would be safe to continue reeling him in. Victoria had been careful, suggesting other remote locations and laughed to herself when she informed him of where she had booked.

The final snatch of the rod was Elizabeth's responsibility. The women knew that Flynn would have to protect himself, in case he bumped into Elizabeth in Cumbria, which was a strong possibility at Victoria's chosen destination. As predicted, Flynn texted Elizabeth, being exceptionally polite and nice, explaining he was bringing up an old flame who wanted to have an expert show her the wall and would be in the hotel. He hoped it would not be too awkward, as the lady was just a friend, but he did not want a scene. He even apologised and said this was not his idea, but did not want to upset his friend, as apparently it was her favourite place in England. When Victoria and Elizabeth conferred on the latest development, the sheer cheek and outright loathing they had for Flynn, merely highlighted their determination. They had decided to change their final assault. They had planned to have a big show down in the hotel, them against Flynn. He would not have known what had hit him, but due to the new levels he was prepared to go to, they decided to destroy him. Just four days after meeting each other, the trap was set in London. And it was foolproof.

Flynn could not believe his luck... not only did he love his wife dearly, there was now a possibility that she might want to experiment in her sexuality. As the days went by, he found he was actually cooking up a plan that would be any man's dream, your wife and mistress at the same time. He tried to avoid the thought, but he got aroused; his foolish plan started to seem infallible. He dismissed the thoughts as best he could and regarded himself lucky that Victoria was talking about a third person in the bedroom. He hoped that it was only a matter of days before something happened. Victoria and Flynn had always had quite a carefree way of living, with an understanding if one of them wanted to try something, they should be allowed to, so long as it didn't break the law, or class as cheating on one another. The day came when Flynn got a text from Victoria, telling him to be ready for a big surprise when he got home and to have a shower at work first.

Flynn rode his bike through the security gates to the mews and noticed Victoria at the window only just visible, lit by soft candlelight. There was someone else with her and judging by the long hair, it was another woman, or a heavy metal fan. *This could either be very very good, or very very bad,* he thought. He entered the house and saw a note left on one of the stairs. He looked around to see a fancy dress suit hanging up. It was of a gladiator, complete with a feather-topped helmet, sword and leather strapped sandals. He could hear an adult film being played upstairs and fell over several times in his haste to get his clothes off and the uniform on. He checked himself in the lounge mirror and with difficulty, marched up the stairs. The bedroom door was virtually closed, so he stopped to listen, his blood pounding around his body, his thoughts and ideas running away with him.

'Flynn, come join us,' he heard Victoria say, in a sleepy, seductive voice.

He pushed open the door with the point of his fake sword and could just about make out his wife, lying on the bed. The candlelight he had seen from the street had gone out, so just a miniature spotlight set in the ceiling of the landing lit the bedroom. There was another person in the room, the one he had seen at the window laying on the bed beside her and both had their hands tied to the bedstead. Flynn entered the room, pushing the door open with the point of his fake sword. Just then, the lights flooded on,

'AH!' screamed Victoria, thrashing around on the bed.

'Help me, please help me!' whimpered Elizabeth, pretend tears streaming down her over-exaggerated, make-up smeared face, 'Please stop him.'

Flynn did not know what was happening. As the lights flashed on they revealed Victoria and Elizabeth tied to the bed. He did not know what to think. Everything happened so quickly. The women increased their acting when Flynn took a step towards them, but with his hands held out in a gesture of calm, he forgot about the sword in his hand, which just happened to be real, borrowed from the museum. By taking a step forward, he saw someone else in the room, but his attention was quickly brought back to the women on the bed, when they started to really thrash about, with petrified, tear-sodden, terrifying screaming, struggling against their fake restraints.

'Victoria, what the fuck is going on here? Elizabeth, Victoria... oh FUCK!' Flynn could now clearly see in the mirror's reflection the third person in the room and saw he was holding a gun and a smartphone.

'Smile, Sweetie, you're on live stream!'

Twenty minutes later, Phil the drag queen stood at the bottom of the wooden sleigh bed, with his arms around Victoria on one side and Elizabeth on the other. The three of them were stood over Flynn, who had been forcibly tied to the bed, with a little persuasion from Phil and his weapon.

'You thought you were clever... everyone thinks you're clever, but now we know. You're not clever at all. How did you suppose we tied ourselves to the bed?' Victoria jeered.

'I wasn't exactly thinking about basic physics. This is entrapment!'

'It doesn't matter what it is. Call it what you like,' said Elizabeth. 'You're finished. It will be a matter of days before you get arrested, in fact, I'll ring them now I think.'

'Wait a minute, darling,' said Phil, in the campest of voices, 'I've got a little treat for our man here; it's in my trousers!'

'Oh God, no way. Vicky, Beth, come on, please!' shrieked Flynn, wriggling around on the bed, as Phil fiddled about looking for something in his trousers.

'Not that silly boy, gosh, you rate yourself. No, lookie what I have here darlings...' Phil continued, holding out a little bottle of something. Flynn was desperately trying to see what it was Phil was holding.

'What is it, what are you going to do?' he wailed, scared, as he didn't know what limits these three would go. He realised that somehow he had been found out and that Victoria and Elizabeth had set out to at least humiliate him, at worse... who knows, but they had already ruined his career, set him up to get arrested, so how much further where they prepared to go?

'Itching power!' squealed Phil joyfully, stretching out his arm he sprinkled it all over Flynn's groin, doing a little pixie dance as he went. 'You know what they say, Flynn, sleeping around can cause nasty itches. As dear Elizabeth is quite clearly pregnant, you obviously don't practise safe sex and now you are going to have to deal with the consequences. Happy pork sword scratchings!' and with that, the three of them left the room, shutting the door and turning off the landing light.

As they walked down the stairs and out of the front door, Flynn could hear them talking.

'Where did you get that gun from, Phil?'

'Darling, a good queen always carries protection. You never know what might pop up!'

'It could have turned nasty, imagine if it had gone off. We wouldn't be walking away with our heads held high!'

'Oh darling, yes you would. If this gun had gone off, we would have all walked away with our heads held very high. Look!' at which point Phil pulled the trigger on the gun. A little jet of liquid flew out, 'It's only Woo Woo lovies, my favourite "cock" tail, it's just a little Woo Woo!'

Chapter Six

May 2011, Lincolnshire

It was way past midnight when Coco and Pod retired for the night. They had sat in the cosy lounge, with Mahoney the house rabbit stretched out in front of the open fire, on a green and blue flecked rug. It was still really cold at night, and they both sat in fleecy dressing gowns and fur-lined slippers. They each sat curled up on a big, cream, body-hugging sofa, watching the flames of the fire dance in shades of orange, white and purple, as different logs caught alight. The room smelt of smouldering apple wood and rich hot chocolate. Heavy curtains decorated with a large floral print in duck egg blue, green and cream hung at the arched window overlooking the country lane, and shorter curtains hung at a small window in the alcove beside the fire. As with the rest of the house, the walls were a warm, buttermilk colour, with a thick dark green carpet. Various floral, checked and tartan prints in the same colours as the curtains accented the room, on the cushions, throws and hearth rug that Mahoney was stretched out on. They drank whilst dunking Jaffa cakes, occasionally dipping into a big tin of Celebrations. All chocolate had to be kept out of bunny reach, as Mahoney was an avid lover of milk chocolate, and would steal any whenever he got the chance.

Coco had always had rabbits as pets, but only once she had a place of her own, could she train them to be house rabbits. It was not as hard as you might think. Mahoney had come from a pet shop, and was already house trained, as his mother had been a house rabbit. He was a huge thing, and when he had first been brought home, his long, lop ears trailed on the ground for an inch or two. It was suspected that he would grow into his ears, and by six months they seemed to fit him far better. The house had to be made bunny-proof, as his sometimes demonic nature urged him to chew electrical wires, and had already rendered useless a hair drier,

Playstation controllers, the Hoover, phone chargers and the fridge. Coco and Art could never work out why he never electrocuted himself; 'secret-magic-bunny-powers' had been suggested on one particular night when she had smoked a serious amount of home grown. People underestimate the qualities of rabbits as house pets, but as Coco had proven to Art, 'once you've owned a house rabbit, no other pet will do.' Mahoney had an inquisitive nature, and would follow Coco or Art around the house. He would lay across the threshold of the room, so they had to step over him to leave. He would then get up, and continue to follow whoever was at home.

'How did he get his name?' asked Pod, suppressing a yawn.

'When I first brought him home, I told him "I'm going to love you so much, my little honey-coloured bunny" and there it was My Honey Bunny, Mahoney Bunny!'

'He's ace. I was thinking of rescuing a pair.'

'Oh defo, they are the best pets. Like a cross between a cat and a dog. If you have time for them, they lap up attention, but if you're busy, they don't mind if their lovings are a little thin on the ground!' Coco got up and collected the massive rabbit in her arms, and sat back down on the sofa with him. His long, silky beige ears were really hot, and as Coco hugged him, there was a faint smell of singed fur. He nuzzled his head under her chin, and lay along her chest and stomach, with his haunches on her lap. She stroked the length of his body, partly petting, and partly collecting loose hairs. 'He's not got rid of his winter coat yet. The climate is definitely changing. It was T-shirt weather in April, and now it's cold again. I'm a bit worried about my fruit trees really!'

'Well, if what we are to believe on the alternative news channels is true, there's a lot more than the climate for the fat cats to worry about.'

'Um, worrying, isn't it?'

'It is, but we should be okay. We're totally self sufficient here, so high food prices and fuel or utilities shouldn't cause too many problems. This wet, cold start to the year will eventually reflect on food prices, and you can bet there will be an excuse to put the utility prices up too!' said Coco.

'Yeah, you're right, but I don't have wind turbines and solar panels, with enough acreage of land to grow enough food to supply a supermarket! Plus, for some reason, your trees look so much healthier than the ones in town, and just up the lane. Are you feeding them something special? I mean, the cherry trees on London Road in Sleaford have got a few, thin straggly flowers, but yours are amazing, show winners even!' replied Pod.

'They do their own thing, the Apple people come in, every now and again; they must just be happy growing here. Anyway, come live here, plenty of room, if it came to it. There's the big guest room, and the den next to the potting shed,'

'How's the den coming on? I didn't think you had started it yet?' The den was an old mobile home stood behind the potting shed. It had been refurbished, with its old tatty plastic and Formica replaced with natural wood. The interior colours were inspired by the colours of the night, including rich blues, greys, purples and cream. Art and his father had clad the exterior with wood and trellis, and made a 'living roof' of herbs and wild flowers. The vegetation was just starting to wrap itself around the den.

'Yes, it's nearly finished inside. You should see the honeysuckles growing up the trellis; they've all taken really well. Besides, I thought you were going to get off-the-grid as best you could?' chatted Coco, still caressing Mahoney's ears.

'Well, we chucked the television out months ago, my small veg patch is doing okay, but I'm nowhere near being self-sufficient yet. I don't believe a word anyone from the government says, don't buy comics, I mean newspapers. It feels amazing not having to read or hear all that crap that comes with the media. It's not until you're not having it pumped into you anymore, that you realise what a load of old crap TV is. State-controlled, propaganda news and adverts telling you how to spend your money. Every advert ever written is asking for money,' said Pod getting quite angry.

'But you're doing something about it, trying to make a change as far as your boundaries will allow you. You're doing okay, mate,' Coco reassured. 'You can stay in the den, if it comes to it, you can lodge here. There's enough room for Logan and Fay too.'

'Nice one! What about Art? Where is he by the way?'

'He won't mind. There's plenty of room here. He's away fishing with his friend. They won a ticket for 48 hours on a lake that's privately owned, and hardly ever fished.'

'He's got one of those here!'

'Yeah, I know, but I guess it's a bit of a break for him too!'

Mahoney woke with a start, and hopped onto the floor. He gave a big stretch and yawn, and then sat in front of the fire, with his back to Coco.

'Take it you've had enough hugs, Mahoney?'

'Has he sat with his back to you deliberately?' asked Pod, not having seen the rabbit become antisocial so suddenly.

'Oh, he knows what he likes. Whenever he's had enough, he turns his back on you. That means "leave me alone!" '

58

'Crikey, he is his own man, isn't he! What do you want to do tomorrow? We've nothing on for a change, unless you're getting on with that drawing?'

'We could do something. I've been meaning to go up to Temple Bruer; it's only about ten miles away,' said Coco, getting a book that was beside her on the sofa. There was a selection of books and magazines in a pile, ranging from *National Geographical, Wonderpedia* and *Weekly High,* along with *Gardening Month by Month.* 'D'ya fancy a bit of history? Have a look at the book,' she said. Coco passed *The Knights Templar Secret Locations in England,* and noticed quickly that the Lincolnshire section was quite full. There were write-ups on The Angel and Royal Hotel in Grantham, where royalty dating back to King John in 1213 had stayed at the then Angel Inn.

'It amazes me about Grantham. It's a nothing town, but its history is immense.'

'I know, when you think Richard III stayed at The Angel, as did Charles I and Oliver Cromwell,' said Coco.

'Bloody hell, you've been swotting up on Grantham history?'

'No,' laughed Coco, 'no, I've just read it in that book!'

'There is quite a bit of history in Grantham. Maggie was born there, and Sir Isaac Newton, and looking at this, the Templars passed through a few times.'

'They would have stopped off there on their way up the Great North Road, the A1 to you and I. It says in that book that they had a big settlement at Byard Leap, a few miles outside of Sleaford. They trained and exercised their horses on the open land. *Bruer* comes from the French word *Bruyere* meaning heath or heather. The area was really dangerous, and when stagecoach travel became popular, insurance could be purchased for the London to York run, but it excluded the Lincoln Heath section.'

'Wow, who would have thought just a few miles from here there was such exciting history. It says here that Temple Bruer was a walled preceptory, consisting of typical classical Templar architecture. It could accommodate up to one hundred and fifty people, from chaplains, servants, sergeants and possibly a few Knights of the Order. There's even mention of secret underground tunnels running to Wellingore, two miles away!'

Mahoney lay back down. He'd had a busy day. He had secretly picked all the flowers of a lavender bush, and then hopped off leaving them discarded on the ground. He had dug a shallow hole to lie in, as it had been quite hot at midday, and the cool earth beneath the surface was a refreshing relief, especially as he still sported a thick winter coat. He enjoyed his freedom. He could come and go as he pleased, and the boundary of his kingdom included all of the house, the herb and rock garden (though he could not reach many of the plants, which was a shame as some of them smelt great, and would therefore probably taste good too!) and up to the wall and fencing that separated the car park area from the patio. It was a safe place to live; he was safe from predators, could dig in his bunny pit that Coco had made him, and had fresh vegetation to eat for a healthy diet. He even had his own parsley bush.

'So, we'll go to Temple Bruer tomorrow. Sounds like a good plan. I'm off to bed. We'll have a good-night-cuppa and hit the sack,' said Coco, as Pod let out a big yawn, which contagiously caused Coco to yawn. 'I'll just text Art, check he's okay. He'll probably be asleep by now though.'

'How's his fishing going?'

'How's his *camping* going you mean!' laughed Coco.

'Ay?' questioned Pod.

'I've been taking the piss out of him because he spends hours preparing his stuff for fishing, lugs all this equipment about, sets up camp, and doesn't catch anything. Therefore, with a serious lack of fish, it is only camping. It becomes fishing when there are fish involved!'

'Bless him. What about your lake? Doesn't he catch anything from it?'

'Yeah, loads, but never the carp he's after. He says he is sure someone is putting fish *in* the lake, as he keeps seeing new ones, but he said they are small. He's never heard of a lake *reproducing* fish. It's baffling him.'

The next morning, Pod woke at seven, stretching out on the wrought iron double bed. As she sat up on her elbows, a dull, grey light barely made it through the white curtains, decorated with artificial daisies. Coco had made them herself, finding a very cheap, nasty sprig of daisies in a charity shop. When she had taken the flowers off the tacky plastic stem, and added little yellow, wooden beads for the flower centres, which also doubled up as a means to attach the daisies to the fabric, the end result was rustic and pretty. In the corners of the room, in massive clusters, large white daisies had been painted, with pastel green leaves and dusky pink centres. The modern day frescos cascaded down the walls in a couple of places, but the concentration of flowers were in the corners of the room, including the ceiling. As the ceiling was white, the daisies stood out against painted green leaves. The carpet was the same luscious green as the lounge, matching the colour of the daisy leaves. Around the feet of the furniture, Coco had stood little daisies on wire, so they looked like they were growing out of the lawn carpet. These looked fantastic, but did need regular attention from a hairdryer, to blow away collected dust. There were many houseplants that preferred a cooler temperature stood on the windowsill and table top. As the guest room faced north, it could be quite chilly, but the plants chosen were thriving and their various different leaf colours finished the aesthetics of the room.

Getting out of bed, Pod left the bedroom, and walked past the studio to find Coco sat at the circular dinning table. She looked up, 'Morning dude, how goes it? You sleep okay?'

'Yes ta, slept well. It's a beautiful room, love what you have done with it.'

'Thanks. Tea's in the pot and bacon under the grill. Help yourself.'

By mid-morning, they were driving through Sleaford, and out towards Lincoln. Temple Bruer was signposted on the left, and they turned down a narrow country lane. The skies were overcast. There was no threat of rain; it was just cold, dark and quite miserable. On arriving in the hamlet, there were five or six large stone houses. Their thick stone walls were visible by the depth of the stone window frames, and ornate decoration had been carved above the doorways and windows. As they drove very slowly through the hamlet, there was no sign of a tower. They stopped the car, and Coco climbed onto the bumper to get a higher view. A distant sound of dogs barking could be heard, and as one dog barked, its neighbours joined in. Coco got back into the car, just as curtains started to twitch.

A lady appeared, in a long green wax jacket, and wax cowboy hat. She was walking a young chocolate Labrador, who was eagerly pulling on his rope lead. As she approached, Pod noticed she had a shot gun thrown over her shoulder.

'This is all a bit spooky, where the hell did she come from? All these dogs barking, it's like the hounds of hell!'

'Are you lost?' asked the dog walker, heading towards the car. She had a cut-glass accent, which was fitting with the big stone houses, and extensive, mature grounds they sat in. 'Where are you trying to get to?'

'Hiya, you might be able to help, we're looking for the Templars Tower,' called Pod through the open car window.

'The Tower?'

'Yeah, it's in our book on the Templars. We just thought we would have a look.'

'No tower here, your book has misinformed you. Try Grantham if you're after Templar history, or Lincoln Cathedral. Some of them were sentenced to death there.'

'It's here, look, page 155. This is Templar Bruer isn't it?'

'Yes, of course, but as you can see, there's no tower here. You being here is upsetting the dogs. As soon as you are finished and leave, the dogs will stop barking.'

'Oh! Right. I guess you're asking us to leave? Not really necessary as we aren't doing anything wrong.'

'No, I have no right to ask you to leave. I am just saying, your presence is upsetting the dogs, which is pointless, as it's quite clear there is no tower here,' replied the dog walker, with a stern, cold stare. Her Labrador sat obediently by her side. She was looking at Coco, who wore black bondage trousers with red and yellow tartan patches, and lots of metal zips that had no purpose. Her hair was short, spiky and scruffy, dyed white with orange, black and red tufts, and an oversized union jack knitted jumper. The red velvet brothel-creepers she wore stood out brightly, in the grey, greenness of the countryside. 'Have a good day and safe journey!'

The dog walker started on her way, after giving the two girls a long, deep stare each. The Labrador was pleased to be on his way again, and bounded forward to the limits of his rope. As the woman walked off, her shot gun still over her shoulder, Pod wound the car window up. They studied the map, and noticed there was a small cluster of buildings just south of where they were.

'What about there? It's only about a mile away and still within two miles of Wellingore.'

'Let's go have a look. This lot here are a bit weird,' replied Pod, starting the car, and turning it around in the lane. The curtains were still twitching, but no faces were visible. 'They are a bit freaky out here. It's a little hamlet, with a problem. They should be used to people visiting!'

Coco drove the car back to the main road, and turned right towards Sleaford. The next right took them towards the buildings sited on the map. As the lane got narrower, and more overgrown, a stone house came into view, followed by a large farmhouse. There, stood in the yard, was a tall, square tower, about three storeys high. Its sides were about 25 feet square, made of darkened yellow stone. A little wrought iron fence surrounded the tower, with hawthorn bushes intertwined with the metalwork. A plaque erected by the local council described the tower with a brief history of the local Templars.

'No tower, my arse,' said Coco. 'Why didn't she just say it was here? Stuck-up old bag!'

'Never mind, we've found it now!'

Coco pushed the small, creaking gate, and walked through onto well maintained grass. On the north side of the tower, there were a few worn stone steps, to an arched doorway. The heavy wood of the door was clearly very old, though not necessarily the original. The decorated door frame had lost a lot of its detail, and had strangely eroded more at hip height.

'They say the wide bit of the doorway is from the Knights in their armour brushing past the stonework. The more scientific theory is inconclusive,' said Pod, reading from the plaque.

It was a peaceful location, and the yard the tower stood in was deserted. There was no one about, not even the sign of another car parked near the few houses that made up the residency. Coco had pre-rolled a smoke, which she lit as she studied the structure. The gap in the door frame allowed her to peer through, and she noticed the ground floor of the tower had alcoves decorated around the walls. There were no internal floors, so the whole tower was illuminated by the weak shafts of light bleaching in through windows of the first and second stories. Coco could just make out the wooden rafters supporting the roof. She stepped back, and walked down the stairs onto the grass and joined Pod, who was now also studying the building. As they both turned to look at the west wall, they noticed a triangle shape cut into the masonry, between the first and second floors. It had a peculiar location, as part of the triangle cut through the second storey window.

'The book said that this is the old marking of where an adjacent building was!'

'I'm not buying that!' said Coco. 'Who would build the roof of a building half over the window of another building. It doesn't make sense. The base of the triangle, which would be the floor of the adjacent building's roof isn't even straight.' She took a long, deep drag and exhaled slowly, whilst she stood looking at the tower.

'The book said it was where they attached a building when they expanded.'

'No. Not having it!' Shaking her head, Coco walked up to the building and touched the stone. As she did, a shot gun broke the silence of the deserted yard. Rooks and crows shouted as they were disturbed, rising in the distance into the air like a black confetti gun. Coco violently jumped backwards, tripped and landed on her backside. She had a glazed look on her face, a blank, vacant expression. Pod looked over to her.

'You okay, dude? What you doing down there?' She held out her hand for Coco to take, but it was ignored. 'Cocs, dude?' There was still no response from her friend. Pod put her hand on Coco's shoulder, and jumped as a static charge flashed between them.

'Ouch!' said Coco. 'What the FUCK was that about? Did you see it? What was it?'

'What was what?' said Pod, rubbing her hand that had received the shock. 'It was just Posh Lady firing off her gun!'

'What gun? Didn't you see the PYRAMID in front of the tower and the sun came out for a split second like a bullet from a gun, shining through that window up there!' said Coco, who had gone a greyish colour.

'You're smoking too much horticulture. Has it been laced with something? There was just a gunshot sound, every bit of wildlife for half a mile shit itself. It made you jump and land on your arse and now you're pulling my leg by cooking up this story! Ha!'

'No, I went to touch the tower, and at the same time, I saw that triangle on the wall become three-dimensional; the tower itself kind of sparkled, and the sun shot through that window like a bullet from a gun. As all this happened, it felt like I had been pulled back, which is when I tripped and fell... I think!'

'Think you need a break from de 'erb mate, it's frying your brain.'

'It's not the weed. If I didn't smoke that, we wouldn't be making the money we are with the drawings I do. You've seen the difference in my drawings. The parts done when stoned, compared to the bits I have done when straight are totally different. The detail I can create when mashed is out of this world. You know how much time I spend wondering where all this stuff comes from. The shapes. The detail. It's like two different people drawing it, the mashed me and the straight me.'

'I know, I've seen you try drawing when straight. And when you're mashed. It makes a massive difference. As you have said, the herbs seem to open your mind, boundless limits, it's unplanned, and you worry too much about where the ideas come from!' Pod helped Coco get up, and they took one last look at the tower. 'The gunshot just startled you, and you probably got a bit concussed when you hit the deck. You went down quite hard, and were in a bit of a daze for a few seconds after. Anyway, weed is harmless. Thousands of people die from fags every year; no one has *ever* died from the herb. Besides, how can they make nature illegal? Crazy! It's medical benefits are endless!'

'Dude, what gunshot?'

Chapter Seven

May 2011, London

It had been six months since the five members had been informed by Uncle Sam and Ed Lizard that the time was coming. Since then, there had been three meetings, where each member had brought their research to verify what was happening. As always they had met in The Palm House, in privacy. A valuable aspect to their meeting place was that there was only one staircase to the high gantry, and as the walls were glass, they were able to see anyone approaching. It had been cleared by the horticulture department of the MBHK. Kew Gardens workers were told the team were studying the plants, as they were palm experts. No one had questioned it, probably because the meetings were so few and far between. It was now May and there was only just over a year left to prepare.

Ed was giving his evidence and research. They had started discussing some of the finer points of what needed to be done. There was so much to organise; contacting the festivallers, preparing the site and sound system, checking the cosmological readings and the aftermath. 'Well, the subliminal messages have started to appear over the last year or so. Some people have really latched onto them, the shapes they keep seeing, and are questioning them.' He was dressed all in black, including skinny jeans, full length leather coat and even a black beret. There had been a few days of warm weather, but it had gone cold and wet again. *By mid-May it should be warm weather,* he thought. He remembered back to his younger days when the summers were a guaranteed four or five months of hot sun. He used to be one of the world's greatest DJs, and had worked in every club from Brazil to Ibiza. He was renowned for his four-deck mixing, which no one since had managed to achieve to the dizzy heights that Ed had.

He had always maintained he could only do what he did, as he never smoked, drank or did drugs. He had been an ambassador for safe drinking and various anti-drug campaigns, but had fallen from grace one night when he admitted to taking marijuana for medical reasons. This had been made public, just as his latest album had been at number one for five weeks. There had been uproar, as it had not only proved that the drugs had liberated Ed's creative powers, producing a record that was way before its time, but the anti-drug groups slated the DJ for double-standards, hypocrisy and deceit. In turn, Ed had fallen apart, until he won his plot of land. He had turned his winnings into a rehab programme, helping people to master their addictions, with gardening, animal husbandry and home grown, home cooked food.

'Are there any coincidences amongst these people? The selection process started four years ago, and so we must be getting to the point where everyone has been brought to our attention,' replied Uncle Sam.

'Not really!' exclaimed Ed.

'What do you mean, not really?' asked Rik with concern in his voice. 'Why haven't these people all cottoned onto it yet? Bloody hell, the communications guys have been flat out!'

'They have been flat out, but some people can't think past what they are going to watch on TV that night.'

'What about the back-up plan?' Rik said, 'has that been considered?'

'Of course, we wouldn't have come this far without ensuring all the selected people know what to look out for!'

'That's all well and good. These folk don't know what to look out for, or indeed that they are supposed to be looking out for anything,' said Robert Eye, the geoengineering expert who was also the second oldest member after Uncle Sam. 'My in-depth statistics are going off the scale. I've never heard of such excessive military action during peace time. The spraying of the skies is getting ridiculous!' Robert had been in the Royal Air Force for most of his life, and had only retired nine months before he won his plot of land. He still had some good, honest connections in the Air Force, and would regularly meet up with his old friends for a pint. They would talk about non-security restricted information, but Robert was able to decipher what was being planned, as his security clearance had been much higher, and he knew what signs to look out for.

'I've got some news on the spraying,' butted in Ed, the Doomsday expert, 'there is conclusive evidence that the trails sprayed in the skies are potentially damaging, even lethal.'

'What do you mean? I know everything there is to know about the trails,' said Robert.

'Yes, but you don't know about the site. We all know that the farm will be protected, and the destruction will come from...'

'Hang on guys,' said Dylan, a very talented musician. 'Anything to do with the site I need to know about. But going back a bit, what scenarios have happened to attract these people? We need them all to generate enough energy. They have been picked for a reason, for their love of music, for the drum beats in their hearts and rhythms running through their veins. How do you get to so many people from so many different walks of life?'

'We have used social networking, tapped into people's phones and run adverts in popular magazines.'

'Tapped into people's phones...'

'Um, yeah!'

'Can they do that? The communications lot! They can do that?'

'Yes, everyone involved. They need to monitor who has responded to the images that have been coming to them, and if needs be, have sent relevant posts to their Facebook accounts!'

'Bloody hell!' exclaimed Rik, 'this is all a bit random.'

'So if everyone is being monitored, how is it going?' asked Dylan, with a puzzled look on his face. 'When do we bring the big guns out, excuse the pun!'

'According to communications, everyone selected has had the image at least four times, sometimes subtly, other times it's obvious. Imagine the lights of a graphic equaliser, Dylan. As each person receives a visual message another of their lights go on. They need to get into the red before they are aware of something happening, before they start asking questions, querying things they experience. At present, we are about ninety per cent ready,' said Ed.

'What's happening on Facebook?' asked Rik, glad that his kids were not interested in social networking, 'can't the selected ones just be messaged, prompted?'

'Yes, and ultimately of course, there are the tickets. Some of the selected ones who don't have access to a computer, or live in areas where news travels a lot slower, will receive flyers in the post. They will be purposely designed to suit the individual, so there will be no doubt that they will attend,' said Ed.

'Just run it by us all again, Ed. I just want to make sure I have it clear, plus Dylan looks a bit bemused too,' laughed Rik.

'I'd go a lot further than a *bit*,' laughed Dylan. They all chuckled to themselves, knowing that their close friendship was rarely questioned.

'Fair do's,' said Ed. 'Here it is. Six months ago, we learned that the predicted date of December 2012 was wrong. When it was all worked out from the information they found on the Stones at the farm, and the Hopi, Egyptian and Mayan information, they hadn't recalculated when Emperor Constantine had rewritten the calendar in 300AD. The stone information was all tested to be 2,000 years old, and so the 4th century change had not been accounted for in the calculations. Constantine changed the Sabbath day and all that, but also the leap year wasn't calculated. Therefore the date is wrong, it's not Winter Solstice 2012, it's Summer Solstice 2012. As you all know, the people selected were naturally chosen. They all have ancestry that can be traced back for thousands of years, to the time of the Ancient Britons. This is a worldwide trend, with many other strains of this DNA being present.'

'Though none of them know that bit!' added Uncle Sam as he nodded for Ed to continue.

'They have a defect on their DNA, which only the first civilised human beings of Britain and various parts of the world have. As humans, we only use about ninety-seven per cent of our DNA, which is very wasteful and inconsistent with the laws of nature. The rest of this DNA must have had a use or purpose at some point, otherwise what *is* the point? We don't know how or what that is, but there is recent evidence our scientists have found that there was a certain vegetation, or animal that inhabited prehistoric times, which had been eaten, giving them the differently developed DNA. Not everyone from this ancient period has this DNA, just those that ate this certain food for a prolonged period of time. They have worked out it took about 50,000 years before the DNA transformation was complete,' continued Ed.

'You saying the ancient UK dudes are aliens, with badass DNA?' piped up Dylan, 'that explains a lot!'

'No, not all of the UK dudes as you put it, just the ones with ancient ancestry.'

'What about these alien dudes that go abroad, not in England anymore? Do they get the calling?' Dylan continued.

'Yes, they would get the calling, but from the nearest source that this DNA has been recorded, not necessarily their homeland,' said Ed, getting a little irritated by Dylan's questions, on a subject that should have been understood years ago. 'And going back to an earlier point, they all do have certain characteristics. This has been noticed by the phone apps and Facebook pages they use. I'll come back to this later.'

'What about everyone else in the UK? Loved ones, family? Who would want to live, if everyone you know is dead?'

'Preparations have been made for that too. The last communication the telephone companies will do via our main computer is to send a "shield" to loved ones and family. It's a complex process, but the IT guys think they have nailed it!'

'Is it just these selected few that are getting the images?' Rik asked.

'Yes,' said Uncle Sam, 'because of this DNA, they sort of have a seventh sense, if you like. They're more perceptive than normal folk. They always get the jobs they go for; have a close psychic connection with their immediately family. They often get a feeling of having been somewhere, without actually having visited the location before; they question everything, and rarely accept what they are told unless it is emphatically proven... there's loads of it, that sets them apart, without it being apparent.'

'Not only is there the ancestry connection, there is the plaque found at the farm about 1,000 years ago when there was a small settlement on the site of the farm. I'll dictate the script on it later. It clearly says that when the time is right, certain things will happen, to forewarn of the event, which is now. Things have been happening on the farm. Nothing electrical works, just battery or generator-powered operated stuff. The productivity is up on the farm about forty-five per cent,' went on Ed.

'Forty-five per cent more cow juice?' stated Rik, 'What are they doing with it? The farm was never in operation to make money, hence the millions spent on it each summer, but it seems a shame to chuck it all.'

'The milk is sent off to make cheese... a small local cheese maker that was nearly going out of business makes it, and it gets shipped out to soup kitchens, homeless shelters and to people living on the street,' said Ed. They all nodded approval over the cheese story.

'It's funny you should say that. My chickens have laid more, the fruit trees are aflame with blossom, the veg patch never needs weeding and I've had no bug infestations yet this summer!' said Rik, 'I thought it was just my excellent green fingers.'

'Do you think your produce is up forty-five per cent?'

'Yes, no, I don't know. We are a bit early in the season to gather anything, so I couldn't say. The chickens are definitely laying more, and come to think of it, Izzy, my wife, couldn't keep up with the bottling, pickling and freezing of the winter crops. I thought she was just slowing up, but it could be that the produce was growing more!'

'It's more than likely up forty-five per cent too. The horticulturists reckon the Earth is getting ready too, making sure there are enough supplies for when it happens.'

'Really? Modern-day-science-man think Earth think?' imitated Dylan, in a mocking ape-man type voice, 'Modern-science-man think earth know? Modern-science-man know Earth knows, but doesn't know if Earth know what man know!' said Dylan laughing, leaning back in his chair. The other four just stared at him in total amusement. Dylan rarely said much, in fact, he rarely strung more than four words together. But when he did, it was priceless. 'What?' he said, as the other four continued to stare at him, each trying to work out if what he had just said made sense, or if he was just bluffing them.

'Moving on…' said Uncle Sam after a few moments of stunned silence, 'The Eden Project in Cornwall, along with here at Kew, have both said they have had an increase in plant production and growth, despite the fact the climate controls have remained the same. They have each had independent investigators look into the phenomenon, but nothing conclusive came back.' They all sat in silence, pondering.

'Going back to the phone and computer monitoring, the characteristics they all have in common kind of signify what requirements might be needed of them, if the event happens as we think it will,' went on Ed, still distracted as he tried to work out what Dylan had just said. 'They are pretty much all unconventional in one way or another. The main characteristics are, most importantly, they all stand out, go against the norm. Creativity; they can all grow or make things; they don't generally follow the "usual" rules, only do things when they need doing, if they need doing, not just for the sake of it; none of them have an affinity with money, they are non-materialistic; they all have some sort of environmental awareness; are open-minded, and investigate things as and when they come across them, proper thinkers, people who do it naturally.'

'That's Dylan out then!' laughed Uncle Sam, 'Proper thinker!' he added, as the others joined in with the mockery.

'He's all about the "natural" though!'

'Yeah, and he's often been "investigated" in his past!'

'All right guys, you gotta love the brothers from another mother!' laughed Dylan, 'You guys are the best!' They sat for a moment, looking at each other, smiling like family would. Even though they had known each other for years, had bonded like no other five people in the country, their knowledge of one another was minimal. The meetings had always been short and to the point, and there was never a social scene between them, as in theory, there was no connection as to how they would know each other. Therefore, they had never really discussed their personal lives, just their professional ones, and of course their sharing of research into the event. Robert never had much to say, rather like Dylan, but whereas Dylan was a pot-smoking, music whizz-kid, prolific as a bassist and drummer, Robert was a former RAF pilot, who had gone straight into the force as an officer, due to his graduation from Oxford with honours. 'Are you telling me, the ones that are selected are conspiracy-thinking, commune-living, lazy-bastard, hippy-naturalists?' he said, horrified. 'Surely our last twenty-five years have not been to collect together the scourge of society!'

'No, no, far from it! The range of people is vast. Every walk of society is represented, though the majority of the age range is thirty to forty-five!' checked Ed, as he recalled the information from Uncle Sam.

'Right O! Sounds like all our hard work is going to be well worth it!' Robert added sarcastically.

'It's not for us to decide, Rob. We all came to terms with that one years ago!'

'I know. I just don't see how it's going to work. I mean, have we any idea what is going to happen? Do we know what to expect? No one has told me anything!'

'We don't know. We know as much as you, in fact, you probably know more with your military background and sources. At present there is more unusual activity on the farm. The stones are covered in wild flowers and mushrooms!' went on Ed.

'Shrooms?' asked Dylan, 'to the farm we go. I've not been for ages!'

'Dylan, please?'

'Sorry. Continue!'

'The Sacred Stones, although they are not the originals, apparently they are made from the same quarry as the originals. The meadow around them is full of every wild flower, all growing fantastic blooms, and it's as if a professional gardener has looked after the patch. It is pristine. The farmer first noticed it when the cows would stand around the stones back in February, and would not graze amongst them as they have always done. The trees around the edge of the whole farm are rich with blossom and there is the starting of fruit, even though the rest of the country is having the worst spring ever. The surrounding countryside looks tired and worn out, as with most of the country, but the farm is as perfect as it could get,' described Uncle Sam.

'Just one point,' said Dylan, 'what about the connection that the new date is now the Summer Solstice, which just happens to be the same date that the festival is always held at the farm?' They all looked at each other in silence, as it was something they were all thinking about. The enormity of this event was becoming realised, as up until now, it had all seemed rather far-fetched.

'Dylan, it's no coincidence. Everything leads to Summer Solstice next year, 2012! All the research shows that the location of the farm, The Tor and The Sacred Stones and the festivallers will be protected. The people who have been chosen will find their way there somehow. When the time comes, everything will be as it should be, and our work will be done!' said Ed, looking out over the cityscape of London.

Chapter Eight

May 2011, Italy

It was late evening by the time Miriam and Sophie had reached Sorrento. The journey had been spectacular, as the little train had followed a track hugging the steep mountainous terrain, occasionally passing over deep ravines on viaducts. To the right, was the Mediterranean Sea, sparkling as the sun started to set, reflecting sun sparkles off the crest of gentle waves. There was no sign of the rain and wind that had caused the Rome train to stop. The sky was clear, with wispy, bright pink clouds drifting across the bay. It had become cooler as the sun sunk lower, and so the girls had put on fleeces. The windows on the train were still open, and fresh clean air filtered through the carriage. There was a smell that came with heavy rainfall, mixed with the aroma of Cyprus trees clinging to the gentler parts of the mountainside. As the journey moved further away from the outskirts of Naples, the track wound its way around the bay, until Naples was visible on the opposite side. Its bright lights, a mirage in the shadowy blues, reflected on the sea along the coast. Passenger ships, ocean liners and yachts were dotted about the bay, and distant dance music could be heard from one of the boats with flashing disco lights.

The track followed the coast to the south, passing through sun-baked villages. Mount Vesuvius loomed in the distance on the left, getting bigger as the train neared, and eventually passed it by. By the time it pulled into Sorrento, it was dark. After a short walk to the hotel, the girls dumped their bags, and quickly freshened up. The room overlooked the sea, with a steep drop down to buildings clinging to the lower levels of the cliffs. Strings of little lanterns decorated back gardens, and the sound of family laughter could be heard. Delicious smells wafted into the room, making the girls realise how tired and hungry they were.

'We could have a quick light tea, get an early night so we're fresh for tomorrow,' said Sophie. Miriam was in agreement, so they changed their clothes, and walked down into the town. A narrow pavement snaked beside the cliff hugging road, slinking around the contours of the coast. It was quite a steep downhill gradient, and once in the heart of the town, there was still more descending to do, to reach sea level. The girls had hoped there might be a pizzeria or café open. Shops selling pottery, liquors and ice cream were still busy trading. The area's lemon industry was evident, with everything lemon available to buy. Lemon decorated plates, bowls, ornaments, souvenirs and sorbets all reasonably priced were displayed in the windows.

At the bottom of a long flight of steps, a winding single track road opened out onto a small bay, with a few shops and fishing boat repair sheds lining the curved inlet. The boundaries of a car park were marked with some big boulders, separating a small shingle beach which led down a short way to the sea. It was quiet, in comparison to the tourist-filled streets above. Lobster baskets were stacked in piles, with random fishing nets and boats stored away for the night. The little bay, only a few hundred feet across, was pierced by a short, narrow wooden pier. At the end, the pier widened, where wooden tables were set out, with yellow checked tablecloths, and candles in glass bowls as centre pieces. A yellow and white stripped canopy hung above the tables, with hundreds of white fairy lights illuminating the family run restaurant.

'Oh my God!' exclaimed Sophie, 'this is beautiful! The sea reflected the twinkling lights, and a gentle lapping of the tide on the shore, dislodged the shingle making a tranquil sound. The salt in the air, and smell of the fishing nets had a very cleansing quality, as the girls walked across the car park to the pier. The shingle was hard to walk on, and it was light relief when they stepped up onto the wooden pier. 'I wonder if they are still serving?' said Sophie.

The smell of garlic butter and the sizzle of hot rock cooking could be heard. Two tables were occupied, with elderly, romantic couples eating bowls of pasta. Twenty minutes later, Sophie was tucking into garlic prawns and warm flat breads, whilst Miriam had a green salad with a tomato and basil pasta dish. They each had a bottle of beer, and ate in silence, savouring their mesmerising surroundings. The restaurant staff could not do enough for them, and it was nearly half ten by the time they had finished homemade lemon sorbets. The restaurant was now busier than it had been when the girls had sat down. In fact, every table was full, with locals and tourists alike, chatting quietly, with the occasional outburst of laughter. Fairylights and stars did an equal job of adding a certain quality to the meal, and the waiters hurried away dirty plates, opened bottles of wine and cooked fresh seafood at the tables.

A young man in black trousers, and an open fronted, tailored white shirt played an acoustic guitar at the very end of the pier. Every now and again, a soft breeze ruffled through his long hair, as he passionately played the instrument. With closed eyes, he played the strings with ease, leaning over his instrument, playing with the expertise of an individual who was prolific in his music. The sweet notes merged with the sound of the ocean kissing the pier supports. One of the couples who had been eating when the girls had sat down, had got up and, holding each other closely, danced under the stars beside the musician. They shuffled around in small circles, both well over 70. Their wrinkled faces close together and their eyes closed whilst the man held his wife tightly. She had her arms around his waist, and they swayed together encapsulated by the music.

'So there is heaven on earth!' said Sophie, lounging back in her chair, looking down the restaurant, past the musician, and out to sea. The sounds and smells of the restaurant, the obliging staff and the beginnings of the alcohol taking effect, she could not imagine a more perfect, happy setting.

'Pardon?' replied Miriam. 'Did you just mention heaven? Bit of a contrast from the outburst at the Vatican!'

'Oh come on, look at this place!'

'What a find indeed! Maybe it's a reward for all that worry on the Naples train?' Miriam was sat with her back to the sea, and could see the little bay, lit up by the coloured lanterns. The rock face was sheer, with houses clinging to its lower levels, until prickly bushes were the only things able to hold on tight. Way overhead, the distant sound of traffic on the coast road, and tourists going back to their hotels could just about be heard. 'It's one of those "right-place-right-time" moments. If we came back tomorrow, it probably wouldn't be the same.'

'You're right. I guess we better go back. Big day tomorrow. Massive in fact!'

'Yes, it should be okay as we can rest on the train trip. It's about five hours to Florence, so plenty of time to catch up on rest,' said Miriam.

They paid the bill, and walked home. It was an arduous climb, hindered by feeling very full but content. As they left the bay, a little shop was just closing. It sold bottles of lemon liqueur, and the girls decided to buy small bottles to take back home with them. The young shop assistant put the bottles in bags.

'Ten euros please,' she said in very good English. 'This is a very good year, there are many lemons this year. The lemon trees growing on the volcano soils are very busy, so the drink is particularly good.'

'Thank you, said Miriam, 'we just had some of this after our meal, down on the pier.'

'It is a good place to eat, no?'

'Oh, it was heavenly!' exclaimed Sophie, 'such a beautiful place.'

'Ah, yes, is bellissimo!' said the shop assistant. 'Be careful if you have had the Liquore di Limoni. Is strong, no? This season is special, the weather has made much juice in the lemons, and everything growing on the volcano sides is good, is rich. Be careful with the drink, it has a fuzzy head for you!'

'Thank you, we will be careful!' said Sophie, leaving the shop through the open door. As they took the steep walk back to the hotel, they discussed how fabulous the meal had been, and the irregularities of the day. 'It's certainly been a strange day. Brilliant. Thanks for being an ace travel companion, Miriam.'

'No, thank you, it has been brilliant. Pompeii tomorrow, can't wait!'

Getting off the train the following morning, the girls had left their rucksacks at the luggage left, and walked the short distance to the ticket office. The worn path, a short walk along the side of the mountain was uneven, dusty and dry, with flowering plants running along beside the path. Large pieces of broken masonry and volcanic rocks protruded from the ground, as Cyprus trees majestically towered above lemon trees, which were heavily laden with fruit. Next to the ticket office, a small wooden barrow had an industrial sized citrus juicer, where chilled lemonade was made from the lemons growing nearby, and snacks could be bought. It was really warm, with deep blue skies mimicking the colour of the sea. It was a cloudless, still day, with the exception of the now familiar long, straight, wispy clouds that Sophie had seen made by aeroplanes many times. She had researched chemtrails and was not impressed. The girls decided to buy some lemonade, and poured some of the liqueur they had bought the previous evening in Sorrento, into the citrus drink. Before they had got on the train, they had purchased bottled water, bread, cheese, ham and some treats. They planned to find a quiet spot at Pompeii to have lunch al fresco.

Once inside the city walls of Pompeii, they wandered around, marvelling at the amount of detail that remained, even after 2,000 years. Most of the town had been preserved for 1,700 years, buried after the volcano had erupted on 24th August, AD79. Burning hot volcanic ash had fallen, incinerating people, as they suffocated from the lack of air, and the ones who did breath in, had their lungs turned to cement. The ash buried the town and everyone in it, regardless of their status. It was a time capsule of Imperial Rome, where 20,000 inhabitants had traded and holidayed. Miriam and Sophie wandered around, not bothering with a map. It was fun to get lost in the many streets and roads, but it would be easy to find their way back to the exit. With the volcano standing dormant, and yet imposing, it was a good landmark for getting their bearings. They visited the Roman Forum, with some of its tall columns still standing. The amphitheatre was intact; a smaller scaled structure similar to the Colosseum. It was possible to walk around the grid system of roads, walking through shops, public baths, temples and brothels. Many of the wealthier homes had frescos on the walls, in vibrant red and gold colours, and the images in the brothels were strictly over 18.

At the furthest, northern point of the site, the girls found a quiet, secluded house and garden. Only the single floor of the two storey house remained, as the roof had collapsed under the weight of the stone and ash. The grey stone was impeccably preserved, with decorative frescos on the walls. There was a damp smell in the rooms; an earthy smell that was everywhere at Pompeii. Their footsteps echoed slightly as they walked over a tiled floor, with shards of brick and plaster in places. Many of the bigger buildings had fabulous mosaics on the floors, but this home was more modest. The light at the far end of the room came from a columned portico. The girls wandered through the columns entering the peristyle, which was a courtyard garden. Originally plants, statues and fountains would have been in the garden, forming the hub of the house. It was here that the girls decided to rest, and have their lunch. Time was getting on, and the train for Florence could not be missed.

'It's so peaceful here. It feels quite spiritual,' said Sophie, making a ham and cheese sandwich on her knee, as she sat on an edge of a sunken, square, stone pond. The water had long gone, but it contributed to the grandeur of the house. 'I wondered who lived here?'

'It's amazing, isn't it!' Miriam had made a cheese and crisp sandwich, which was making a bit of a mess. 'Something for the birds to nibble on!' she laughed.

'You tried your lemonade yet, it's really good. Got a bad-ass kick to it! Really sour too, which is alright if you like lemons!'

'Not yet. Was going to have it after lunch, as I thought it might help me have a nap on the train.'

'Good idea, I've nearly finished mine. That shop assistant was right, I've got tingly legs.'

After eating, they cleared up all their rubbish, and sat for a moment, letting the sun warm their faces, with their eyes closed, imagining how the house would have looked and felt before everything had been destroyed. They imagined the head of the house on a plush chair, talking business with fellow traders, and the children running in and out of the columns playing, totally unaware of their pending doom. The complex, formal garden would have been planted with fruit trees such as lemons, olives, nuts and soft fruits, as well as vines.

'I'm surprised there is so much evidence of a lavish, hedonistic lifestyle in so many of the homes. It must have been a real sensory experience, all the decoration and attention to detail, whilst keeping the rooms minimalist. I didn't realise too, that they were such patrons of the arts.'

'It must be something to do with the long standing beauty of Italy, as 1,500 years after all of this was buried, you have the Italian Renaissance, which ironically, means "rebirth", when the artists of the time were influenced by the ancient Greek and Roman styles,' replied Miriam. 'I've also noticed there is a Greek influence in some of the architecture and style of decoration here at Pompeii, so Michelangelo and his cronies weren't the first really.'

They started heading back towards the exit, to collect their bags and catch the train. They found themselves in a series of narrow streets, with high kerb stones. The buildings were clearly single storey, as many of them still had their roofs. Some had open fronted areas, indicating they were shops, where the owners would live behind the serving area. There was none of the finery that had been evident in the larger, atrium homes of the rich. Even in what was clearly a poorer part of the town, there was still a place found for a temple. Although there was only one pillar, and none of the walls left, the large marble stones were all that was needed to suggest that this had once been a magnificent building. This ruin made a lovely photograph, with the volcano rising up behind the town. As they walked on, Miriam started drinking her lemonade, with the lemon liqueur in it.

'Bloody hell, it's well strong. Have you quaffed yours, Sophie?'

'Nearly. I think I will buy some more lemonade, and make some more up for the train.'

'Wicked idea! This lemonade is just so good, it's really sour, but you can just taste the goodness in it. All those lemons growing out here in the fresh air, on the side of a volcano.'

Miriam walked on, aware time was running out, and they did not want to have to run for the train to Naples in order to make their connection to Florence. She suddenly felt lightheaded, and swayed a little, putting her hand out to steady herself. She had both palms flat against the wall of the shop.

'Jesus, it's well stro...'

'Miriam you okay? MIRIAM!'

'All these people, where did they come from? Is it a fancy dress day here or something?'

'MIRIAM, mate!' Sophie rushed to Miriam's side. She was coherent, but seemed to be in a trance. Her eyes were glazed, and she had a far away look on her face. 'Miriam, dude, you're scaring me, what's wrong? Have you drunk too much too quickly?'

'Yes, okay!' Miriam said, as she leant against the wall of the open fronted shop. 'Where? On the wall? There?'

'MIRIAM!' Sophie was getting frantic. Was this an alcoholic reaction? They had eaten properly, were not dehydrated, and Miriam had only just taken her first sip. 'Shit shit shit... Miriam, dude?'

Sophie stepped off the kerb, and looked up and down the empty street. There was no one about at all, and looking at the location of the towering volcano, they were still a little way from the exit. She knelt down beside her friend, not knowing what to do. Miriam looked at Sophie, but looked straight through her.

'There's writing on the wall? Okay. You with a tour or back-packing like us? I wish we'd thought about dressing up in togas to look like a Pompeian inhabitant,' Miriam continued, really calmly. For as calm as Miriam was, Sophie was tearing her hair out. She made the decision to stay with her hallucinating friend, rather than getting help. If she left Miriam, she could wander off and lose herself in the maze of narrow streets that made up the shopping district of central Pompeii. She took a few steps to a nearby crossroad, keeping Miriam in sight. As she got to the junction, she looked up each road, hoping someone English-speaking would be within shouting distance. Just then she heard a familiar voice.

'We'll miss the train if we don't get a move on,' said Miriam.

Sophie spun round and saw Miriam balancing on the kerb, pretending it was a tight-rope, with her lunch bag in her hand, and Sophie's in her other out-stretched hand. 'Stop pissing about and let's get going!'

'Miriam?' Sophie said softly, jogging over to her friend, 'Are you okay?' She gave her a big hug, bags and all. She looked into Miriam's eyes, which were now normal again, shining dark brown, as they should be.

'I'm fine, what's up? We going or what?'

'Miriam, you just had a funny turn. You were talking to someone, blabbing on about lots of people in fancy dress!'

'What?'

'Mate, honestly, you were talking, but you definitely weren't with it, you were miles away!' Sophie explained. 'You were all confused about something, and pointed over there!' After debating the craziness of the idea, they decided it did not hurt to take a look, not expecting to find anything. They walked to the corner of the ancient shop. It was quite dark and hard to see, with the shadows casting coolness in contrast to the warmth of the day. They searched the worn flaky plaster walls with patches of bare bricks showing. 'There's some writing over here.'

Miriam walked over to where Sophie was looking. There was some old Roman graffiti scratched into the plaster near the door frame. There was a circle, then a rectangle resting on its short side, with half a diamond laid in front of it.

'I'll take a picture of it. It's curious. I'll look it up later. We really need to crack on and get the train!'

'Do you feel okay to travel, Miriam? We could always book into a hotel here?'

'I'm fine, mate. Besides, if we did that, it would mean having to lose the payment for one of the other rooms, which we can't really afford. I'll be fine, honest. I don't know what came over me!'

'You just took a sip of your drink, wobbled and started talking bollocks,' Sophie recalled, 'you swayed and grabbed for the wall, which steadied you, then you turned and leant against it, talking nonsense!'

'Did I? I don't remember any of that. What do you think happened?'

'I don't know, but we drank the same drink, and it hadn't affected me at all, and I've been knocking it back all day whilst I've been walking about. It's very sour, but also refreshing, like a super-charged starburst!'

'Well, I feel fine. Let me get a picture of this, and you have a quick look to see if there is anything else. I don't know why we're bothering really. It was just some hallucination brought on by some dodgy lemons!'

'You were pretty serious about what you said. It seemed important and it was as if you trusted what you were being told. You were very sincere.'

They got the pictures of the strange writing, as there was nothing else in the room and headed towards the train station. The full heat of the day was starting to wear off, but it was still warm. By the time they reached the lemonade trolley, they were quite hot and sweaty. They bought some more for the journey, though Miriam was dubious about adding some of the lemon liqueur to hers. Sophie had no such reservations, and looked forward to a cold drink on the train, and some sugary snacks.

Chapter Nine

May 2011, Egypt

Annie had never felt heat like it. As she walked out of the airport, the scorching sun relentlessly beat down on an arid, sandy landscape. The airport had formally been a military air force base, therefore it did not have the home comforts of the departure lounge at East Midlands. Her friends, Charlie, CT, Deano, Kay and Kay's boyfriend Bobby, walked behind her into the punishing heat. They put their bags down, and looked around for a taxi. Being the adventurous types, Annie and her friends had not booked the holiday through an operator.

'I'm not paying loads extra for someone to do what I can do myself!' she had stated, and proceeded to research various holiday sites, and booked the hotel and flights independently, saving everyone a fortune. They had successfully arrived in Taba, Egypt, at the top of the Red Sea and they just needed to get a taxi to the hotel, for a week of sun, fun, and relaxation. The guidebook had said the taxis were cheap, and with the exception of the tourists' coaches slowly filling up, there was just one other vehicle to be seen. That was a leather seated stretched executive car.

'That'll do!' said Charlie. He was tall, slim and young, wearing designer shorts and a pink, designer T-shirt, with expensive sunglasses resting on a pointed nose, 'Let's do it!'

'It'll cost a fortune!' replied Annie, picking up her bags and heading for the waiting car.

'Be great to arrive in style, plus I bet it has wicked air con!'

Fifteen minutes later, the six of them, and their luggage were travelling in the climate controlled, comfortable Mercedes. The road was bumpy, and wound in-between the high, barren, orange-coloured mountains.

Officially being one of the most barren landscapes on earth, there was no sign of obvious life. There was the odd spiky bush, with dark, waxy leaves and small white flowers. The light changed as they travelled between the mountain shadows and the burning sun, as the road continued to descend.

The gradient gradually levelled out, and the canyon they had been driving through widened. It was just as barren, but there were signs of civilization. Bedouin camps were set back from the road, dotted at regular intervals. Donkeys, goats and camels were tethered on ropes, but there were no signs of people. It was midday, and the sun was at its hottest. Rounding the last bend, the landscape transformed into one of luscious green beauty. Low level hotel complexes could just about be made out amongst the palm trees and flowering bushes. It was a riot of colour; purple, blue and pink flowers intertwined with cacti of all sizes and shapes. Beyond the fertile land, was the bluest sea, looking inviting and cooling.

'I'll be taking a swim in there later,' said CT, 'I'm definitely going to snorkel as much as I can!'

'I've brought my diver's licence, so I'll be going down onto the corals,' exclaimed Bobby, as he gently held Kay's hand, and gave her a smile.

'Sod that,' said Annie, 'all those little fishes... they might get stuck in between your toes. Nasty!'

'They won't get stuck between your toes, Annie,' Bobby said reassuringly.

'Really? Why are you so sure?'

''Cause they're far too big for that!' laughed Bobby, as everyone else joined in. 'Explain the toe-fish phobia, you've mentioned it a few times on the way out here.'

'I can't go in the sea, because a fish may get stuck in-between my toes. The thought makes me nauseous,' Annie said, giving a little pretend shiver. 'When I was about eleven, we went on holiday for a week.'

'And you got attacked by a fish?'

'No, '

'You trod on a fish, and put your foot through it?'

'No, let me finish,' laughed Annie.

'A dead fish got wrapped around your legs?'

'NO! LET ME FINISH! We came *back* from our holiday, and I went to put my foot in my slippers...'

'And it turned into a big fish head, and you thought you would lose your foot?'

'...I put my foot in my slippers, and felt something hard around my toes. When I took my foot out, my pet goldfish, all dead and dry was stuck between my toes!'

'Ew that's gross,' said Kay.

'No, that's nasty. How did it get there?'

'We think it had jumped out of its bowl. We'd given it a holiday block, which would slowly dissolve and release food. Not good enough for old Gilbert Goldfish, he was proper dead and poking out of my toes. I nearly died, it was vile. And, so you see, I now can't go anywhere that has fish!'

The others looked at Annie, laughing. She had never told the story before, and now that they understood the phobia, a few situations now made a lot of sense. The deep blue sea shimmered in the distance and then turned slightly pink, where the land mass on the opposite side of the sea to Taba, Saudi Arabia, also shimmered in the heat. It was an exotic location. Taba was favoured by the tourists who just wanted to relax, and possibly take an excursion. It was nothing like the thriving town of Sharm El-Sheikh, further to the south on the coast. They had all already holidayed at Sharm, on more than one occasion. Taba had been chosen as it was a new development of five brand new hotels. The bay it had been constructed on was only a few miles across, and had a backdrop of steep mountains, so any further development would not be possible. It was an idyllic location and a good choice for the holiday.

The Mercedes continued onto the immaculately cultivated hotel landscape, and came to a halt at a grand, white gatehouse, with a barrier and armed guards. The driver wound down his window, and said something to the guard, who lent in to look in the back of the car, as the tinted windows did not allow him to see who the passengers were. As the driver's customers where quite clearly holidaymakers, they were waved through once the barrier had been lifted. The road had changed to a smooth, modern tarmac, and beautifully landscaped gardens. The well maintained lawns could have been in the heart of England, with the exception of the massive, unusual flowering bushes and palms. The road passed in front of the other four hotels at the resort, and pulled up at another gate house. The driver had to get out, and open the boot for the guard to check. He then opened one of the back doors to the stretched car, for the guard to check who was travelling. There was a five minute conversation, and then they were allowed to enter the grounds of the five star hotel.

Influenced by Islamic architecture, the hotel entrance was a myriad of smoked glass and dark terracotta walls, with a remarkable resemblance to the Brighton Pavilion. There were different sized domes indicating the reception area, dining room and spa of the hotel. The driver pulled up outside the main sliding door, and everyone got out. As they had travelled to Egypt before, all of this security was no surprise. They left their bags at the side of the door with a guard, and went to check in. Once it was confirmed who they were, a tag would be put on their bags, and the security would put them on a golf buggy, ready to be taken to the rooms on the spacious site. Straightaway, the coolness of the hotel was an immediate relief from the 49 degree sun outside. No expense had been spared on the interior decoration of the resort. Massive curving stairs led down to sunken ponds, which had been positioned beneath each of the domes of the main building, giving a cavernous feel, with trees and plants growing in and around the water. Fountains jetted water high into the roof, made magnificent by the great height of the dome from the water's surface. Every surface was highly decorated, yet it was tasteful.

The reception had huge blue and cream sofas, reading chairs and poufs, with long cream voile curtains. Through the glass wall opposite the main door, a view of immaculate gardens, one of the pools, the sea and Saudi Arabia were framed by tall indoor palms. Huge vases of sweet scented flowers stood at reception, and the English-speaking receptionist efficiently checked them in. The receptionist stopped typing on her keyboard, and spoke to her colleague.

'We can upgrade your single rooms to an apartment if you wish? It sleeps four, but has a pool view, not sea views. Would you like it, or stay as you were?' she smiled.

'Upgrade!' shouted Deano. Being an only child, and not socialising too much back home, he cherished group activities, and the company of his friends. 'Upgrade, it will be better!'

'I'm up for the upgrade. It would be more pleasing, to all be together,' concurred CT, in his ex-military voice. He was a successful businessman and was single by choice. He had happily joined the trip to Taba when Annie had asked him. While all of the others, with the exception of Bobby, still worked together, CT had left a few years ago, when he became an executive salesman. He had found his true vocation, and now lived a very comfortable lifestyle. He had just been promoted at work, and so the trip seemed like a perfect reward. He was the oldest in the group at 45, with Charlie the youngest at 19.

'Oh, yes, yes, let's upgrade, that would be ace!' said Annie, hopping from one foot to another, as the receptionist nodded and typed again on her keyboard,

'I'm easy,' said Charlie.

'Yes, we know!' laughed Kay, as the others joined in. Being young, fit, well-dressed and wealthy, Charlie was renowned as a bit of a ladies' man.

'Ha ha, think you're funny? I meant, I don't mind, yeah, let's upgrade,' he shyly replied, with a glint in his eye and flushed cheeks.

Kay and Bobby were separately checked in, and the group agreed to meet in reception in an hour, once they had sorted out their rooms. Bellboys led the friends out of reception, onto a colourful terraced area of Bedouin throws, rolled cushions and smoking pipes. Low tables, just a few inches high sat between the seats. It was a cool shaded area, as the hotel made up three of the sides, and the view of the sea was the fourth. Overhead, wooden struts acted as a framework for plants to grow over, ensuring the people sat beneath were in a pleasant shade. The delicate leaves of the canopy whispered as a gentle breeze combed between them.

They walked off the terrace, past swimming pools attached by narrow channels, and crossed by small, arched bridges. The plant life was in abundance, and birds chattered amidst their protective foliage. The crazy paved path passed between raised flowerbeds where occasionally a two-story, square, dark terracotta building could be seen. They had a ground and first floor, accessed by an external flight of stairs. The upstairs balconies were decorated with lattice patterned panels, keeping within the theme of the main reception. Trailing plants hung down from the upstairs balconies, some nearly reaching the floor. As the blocks were low, they were well hidden by palms, tall plants and climbing or trailing foliage. Behind the hotel and beyond the other hotel grounds, the almost Martian landscape of the uncultivated foothills of the mountains, looked down with a menacing, hostile appearance of deep shadows and the unknown.

Annie stepped into the apartment first and marvelled at the luxurious surroundings. She walked towards the window, and looked out onto a circular swimming pool. There were six empty sun loungers, each blue and cream striped, with cream, canvas umbrellas folded away in-between each pair of chairs. The small pool, about ten swimming strokes wide, had a channel leading off it, to another larger pool. A small bridge crossed the channel. On the opposite side of the pool to the loungers, were flowering plants, hiding a path that led over the bridge to a small bar area, serving drinks and snacks.

Charlie and Deano had joined Annie at the window. Deano yanked the mosquito netting back, to get a better look. 'Is that ours too?' he asked, 'Pay the man... ask him to save it for us.'

'Wow, here, give him this,' said Charlie, handing over 200 Egyptian pounds, which worked out at £20, more than the bellboy would earn in six months. 'If we keep the staff sweet from the start, we'll get a better service!'

'Yes, I always do that,' said CT, as he handed the bell boy another 100 Egyptian pounds. The young hotel worker smiled broadly, displaying surprisingly perfect, white teeth. He nodded his head, with a little bow in gratitude. CT started doing swimming actions with his arms, and pointed to the pool. 'Could you save us those chairs please? Save chairs?' There was more swimming actions and pointing, until the bellboy picked up the beach towels neatly stacked by the door, and pointed at them, then the pool area.

'I put out for you, Sir. Towels on chairs, Sir. I put umba-rells up too Sir, for you!' He darted off down the stairs of the first floor apartment, stuffing his money into the deep pockets of his white, formal, deck shorts.

Annie and Deano, who were still sat in the bay window, watched as the bellboy hurried around, opening the umbrellas, and laying the towels out on the loungers. He picked up a bristle broom and swept a few loose leaves and petals so the patio was perfect.

'One of us needs to tell Kay and Bobby that we are crashing here. Sod going to reception, I'll text her,' said Annie.

'Beers, beers and maybe a beer is in order I think?' said CT, walking through an arch to one of the two bedrooms and the bathroom. The bedroom CT had walked into had two single beds, and a balcony overlooking the pool. Deano walked in behind him, having already investigated the other room, which had a double bed in it and an en suite bathroom.

'I'm in here with you; the other room is a double. I don't think Annie would want to share with me, and I don't want to share with Charlie, so here I am, roomy!'

'Great, what a lucky man I am,' said CT, sarcastically. Having been on holiday with Deano before, he knew he could be quite mischievous if he became bored.

'You are indeed. Very lucky!' replied Deano, secretly knowing CT was being sarcastic.

Annie walked through to where CT and Deano were settling in, admiring the view on the balcony. 'You boys will be cosy in here,' she mocked. Turning round, she went through to the other bedroom. 'Charlie... Charlie!' she called, but Charlie was bringing in the luggage with the security guard who drove the golf buggy.

'What?'

'Top or tail?'

'What?'

'Top or tail, we're sharing!' shouted Annie, as Charlie walked up beside her. 'Oh, 'ello. We're sharing. The two lovers in there have nabbed the single beds. We'll be okay, I'm sure you can keep your hands off me for a week!'

'No problem there, Cupcake,' said Charlie, dumping his bag on the king-size bed. 'It's big enough for all four of us!' He found his swim shorts and sun cream, and headed to the bathroom. 'I'm off down the pool!'

The next few days passed in a hazy, lazy fashion. They would all rise and go down for a buffet breakfast. The food was standard, but good. Various Egyptian dishes of fresh fish were avoided, or anything washed or made with water. Although the complex was brand new, and the water filtration system was state of the art, there was no point in risking Ramasis Revenge. After breakfast, it was down to the pool. The biggest decision of the day was which swimsuit to wear. They would lie out on the patio, on the chairs Alfred would have prepared for them. Deano had asked the bellboy's name, and could not understand what he had said, and so nicknamed him Alfred, after the butler in the Batman films. The 'umba-rells' would be up, and menus for the snack bar would be neatly left on each of the little shelves hugging the umbrella posts. Even at nine in the morning, it was already in the high thirties.

The day would be spent sleeping, reading and swimming. They invented games to help pass the time in the pool. The little circular pool had a hot pool besides it. The water was only a foot deep, and very warm from the sun. A small slope at the water's level caused a semi-circular waterfall to drop into the main pool. CT, in a moment of madness, sprung up off his chair, jogged on tiptoes over the hot floor, to the shallow pool and splashed in. He lay down on the slope, rolled over and over until he fell off the edge, hitting the main pool with a massive splash. They had all laughed at his spontaneity and youthful antics. For someone who was usually quite prim and proper, it was out of character.

By about one, they would start planning lunch. Deano would go over the bridge to the bar, and order meals for everyone, bringing back more drinks. They did a lot of drinking. A lot. Back home, not only did they all work as drivers, warehouse staff and management at a national courier company, they also went out together every Saturday night. Deano would buy rounds of drinks before the previous ones had been drunk, and so they would all be playing catch up all night, getting totally mashed in a local club. 'You know it's been a good night, when you're leaving the club as the birds are getting up!' Deano would always say. They all had the belief that as they worked hard, over 60 hours a week most of the time, they should also play hard at the weekends. Although they all had very different backgrounds and characters, they enjoyed each other's company, and valued their relationship with the rest of the group. They had led this lifestyle for over five years, though Charlie had only recently joined the company after leaving school.

The afternoons were very much the same, with drinking and messing around. As the sun set behind a headland of tall, dark brown mountain tops, they would go back to their rooms, shower, change and go lay on the Bedouin terrace before dinner. They had explored the complex, and Bobby had had a couple of days diving. Kay was happy lounging beside the pool, and would go for walks with Annie to the little boutique shops inside the hotel.

'How's it going with Bobby?' Annie asked Kay one afternoon.

'Um... yes!'

'As good as that,' laughed Annie. 'If you get that fed up with him, you can always crash in our bachelor pad!'

'You're not a bachelor,' said Kay.

'No, but with three against one, I was outnumbered.' Annie had worked for Kay for over seven years, and they socialised a lot outside of work, frequently going out for tea after work with Deano. Chinese buffet was the favourite choice. They would also cycle to the fruit farm every summer, to eat and pick berries.

'I'll have to move in and pull rank on them all. Boys drool, girls rule!' she mocked. At work Kay got on with everyone. Well, everyone who pulled their weight. In exchange for honest hard work, Kay would do anything to help a struggling employee, no matter how serious or trivial it might sound. She was a fantastic organiser, letter writer and listener. She was almost a surrogate mum during work hours, though she was younger than most of the staff.

They discovered the spa when they first arrived at the hotel which had an indoor pool. It was freezing cold, and set in the basement of the reception, accessible by a wide, spiral staircase. The indoor pool was of white marble. It was only a few feet deep, and had lots of pillars in and around it, in rows, supporting a low ceiling. There were big, fluffy blue towels in neat piles, and mood lighting in various shades of blue gave the effects of swimming in an ice cave, as the water reflected off the ceiling. It was a stark contrast to the hot oranges and browns of the landscape outside. Glass doors led to hot tubs, saunas and steam rooms. It was very luxurious, and the girls made a point of visiting it at least once a day.

They would all take walks around the grounds, and down to look at the coral in the sea. There was a pier passing over the shallow water, where it was possible to look down on the top of the coral, and all the marine life it supported. This private beach and pier were busy with people from the hotel snorkelling and sunbathing. The beach had rows of loungers under cream umbrellas, and hotel staff in the same uniform as Alfred offering a waiter service to the residents. Walking off the beach, through a desert garden of cacti, aloe vera and other succulents, the heat was punishing. It had been the hottest May since records began, with the midday temperature reaching 57 degrees. Deano had had to be physically removed from the sun, as he had refused to take shade. He had lain in the sun and sweated, until he had run out of body juices. At that point, CT, Charlie and Bobby had dragged his lounger under the shade of an umbrella. He had felt really ill for the rest of the day, and resigned himself to just drinking water. It was not something he would be trying again.

Chapter Ten

May 2011, Egypt and Jordan

On the fourth day, Charlie, Annie and CT were collected by a shuttle bus at the front of their hotel. The sky was a bronze colour, as the sun started to rise over the horizon. It was cool enough for light shirts to be worn over T-shirts, and they carried bags with sun cream, cameras and reading books. They had planned a trip to Petra, the Rose Red City carved into the rocks in Jordan. It was better known as the temple where Indiana Jones and the Third Crusade found the Holy Grail. The pink, stone treasury façade had been carved out of the rock face, and had only been discovered in 1812, due to its inhospitable, isolated location. Getting there was going to take nearly five hours. The shuttle bus ran the tourists to the other end of the bay at Taba, a ten minute ride away, picking up from the other hotels along the way. A boat then took them up to the top of the Red Sea, to a point where Egypt, Israel, Jordan and Saudi Arabia all meet. Once passing through customs in Jordan, a coach then drove through very dry, dusty plains and through rocky, twisting mountains. They had passed ochre-coloured pinnacles, rising up to 2,000 feet off the desert-like landscape. They stopped off for a leg stretch, and to experience the natural, inhospitable environment. The wind whipped across the plain, sandblasting bare legs. Even with the wind, the heat of the sun was unbearable, after the comfort of the air conditioned coach. It had been quite scary, to imagine the coach driver leaving them all stranded miles from anywhere. The coach had waited for them all to get back on, and drove on to Wadi Muso, the nearest town to the ancient city of Petra.

'It says in the guide book, that *Petra* in Greek means *rock*, and it was built in the first century AD,' Annie had informed Charlie and CT.

'I read it was still inhabited until the 1980s!' said CT.

'Wow, while I was bopping away to Boy George and Culture Club, people still lived in these caves. Amazing!' marvelled Annie.

The tour operator had organised a meal before the long, hard walk to Petra. Everyone had been advised that they needed to bring plenty of water, sturdy walking boots and to be in good health.

'Good job Deano isn't here then,' CT had laughed, as they were all aware that Deano and exercise were never a combination found together. They had dined at The Petra Kitchen, where they sampled traditional Jordanian meat and rice dishes, some almond type biscuits, and drank fresh fruit juices. Once fully refreshed, they started their trek to Petra. The walk would be about three hours, with no point of refreshment until they reached their destination. Before they set off, they called into the visitors centre, went to the bathroom, bought ice creams, and browsed around the shop. They bought postcards and books on the history of Petra. There was a little flat cart selling rugs, smoking pipes and little snow globes. Annie took a shine for one of the little spherical gifts, and bought it for Deano. As he had not made the trip, she would give him a souvenir. She picked a dome with a little model of The Treasury in it.

'Deano will like this. All he will go on about is the Indiana film. I'm still not sure about him; he thinks this is a movie set, not the other way around!'

'He'll like it. Bit inaccurate though,' said Charlie.

'Why, what's up with it? It looks fine to me, just like the pictures and film!' said Annie, indignantly.

'Annie, when did it last snow here?' replied Charlie, raising his eyebrows, and looking down at her, through the corner of his eyes. He liked taking the mickey out of Annie.

'Don't laugh at me, Charlie. It's nice, and only a quid or so!'

'I'm not laughing at you, I was just thinking about CT!'

'Maybe I should swap beds with him then?'

'Not like that, muppet. I was just thinking how well we all get on, and how great this trip has been!'

'It has been brilliant, hasn't it?'

The cart owner bagged the little gift, and Annie put it in her canvas beach bag. He was speaking fluent Jordanian at her, but she had no idea what he was talking about. He kept pointing at the globe, then putting the tips of his fingers together, so they formed an inverted 'V'. Politely, but somewhat bemused, Annie smiled and thanked the man as she walked off. They left the shop area and passed through the gates that led to the entrance for Petra. The sandy, scorched open space gave way to narrowing rocky walls of the surrounding peaks, until the path passed into the canyon, exactly like the Indiana films. The *Siq* is a long canyon snaking through the rock, with dangerous overhangs and loose falling stones, carved over generations by flood waters. The hues of pink were various, with a closeup inspection of the stone, clearly showing all the different shades of purple and dark red. Most of the canyon was in the shade of the surrounding rock fascias, which had sheer heights of 300 feet. As the friends trekked on, they thought about the many different walks of life that had passed between the canyon walls over the centuries.

The clatter of hooves on the stony ground could be heard regularly, as Jordanians drove their horses and buggies aggressively up and down the *Siq*, between the visitors centre and Petra, taking passengers who were either too scared or too weak to make the testing walk themselves. The horses looked thin and overworked, though Annie did notice they all had well trimmed hooves, all with well fitting metal shoes on. The carriages were tatty, though simple efforts had been made to decorate them, by a bright coloured throw on the seats, or tassels hanging off the roof.

Unexpectedly, as they rounded a bend, the 130 foot high treasury building came into view. Dark purple sandstone in the shadows framed the view, with the bright apricot pink, two storey masterpiece across the narrow gorge floor illuminated by the full sunshine. The spacious portico of the lower floor was entered by two doorways underneath a colonnade. There were remarkable resemblances to the architecture of Ancient Rome. Pillars supported the second floor, where in the centre stood a round kiosk with a tented roof, placed between two carved pavilions. There was incredible detail carved into the soft stone, which had been protected from wind and rain erosion by the narrow canyon walls.

'What do you think the inside will be like?' asked Annie, as they strolled out of the canyon, across the deep, sandy gorge, to some shallow steps. 'D'ya think it will be all tunnels and cob-webby, like the film?'

'Sorry to shatter your illusion, but I've been before,' said CT, 'it is just a square room inside. Spielberg has a lot to answer for! They don't even think it was ever a treasury, probably a tomb. There's a myth that there is treasure buried here somewhere!'

Having explored the treasury, they proceeded to walk down the 4,000 foot long gorge, which got wider and wider as they went. Untethered donkeys wandered about, looking like free beasts, but were probably just waiting for a return customer back to the visitors centre. There were steps leading up to higher levels of the rock, where doorways led to darkened, square rooms. These tall, rectangular cave fronts were decorated with a triangular pattern, with a doorway in the centre. The surrounding rock had been chiselled away, making the dwellings look like they were jutting out of the rock. A whole city inhabited the gorge walls. It was unbearably hot, as they were now walking with no shade. Taking a short walk up to one of the caves was hard work, and CT was sweating quite profusely by the time they rested at the top, in one of the shaded rooms. With the higher elevation, the gorge could be seen stretching out, with numerous cave dwellings at different heights. There were no trees in sight, just hard, scorched rock, stone and sand. Annie had drunk all of her water, as her mouth was so dry. It was like a sauna heat, where every suffocating breath warmed her lungs. There was zero moisture in the atmosphere, and they were all starting to feel it. Charlie, being the youngest and fittest was coping, but he was getting tired, and they were all aware they had the three hour walk back, which they needed to start soon.

They sat on stone steps and looked out over the city, studying the formation of caves on the opposite wall of the gorge. Some little rose finches hopped about on the hot stone floor at the entrance to the cave. The lower level had a long row of terraced, decorated rectangles sticking out of the stone, with open doorways showing as very dark, cooling spaces, but higher up the gorge wall, on the fourth row, there were just a few doorways. The final fifth level had just one house in the very centre.

'It's just amazing, fancy living all the way up there. Bet the rent was cheap, and you would be dead fit. Can you imagine if you forgot a pint of milk, it would take you an hour round trip!'

'I think I could handle cave life,' said Charlie.

'Pull the other one. You can't be away from Sky TV and your iPod for more than a day. I bet it's in your bag now!' joked Annie. She went to grab his bag, to prove herself right, causing her own bag to tumble to the floor. 'Oh no, my snow globe!' She knelt down on the stone floor, and examined the little gift.

'It's okay, I think,' said Annie, closely examining it. 'Shit, it's got a tiny crack, but it's not leaking.' As she stood up, the rush to her head was severe, and she felt light-headed. She steadied herself, and sat back down again. As she did so, she inhaled some of the dust from the floor, kicked up during the skirmish. Before she could put her hand over her mouth, or turn her head away, she had inhaled the dust, and immediately felt sick. 'Oh, man, what the hell...?'

'You okay,' asked CT, crouching down beside her, just as Charlie joined them.

'Yes, I'm fine thanks,' Annie replied as she went to stand up. She wrapped the globe back up, and put it back in her bag. There was no real damage to it.

As they left the darkness of the cave dwelling, Annie held the stone corner of the doorway, to steady herself for the big step down to the rugged path outside of the house. Immediately when she touched the rock, everything she looked at became a sepia colour, except for the triangle of the portico to the treasury, away in the distance. She was aware of Charlie and CT walking off in front of her, but was rooted to the spot. She felt nauseous, but was intrigued by the spectacle unfolding in front of her. The sky was a translucent black, and she could clearly see all aspects of the universe above her head. The planets were there, all laid out slowly rotating above her. The colours were fantastic. Gas clouds of red, orange, purple and blue, white shining stars, and the Milky Way stretching out as far as she could see. And there was silence. All Annie could hear was a faint whirring sound, like metal sliding over metal, as the discs of Saturn turned. It was as if time on earth had stood still, though she was able to recognise Charlie and CT as they came over to her.

The portico of the treasury started to rise, as did one of its columns. Annie stared in wonder as the two huge, ancient pieces of masonry realigned themselves, so the pillar stood behind the portico triangle, and came to a rest once the sun was shining in the space between them.

'Annie... Annie... you okay darling?' asked CT, holding one of her hands and standing in front of her. Annie, still steadying herself against the doorframe, craned her neck so she could see over CT's massive shoulders. He gently put his hand on her cheek, and turned her head back to him, 'You okay flower?'

'Annie, mate?' said Charlie, showing signs of concern.

'Hey guys, look behind you, those stones look like a giant pyramid... the stones above the portico of the Treasury? That cart seller kept making a pyramid with his hands. Do you think he was telling us not to miss this?' she said, pointing up the canyon to where they had just walked.

CT looked at Charlie, and they both turned to see what Annie was looking at. CT, still holding Annie's hand, with his other arm over her shoulder, turned to look at the treasury, and could not believe what he saw. A giant pyramid of stone was floating in the sky, shimmering in the punishing heat, with a portico tower besides it. The sun shone in the space between them.

'What am I supposed to be looking at?' said Charlie, 'I can see donkeys and camels... lots of donkeys and camels, and a shit load of tourists.'

'Can't you see what I can see?' said CT, as he stepped forward to point at the sky above the treasury, letting go of Annie's hand and removing his arm that had been comforting her. 'Look at the tres...!'

Just then, everything went back to normal. The stones were where they had been for the last 2,000 years. 'What in God's name!' he wondered.

'Will someone please tell me what's up with you two?' asked Charlie, getting frustrated that his two friends were sharing something he could not see. Annie turned to Charlie, 'The Pyramid Festival,' she said. The universe was still displaying its full magnificence above her, and she smiled and giggled as the stars and planets slowly moved. She could see for thousands of miles into outer space, so many stars, gas clouds, colours and planets. She took his hand, and turned him to look in the direction of the floating stones.

'Come on, pet. Let's get you back to the bus. It must have been something you ate. There are all sorts of hallucinogenic plants in this part of the world, maybe you ate something at lunch,' said Charlie as he turned and started to walk away from the cave dwelling, to the stairs that led to the gorge floor.

'Oh. My. Fucking. God!' he whispered, 'what the fuck is going on?' With Annie holding his hand, he could see what the other two had been marvelling at. Everything went a sepia colour, and he was aware that the stones were suspended in the sky. Being rational, Charlie stopped. There had to be an explanation.

'Charlie, let go of Annie's hand,' said CT. 'What do you see now?'

'Well, bugger me! it's all gone back to normal!'

'Right, now touch Annie again.'

'Ahh, cool. Annie is a portal to another dimension!' jested Charlie, in a stoned, hippy type of voice.

CT got some water out of his bag, 'Here Annie, have a drink. It's probably Qat or something, just harmless leaves that if chewed can have the same sort of effects as speed mixed in with something. I don't know, but have a drink, Annie!' She took the bottle and drank, still with an astonished look on her face, as she studied the fantasy world in front of her. CT took the bottle back, then poured the rest of it over her head.

'What you doing, you freaking arse!' shouted Annie, putting her hands to her head, trying to protect herself from the downpour, which in actual fact was really refreshing, 'Not only am I now soaked, but you've used all the bloody water and it's a three mile walk back!'

'…and welcome back, mademoiselle!' smiled CT.

Charlie could see the pink mountains with the treasury in the distance, and once again the donkeys and camels wandering about. All aspects of the phenomenon had disappeared. Everything was as it should be. Annie's own vision had been rectified, and she too saw the landscape as it had always been, in a rose pink colour, all dusty and parched.

'Did I just see what I thought I saw?' asked Charlie.

'It was a bit odd!' said CT. Being a former high ranking military man, having experienced hostilities in many European countries, and the jungles of South America, there were not many things that shocked him, but this incident had taken his breath away. 'If everyone feels okay, we need to get a move on!'

'What was a bit odd?' asked Annie, as they started their descent from the caves, 'what you guys on about?'

'Don't you remember, Annie, you saw things, and said "The Pyramid Festival!"'

Chapter Eleven

May 2011, Italy

A week later, Sophie and Miriam were an hour away from Venice. The last week had been very busy, and they were looking forward to their last three nights in one location. Living out of a packed rucksack can be hard work; washing out smalls each evening and drying them on windowsills, or hanging them in the bathroom; keeping their souvenirs on the smaller, lighter side and having to wear the same clothes for the whole trip. The photographs they had taken looked amazing, but they looked like they had been taken in one day, as they had the same clothes on. To pass the time, Miriam got her phone out, and looked back over some of the pictures she had taken. Rome, Sorrento, Pompeii...

'Look at this one at Pompeii, of the graffiti I took,' said Miriam, 'I can't rotate the picture, so it's permanently on its side.'

'The one after, of the volcano and that column, look similar... the shapes are the same. Look!' Sophie used the phone's curser to jump from one picture to the other. 'See, the graffiti picture, which is on its end, is like an exact outline of the volcano picture,' she explained, stopping on the picture of the writing. 'Maybe that's why it won't rotate, because it's meant to be that way round.'

'Maybe, but... it's a bit spooky that... how is that possible? They are identical. Look!'

Miriam continued to view her pictures. Florence had been just breathtaking. They had done the usual of buying tickets for the open-topped, double-decker bus, and toured the city. They had visited the Piazza della Signoria and Palazzo Vecchio. Here, they had admired the replica of Michelangelo's marble giant *David*. The original had been moved to the Gallerie dell' Accademia, and although they had queued for three hours, they did eventually get to see *David*, in the flesh. The intricate detail, to the extent that he had dried skin around his fingernails, and even the veins in his arms and legs, had been carved into a piece of white Carrara marble. He was magnificent, a very fine specimen of manhood.

'He's stood in that position as Michelangelo wanted to capture the moment that David realised he was going to have to fight the Giant. All previous Davids were shown as being triumphant, after winning the battle. He was also placed facing south, looking towards Rome, to ward off the evil of the Pope, protecting the Florentine Republic,' said Sophie. She had written a piece about David for one of her classes, and so was very knowledgeable about him. 'He's 18 feet tall, the exact length of the flawed piece of marble the church gave him to make the statue,' she continued.

'How do you know?' replied Miriam.

''Cause Michelangelo used the flat ends of the block in the sculpture. If you were to look at him, *David*, not Michelangelo, from above, you would see his head is flat on the top. It had deliberately not been worked, to show the entire block had been carved.'

'I thought David was meant to be looked at from below? His big hands make him seem taller than he is.'

'He is, that's why no one ever sees the top of his head! Clever, eh?' laughed Sophie.

They had also visited Santa Croce, a massive black and white marble church in Piazza Santa Croce. The largest Franciscan church in Italy housed the tombs of Michelangelo and Dante. It also had beautiful cloisters, which were a refreshing rest from the bright sun. They'd had a pot of tea at a little café, just across the square opposite the church, and admired the detail that had gone into the architecture.

Once they were back on the tourist bus, they were taken a little way out of the city, crossing the Arno on a bridge next to the shop-lined Ponte Vecchio, and out of the city. The bus climbed the steep hills, winding up a twisting, narrow road. It was early evening, and the sun was setting. It had got a little colder, but the warm breezes whispering past the top of the bus carried with them scents of pine, jasmine and wild rose. As the bus climbed higher and higher, the flutter of small bats could be heard as they caught insects in flight. Once the bus came to a stop at the end of its tour, before turning around, the passengers got off and had a wander around the tiny square of pretty Fiesole. With Etrusian roots, and Roman ruins, it was a day out in itself, but time was of the essence, so the girls took photos, and then rode the bus back into town. The views over Florence were magnificent, with the bronze sky causing the city to almost shimmer in the fading light. The Arno shone as a silver and golden thread running through the shadows of the Tuscan countryside. Maria del Fiore, the famous Florentine Duomo, with its tall terracotta dome and the Campanile standing as important and majestic as it had for over 700 years, dominated the skyline. The views on the way back down to Florence were spectacular. Sophie played *Madame Butterfly* by Puccini, something she did every time she visited Florence, having seen the film *A Room with a View*. The beautiful, haunting operatic music serenaded the silent passengers of the bus, as the warm air gently carried the sound. It was a poignant moment. Sometimes the simplest of moments can make a lifetime's impression.

Miriam had then moved onto the Milan photographs. She had taken over 400 on the trip so far, but every now and again would erase the ones that were of nothing special. Milan had been a very special part of the trip. They had ordered pizza from a tiny café, sitting outside with a few glasses of beer. The chef had turned up, and made gestures to Sophie. Using his Italian charm, he had her laughing, as they tried to communicate. He seemed like a good man, as he also made Miriam feel special, not leaving her out of the misunderstood flirting. When Sophie's pizza had been brought out, it had been freshly made in the shape of a heart. *Romance is not dead, after all!* thought Miriam. The Italians in Milan had a clear lust for life, with everything being tasty, tasteful or aesthetically pleasing. There was a celebration on in the city, and all of the shops and museums stayed open for 24 hours. Miriam and Sophie had walked down into the centre of town after their meal. They discussed the beauty of the Italian people, not just in their personalities, but also with their love of fast cars, high fashion and well-groomed, romantic citizens. By the time they had reached Piazza Duomo, the usual ochre colour of the largest Catholic church in the world, had turned a dusky pink. Music was being played, and as they walked to the side of the church, they saw a full orchestra and choir singing the scary *O Fortuna* 'Omen' music in the square. Sophie's music taste varied from punk and indie bands, to heavy rock, and Miriam was a classic rock chick, who always went to watch her husband when he played local venues. They were used to massive guitar rifts, ear-splitting drum solos and sweaty moments in the mosh pits (before it got too rough!) but the power of the voices and instruments caused goosebumps, as they stood and listened.

They browsed through the windows of the designer clothes shops in the Galleria Vittorio Emanuele II one of Europe's grandest shopping malls. The tall, glass vaulted pedestrian walkway acts as a convenient cover during inclement weather, as it ran between the Plazza Duomo and the Milan theatre, Castello Sforzesco. Due to the extended opening hours, they had managed to visit Santa Maria delle Grazie, where Da Vinci's *Last Supper* had been painted. There was usually a three-month waiting list to view the masterpiece, but as luck would have it, there were two vacancies available just before midnight. Milan had been a cultural delight, with everything being so elegant and flamboyant. There were the expressive hand gestures and the confidence of beautiful people in expensive, designer clothes. Sophie imagined it would be a hard place to live, if you didn't fit in.

As the train neared Venice, Miriam moved onto the pictures of the Italian lakes. They had travelled an hour on a local train from Milan, and gone north to the start of the Alps. The pastel coloured villas nestled into the wooded mountain slopes, with boat jetties, and matured, manicured gardens were evidence that this was the place rich Italians came to, to get away from the heat and pollution of the cities. They had taken a boat ride from Como, up to Bellagio, arguably the prettiest town in Italy and had a few beers sat on the water's edge, dipping their toes in the icy cold water.

'It's so... how can I put it... it's so... clean. The air, the water, it's all so fresh!' Sophie had commented. And she was right. The cooler mountain air allowed for sharp, clear views into the distance without the distortion of smog. The tall, dark grey mountains towered over the lake, with green vegetation on their lower levels. The greenery looked fresh too, which considering the pollution-free air they were growing in, was bound to make them look healthy. The clear water of Lake Como, which was fed by the melting ice and snow of the Italian Alps, was clear and cool. Small fish came quite close to the water's edge, 'It's just such a different world!' said Sophie, taking in the natural beauty around her, thinking of the busy A1 trunk road that passed quite close to her home. 'It's all very well, living in the city, with take-aways, and frequent public transport, but wouldn't it be great if life slowed down a little? Miriam... life needs to slow down, doesn't it?'

'Yes, it does. Modern culture requires that everything is bigger, better, faster, but there is no real need to fly through life. It's just how things are where we live. This is available in England, a slower way of living, mountains and lakes!'

'It's something I would like to think about,' said Sophie, taking in the fresh smell of flowering shrubs, pine of the mountain, and the fresh air hanging over the water. 'Alpine fresh!' she said.

The train started to slow, as it neared its destination. The shallow turquoise waters of the lagoon started to come into view, and an air of excitement rippled through the train. People stood at windows, looking as the iconic landscape came into view. The Campanile of St Marks stood out in the distance, like a solitary Redwood, its red terracotta stonework piercing the blues of the sky and sea. In the distance, out over the Adriatic, huge rain clouds were forming, large purple clouds, climbing to great altitudes, looking menacing as they crept towards Venice. The train rattled beside cars travelling out to the Venetian Island on the mile long bridge. Until the latter half of the last century, the only way to get to Venice had been by boat. Once on the island, both cars and trains would have to turn around, and leave the island by the same way they had come, as the only form of transport in Venice, was by boat or feet.

Half an hour later, they had checked into their cheap, backpackers hotel. All of their hotels had been hostels, which offered private rooms. It was in the very centre of Venice, near the Rialto bridge, on the Grand Canal. It had been easy to get to, first on the *vaporetto* (the public water bus service), and then on foot through narrow lanes and the very old food market. Built in white marble, the Rialto Bridge had stood at this pinnacle point in Venice since 1588. It had originally been some boats strung together, then a narrow, wooden footbridge, and later a full size wooden bridge. Even today, only three bridges span the Grand Canal. The hostel was behind an elegant palace, which had its main entrance on the main waterway through Venice. Sophie and Miriam had had to negotiate some very narrow, twisting stairs to get to their room, which had the added danger of being dimly lit. As they had opened the bedroom door, blinding light shone into the hallway.

'Jeez!' exclaimed Sophie, as she put her only free hand up to her eyes. 'What the fu…'

'Sophie!'

'Sorry. Bit bright that sun!' She had walked over to the window, just as the room fell back into a dusky darkness. 'Bloody hell!'

'Soph!' repeated Miriam, starting to sound like her mother.

'No, Miriam, this is a "fuck me" situation. Look!'

Miriam walked across the little, clean bedroom, and looked out of the tiny window. Their room overlooked a small wooden bridge, spanning a narrow, deserted service canal for the bigger hotels. As she looked up the little canal, she saw the wildest sky she had ever seen. The black clouds had reached the city, and as they rolled across the sky the sun was swallowed whole. 'What is it with us and bloody bad weather, Mirry?'

'It is a bit odd, but Italy has been having heavy rain, same as the rest of Europe this year. I'm sure there were severe rain storms before we came to Italy, and I'm sure there will be many more when we've left!' Miriam said, lazily shoving her rucksack off her bed onto the floor, and flopped down on it. It had been a very long day. 'You know the incident at Pompeii?'

'Yes, could hardly forget!'

'Well, this might sound a bit odd, but I keep seeing the triangle-circle-rectangle thing...' Miriam quietly said, as she thought how stupid it sounded, now she heard her own words. 'I mean... I just seem to keep seeing those shapes together!' It still sounded crazy.

'What do you mean?'

'The photo of the writing that wouldn't rotate in my phone, in that formation... I keep seeing those shapes, you know, restaurant logos, adverts on buses, mountains, towers and the sun!'

'Well, are you sure? It was a week ago, could it be we're really tired, and you're just imagining it?' Sophie said, perching on the edge of her own bed, facing Miriam. 'Have you had headaches or dizziness, or anything like that?'

'No, I haven't, if anything I've felt really well, better than I have for years, but I just put it down to our trip with plenty of exercise, fresh air and delicious ice cream. Talking of which, I've only had two today, so I need my third. Shall we go out for half an hour?'

'Are you crazy? It looks like Armageddon out there, we don't know where the nearest shop is, and it's getting dark already. Hang on, how can it be getting dark, the sun was blinding us a moment ago!' Sophie went to look out of the window again, and whistled. 'Whoa...!'

'Whoa what?' said Miriam, heaving herself off her bed. 'Whoa, my, that's a big 'un!' The ferocious looking weather front was directly over Venice, but from where Miriam and Sophie were, their view of the sky was limited, with three or four-storey buildings packed tightly together. 'Come on, let's be adventurous. Even if we get soaked, this room is lovely and warm. Let's go get an ice cream?'

Ten minutes later they had crossed over the Rialto Bridge, onto the north bank. They had stood and looked out towards the Adriatic at the enormous storm clouds, and even saw a few flashes of lightning, way out to sea. The water on the Grand Canal was surprisingly calm, but that was because there were hardly any boats using it. Many of the shops had started to close, and many had put sandbags against their doors. Some shops had metal floodgates: simple metal boards that slid into a tight frame fixed to the doorway. *These people are prepared,* thought Miriam. Having walked straight ahead once they had stepped off the bridge, they came to a T-junction. It was a main thoroughfare through Venice, and expensive shops selling glass, handmade paper and carnival masks were starting to close. In the distance, there was a arched bridge spanning a canal, which the girls walked towards. They stood on its summit, and looked at the buildings making up the canal walls. Every colour had been eroded into the red and brown brickwork and flaking plaster, with different layers of colour and textures making up a surreal scene. Whilst the architecture was stunning, with ornate metalwork and balconies, the shabby exteriors did not seem to matter. The walls were in dire need of some attention, but the shabbiness and crookedness of the environment only made the place more enchanting. Looking to the left, towards the Grand Canal that was running parallel to the path they were on, the buildings were in stark contrast. Although there was not a right angle on these buildings, they were immaculately painted, with heavy, expensive drapes hung at the windows, lit by blazing chandeliers hanging from high ceilings. Powerful speedboats were moored at the entrance to the canal, exclusively for the hotel residents, should anyone need some private transport.

They continued walking, and at the next bridge saw along the pavement beside the water, a tiny Chinese restaurant. There were a few oddly matched tables outside, with some Chinese lantern lights threaded between the building and some long poles. The exterior was run down, with flaking green paint on the door, and the subsiding walls were leaning in on each other, with crumbling cream plaster and paint completing the neglected façade. There was nobody eating outside, but the hustle of a busy restaurant could be heard, and delicious smells wafted over the cooling air.

'Wow, that smells good! How weird would that be, to have a Chinese meal in Venice?' said Sophie, walking off the bridge, down some long shallow steps to the pavement beside the canal. Miriam was following her, obviously thinking the same thing. Just then, the distant sound of rain could be heard, and as quickly as someone turning on a tap, the heavens opened, and the downpour began. The girls ran a few yards to the crooked restaurant door, and stepped down into the small, quaint restaurant, full of oriental people eating heartily. Their entrance must have been quite dramatic, as everyone looked around and stared, as the girls shook themselves dry.

'Oops!' whispered Sophie, as she looked up, mid shrug, to see the whole restaurant looking at them. 'Ah, no Italians... hope this isn't like a private club,' thought Sophie, tugging on Miriam's arm as she busily brushed herself down.

An hour later, Sophie and Miriam were sat back at their little corner table, a mountain of empty plates and bowls littering the table. The candlelit room was warm and cosy, as the torrents of rain lashed down outside. Shortly after they had been shown to their table, a troop of kitchen staff came out with sandbags. They started stacking them up at the door. People stopped eating, and helped the staff to build a flood defence at the old, rickety door, with extra sandbags supporting some old battered boards that acted as a dam. It was all very basic but the community spirit amongst the Chinese in the restaurant was astounding to Sophie and Miriam. As a sign of respect, and not being sure of what Chinese restaurant customs were like in Italy, they helped too, passing the sandbags as part of a chain from the back of the restaurant to the front door. It had been a spirited event, random, surreal, but at the same time seemed totally natural. It was in everyone's best interest that the restaurant did not flood, so everyone helped. The restaurateurs had thanked their customers with a round of strong liquor, and everyone had toasted, though the girls were not sure who or what the toast was to. Some quiet Chinese music played in the background, and the restaurant carried on, as if nothing was happening outside. The girls ordered a set meal, and could not believe how much food they got, nor how cheap the bill was.

'Check it,' said Sophie, 'I know we're going home in a few days, but I don't fancy spending them banged up, 'cause we didn't pay for our tea!'

'I have, it's the correct price according to the menu. What a wonderful meal, amazing value. She laid out the money on top of the bill on a little ceramic plate. They got up and put their coats on. The head waiter came rushing over to them.

'Told you it was wrong, they think we were leaving without paying the full amount, it's probably a huge insult,' whispered Sophie.

'Excuse me, your bill?' said the small Chinese lady, in a beautiful embroidered Chinese dress.

'Told you, told… you, oh crap!' exclaimed Sophie, looking down at the ground as she pretended to rearrange her coat, trying to avoid eye contact with the restaurant manager.

'Yes, is there a problem?' said Miriam, in a schoolteacher sort of voice, trying to sound confident as she was sure they had not done anything wrong.

'Your bill. You no pay!'

'Oh crap,' said Sophie.

'We have, it's on the little plate, I even checked it. The money…'

'You no pay your bill. Chinese custom,' repeated the Chinese lady, waving the girl's bill, pushing it into Miriam's hand.

'Excuse me, ladies, may I be of assistance?' said a young oriental lady, standing up from her table.

'They are saying we have not paid our bill, but we have,' said Sophie, pushing in front of Miriam, pointing to the restaurant manager. 'She's saying we haven't pa...'

'Excuse me,' repeated the young volunteer translator, 'they are saying you don't have to pay your bill. It is a custom at this restaurant, and many in Italy. You showed a compassion for a family that is not yours. You helped with the flood barrier. You showed no prejudice, having conquered an initial confrontational situation. They wish to thank you, and have fortune cookies for you. Look!'

Miriam and Sophie looked at their bill in the manager's hand, and saw their money wrapped in it. Then, on the counter, they saw two tiny boxes, with the restaurant name on it.

'Fortune cookie,' said a young male waiter, as he handed over the two boxes, with a polite nod of his head.

'You are honoured. This restaurant is the busiest non-Italian in Venice, and yet no tourists or Venetians come here. They judge a book by its cover. Outside, it is simple and plain, but people who visit here, will never forget it. It is discreet, gets passed by. It is a family run business, and has been here for generations. Only Chinese people notice it is here, and people like you. It called to you, to protect you from the heavy rain. In return, you helped protect it with the sandbags!' exclaimed the translator.

'Thank you,' whispered Miriam hoarsely, seriously taken aback. The restaurant staff had continued with their business, as for the second time in a few hours, Miriam and Sophie had brought the place to a stop. Miriam took the cash, and put half into a tip bowl. She smiled at the manager, who gave her a huge smile back, and a shallow bow. Miriam in return, bowed back, and poked Sophie in the ribs to get her attention, to do the same.

'It is safe to go. The rain has passed by quickly, so we will not be flooded. Be safe, your path is laid.' With that, the manager turned, and started tending to other customers.

They took their fortune cookies, and Miriam noticed the box first. There was a little drawing of Mount Fuji, with a pagoda, and the sun shining between them.

'The drawing,' whispered Sophie, as she noticed her box, 'the drawing from Pompeii, is Mount Fuji too!'

'But Mount Fuji is Jap...' Miriam's thoughts trailed off, as she tried to understand what was going on.

Chapter Twelve

May 2011, Egypt

By the time the little shuttle bus got back to the hotel, it was nearly midnight. Charlie, Annie and CT trudged through the hotel lobby, totally exhausted. They walked out onto the Bedouin terrace, to see the others having a heated argument.

'Hi guys,' said Annie, flopping to the ground on a purple and red cushion, 'What's happening?'

'Hello fellow campers! Is it a heated debate on the infrastructure crisis in the Middle East, or has someone stolen Deano's ice cream?' mocked CT, knowing too well his friends would not have been discussing topical political issues.

'You tell 'em Deano,' said Bobby, clearly agitated.

'I'm not telling them, it isn't my fault!'

'It is, you dickhead!' shouted Bobby, clearly not as tolerant of Deano as the others were. Turning to CT, he started, 'This thick fuck...'

'Oy! Oy! Oy!' the others all said in unison.

'Bobby, let me sort this,' said Kay.

'What's he done now?' asked CT, quite expecting the unexpected.

'Bobby asked Deano to go see how much the wine was...' she started.

'There you go then. Bobby's to blame. Never ask Deano to do anything, unless you want it arse-about-face,' joked CT.

'Ha!' said Deano, pulling a face behind Bobby's back.

'What did you say, you fucking wan...!'

'ENOUGH!' shouted Kay, loud enough so the other few stragglers out on the terrace looked around. 'Deano got the figures the wrong way around. He knew it was twenty-three pounds, but thought it was Egyptian pounds! 'That's cheap, says Bobby, let's get lashed!' which is what we started to do. After three bottles, we noticed the tab. It was twenty-three *English* pounds a bottle, so we now owe seventy pounds, and Bobby says he's not paying, Deano says he will pay it all, and I'm saying we should split it three ways, as we're all at fault!'

'Seems fair to me,' said Charlie.

'Me too,' said CT.

'Easy mistake to make!' commented Annie, as she rummaged through her bag for Deano's gift, 'I've nearly done that, worked it out the wrong way!'

'You're as thick as that dickhead then,' said Bobby, standing up. 'The fucking lot of you are nuts!'

'Ay, mate, NO need! I'm hoping that's the wine talking,' said CT, also standing up.

'Expensive wine,' said Deano, laughing under his breath.

'What did you say? Don't mock me you...'

'Bobby?' said Kay, in a very stern voice, 'we need to have a chat.' She led him away from the group, though at first he had protested and said he didn't want to go anywhere. Anything Kay had to say to him, she could say to him at the table. However, the others all knew what 'I think we need a chat' meant. Kay used it when disciplining or firing people, and it had become a bit of a saying in the office, whenever things were going wrong.

The group was distracted as they tried to overhear Kay giving Bobby the push, when Deano shouted, 'Wow, I didn't know you went there. I thought you went to the Indiana Jones film set?'

'We did, buddie,' said Charlie, smiling at his friend, who he knew would be a little upset after the shouting, 'the one where he rides horses through the path in the rocks, to a temple carved in pink stone.'

'How big were the pyramids?'

'No pyramids, dude, you're thinking of Cairo.'

CT came back from going to the bathroom, and looked a little flustered. 'I've just seen Alfred!'

'We saw him earlier,' said Deano, 'he set out all of the towels, so no one would sit in your chairs while you were out for the day!'

'And he had made a towel swan for Annie, I got a flower!'

'Nice, I'm sure. Deano, where are your trainers? I've just seen Alfred in them,' he said, not waiting for Deano to reply, 'I've told him to give them back. I know they're yours because they have different coloured laces! Cheeky bastard nicking them, after that huge tip we gave him. I'll be back in a mo, I'm going to report him,' he said, walking back towards reception. Deano carried on looking puzzled at his snow globe.

'Wait, CT...' said Kay, jogging after him, 'Deano gave them to him!'

'Who gave what to whom?' asked CT, stopping so the sliding door kept opening and closing. He stepped aside, and listened to Kay.

'Deano went for a walk…'

'Deano doesn't walk anywhere!' said CT, laughing.

'Deano went for a walk, because he heard there was a sports bar at one of the other hotels, which this hotel is allowed to use. On his way over there, he saw Alfred off duty walking with his mother. He was in his civilian clothes, a long smock and trousers, but no shoes. Deano found out that Alfred only wore his work shoes at work, so they lasted longer and did not get scruffy. Deano chatted with him, and found out that Alfred's mother is sick, so all of his wages and tips go on her medication. So, catch this, right there and then, he took off his shoes, and gave them to Alfred. And all the money in his pocket, which was about 1,000 Egyptian pounds, £100!'

'Bless him, did he?'

'Yes, he knows it's £100, and he's explained the exchange rate to me. The wine thing was to piss Bobby off, 'cause he saw him flirting with a girl on the beach. Can you believe it?' said Kay laughing.

'He's a simple guy, kind-hearted. Decent, far cleverer than we give him credit for but what a total star,' said CT, surprised how choked he felt.

'THE PYRAMIDS!' Deano was heard shouting. Kay and CT looked around, and walked over to the others.

'You guys still fighting?' asked CT.

'Deano can't get it into his head that we didn't go see the pyramids today.'

'What's up Deano?' asked CT.

'Look at my snow globe, my gift from Annie. She said she would bring me something back from your trip, but Charlie says you didn't go to the pyramids!' replied Deano, indignantly.

'We didn't see the pyramids dude, we went to Petra, the Indiana film!'

'So what's this then?' Deano replied, showing his snow globe to the group. There was the little gift, with the rose coloured stones of Petra rearranged to look like a pyramid and a tower in fluttering snow.

'Well I'll be…!' said CT, Charlie and Annie, all at the same time, as their uncompleted sentences remained unfinished.

Chapter Thirteen

September 2011, Somerset

There is always something new and fresh about a warm autumn morning. It is probably contradictory, considering the trees start changing into their tired, dry, winter attire, but for some reason, even at Rik's age, it still reminded him of going back to school, with new uniform, books and a school bag. This particular morning, sat on the farm in Somerset, drinking fresh milk from a glass, he watched the dairy cows happily munching on the overly rich grass, with The Tor still shrouded in early morning mist, its purple stone being kissed by the first rays of sunlight. There was definitely a different feeling on the farm. The poor spring had eventually given way to five weeks over June and July, that had become known as the 'worst summer on record'. It was the worst for two reasons; the obvious being it had been very short, and the other was that it had been the hottest. In June the music festival had gone ahead as usual at Pilton Farm. The excessive heat had saved the land from getting churned up, so recovery from the festival was already nearly complete. All of the rain of the spring had disappeared, leaving the land parched. The weathermen were struggling with their figures to try and work out what was happening.

Despite the last few hot, dry weeks, the grass on the farm was still healthy, which was both unusual and yet expected. Well, expected by those in the know of course, and there were only five of them, plus the farm workers. Just the five of them, though they had an unknowing team of hundreds, number crunching and speculating as to when exactly the event would happen. It would be the cows who would know when the time had come. Strange, but true. Humanity in England partly rested on the cows!

'They don't look any different,' said Rik to Dylan, who was sat on a bank, by a very small trickling stream, that split the farm in two. The peace of the countryside was punctured with the gurgling trickling of the stream and the munching of grass by the cows. Dylan was drawing heavily on a long joint, lazily squinting against the bright sun, as the leaves and branches above him offered him chilling shade, until the wind moved and disturbed the foliage, allowing a weak sun to warm his face. The wind had picked up over the last few days, but as it had been so hot recently, it had been a welcome relief. Although the mist was still in the valley, the wind was lifting it, to reveal another clear blue sky.

'What doesn't?'

'The cows! They look the same as our last visit,' replied Rik, 'How do they know, anyway?'

'Know what?'

'How do they know when the time has come?' said Rik, taking the joint passed to him by Dylan. 'Don't smoke this on the farm. Show some respect!'

'What time?' said Dylan, totally unaware that Rik was staring at him.

'How much of this stuff have you puffed, Dylan? It's fried you!'

'Fried what? We having bacon?'

'DYLAN!'

'Shit, what?' he said, sitting upright with a start, 'What's up man?'

'Chill dude, I was just saying, how do the cows know when the time has come? You're the site expert.'

'It's as I keep telling Uncle Sam and Ed, it's not the cows themselves, but the land the farm is on. Obviously, cows can't talk, but their actions and interactions with the farmland around them would signify when we should start planning the final stages. There's also the Sacred Stones on the southern hill covered in wild flowers, with a healthy fringe of trees lined up along the crest of the hill. The cows have started producing a lot more milk, due to the increased richness of the grass. We're making so much cheese from the surplus... it's madness. Look at this place though, it's paradise!'

They both sat and looked around. Everything they could see was green, vibrant and... well, had a well-being feel to it. It was early September, but there were no signs of autumn colours at Pilton. The shallow valley the farm was situated in, ran in a southeast to northwest direction, and so basked in sun all day. The tree-lined ridge in the distance had mature trees closely growing together, providing a natural defined perimeter to the plot. On the opposite slope, there was a circular patch of colour, just visible through some small trees and bushes.

'What's that colour over there. It's really bright, in the middle of the other side?' asked Rik.

'You been doing mushrooms too, Rik?'

'No, man, not at all. Look over there, you'll see what I can see!' said Rik, pointing.

'Oh, yeah,' said Dylan, ducking and swaying to get a better view through the Weeping Willow that was on the bank opposite them. 'That's the Sacred Stone Circle. Shall we go over there? I've not been up there in a while. Ed said it's a sight to see, "unbelievable" he said.'

'Come on then, let's have a look. Go through how they found the poem and plaque. Ed never explained it all at the last meeting,' said Rik.

'I don't know the exact details. When they examined the original Sacred Stones, they each had a minute symbol of a pyramid, circle and a tall rectangle. When they photographed them and studied them in the lab, they were identical. Not a slight deviation. Even under high definition, when they were superimposed, the carved symbols were exact. The experts said that although they had carbon dated the drawings as two thousand years old, we're talking "times of Christ", they would not have had the technology to repeat them with such accuracy. That's why the original stones were moved and replaced with replicas in 1990,' Dylan explained, as they walked over a reinforced wooden bridge, which farm machinery used to get about the farm. Larks swooped and caught insects as they flew, and the sound of many different types of birds could be heard close by, and in the distant trees. It was peaceful and tranquil, how an idyllic portrayal of England might be.

'That was twenty odd years ago!'

'Yes, the time when the team first got together. They had put all the pieces together by 1993, which is when they started searching for us,' said Dylan.

'So they had these two thousand-year-old, exact minute drawings. I take it that's why they weren't found sooner, 'cause they were so small. What about the plaque, when was that found?'

'A farm of sorts has been here for one thousand years, and in 1969, the year before the first festival, they found a plaque that had been used as building material for one of the barns, or so they thought. It had been handed down from generation to generation. It was known by the family that it was important to keep it safe. The official story was that it had been hidden to keep it safe, and was not just part of the barn wall. However, over the course of time, its location became lost. It was rediscovered when a long, lost family relative visited, and asked about it. We've had it carbon dated to be about 700 years old.'

'It still doesn't explain why we are doing what we are doing now. Let's face it, no one would do what we are doing, unless there was more than a plaque and a few stones. Besides, one thousand years ago when the first settlement was here, they wouldn't have recognised the significance of the exact drawings, and certainly wouldn't have been able to check how accurate they were.'

'No, they didn't know about the drawings on the stones until recently. It's the wording on the plaque, which also has the same symbol as on the stones... in exactly the same size. It's the plaque that tied everything together here on the farm.' There was a long silence. 'There is also the Mayan Doomsday conspiracy, but what people haven't been told, is that the symbols on the stones were also found throughout the ancient Mayan cities. The three shapes could be found repeatedly, but only two of the three at any one time. Again, recently, they copied all these carvings from around the world, and found when they were laid over each other, they were perfectly identical. Some had the triangle and circle, others had the circle and the rectangle, but none had all three. The only place archaeologists in the UK have found the symbols in one drawing, is here.'

'So the Mayans, Hopi and Odin's lot have something to do with this. I thought the five thousand year Mayan calendar being calculated to the date of December 21st 2012 to be the end of the world was rubbish!' said Rik, puffing a little as they started to climb the upper slope of the valley, which was getting quite steep. The long grass made it heavy going, as their shoes had to rake through the long, strong stems as they walked.

'Well, the calendar and date exist; there is no doubt about that. Of course now we know the date has changed to June 2012, but all the calendar was, was a countdown to a new era, or time. It's to do with the alignment of the planets, and a new cycle was calculated to start in 2012! We're moving from the Age of Pisces, which values money, power and control, to the Age of Aquarius. The new values are love, brotherhood, unity and integrity. The Mayans and the Egyptians had predicted the exact year that the Great Age will change, by studying the stars. The fall of Rome happened at the start of the current Age of Pisces. Every new age starts with chaos, but with this new age there is also a rare astral event at the same time! Double trouble!'

As they rounded a small dip, filled with flowering bushes, they saw the paint-colour-card display, as nature showed off all of its colours to excess. The Sacred Stones were surrounded by every type of wild flower imaginable. The two friends approached The Stones, but could only get within 50 feet of them. The grass was nearly white, with small pink-tipped daisies growing close together. Dandelions then grew, mixed with the tufty white flowers of wild garlic. Dylan walked clockwise whilst

Rik went anticlockwise as they circled the wild garden of flowers. They were looking for a gap among the flowers, so they could walk into the centre of the stones where there were no flowers, just lush grass.

'Here's a way in,' said Rik, at the very top of the slope. Dylan walked over to him. From this elevated position, the colours had all merged into one. 'My God, it's amazing. I've never seen so many wild flowers packed so closely together!'

'It certainly is amazing,' Dylan replied, as he led the way through the narrow gap between the flowers. They were looking down onto the valley, with the stream and farm building nestled amongst the trees and bushes. 'Look here! There are Cheddar Pinks and wild Sweet Peas around the bottom of the stones. There are even Bluebells, which shouldn't even be flowering still, they are a May flower.'

'You're very knowledgeable about your plant life mate. How come?'

'My nana was a keen gardener. She always told me the names of plants. She had a wildlife garden too, and loved all wild flowers. She taught me the names of butterflies and insects. Oh. My. God!' he shrieked.

'What... what? What's wrong, you okay?' Rik said, turning to Dylan, who was crouching down on the ground, studying something.

'Yes, I'm fine. Look what I've found!'

'Magic mushrooms?'

'Yes, how did you guess?' said Dylan excitedly, looking up at Rik.

''cause they are here too, they're everywhere. There is a perfect circular path of them, about a foot wide, running just inside the edge of the stones,' said Rik, who was stood in the very centre of the circle. Dylan got up and met him in the centre, turning slowly round, until he had done a full 360 degree turn. He then crossed his legs and sat down, without steadying himself with his hands. Rik flopped down beside him, and they sat side by side, looking out at the rolling hills of Somerset, with The Tor on its mound in the distance on their left. A sweet smell of fresh grass lingered as they shuffled around and got comfy.

'What was the poem on the plaque?' asked Rik after a 15-minute silence.

'I've got it here on a piece of paper.'

'You always carry it with you. You're taking it all far more seriously than me. I don't even know what it says, but you have a permanent copy. Is it laminated?' Rik joked.

'No, it bloody isn't. Nob!' replied Dylan, laughing. 'Here we go!'

'I'm sitting comfortably, please begin,' said Rik, lying back in the tall, dew-touched grass, with a little purple and cream clover flower twiddling in the corner of his mouth.

'Just remember that it's had to be translated, but it's the way the poem rhymes, after translation, that made the linguists sit up and shit themselves. When this was written, most of the words in the modern version didn't exist, so the mystery is that a seven hundred-year-old script could be translated to modern English that not only makes sense but rhymes too!'

'Go on then, I remember reading it, but never realised the significance.'

If the yield is great, beyond all doubt doubled
Prepare for a time as it turns to rubble
Protect the fold, from powers that be
Prepare for hell destructive heat.

As the pyramid stands, to protect and serve
Allow the stars, to deliver their verse
Jupiter and Mars, big or mightiest
Chant in unison, hold hands united.

With swaying vibration, emotions of tears
Joyous loving total devotion, as one, no fears
If the yield is great, when all else failing
Economies politics environment waning.

Prepare for the change here at the farm
Call unto the ones to save from harm
Test them check them they must be right
For in their hands lies humanity's plight.

'That's right, I remember it now. So when the land and everything on it has an increased production, the time has come. The farm and land will protect the ones chosen who will have to gather here, led by their stars, or in this case, musical idols. Basically, when the time comes, two of the biggest headliners, Jupiter and Mars, will get the crowd going so well, their emotions combined will be the energy to ignite the protection of the site, powered by the sacred waters and stones that litter the farm!'

'That's it, the basics anyway. No idea how it's all going to work, but I've done my bit. So long as we all do our bits, it should all work!'

Just as Dylan finished, a strong gust of wind whipped the piece of paper from his hand, and the tall grasses whispered. Petals from the wild flowers were caught in the updraft ascending from the valley, which then cascaded down into the circle like wedding confetti, carrying with it a delicate flora smell. Like lightning, Rik went to grab the fluttering paper a few feet above his head, catching it with ease.

'Bet you wouldn't be able to do that again, good catch,' said Dylan as he laid back to look up at the clouds racing in the wind. The trails in the sky were bad today. They criss-crossed over the sky, being dispersed by the wind. The usual early morning clear, blue sky was already turning to a white haze.

'Look at that! How can they think we wouldn't notice. You see planes leaving those trails, and people just think they're clouds,' said Rik.

'Robert knows more than he's letting on I think. He's high ranking ex-military, he knows what they're spraying.'

'Yes, he probably does. He might not.'

'Yes, but he also said they've been spraying our skies for decades, but with the instant knowledge of the internet, it's been brought to a lot of people's attention. He says they're spraying aluminium bariums up there and it costs billions!'

'The internet is probably the government's worst nightmare. All information, on everything, available to everyone, all the time!'

'That's probably why they use it to monitor what everyone does. We all know that Facebook was only created in order to monitor what information people are reading about. Prior to 1989 and the net, all secrets were safe, unless published in print or spoken by those in the know. Any shenanigans the Governments were up to would have been regarded as safe, but then when the net was born, the governments of the world had no means of monitoring who was investigating what. That's why Facebook was created in 2005. By having seventy-five per cent of the world categorising themselves into groups, by "liking" pages, sharing articles and publishing to the world what they are into, the powers-that-be were then able to gain control again, as they had done pre-internet. Social networking was designed by the government, to keep an eye on troublemakers! Age of Pisces... control'

'The governments are just playing god, looking to see who will take a bite of the "apple" from the tree of knowledge,' said Rik, which was followed by a ten minute silence, as they both thought about the relevance of Rik's statement.

They sat quietly, as butterflies and bees busied themselves amidst the flowers, thinking about the poem, the trails in the sky, and the situation they found themselves in. A loud chirp caused Dylan to sit up. He startled the blackbird that had been sat on top of one of the stones. He sat and watched it as it circled, then came back and sat on the stone. It hopped about, chattering away. It turned to look at Dylan, and tilted its head.

'Rik, slowly sit up, or just look at the stone just in front of us,' Dylan whispered.

'Look where?' said Rik, sitting bolt upright, just to see the blackbird fly off. He too then watched it circle, and sit back on its stone. 'I'll be...' he exclaimed, but stopped as a thrush came and sat on one of the other stones.

'Look left slowly, very slowly,' said Dylan, as Rik turned to look to his left. A green woodpecker sat on another of the stones. 'What are they doing?'

'Having a chat!' whispered back Rik, as a tiny, brown wren joined the gathering, 'how the feck do I know!'

'I've seen Hitchcock... I never thought this is how I would go!'

'Prick, they aren't going to attack. Look at them, they're just sitting, looking at us, looking at us very intently... intently and intimidating. Do you think they're going to attack?' asked Rik, getting ready to make a run for it.

Dylan slowly reached out and held Rik's arm, 'Wait, look,' he said, nodding his head at the blackbird. It had flown down, pulled a worm from the ground, and hopped over, half flapping its wings, having difficulty with its wriggling load. Rik and Dylan sat perfectly still, mouths wide open, as the bird placed the worm on the grass, by their feet. The thrush flew forward and brought a snail, the woodpecker brought a grub and within a few minutes, a different bird was sat on top of each stone having flown forward, placing its favourite delicacy in a circle around the stunned visitors. Each bird then sat back onto its own stone.

'What the FUCK is going on,' whispered Dylan. 'All the stones but one, wonder whose throne that stone is?' Just then, all the birds flew off squawking, as something startled them all, leaving Rik and Dylan surrounded by various grubs, insects, berries and seeds. A quick, large shadow passed over them, and looking up, they saw a buzzard circling directly above them. The bird gracefully glided in a perfect circle, the same size as the wild flower garden, about 60 feet above them. With its massive wing, it rode on the thermals, slowly getting lower.

'That will explain why the others scarpered,' said Rik. 'Oh crap, what bird is that, just wondering what it might eat for tea?'

'It's urm... dude... it's a buzzard. A great big, massive, bunny-eating bird of prey!'

'It's a big bastard, isn't it?'

'Dude, these are badass birds, and yes, big is a word I would use. Fucking gigantic would be more appropriate. What's in its feet?' asked Dylan, putting his hand to shade his eyes from the sun, watching the bird getting closer and closer, 'Looks like a rabbit, but... but... but the rabbit doesn't appear... doesn't appear to... be actually attached to the bird, there is sky in between them!'

'It is a rabbit... oh God... this is going to be gruesome!' exclaimed Rik, 'I don't really want a lap full of rabbit carc...'

'No, look, as it's getting closer, there's an inch or so between them, the bird isn't holding the rabbit. Look mate, honest, it's okay!'

They watched until the breath of the bird's wings could be felt on their warm faces. It was still circling, but only about ten feet above their heads. They could see its eye, its feathers, the skill in which it used its tail and wings to change speed and direction. The little, baby rabbit was hanging from the bird's massive claws, but not by its fur or skin. For a fleeting glimpse, it made eye contact with Dylan, a silent cry for help. They could see it was trapped in a plastic beer can tie, the ones that hold a four-pack together.

'Oh. My. God!' said Rik, not sure what to make of what he was seeing, once again totally bewildered over what was happening.

Just then, the bird let go of its cargo. The rabbit and its bounds plummeted to the floor. Before Dylan knew what he was doing, he had propelled himself off the ground, and with outstretched arms threw both of his hands in the direction of the falling rabbit, catching it a few feet from the ground. He rolled over, holding the rabbit aloft so as not to squash it. Rolling onto his knees he then sprung onto his feet, with the agility of a gymnast, and the eye of an international cricketer. He cupped the tiny rabbit, looking closely into its face.

'Bet you couldn't do that again?' Rik said, mimicking what Dylan had said earlier. 'Is it okay?'

'Yeah, seems to be, it's just got this plastic shit around its middle. It probably might have been stuck for a week, got in there when it was smaller, and now it has grown, it's caught tight around its middle. While Dylan gently dealt with the quiet rabbit, releasing it from its bondage attire, Rik looked for the bird. It was a few hundred feet away, soaring and gliding across the meadows. The sky had become a bright white, as it always did in the afternoons when they had been spraying it. With the extra windy conditions, the white haze had come earlier. *What are you fuckers spraying us with?* thought Rik, looking at the magnificent countryside about him. 'I know one thing for sure, if it was something good you bastards would be making a point about it, but as it's always denied, we have to assume that you fuckers are slowly destroying us and, or, the planet.' He turned to see Dylan with the baby rabbit. The plastic was not as tight as it had first seemed, and so with a little help it was now free. Dylan sat back on the grass, as before by crossing his legs and lowering himself down, with the rabbit clutched to his chest.

It showed no sign of panic, but instead sat peacefully in Dylan's hands. He lifted it up so it was level with his eyes, gently cupping it. He didn't want to restrain it, the plastic may have been uncomfortable, and he didn't want to exasperate things. The rabbit sniffed his fingertip, then another fingertip, then looked up. It stretched its neck out, so that the end of its whiskers tickled Dylan's nose. He tried not to laugh, in case it was startled. Suddenly, it leapt from Dylan's hands to his chest, and clung onto the material of his original Ramones T-shirt. It crawled its way up so it could bury its head under Dylan's chin. He considered it might have parasites, and so quickly supporting it, he lowered it on the grass in front of him. It immediately hopped off into the wild flowers.

'Joint!' said Dylan, as he got his pre-rolled out.

'Not at the *farm*, Dylan!'

'What was all that about? Are we in a Dreamworks production?' Dylan asked Rik.

'I have no idea… no idea whatsoever. The birds, the rabbit. Maybe the power of the Sacred Stones is true… but the birds…'

'I never believed it. I started studying the site properly fifteen years ago. There is documentation about these stones. They were replaced when the prehistoric circle was moved, but this was not made public. The originals are safe in a cellar under the main meadow, the triangular field over there beneath the permanent Pyramid Stage framework,' said Dylan, pointing just to the left of them, 'Where that steel frame of the main stage is. They are under there, in their original formation, surrounding an underground well. The recent history of this site is amazing. Do you know of it, Rikky?'

'Only the basics. The first music festival was 1970, the year after the plaque was found, the fence had to be put up in 2002 and costs six million pounds each erection, excuse the pun!'

'It's okay, I get a hard on too when I think about the site, excuse the pun! When it's in full swing, the atmosphere, the sights, the smells, the sounds! Gives me goosebumps!'

'Oh, and the cows weren't moved for the first one.'

'Yeah, it's all true. The first festival was in 1970, and the first pyramid stage was built over a blind spring in 1971, which they found by dowsing. Some old boy who'd lived at the foot of The Tor found it, and he'd traced it from The Tor to the site down there beneath the framework. This is the significant part… in 1981 the pyramid was replaced by a new one, with materials acquisitioned from the MOD. It was also the year that CND were supported. Ironic, isn't it?' said Dylan, hoping Rik wouldn't notice he was lighting a joint.

'So you're saying a festival supporting anti-war had its infrastructure built using Ministry of Defence steel and wood?'

'Wicked, isn't it? Well, here's the thing. There have been a few other pyramids built on that spot,' he said pointing, 'and each since has been built using bits of all the previous ones, so that even that one down there, still has some of the original building materials. Plus the Sacred Stones are underneath it and the blind well in a cellar, the trace to the Tor, and the military materials,' Dylan said, excitedly. 'It's amazing, just the history of... Well, bugger me, look who is here!'

Rik turned to see the baby bunny hopping back towards Dylan. It sniffed his shoe, poked its nose into his calf, and lay down in the long grass, a foot or so away from a stoned Dylan. It lay with its front feet in front of it, and its back ones stretched out behind it.

'Did everything just happen like we think it did?' asked Rik.

'Yes, think so. That rabbit is real, and I saw it drop from the sky thanks to a buzzard, that would normally have eaten it, so that I might set it free from one of the worst plastic inventions known to man. Birds offered us their teas, and even the wind showered us with nice smelling petals. Normal day for me!' mocked Dylan, 'those trails are definitely in the sky, and we know they're real. If this was a dream, those wouldn't be there. No, it all definitely happened. There have always been rumours that this spot has special powers!'

'Well, I would have said what a crock-of-shit, but looking at you, with that tiny rabbit and all the weird bird behaviour, yes, maybe they do have secret powers!'

Dylan slowly stretched his arm out, and the rabbit let him stroke its head and back. 'These stones have things under them you know?'

'Really, like what?'

'All sorts; water from the Ganges, crystals from Stonehenge, stone from the pyramids in Egypt and there are healing herbs among these wildflowers!'

'I didn't know that,' said Rik, looking around at them, 'Maybe the bird and rabbit thing was meant to happen. You know... an "at-one-with-nature" episode?'

'I've been here before, dude,' said Dylan sternly, the tone of his voice causing Rik to look around at his friend. 'The bird thing happens every time I've sat here. I was worried telling anyone else. I was worried you would all think I was nuts...'

'You are!'

'Thanks. I chose to show you it, as I thought you'd be best to be able to handle it, and you have. It's definitely happening mate, not the buzzard and rabbit bit, that's a first. But every time I've sat here, birds have sat on the same stones and brought stuff.'

'So, I would say that this is definitely the right site. Everything is falling into place. The only thing we now have to do, is to persuade one hundred and eighty thousand people to all come here for a summer festival, even though they all know 2012 is a lay year.'

'Ever thought *why* 2012 works out to be a year the festival isn't scheduled to be on?'

'No, why?'

'It was scheduled from the very first festival to be a lay year, so we could handpick the festivallers. We can tell each of them that there is a tailor-made event happening... here are free tickets...' Who would refuse? Because it is a fallow year, there won't be the usual buzz and speculation amongst the Pilton faithful. The one thing we know for sure is that the festivallers of 2012 not only all have a love of music, and are, all in fact, related by an ancient DNA strain. Once the potential festivallers have passed an audition to their viability, the event is going to be billed as so massive, no one will want to miss it!'

'But surely with the internet, if you are going to get one hundred and eighty thousand people all going to a different event, in the same location at the same time, someone will twig.'

'Well, I am ashamed to say, but Ed was saying they have installed the technology, so that key words that flag up on the net or social sites will be blocked, censored or the sender's signal will simply fail.'

'People still talk though. People will tell their friends, use a telephone, and on the rare occasion write a letter.'

'Yes, they will, but that's where the vetting auditions come in. The ones who have been chosen are so few and far between, only one hundred and eighty thousand. You wouldn't expect to know someone who is also going. Besides, they are all chosen in pairs, as the research on the phone apps and social networks show that strangely each chosen person will be bringing a close friend, who also just happens to be chosen too. It's something to do with the defective DNA. Just as the chosen ones will eventually get here in time, they have already bonded with someone who is the same. That's one of the few things we are definite on, the chosen ones have naturally found the other half to their pair. Not necessarily one man and one woman. Best friends of the same sex are also connecting together. This is something that nature planned thousands of years ago, totally out of our control. This is why it's so important that 2012 happened to be a lay year, a fallow year. A Winter Solstice festival had been planned instead of a summer one. All the friends they tell can research for themselves, and all they'll find is that there isn't going to be the usual festival of performing arts, on this site, on the Summer Solstice and so would have no reason to question anything.'

'But as you said, you are billing it as an individually tailored event. Not everyone wants to go to a five-day music festival. What happens when Joe Bloggs gets down here, and decides he's going home. Then what?'

'He won't be able to leave!'

'What, you're imprisoning them?' said Rik in a raised voice, wondering if he actually knew what he was involved in. *Protecting a chosen few doesn't sound like it should involve imprisonment,* he thought.

'No, not lock them in the site. They won't want to leave. It has to be a music festival with the biggest names to produce the greatest energy needed to set the event off, but due to the vetting process, we will know what floats everyone's boat, so they will remain here, once we eventually get them here. We're running scenarios through the computer, and the best festival we can come up with is to have the top 50 musicians playing a medley of songs. You know, four to six musicians playing each other's music, covering all genres, swapping artists every hour or so. That way we can feature more songs and more bands will be represented, ensuring all tastes are catered for. Oh, and we're thinking of using holograms to get the likes of Hendrix, Lynott and Vicious playing too.'

'Wow, hope that works out, it would be amazing! It means the deceased members of the original line-ups of Sex Pistols, Thin Lizzy, The Clash, Nivana and Queen will perform! What about the families, the loved ones who aren't invited to the festival?' asked Rik, looking a little sick at the prospect of Dylan's reply.

'We don't know, Rik. The IT guys at MBHK are developing a warning system for the festivallers' relatives, something to do with a viral text message that will connect family and some friends to the energy of this site, therefore protecting them.'

'So, let me get this right. The amount of modern technology and burning of fossil fuels et cetera is changing the magnetic energies of earth, destroying it. We're going to borrow that power, to save people, but we're not letting the people who make the technology know?' checked Rik, 'It's kind of like a giant grand finale, with two fingers up at the people who thought they had it sussed, because they've always relied on their extreme wealth for elitism and safety. All these massive corporations think they have the world in their hands, holding it to ransom with a population of slaves... but none of those people will survive?'

'Basically... yes. It has been possible to send viral texts for over three years, which isn't long when you consider mobile phones were the size of house bricks in the late eighties. No one knows what is going to happen, but from what you have witnessed today, I'm sure you now realise the magical possibilities that can happen.'

'And so what will happen here in just under a year is...'

'Is going to be... well... biblical!'

Chapter Fourteen

September 2011, Lincolnshire

As autumn came to Railway Cottage, the last few finishing touches were put to its decoration. Since the spring, things had been very busy. Shortly after their trip to Temple Bruer, both Coco and Pod had been flat out. Coco had managed to sell some of her bigger pieces to a company who would make them into posters, so they might be used as relaxation aides, in doctors, hospitals and dentists. Even a few solicitors had purchased them. They were popular, sold well, and had increased the funds in the bank account. Pod had been very busy, as she liaised with Coco, the printers and the companies who had bought the drawings. It was hard to believe that three years ago, Coco could feed her and Art for £20 a week, and could live off £500 a month. Although they now had enough money to get by with, they actually needed less money, as they were growing so much of their own food, and producing their own power. Art had been really successful too. He had finally given up the driving job he hated, and spent his time down by the lake fishing. He was writing his book, taking photographs and keeping a record of everything he found. He even made a note of the trees, flowers and animals he saw as the seasons changed. As the summer progressed into autumn following closely behind, he started to notice strange things.

As he drove down the country lane to get back home, the lane was strewn with fallen leaves, of all colours of red, orange and yellow. A damp fog was starting to form, so he was glad he was nearly home. He liked autumn, because as the nights got shorter and colder, he could start to concentrate on pike fishing, rather than carp in the summer. He turned off the lane, and onto the newly laid drive. He had spent July with his father, collecting waste bricks, cleaning them up, and using them to make the drive. The bricks had come from the back of the wood, where stacks of them had been left next to what had been the railway track. There were underground brick ovens at that side of the wood, which had been used to bake newly made bricks before they were loaded onto the train trucks to be carried away. They had used slightly raised railway sleepers too, to make large squares that were filled with a herringbone brick effect. In the centre of each square, round white pebbles had been sunk into the cement. Once finished, it looked fantastic. The wall beside the road, which ran along the front of the house, curved into a wide, open drive and had been painted cream, to match the outside of the cottage. Coco had laid glass jars at different levels within the wall as it was built, at different heights and placed an LED light in each. She had decorated the inside of the jars with coloured glass paint, so when the little solar panel lit up the lights, the wall appeared to have coloured, patterned discs fixed into it. The effect was staggering, with the complimentary colouring of the jars running through the cream wall. Along the top of the wall, pots of trailing white lobelia, with white and pale pink geraniums had been planted, which cascaded over the newly painted wall, and although it was coming to the end of summer, they still looked surprisingly good. Trellis also ran up the front of the house, with a climbing, white *Iceberg* rose leaving its strong scent along with the white jasmine. Various coloured sweet peas, which twined themselves around the rose and jasmine added an accent of colour. The old house had been brought back to life, with the sensitivity and care that the previous owners would have liked.

The finishing touch to the actual house had been when the previous owner had left a parcel on the back doorstep. Art had found it, and opened it on the dining room table. It was a framed pastel picture of a hare. The original picture had hung opposite the back door, and had been drawn by one of the previous family's siblings. Coco had asked for it to be left, but it was a much loved picture. However, when they had seen how much work had gone into the old house, they'd had a copy done and framed it. A little note fell out, as Art turned the picture around and smiled. 'Thank you.' He had hung it in the same place as the original, though he had to move a framed Sex Pistols poster, but he knew Coco would be totally over the moon with the new acquisition. The hare was a fabulous drawing, with a wild glint in his eye. The dark green paper of the drawing added an air of intrigue, as the hare looked like it was peering through luscious vegetation, with a 'catch-me-if-you-dare' hare look! Art stood back and smiled once again. He had done a lot of smiling recently. He had a simple but cosy home, miles from anyone. He did not enjoy the company of other people, which had been the main attraction of the house. Now, although they were not wealthy by any stretch, they had made themselves a happy place to... well... to live. They lived in the house surrounded by nature. They had a few visitors, but not on a regular basis. They had so much to do at the property, with all the fruit needing to be harvested and preserved; friends would often lend a hand.

Coco and Art had painstakingly collected together all the ripe apples, and cooked and frozen them. They had also managed to make about eight barrels of homemade cider and perry, with mixed berries, and some with honey from the orchard. Some of the apples had been taken by The Apple Society, as there were so many of them, and they needed to keep samples of them. The double garage had been to put to good use, with Coco's 1989 Astra GTE in the front of the garage, slowly being renovated, and the work space behind had been converted into The Brew House. A new barn door had been put in the end of the garage, as the only way in had been to shimmy past the Astra. The barn door opened onto the drive, opposite the back door to the house. The rock and herb garden curved round, from the back door to The Brew House, completing the backyard landscaping. Considering how impressive the yard looked, it had hardly cost a penny. Nothing really matched, with lots of different pot sizes and shapes, but there had been clear thought with its layout and design. As the hard landscaping had started to soften with newly planted shrubs, it started to have a lived-in feel.

All the fruit and nut trees and bushes had started to ripen, and so they had been preserved, frozen and made into jams and chutneys. It had been a very hard few weeks, and there was still another month of it, at least. They were comfortable, with neither of them really having to work, due to the lucrative deal with the poster company. Friends had come over to help, where in return for help with the harvesting Coco would cook a big homemade stew. They would eat it beside the outdoor heater on the patio among the herbs. The patio was decorated with lots of tealights in coloured holders, whose colours danced as the chilling autumn wind caught their little flames. They drank homebrew, discussing how things had moved on. Most of their friends liked the idea of living miles from anyone, but the amount of work the small holding needed was astronomical. There was so much soft fruit, strawberries in mid-June, then raspberries and red currents, followed by blackberries. Then all the veg; with onions to harvest, plait together and hang; root vegetables to freeze and potatoes to put into store. It was a never-ending cycle. As soon as a crop was harvested, the ground would be prepared for the next batch of seedlings. Before the first frosts came, the garden needed to be prepared, and so ultimately it was the busiest time of year for the gardener, especially with new seeds to sew and tend to.

The little greenhouse had been very successful too, with tomatoes and peppers, chillies and cucumbers all producing good crops. Coco had boiled all the tomatoes as Art made them into bolognaise and chilli sauces, removing their skins and adding different herbs, ready to use over the winter. They had been collecting jam jars all year, as had family and friends, so whilst Art made sauce, Coco would decorate and make labels. All the jars were stored in the cool of The Brew House, where racking spanned the back wall that led onto the garage. It certainly looked impressive, with six barrels of flavoured apple cider on the floor, with the preserved jars above. Art had managed to find oak casks for his home brew, which he salvaged, cleaned and restored. They stood on their sides, on little pegs. On the right, there were two bigger, heavier barrels, which each had a plain apple cider, one dry and one sweet. Coco had even collected thousands of bottle tops from the local pubs, and made a mosaic floor with them. One weekend when her son had visited, they had spent the whole time washing and sorting the bottle tops. They had put them in a duvet cover and soaked them in the bath. Then they were spread out on the duvet cover in the sun to dry. Once completely dry so they would not rust, they were sorted into colours. Coco and G'orgie had sat under the apple trees in the orchard drinking snakebite. Their bond was very close, and they could openly talk to each other, more like best friends than mother and son. There were over 500,000 bottle tops to sort into colours and store in shoe boxes. Coco counted over 130 different designed tops. She then spent a week designing a pointillism mosaic design, of an underwater scene, of bright shellfish and cresting energetic waves. To stand back to see the bottle-top mosaic and all the shelves full was very rewarding. All the year's hard work, nurtured, harvested and then preserved. *This was definitely the way to live. Good, healthy, homemade, home grown food. Everyone should do it, but others don't have time as they are too busy working to save for the next big TV, or next iPhone,* thought Art, *to need less, is a richer life,* he mused, as he parked the car behind the house.

As the property was quite large, they had created a messaging system. They had gotten fed up leaving stone and twig notes by the back door so Art had carved some soft wood pieces into amulets which hung on hooks on a labelled frame. He had a fish, with its scales intricately carved and a rabbit with long ears and big eyes for Coco. There was a daisy, an apple and a strawberry for guests. Whenever they were working somewhere on the property, they would hang their amulet on one of five hooks: lake, orchard, greenhouse, den or garage. The potting shed, vegetable beds and The Brew House could be seen from the back door, so they did not need representation. Coco's 'rabbit' was on the little hook titled 'Lake', so

Art made his way there. He noticed that everything was still really green, even though he had just seen all the colours of autumn on the lane. He had an alternative appearance, extremely stylish, with a quiet, gentle, pleasant persona. He always wore a hat, woolly in winter, or a canvas cap in the summer. Whatever the weather, nothing would put him off. His sense of humour totally matched that of Coco's and they could have a conversation together that no one else could ever understand. They would laugh at the silliest things, and come up with conclusions they discussed until the late hours of the night. It was common knowledge, it was never a good idea to 'dare' Art, as his courage was boundless and was always up for a challenge or a new venture.

Art called for Nicholson, his hyperactive Jack Russell. Nicholson had been in the car, but he had shot into the house to find Mahoney. An odd relationship as it was, the little dog had bonded with the rabbit, which went against the instinct of both animals. Neither animal was allowed upstairs, so at night Mahoney slept under Coco's drawing board whilst Nicholson would sleep in Art's fishing room. Nicholson was one of the reasons it was safe for Mahoney to wander freely in and out of the house. Once, the gate to the car park had been left open. Nicholson had followed the rabbit everywhere it went. They did not stray far, but the little dog made sure his friend was safe.

Nicholson trotted out of the house when he realised Art had not followed him. They walked down to the lake where Coco was sat with a very thick knitted coat on, fingerless gloves and a woolly hat. She was sat on a log seat they had made in the summer near the water's edge. It had been made from a short, very fat log, laid on its side. They had cut a quarter out of it, creating a bench seat with a short back to lean against. It had been placed facing the lake, on the edge of the undergrowth. As blackberry runners had grown, they were shaped around a handmade trellis fixed behind the log, which allowed the brambles to form a high, woven back to the bench. The evening was getting cold, with only a few hours of daylight left. A beige mist tinted by the last few rays of sunlight had quickly fallen hugging the still surface of the lake. It was very quiet and tranquil; no ripples on the water or sounds of bird chatter. Little drafts of wind swirled through the mist, sometimes thinning enough to reveal the opposite side of the lake, occasionally being strong enough to rustle through green leaves on the trees. The whispering sound of disturbed dry leaves was amplified by the moist atmosphere, sounding like harmonious singing voices. The sun was low in the sky as it dropped behind the woodland. Olive coloured misty shadows started to envelop the lake as the final hours of the evening passed.

Mahoney was sat on the floor beside Coco, but would occasionally hop off for a bramble treat or a dandelion snack.

'If this was all you owned in the world, you would be the happiest person in the world,' said Coco, almost silently, looking around her, then down at the honey-coloured rabbit. Just then, Nicholson came running down the path from the house, startling Mahoney, who still maintained some of his 'flight' instincts. He shot off into the undergrowth. 'Mahonnn...ey!' called Coco, tutting, 'Nics, Nics... Nicholson, where's Mahoney, go find Mahoney!' The little dog stared at Coco as she spoke, and did a little skip, and took a few steps in the direction of the bolting rabbit. 'Go find Mahoney!' Coco repeated, standing up and pointing after her scared pet. Nicholson looked in the direction of the pointed finger, then back at Coco, before shooting off in search of his housemate, just as Art ambled through the thickening fog. He walked to the water's edge, leaning to kiss Coco as he passed. They chatted about their days, as Mahoney and Nicholson came back to join them.

'I've been repotting all the offsets from my aloe vera and spider plants. There are so many!' said Coco as Art came and sat beside her.

'We have loads!' replied Art, who was not a big fan of talking much, 'Where you gonna put them?'

'Well, some I'm going to give as gifts in December, in pots I shall decorate,' said Coco. Neither of them liked Christmas and so would rarely use the 'C' word. Art would fish all day if he could, but had enough respect for his parents to ensure he spent some of Christmas with them. However they happily went to Coco's mother in London for Christmas Day, and Art's parents on Boxing Day.

'Cool,' replied Art.

'I've also been talking to the local Alcoholics and Narcotics Anonymous group in Nottingham...'

'I'm not that bad... with all this home brew it would wrong not to drink it! I don't need to go to meetings!'

'I know you don't, it's not for you.'

'Wicked!'

'I heard that as part of therapy during rehab or meetings, at a certain stage the members are asked if they want to look after a plant. It's sort of to show they're recovering well enough to be able to care for something else.'

'Cool, sounds good!'

'Yeah, that's what I thought. So I rang them to say I could supply some plants if they wanted.'

'Make sure you don't give them the wrong ones... you'll have Narcotics

Anonymous after you!' Art said, as they both laughed.

'So that's what I thought. What do you think? Do our bit? I said they could come over sometime to pick them up. I'll ring them tomorrow if you like the idea.'

'Yeah, it's wicked. This is what it's all about, not having to buy stuff unnecessarily. Giving them as gifts in a decorated pot is ace. It's a totally-homemade homegrown gift. As for the AA, that's such a cool idea. It hasn't cost us anything to grow them. How much will soil and pots be?'

'Not much, about five pounds to pot fifteen plants. The offsets are quite small, and I've used pots that are a bit too big, so they literally will just need putting in a sunny spot and watering. They're dead easy to grow!'

'That's wicked. A nice thing to do!' said Art, putting his arms around her. It was getting quite cold and dark, so they made their way back to the house. The evening continued as most of them did. They ate a homemade chicken stew, with vegetables from the garden, sat at the dining table. Music would range from Black Sabbath and Down, to The Clash and The Ruts played from the stereo in the lounge. Art had opened up the cupboard under the stairs, and built perfectly sized storage to store all of their CDs. There were hundreds of them, and as the cupboard was so deep, the discs were stored in long, CD-sized drawers, which was the only way they would all fit in the unit. Each row of drawers had a wooden name carved out of a different wood, to act as some form of identification as to where a disc might be found. The largest genres were heavy metal and punk, but there was also a carved 'gypsy punk' in walnut, 'death metal' in oak and 'chillin' in birch. The unit was beautiful, and showed a high level of craftsmanship. The stereo itself was a really good one, which Coco had been given by a former housemate, who had broken hers by mistake. It was quite old, but a really good make and its maximum volume was a perfect match for the isolation of the house. Once they had finished eating they each had things to do. Coco went to her drawing whilst Art went to his fishing room next to the studio.

'How's it going?' asked Coco, walking in to see Art. She slumped down on a sofa near the door, watching her partner tying fishing line rigs. 'I can't get into my picture!'

'I'm just making these, as William is coming fishing tomorrow,' said Art, concentrating on his threading of fishing line.

'Excellent. I'll bring you both down some of the stew that's left. Saves you coming back to the house!'

'Thanks that would be nice. How you getting on?'

'Not good, my mind's not working. I keep getting distracted. I keep seeing this shape, everywhere I go!'

'Really, what sort of shape?'

'From when Pod and I went to Temple Bruer... I keep seeing pyramids and towers. Even in my drawings, I'm finding I seem to be creating that image I saw, even though it has nothing to do with the picture I'm doing!'

The next morning, Art was up before it got light. Mr Idol turned up, and after a cup of tea they made their way down to the lake for the day. Coco continued trying to finish her picture, but it was no good. She decided to check all the fruit trees and bushes to see how the fruits were coming on. There were already more plants ready for harvesting, and Coco was wondering how much more fruit they could store. It was another misty day, with the smell of bonfires hanging in the air. It was cold too, and her breath could be seen as she walked around the orchard. She would take some stew down to the lake, and later she would ring the AA group about the plants. She picked a pear to eat as she walked, then stopped suddenly as she looked through the tree branches. There was a triangle of countryside framed by the tree, with the church spire of St. Denys way off in town. The sun was a light grey fuzzy disc, trying to break through the fog. *There it is again,* thought Coco. The shapes had been coming to her more and more since the vision at Temple Bruer. It had come to her attention when she was trying to draw a label for one of the preserving jars. She was just absentmindedly doodling, but when she looked down at the page, the shapes were there in different combinations and sizes, and she instantly realised where she had first seen the images.

While the stew was warming, she made a berry and apple pie and rang about the plants. They were coming to pick them up in a few days, and so she made sure they were all well watered in their new pots, ready for collection. Putting the stew into a huge, wide topped thermos flask, and collecting two bowls and spoons; she went down to the lake. Mahoney had chosen to have a nap, but he would follow her later, using his 'rabbit hole' cut into the back door, which was actually a small 'dog flap'. As she neared the lake, she could hear excited talking, as Art and William fished.

'Hiya Mr William, I've brought you both some stew. Brrr, it's quite cold today, and so damp!'

'Good afternoon Coco dear, how are you?'

The conversation continued as they chatted about the weather, until Art mentioned the fish.

'Can you believe it, we have both caught fish over thirty pounds!'

'Carp or pike, are you both piking?'

'Both, we have caught both. The fish have been massive!'

'Aren't they usually big? I thought you always caught big ones out of here?' asked Coco.

'Yes, well, yes we do, but for some reason, the *proper* big ones are biting today. In all my years of fishing, I have never caught so many big ones in a morning!' said Art, showing a rare excited side to himself.

'Brilliant! Well done. I've made a berry and apple pie, and the AA people are coming in a few days for their plants.'

'What plants? The AA?' queried William, looking concerned, 'drink or drive?'

'Drink! Coco is giving some of her aloe offsets to the AA guys, it's part of their recovery and rehab, to be able to look after a plant. We had loads, so Coco is giving them away! Plus with them being healing aloe vera plants, people can use the sap too. Handy plant to have!'

'What a marvellous thing to do. You two really do have a fabulous place here,' said William 'and I would just like to say, it doesn't matter *what* plants you are growing,' he winked. 'I have grown a few "plants" in my time!'

'Really?' asked Art, turning to look at the old man, with his black woolly hat, scarf and fingerless mitten gloves keeping him warm in the damp fog.

'Well yes son, I grew a lot of plants in the sixties,' William said, with a sheepish smile on his face, 'My friend was a heavy smoker. Bless Tarquin, I wonder what he's up...' he did not finish his sentence as he began to reminisce, winking a twinkling eye at Art. 'Tarquin and I were best friends. I should look him u...'

'Tarquin? Tarquin who?' interrupted Art and Coco at the same time.

'Mr William, are you saying what we think you are saying?'

'Do you mean *the* Tarquin, Tarquin Philbert?' asked Coco, with a shocked expression on her face, '*The* Tarquin Philbert who was the UK's most successful weed importer in the sixties?'

William smiled, 'Please, you don't have to call me Mr William... just William my dear. You two have shown me more respect in the short while I have known you, than the rest of my family put together. It's too much for them to order my shopping on the internet, never mind come and see me. I don't have a computer, and don't have the strength to carry the bags myself, so I order it in. They moan and carry on... Call me William... I know, yes, my friends used to call me Billy, but quite clearly I am not *the* Billy Idol. It stood me in good stead though, as I could always get a good table at a restaurant when I booked by telephone,' he laughed.

'How cool,' said Coco impatiently interrupting. 'So, William... you knew Tarquin Philbert?'

'No, I didn't know him,' said William, looking at Coco's face as her smile faded slightly, 'I worked with him!'

For the next half an hour William told his avid listeners of how he had helped Tarquin in the beginning. He worked for him in the early years, before everything got too big. He would meet a boat just before it docked at Boston Port. Here, he would offload a couple of kilo of green, and take it to his house to hide. He had the best secret place, which nobody knew existed. There, he would store the majority of the stash so he only had a moderate amount on him. William distanced himself from Tarquin when he started to plan some really big hauls that could not come through Boston. William had been happy to continue collecting the small amounts, but did not want to get involved in anything too serious. They had met at Oxford, and had been good friends. 'Tarquin was a really nice guy,' William had continued. He had even spent some of a summer holiday with William in Lincolnshire, which is when the idea had been cooked up. Tarquin had good connections abroad, and could get his goods onto boats coming into Boston. It was an ideal port due to its remoteness, and the fact nobody had cottoned on to watching waterways for drug smuggling. It was especially handy that the farmhouse William lived in with his parents had such a good hiding place.

'You have to seize the opportunity when it comes by, but know when it is time to walk away!' William said. 'You people are doing just fine. You're sharing your surplus, you are preparing for winter, storing all that you can. Just like the squirrels.' Just on cue, a grey squirrel ran across the clearing they were sat in. Nicholson shot off after it, as Mahoney carried on digging a hole.

'It's hard work,' said Coco.

'Yes, but it has to be, my dear. It has to be a little tough, so you really appreciate what you have. If it was easy, everyone would be doing it,' said William understandingly. 'Love the hare pastel drawing in front of the back door!'

'Oh I know, isn't it a fabulous picture! Our way of life is perfect, and we both understood before we took it on just how much work there would be. The thing is...' Coco paused as she leant down and stroked Nicholson who had returned after his unsuccessful squirrel chase, 'The thing is, there is so *much* fruit. All of the plants have just been harvested, and they will need doing again in a few days. It wasn't like this last year.'

'There can't be much more?' asked Art, 'we only did them a week or so ago.'

'I've just had a look, and there's loads more fruit to come, we have so much. The freezer is nearly full, and the one in the garage is rammed. I can make more preserves and some different sauces, but there is only so much we can eat!'

'The one thing I learnt a very long time ago was that you have to take what you can, when you can. It's true, you might not need more now, but none of us knows what is around the corner. Harvest. Make. Store. At the end of the day, if you find in a year's time you still have lots left, swap your surplus to friends and family in exchange for things you need. You guys are sat on a gold-mine. It's the ultimate way of life, exchanging what has cost you next to nothing to make for goods you are not able to grow. You know, toiletries, baking ingredients, meat...whatever you need.'

'Harvest. Make. Store. That sounds so much better than work, buy, sleep... work, buy, sleep!'

'My daughters wouldn't agree with you there. They are all for the buying, buying, buying! Shame they don't work as hard as they shop!'

'I guess we could always get another freezer from somewhere... just an old crappy one to put with the other in the garage. We got the last one free, so I'll keep an eye out for another,' said Art.

Late in the afternoon, just before it got dark, Art walked William back to his 4x4.

'Thank you, young man,' William said, holding his hand out, 'it's been a pleasure, as ever!'

'Yes sir, thank you, it has been a good day. Bumper catch too!' replied Art, using both of his massive hands to shake William's hand, in a gesture of admiration and respect. 'Just one thing, how did you know to talk about Tarquin?'

'I just knew, son. I just knew,' he said, climbing into his car. 'Some people are destined to be great, others are destined to discover the power of nature, and become far greater than any man that doesn't!'

Chapter Fifteen

The squat, Nottingham

John and Rev stood looking out of the window of their new attic flat. It was very foggy outside, and their altitude made it difficult to see the ground clearly. Things had made a turn for the better, with Rev getting a little cash-in-hand job. Over the summer he had managed to save up, which had been very difficult with the temptation to buy drink instead. He put a deposit on a little, one-roomed flat. He still claimed his benefits money, 'everyone does!' he had said, trying to justify himself. He refused to sign off, as the cash-in-hand job was not enough to live on and so he would have been no better off if he was on benefits. He also knew the consequences of being caught, but as his circle of friends was small and nobody actually knew about his cash-in-hand job, he was prepared to take the risk. It was not exactly a 'proper' job either.

Two or three times a week, he got picked up by a little van with 'Seed Mastery... if you want to succeed, it's us you need' written on the side, with a picture of a seed growing in stages to becoming a plant. He would be driven to Doncaster airport were he would be taken to one of the courier depots, where goods from abroad were housed and sorted, to then be distributed around the country. He would have to go to the collection point, sign for three or four boxes and take them to the van. He had fake ID saying he was a horticulturists and no questions were ever asked. He knew he had become an international drugs runner. He handled traditionally decorated Dutch bowls containing a small bag of compost and a flowering bulb in them, doubling as a carrier for the strongest skunk weed from Amsterdam. As both the bulbs and skunk were organic, as were the little bags of compost the weed was secured in, the drugs were never detected if scanned. It was not so much the weed that was important, but the seeds which were very precious. Although the bulb parcels had come directly from Amsterdam, the drugs had originated from the Middle East, and the complicated set-up ensured no real suspicions were raised. John had no idea what his flatmate's job was, and asked no questions. Rev had to keep it quiet, as no doubt John would want to try and persuade him not to do the job. Rev knew it would open a right can of worms if his flatmate got wind of what he was doing, especially as John was finally showing signs of beating his addiction. Knowing his flatmate was an international drug runner would not help his stability. Rev's boss was anonymous; he did not know who he was working for. The driver of the van would pay him £50 when he was picked up, and then another £50 when the goods had been booked in to be forwarded by a different courier. Rev's main task was not only to collect the goods from the airport, but also to drop them off at the couriers. All but one box was sent on to a different address, usually within a radius of about 150 miles. The remaining box stayed with the driver of the van. Rev was not the only one with this job. He had unknown colleagues working out of London's Biggin Hill airport in Kent, Bristol airport, Anglesey Airport in North Wales, Newcastle-upon-Tyne International Airport in the north of England and Inverness in the North of Scotland.

Although the wage was quite good, it was a novelty, and so Rev did not plan on saving any just yet. Their attic flat was not the best place to live, but it was secure, warm, dry and inconspicuous. He started to buy little things for the flat, like new duvets and sheets, rather than having to use the bedding they had found and collected over the last year. It had been a really hard thing to conquer, not knowing where the sheets they were using had come from, the filth and disease that might have been on them. The sheer depravity of it! They now had new duvets, pillows and sheets, and Rev's next purchases would be new beds. Their room was above a hairdresser's, in the old part of Nottingham. The building was 400 years old and the attic rooms were uninhabitable, due to its construction being a little unstable. The middle floor where they lived was comprised of a large room of an unusual and irregular shape, with a small kitchen big enough for one person to stand in, and a toilet. There was no bath or shower, so they had to either wash in the back room of the hairdresser's, or have a flannel wash in the tiny wash basin in the toilet. The windows at the back overlooked a series of courtyards for the other shops, but they were the only windows. There had been two large sash windows at the front overlooking the street, but the room had been used as a band practice room, and so the windows had been boarded up with carpet and cardboard, to reduce the noise. When they had moved out of their squat they had taken the furniture with them.

Their new place was far from a palace, but there was running water, a toilet that worked, and they were warm. The heat from the blowdriers in the hairdresser's ensured they had a constant supply of free heat so they only needed to use their own power to heat the flat at night or when it was really cold outside. As September trundled on by, the nights became quite chilly. The room was big enough that they each had a 'bedroom' area at opposite ends, with the unusual 'L' shape giving them a certain amount of privacy. The sofa sat facing the gas fire in the centre of the room, where they would sit with a little lamp on in the corner. It certainly was a step up from the squat, but by no means was it a particularly healthy place to live, with no bath and no windows in the main room. However, to Rev and John it was a proper home, something they had not really known for many years. The rent was incredibly cheap, which it needed to be considering the lack of amenities.

They both religiously went to their Alcoholics and Narcotics Anonymous every week, though their meetings were on different days. John came home after one of his meetings, with a smile on his face. He had two bags in his hand, and insisted Rev guessed what he had.

'Did you pinch it?' he asked, which was always one of his first questions.

'No, given to us.'

'Can we eat it?'

'No!' replied John, getting restless, 'I'll give you a clue. It's green!'

'Bloody hell, John, you go to NA and come home with a carrier bag of weed. I can't belie...!'

'No, no, no, Rev! It's green in colour, not *green*!'

'Is it an Incredible Hulk toy?' he seriously asked, knowing that what John considered to be fabulous, would probably turn out to be totally useless.

'No. Better than that!' John beamed.

'Is it a Ninja Turtle?'

'No, be serious, will you?'

'I am being serious.'

'You're mocking me... Look!' and with that, John gently got a little plant out of one of his bags, and put it on the floor in-between them. 'It's a plant!' he said triumphantly.

'Um, yes, I can see it's a plant. Did they give you that to look after? Doomed in this place as we have no windows!'

'Oh shit, I didn't think of that!' said John through a fading smile.

The little plant ended up on the kitchen windowsill, being the only natural light in the flat. The narcotics group had given him the plant as part of his rehab. The small aloe vera was in a pot a little too big for it. He had been told to keep it in full sun, and water it regularly. If it started to lean towards the light, he had to turn it around, and if its lower leaves started to turn brown, it needed more water. It would be a challenge, but mighty oaks come from tiny acorns, and John knew the survival of this little plant was important.

The Apricot Mews, Chelsea

Victoria and Elizabeth had stayed in London until Elizabeth's return ticket needed to be used. Strange as it was, the ordeal they had shared had brought them close together and so Victoria had booked a week off work from the museum and had chosen to go to Cumbria with Elizabeth. They had returned to the mews the following morning, after Flynn had been arrested. The police had the fire crew called in, to remove his handcuffs, after which he was arrested and taken away, for the crimes that had been viewed by thousands of people on the internet. His career was totally ruined, he had been stood down by the university and his assets had been frozen until a full investigation was made. Victoria had been allowed to move back in, once she had given the police a statement, though there was an understanding there would still be questions to answer. Elizabeth had also made a statement and each of the women had got their stories spot on. They were not implicated in any way and even Phil gave a perfect performance, saying how he had gone round to see Victoria, 'just watching out for her as her father had always requested,' he had stated, playing his full deck of drama queen cards.

It was now September and the rich autumn colours over on the moors of mainland Cumbria looked like a roaring bushfire. Elizabeth had given birth to a healthy baby boy in June and Victoria had transferred to Durham where she was part of the team working on Hadrian's Wall. It had taken a while before everything had gotten sorted, as she had to find someone suitable to rent the mews house. A young professional man had taken it on, turning up in a new Porsche, wearing a tailor-made suit from Saville Row and Armani sunglasses. Victoria had been very pleased to find such a polite, well-to-do tenant. 'You watch,' she had said to Phil, 'knowing my luck he's a bloody arms-dealer or drug baron. Mr Keiffson seems like a really nice guy! An authoritative type!' Since the harrowing experience she'd had with Flynn, her trust in people had been totally shattered and she found it really difficult to settle into her new job. She felt it was one of the reasons she got on so well with Elizabeth, as they had shared the same experience. She felt in her heart of hearts that Elizabeth was probably the only person other than Phil who she could truly trust.

From her elevated position in the little castle, sat on a bed of rocks accessed by a causeway, she looked down at the Walled Garden and the large, brick and glass greenhouse. Victoria could see all of the flowers and herbs growing really well, with green leaves and pretty flowers. It was a contradictory scene, as the trees at the end of the causeway were brown and orange, with more leaves blown on the floor than there were on the trees. The North Sea surrounding the small island was quite choppy, with foaming waves of a dirty grey colour washing over the shallows. It was hard to see where the sky ended and the sea started on the horizon, as there was a thin mist out to sea. People could not decide if it was a mini castle or a fort, but as it had originally been a lookout for invading Spanish Armadas, it was best described as a 'mini-castle-looking-fort'. It was situated half a mile out on the sandbanks from the mainland, the only access being a tarmac road, which was submerged during high tide. This made the location remote and wild, with gale force winds battering the foot thick stone walls, whipping at the windows with sea-salt spray.

Despite the chilling wintry weather, inside was cosy and warm. A massive stone fireplace at the end of the room had a warm fire flickering away in it, with low, stone vaulted ceilings holding all the warmth in the room. Two large old sofas, both slightly shabby, had been placed at angles in front of the fire and several lamps stood on tables around the edge of the room, casting restricted shadows around the alcoves and pillars supporting the ceiling. Heavy, threadbare Persian rugs in burgundy and gold matching the sofas lay over a red herringbone brick patterned floor. When Elizabeth had described her family home, as 'a mini castle on a remote island occasionally accessible by road', this was not what Victoria had imagined. Each room of the stone constructed building was full of old furniture, some of which had been built specifically for the little castle and had not been used in any other building. Most of the tapestries on the walls and heavy rugs on the floor had quite clearly been there several hundred years, but their signs of age added to the charm of the place. Holy Island had been in Elizabeth's family for generations as it was one of her ancient ancestors who had found an artefact-rich Roman ruin, which housed gold, jewellery and writings from Roman times. The find was priceless. There had been golden goblets, plates and coins, all worth a fortune. Great Great Great Grandpa Claudius had bartered with the Crown. He offered over the haul of golden artefacts, in exchange for a

1000-year free lease on Holy Island. Due to the remote location of the island, with just a dangerous section of the Great North Road 20 miles away, the Crown was glad to have a sitting tenant who would maintain the castle, relinquishing the Crown of all the inaccessibility problems and perilous crossings to the property, where many people had been drowned by the fast-rising tide. Great Great Great Grandpa Claudius had been very smart though and had not handed over all of the things he had found. Some of the goblets and plates he had sold to the Roman Catholic Church in Rome and with the money had gone on a spending spree, buying furniture in Italy, rugs in the Middle East and tapestries from Istanbul. Everything had been shipped directly to Holy Island and ferried across the shallow sand-flats in little boats.

The family Claudius had continued to purchase several inns around the Cumbrian countryside and soon had a good reputation for good stabling, quality ale and comfortable lodgings. A few of the less successful places in the more remote locations had been sold, but the remaining five brought in enough business to keep the family comfortable on Holy Island. Many generations had been born on the island, with Elizabeth's son being the most recent, nearly two months ago. Baby Adrian was asleep in his room, with his baby monitor placed in-between Victoria and Elizabeth on the sofa.

'Shall we have a bottle of wine tonight?' Elizabeth had suggested. 'There's plenty in the cellar to choose from!'

'Okay, you check on tea, and I'll go down and get one. Any particular one?' said Victoria, getting up and putting on her thick jumper lying on a nearby chair.

'Any you like, surprise me. I'll make up Addi's bottle while I'm at it,' replied Elizabeth.

Down in the cellar, Victoria had been surprised to find it was quite small the first time she'd had to go down there. There were the usual things such as trunks and boxes, some with writing on them. All of the walls of the cellar were bare rock with a very uneven floor of natural rock. She found a rack of wine bottles, all laid on their sides. She walked to the end and noticed there was a gap in the racking, revealing a huge wooden cupboard, made up of small drawers set behind the wine. 'Strange,' she thought, as she had not noticed it before. Walking through the gap, it suddenly went very dark, as the light from the main room was restricted by the rack of wine she had just passed behind. It was hard to see in the poor light. 'Ouch, shit!' she said, rubbing her arm and shoulder, 'where did you come from?' She squinted trying to see what it was she had walked into. The top of the offending object, a foot-wide metal pillar, seemed to go up into the main body of the house and the base went straight through the rock floor. It was very cold to touch, but quite solid. Looking around, it was the only one. Victoria could not work out what its function was, especially as it did not seem to be supporting the ceiling. She walked back through the gap and started to choose her wine, whilst still rubbing her shoulder. Many of the wine bottles were dusty and as Victoria scanned the bottles, occasionally taking one off the shelf to read the label she noticed they were all old, maybe expensive and rare. She decided on a Spanish red, from the early sixties. 'Blimey, they all seem to be old. No supermarket special down here!' she said under her breath.

'I bumped into that metal post in the cellar, I'll get a massive bruise,' Victoria explained when she was back by the fire, with two glasses in her hands. 'What is that pillar? It comes into the house and goes into the rock. Is there another room below the cellar?'

'It's the support to the weather vane above the main fireplace in the foyer. You know, when you walk through the front door, you have the four stone pillars and there is that huge stone fireplace to the right?'

'Yes, I know it. It's something that has amazed me since I've been here. The hall is so grand, with those huge stone columns and the impressive stone hearth and yet the rest of the rooms are really modest and cosy!'

'Well, above the fire is a painting of a map with a big dial and clock hand on it.'

'Yes, I have seen it. It has compass points on it!'

'Well, it's a map to show what direction the wind is blowing on the weather vane which is attached to it up on the roof. You know, if it's a northerly wind, the hand will point to the 'N'. Living on this island with the shallow sandbanks it is important to know which direction the wind is going. It's easy to get caught if there's a fast tide!'

'It must be a horrible way to go, getting caught on the causeway, getting cut off from land and being swept out to sea in your car. Has anyone been caught recently?'

'No, not recently, I think it was the late seventies they built a wooden tower halfway between the island and the mainland that's a few metres taller than the high tides. People have had to use it when they had been walking out to visit the Walled Garden, or to take pictures of the mainland from the island. It's easy to misjudge how long it takes to walk the causeway.'

'Why don't you just put a gate up and stop people coming out here. Surely the Walled Garden doesn't bring in enough revenue as an attraction and you could afford to miss it?'

'Yes, it's not that. It's to do with the rare plants in the garden. There are all sorts of unusual plants that have survived down there and many of them are not indigenous to these parts. My Grandpa Claudius brought them back with him when he travelled around Europe and the Middle East, looking for things to furnish this place. There's a diary somewhere logging what's down there and where they all came from. We should look out for it. It's about 250 years old. That's why people come to the island, to walk around the garden.'

'That diary would really be interesting. I'd love to see it!'

'I'm not sure where it is. Mummy and Daddy are in Peru at the moment, but when I speak with them next I'll ask where it is.'

Elizabeth had been living at one of the hotels she was working at, but since the arrival of Adrian, she had moved back to the family home on the island. Her parents, who were now retired, had taken to travelling and spent most of the winter in warmer places. Although it sounded glamorous living in a castle, there were many drawbacks. Not only was there zero access once the tide had come in, there was no internet or mobile signal. The castle had a landline which was the only form of communication with the outside world. The television only had four channels with an occasionally fifth if the wind was blowing in the right direction. However, there was so much to do in the castle, there was rarely the time for social media or satellite television. The room that faced the mainland of the narrow, slim castle was the music room. It had dramatic views of the steep cliffs dropping to the sandbanks surrounding the rocky island. In front of a large window was a raised platform with a few stone steps leading into an instrument-adorned room, with a large stone corner fireplace. A cello stood on a stand, with other various wood, brass and string instruments hanging on the walls and on the table top. At the other end of the room was a big drum kit and an expensive stereo. Stone beams ran the width of the room, but again, due to tapestries and rugs it was a cosy room that did not give away any secrets as to what the weather was doing outside.

The two-storey castle had been built on undulating rocks, over three levels. The cellar therefore had an uneven floor, with little steps and platforms built over rock peaks. Some even nearly touched the ceiling above. Learning the layout of the castle was interesting, as small flights of stairs, corridors with sharp turns in them and large open spaces along various hallways could become baffling. There were several twisting, stone staircases with little rooms halfway up to the next floor. Their greatest pastime was to look out from the small courtyard at the front of the island, which had a low thick wall around it and magnificent views out to sea. This was the only side of the island where the gradient was gentle enough to have a path that twisted around to the other side of the island meeting the tarmac causeway, as the other sides were all perched on steep rocks. Bracing sea salt and sand particles relentlessly attacked the little castle, but due to its long, narrow design that lay in the direction of the prevailing wind, much of the castle's windows and walls were protected from the full-on force of the sea. On a hot summer's day, the view would be magnificent, with cooling sea breezes allowed to waft through the open windows, carrying the scent of salty seaweed or herbs from the garden, depending on which way the wind was blowing.

Victoria had managed to work her hours around the tides, in order to access the castle. There was usually one, sometimes two days when she would have to stay away and would often try and get to one of the family's hotels for the night. She was starting to like her work colleagues, but could never sit in the bar for long after her evening meal when she stayed away. When she had times away from the castle, the nights were so much lonelier. The memories haunted her of what Flynn had done, of the happy times they had spent together and how he had betrayed her. Often she went to sleep with tears in her eyes. Even when she thought of Elizabeth and Baby Adrian, a certain amount of resentment came through. Elizabeth had Flynn's baby, something of his to keep forever. She was not sure if she was envious or sorry for her new friend. Elizabeth had the same thoughts once she had gone to bed. No matter how hard she tried to get Flynn out of her mind, he would always be there, because she saw him every time she looked at Adrian. The wind would whistle around the castle, intensifying any lonely feelings. On very windy nights Elizabeth wished she had someone to keep her warm. It was equally lonely when the wind was silent. The only sound then was maybe a passing ship blasting its horn, but other than that, at night, the castle was totally silent.

Regardless of battling with extreme bouts of loneliness, Victoria and Elizabeth started to rebuild their lives. They both had a new home and each had something to take their minds off the past; Elizabeth now had Adrian, and Victoria had her new job. Summer was rapidly fading and the forecasters had suggested the winter was going to be harsh. Elizabeth and Victoria helped to cut the herbs in the Walled Garden, so they might be bundled up and dried above the open fire in the kitchen. A specialist horticulturists supervised the pruning. They would take samples of each plant, putting them in an identification bag, ensuring the date and plant name was written clearly. This was something that had happened at the Walled Garden since the middle of the eighteenth century. Grandpa Claudius had insisted that this had to be done, and experts from one of the many Royal Horticultural Society locations around the country would take it in turns to perform the task, which usually took about a week. Once all signs of summer had gone and the trees on the mainland stood naked of their leaves, extra provisions were bought each time a food shop was done and the freezers and pantries slowly filled up. There was no way of knowing, with the autumn winds due, how many days they might be isolated. In the past years there had only been a few days when crossing the causeway had been impossible either by boat because of the high winds, or by road because of a higher than usual tide. Extra wood was brought over from the mainland on a big truck, which took the best part of a day to barrow up to the log store by the front door in the stone courtyard. Victoria swapped her little 'city slicker' Audi for a hefty 4x4 to improve her chances of getting about in the Cumbrian highlands when the snow and ice came. She was not looking forward to coping with the heavy snow, but knew when she agreed to the job it would play an integral part of her life for a few months of the year. That was why Elizabeth's father had helped her pick the right vehicle for her. Little did she know that in ten months all the efforts of picking the right car would be a complete waste of time.

Chapter Sixteen

October 2011, Cauldy Island, South Wales

'Gentlemen, welcome to this meeting, I am sure you are all eager to get back to your research and preparations, but we, at the Final Decision Committee, felt you all needed informing of everything that has been prepared so far, and how we see the whole system will work. Please, take a seat everyone. Sit down, please, sit down,' said Dave, a middle-aged man with the appearance of a successful and respected scientist. 'How's the ones and twos doing these days, Ed? Or should I say ones through to fours?' he chuckled, shaking Ed's hand with excitement. 'It's great to finally meet you. Big fan, bugger about what happened though. You still making records?'

Ed and his fellow MBHK members were all on Cauldy Island, just a few minutes boat ride from the little seaside town of Tenby on the Pembroke coast of South Wales. Famous for its quaint holiday cottages and busy, medieval streets, the little fishing village rested between dramatic Pembrokeshire peaks. The island had been inhabited by monks since the sixth century, and although it made an interesting tourist attraction, the monks still worked on the island. Due to the harshness of farming such a small island, they began making perfume, and to this day relied on tourism and their perfume industry as a source of income. Whilst the Cistercian monks, a stricter offshoot of the Benedictine Order, lived in the monastery, a very small village also occupied the island. Ed and his friends were sat in one of the empty offices at the monastery on surprisingly soft chairs, each with a tall straight back. The seats were padded, but lumpy due to losing some of their horsehair stuffing over the years.

'Hope you all travelled down here alright, bit of a trek for some of you. Thank you for coming. I'm going to plough right on, tell you everything we know, then, if you have questions, please feel free to ask them at the end. This is complicated, so pay attention,' said the FDC representative. 'As you all know, from the research you have all submitted, we are heading for a Bio-Armageddon scenario, a global catastrophe. The outcome will not be helped by the misuse of the earth's resources and gross neglect of this spinning rock. It's something that has happened before, every five thousand years!' Stunned faces stared back, disbelieving what they were hearing. 'The spark, and I literally mean spark, was forecast by the Egyptians, Hopi and Mayans whose calendar finishes... restarts... depending on your point of view about 12.21.12, which is now 21.06.12. Our research has shown that the reason why these ancient civilizations made the calendar was so that their future generations were prepared. By watching the stars, they quickly learnt there was a celestial clock, which is something even our scientists do not fully understand. We only know what we know because of these ancient cultures all saying the same thing. They worked out when the next complete planetary alignment would happen, which only occurs every five thousand years or so. The last time it happened was after the completion of Stonehenge, the Egyptian Pyramids, all that sort of stuff,' he said, looking around at the expressionless faces. 'Here's the very scary bit. Are you ready for this?'

Everyone nodded, not knowing what to expect next.

'Those ancient structures, the Pyramids and Stonehenge for example, are all that remains of those thriving, technologically advanced races. They are remains of buildings and structures built by a previous human race, all of which were extinguished at the last alignment. After the planetary alignment, the rays of the sun were greatly magnified, as was all of its energy. This was then all pulled in one direction, towards the aligned planets. The Mayan cities, Egyptian pyramids, Stonehenge and the Nazca lines are *all* man-made, but of natural stone.' A stunned, unbelieving silence hung heavily in the room. 'In summary, the planetary alignment caused so much energy and heat, that the only things left on earth were things made of stones with a certain compound that is found in water. The land, however, was not damaged. Just man and anything he had made, which is why there is absolutely no record of any of this advanced technology. It answers the question as to how the Pyramids in Egypt are a replica map of the stars, namely the exact layout of Orion's Belt! Animals and some humans survived because they came "of the earth", you know; something they ate affected their DNA. To clarify, the last time this happened, the civilized world was far more advanced than the people of today. Everything was destroyed five thousand years

145

ago in the last planetary alignment, with only pieces of sculpture such as Stonehenge, the Nasca Lines and all of the various pyramids around the world surviving. Now that you know the severity and complexity of the situation, you can appreciate why we had to keep it quiet!'

The six men sat in total silence; even Dylan was paying very close attention. This is what they had wanted to know about for many years, but now they were hearing it, it was the last thing they wanted to know. All of their research now made complete sense and the enormity of the task they still had to achieve, made everything even more impossible.

'So, big shit hits the fan, eh? People of this earth were just as civilized as they are now, probably more so, maybe even seriously more advanced. That explains the fact they could build Stonehenge and the pyramids... they had better technology than we do. So, coming back to 2012, basically, it is going to happen again. Everything man-made will be incinerated... except certain groups of people.' He paused for a moment, letting the information sink in. 'Now, as you all know the event site is held sacred, because of its stones, and the blind spring. Here's the "holy shit" bit... that spring that surfaces at the site from The Tor, runs all around the crust of the earth, and holds the purest water to exist on this planet. This water is collected deep inside the earth in underground oceans, collected from years of steam pockets created by the heat generated through the rotational spin of the inner core. It is the purest substance known to man, more pure than a flawless diamond or 24-carat gold. Look at it as a preserved bit of the earth from when time began. We are talking billions of years of filtration; this water is virtually invisible it is so clear. As it makes its way to the surface of the earth, pulled by an invisible force which is the pressure caused by the spinning of the earth, it eventually reaches the springs. The spring surfaces at certain places, some odd, random places, others more predictable. Off the top of my head there is here, at Cauldy, a lake in Lincolnshire, Skomer Island on the most southerly point of the west coast of Wales, and then the likes of many ancient sites such as Petra, Pompeii, Machu Picchu and such. Rik, that stream running through your homestead... it's part of this spring.'

'Bloody hell!' exclaimed Rik, thinking what this might mean for himself and his family.

'The people who are going to survive, as you have been told, are those who have the defective DNA, all of whom will be at the festival on the Summer Solstice 2012. We have recently come to believe the vegetation or animals the first ancient Britans had eaten, had been watered by this pure water. Nobody died during the first alignment, as they were primitive, and already had the protecting water minerals in

146

them. In 2012 it is a very different situation as most of the population of the world will perish. Festivallers' loved ones and family friends will also be saved by the viral text which will transfer the energy from the relative or friend at the festival to anyone they truly love... or have compassion for... admiration... anything like that. The energy field generated here, and transferred to them will act as a barrier, protecting them.'

They all sat motionless and in silence. This could not be happening.

'Now, there are other people who will survive too. Anywhere without internet in remote locations will be safer, as that is where most of the heat comes from during the alignment, as the satellites will be affected before the land is. Basically, the more gadgets you have, the more you're going to fry. Traditionally built houses will survive, better than modern ones, depending on the amount of technology is in said house. Then there are the places where the springs come up. We have identified about 90 locations in the United Kingdom.'

All this was too much to take in all at once. Although they were educated men, who had been working on this project for years, it was not until now that the secret history of the world was being revealed to them. This was going to take weeks to divulge and accept. You can't just change the way you think about history instantly. All the unanswered questions. Who wrote the history everyone is taught? How could they possibly keep all this a secret? Newspapers would pay handsomely for the proof!

'How has this all been kept a secret, I bet you're thinking? Well, it's so simple. The world's media is owned by just seven companies, controlling what the public is told. Gambling, celebrities and sports all shown on television keep citizens in line, brainwashing them. Why do you think hunter gatherer civilisations without TV have zero crime, communal living and rely on the land they live on, to sustain them?' They all sat uncomfortably, shuffling about in their chairs not knowing what to think, or how they should feel.

'This is where we had the help of the Knights Templar,' Dave said, noticing everyone suddenly pay a little more attention, 'Everyone knows of their story, thanks to Dan Brown, but most of their *true* history has been kept from the public. The Knights had the knowledge of the alignment which they found in the Middle East, and knowing what they did, they became very rich very quickly, providing evidence to rich patrons, offering the elite a means of safety when the calamity came, earning the Knights a fortune in the process. The Templars built their churches and preceptories where the spring was nearest the surface, and made maps of natural lakes that contained a percentage of this water.

All this was done to protect the people who would need protecting, even though the Knights knew it would not be needed for generations. However, the Knights failed to mention to the patrons that the next alignment was not for another 700 years, at which point all who had invested would be dead anyway. As the King of France had donated a lot of money to them, he was not best pleased when he found out he was funding an event that wouldn't happen until 2012. It was eventually the King who got his revenge, by reporting the Knights to the Pope. The rest of the story is as everyone knows it. Of course we have worked out the date difference, making the date June, not December 2012.' The representative rearranged the rest of his papers, as he tried to keep it as simple as he could. It was a lot to take in all in one sitting.

'These little oases were easy to spot as they all had the same characteristics; healthy plants, increased natural produce, all that sort of thing. This came about as the ground these areas are on, are fed by the pure water from the underground springs. Most of the springs may not be overly apparent at the moment, but when the event takes off at the site, the pressure in the spring will push all the water to the surface, with various degrees. Some might just get soggy underfoot, others may be in the middle of a fountain, we don't know yet how it will go, each place will be different, but the result will be the same. Being near one of these pure, subterranean springs will offer people protection, because as we all know, "water" beats "fire"!' he said, making the stone, paper, scissors shapes with his hands.

'I'll summarise, it's a lot of heavy shit to take in. Lots of people will survive, but only if they're connected to the site via a viral text enhanced by the emotions of the festival goers; have no or little internet and technology; are protected by a spring opening and one other factor will save people. The remaining factor is... anyone who has eaten anything that has grown on the ground where the springs are will be protected. They will have developed their own immune system, and so will also be saved from the heat unlike those who have not ingested food stuffs or drinks made with the pure water. The goodness of the elements in the pure water gets transferred through the ground, into plants, then fruit or animals et cetera and on to the person who consumes them. About eight-five per cent of human life on Earth will *not* have any protection!'

Stunned silence filled the room, even the sound of seagulls outside the window, or the church organ in the Priory went unnoticed. Five minutes passed, as they all took in the madness they had just been told, some pacing the room while others held their head in their hands.

Silence.

'So, aliens didn't build the pyramids?' asked Dylan after the very long stunned silence. Everyone looked at him, as it was not the first thing they were thinking. 'What...what?' he stammered, looking at all of their faces.

'Is there any chance that any of all this is a load of old bollocks?' asked Uncle Sam.

'No. I'm afraid not. It's probably the one thing Hollywood never came up with,' Dave said.

'The Templars... this is a new one on me! I know their story, defenders of the faith, the Pope's army... whatever, Holy Grail oh... shit!' said Ed, his voice trailing off.

'The Holy Grail?' said Dylan, looking quizzically around the room.

'The Holy Grail...' said Rik.

'Holy fuck!' said Dylan, when he realised what the Templar Grail was.

'No dude, *grail*, Holy Grail!'

'Yeah, I meant Holy Grail, fuck!'

Each man realised the extent of what he was responsible for. They sat, thinking about all the information they had just been told. *The pure water was the Holy Grail the Templars were trying to protect. Wonder if any of the critical thinkers came up with this one?* thought Rik.

'So...!' said Uncle Sam, not entirely sure what to say or ask. There was a lifetime of questions to ask, but only ten months to ask them, 'I don't know what to say!' They all nodded in agreement with him.

'Anyone fancy a beer?' asked Dylan.

'Are you crazy? You've just been told the planet is going to be incinerated, and all you can think about is having a beer!' said Robert, quite agitated with Dylan's response.

'Well, firstly, all this has been planned five thousand years ago, intensified seven hundred years ago, and we, well I certainly, am ready for this. If we can't be ready with five thousand years' notice, we don't deserve to survive it! I know all of my responsibilities are on standby, everything I am responsible for is ready and so there's not much I can personally do right now. Secondly, if mankind is coming to an end as we know it, I would like to enjoy a pint in a pub with no juke box, no gamblers and no televisions. If you lot want to sit here wasting time crying over something you have *no* control over, carry on. I intend to enjoy the island for a few days, you know, remind us what we are doing this for, and then go and treble-check everything, so this speech never comes back to bite me on my arse!'

'You know what, you're right,' said Robert, 'I have often thought that your morals were a little self-centred, but after that little insight, I believe you have the morals of a saint, Sir!'

'Before you all go, obviously this is still a category A situation, top secret to everyone except a handful of people... a handful of people who... are monitored... a handful of people who know the situation well enough not to say anything to anyone!'

'You insult our intelligence?' asked Uncle Sam, leaning forward, looking through his half glasses, balanced on the end of his nose.

'No, not at all, it was just something that the top brasses insisted I reminded you all,' said Dave, a little nervously.

'One thing! Please, before we go for a pint or ten...' stated Rik, 'there's one thing I don't quite get. We, on the inside know what is happening, and are preparing for it, preparing the site, making one hundred and eighty thousand survival packs for festivallers and staff, storing two hundred all-terrain vehicles on the farm, with a further five hundred to be crammed in once the festivallers have all parked their cars and of course food and water. We will all be safe, protected by the spring, which will be activated into action by the energy of the crowd at exactly the right time. Then when the heat comes, a ray of sun intensified because of the planetary alignment, will incinerate the Earth.'

'Totally correct so far,' said Dave, nodding.

'What happens on Earth when it's incinerated? I mean, if we are going to walk off the site after the event to a charcoal moonscape, what's the point? If the end is quick!' Rik continued.

'No, far from it! Scientists all around the world have been working on this. Our section covering Britain includes about one hundred people but the overall committee is about one thousand. We don't... we don't really know what will happen, we can only simulate the conditions through a computer...'

'If it's a big, energy-sapping powerful one, don't be standing next to it when the big bang comes!' Dylan interrupted.

'The closest simulation we could get was at the space industry's Max-Planck Institute in Germany. They study solar flares, asteroid strikes and the likes of impact and nuclear winters on the atmosphere. The start of the process will begin with an increase in solar storms. The magnetic activity of the planet will have to be closely monitored, with backup generators on standby, as there will be a period of time from when it all begins, to the grand finale, when we will need power. Generators will keep observation centres open and communicating with each other until the very end. After the increase in solar flares, the surface temperature will increase, anything running on electrical or fossil fuels will stop working.'

'Aeroplanes?' asked Robert, 'What about trains, and boats?'

'I am afraid the first sign of the final phase will come after the power shortages. Electrical circuits will literally dissolve through the radiation passing into our atmosphere and down to the earth's surface. Planes will literally drop out of the sky along with any satellite debris. As the satellites are dissolved, mobile phones, radios, and the internet, all of it... all of it will be saturated with this intense energy from the sun, everything will stop working. All clouds in the sky will evaporate really quickly as the extreme heat heads to Earth, then a matter of minutes later the full force of the heat will reach the Earth's surface. Trains, cars and boats, mobility scooters, motorbikes, cranes, diggers... everything. Everything will stop working, and as the radiation and heat increases, things will start to melt, explode... gradually shrivel to dust. There will be a period of about ten minutes, for the full heat to reach the surface, after the radiation from space connects with the planet's surface energies...'

'What surface energies?' asked Robert, knowing what the answer was going to be, after all his secretive delving into the chemtrails being sprayed by all of the world's governments in the sky.

'The surface energies include all of the energy created by the people, batteries, combustion engines, computers and the like...'

'And what else, Dave?' Robert asked, interrupting a little too sharply. 'Sorry, Dave, tensions of the moment. Please tell us, is there anything else that is going to contribute to this heat?'

'Um, yes,' Dave took a long pause. 'Sit down gentlemen, you might as well know it all, the pub will still be open in thirty minutes.' They all sat back down, having been putting coats and hats on, for the short walk to the inn.

'Since the fifties, the world's major governments have created a barium, which they'd planned to use in the event of a global attack... from space.'

'What the fuck is a global attack?' asked Dylan, '...the space of WHAT!'

'A global attack, is when the Earth is attacked by... by beings from other worlds.'

'The alien dudes with the wrong DNA again?' joked Dylan, receiving disapproving looks from Robert.

'Well, sort of yes,' said Dave, nodding at Dylan. He liked this guy, even in the face of all the information he had just been told, he was not disheartened. He smiled at an indignant Robert, also noticing Dylan's smug look, 'Yes and no. Governments intended to protect the planet, by spraying highly flammable, explosive, aluminium barium into the skies. Those trails you see the military planes leaving... that is what they were doing. Robert, obviously we are aware that this is one of the fields

151

you are knowledgeable about. The idea was that if there was an attack from another world, they would fire up a rocket to ignite the upper atmosphere, preventing anyone getting to the planet's surface.'

'What a load of boll... what about the people? No point saving a planet, if you're killing everyone and everything at the same time,' said Ed.

'That's where all those massive underground bunkers come into play. There would be places for people to go, to save themselves from the manmade space defence system.'

'Underground bunkers?' asked Rik.

'Yes. Since Roswell in 1947, the military have been preparing for an attack. They found out a lot more than they are letting on, hence the development of Area 51. There's basic information out there on the net, for those that bother to look or think,' said Dave. 'I'm sure you all know the facts about the Groom Lake Research Facility?' he asked, looking around the room. Everyone nodded half-heartedly.

'By the late fifties, the US government had developed a barium vapour they could spray in the skies. Bear in mind, the internet did not exist then, and so the government felt secure that their obvious activities would go unnoticed, especially as commercial aircrafts were just starting to be commonplace in the skies. People did not take any notice of the vapour trails and didn't distinguish between contrails made by planes, and chemtrails made by deliberate spraying, until the current time when people use their camera phones to film commercial planes and spraying military planes in the same shot, they then started to ask questions. People began to wake up, think more, noticing that the vapours left by the planes did not disperse, but instead would spread out, so the skies became permanently white by most afternoons. By the morning the barium would be dispersed into the atmosphere, so the next morning there would be bright blue skies again. They sprayed the skies except for one area above Alaska, in case a rocket was needed to be sent up to ignite the barium. They would fire it through the hole in the "protective" vapour in the ionosphere near Gakona, programming it to explode above the chemicals, thus setting it alight. Underground bunkers were built, whose construction intensified with the threat of the Cold War. They made no point of hiding the bunker construction, as people thought they were for protection against nuclear fallout. The Cold War ended, as the bunkers were finished.'

'Are you saying the Cold War between Russia and the USA was a bluff?' said Ed.

'Yes. Yes it was. A false flag I'm afraid,'

'Well. Fuck. Me!' said Robert, with everyone looking around at him,

'I'm just saying... I worked for the Air Force, and did not know a thing.'

'There is so much we don't know. The bunkers were ready, the skies were being sprayed, then the internet and recently social networks helped to bring awareness to the masses,' concluded Dave.

'So instead of the Earthlings setting off the barium with a rocket, pre-planned once the rich and elite were safely underground with zero consideration for the populace, nature is *actually* going to get there first? Mother Nature is going to save the "Earthly" people with her own life force?' said Ed, 'I quite like the idea the so-called elite fat cats have invested all their blood money to build themselves safe, underground bunkers, because let's face it, those places weren't for ordinary people, but in reality, those rich folk would be the first to go, with their flashy, pre-programmed, electronic homes, with thousands of pounds of electrical goods... gone... in a puff of smoke!'

'It's sort of karma for the ecologists!'

'It's nature getting its own back on all those thieving bastards who plundered the world's resources for their own financial gain. I always said, what goes around comes around,' said Ed.

They left the monastery and went to the inn for the evening. They had a few more meetings to attend to over the next few days, and so felt it would be good to get into village life, and enjoy a small community isolated by the sea. They ordered their drinks at the bar, and sat in a booth away from the other customers. They would not be openly discussing their knowledge on what was going to happen, but there would be the odd reference, and they did not want to be overheard. They chatted about the tourist sites they had visited, or planned to see. Once the barmaid had delivered the food they had ordered, they relaxed slightly, as there would not be any more disturbances.

After finishing plates of corn-fed chicken, new potatoes and vegetables grown on the island, fresh fish caught that morning with homemade wedges or vegetable hot pot, again, made with produce from the island, they sat back and ordered more drinks. The fire in the middle of the room was stoked, and the heat filled the low-ceilinged pub.

'How was the food?' asked a full figured lady in chef's clothes.

'Fabulous, thanks!'

'Outstanding!'

'I'm so full, the portions are huge, beautiful flavours though, thank you,' said Dave.

'Are these your plant friends, Dave?' she asked, as she started to stack the plates.

'Yes, yes they are. Gentlemen, this is Gwyn, she does all the cooking here, single-handedly.'

'Wow, that's amazing,' Dylan said, taking the pile of dirty plates to the bar for Gwyn, 'What an amazing woman you are, Gwyn,' he continued. She was slightly taken aback by him, with his alternative clothes, very skinny black trousers, and massive chain and buckle decorated boots.

'The food was fabulous,' repeated Robert, smiling, 'and the portions were massive!'

'That's because we have so much fruit and veg. So much. In all my years, having looked back over the shopping budgets, we have never spent so little on food ingredients, with so much growing in the yard. The fish are big enough to do two portions. And the weather has been so bad this year, it doesn't make sense.'

'That's why these good gentlemen are here, Gwyn, to take soil samples and things. They are a private company, whose reputation is based on their clients' privacy. If you're sat on a gold mine, we won't tell anyone!' laughed Dave, walking Gwyn back to the kitchen, as he went to the bar for more drinks.

'So gentlemen, now you know everything there is to know. Keep researching as you have been doing, submitting anything you consider useful,' said Dave, as they got down to the last of their drinks.

'Can I ask one thing?' asked Rik, checking nobody was near them. They had sat at the end of the inn all evening, with just a few locals and tourists popping in. The inn was nearly empty, and the embers in the fire were dying down, though still omitting a fair amount of heat. 'Is that what HAARP is for? That one has always baffled me.'

'Yes, HAARP, or America's High Frequency Active Auroral Research Program was created to monitor what the barium was doing. It's based in Alaska, where their scientists transmit a 3.6 million watt signal into the atmosphere. Its official story is that it's searching for ways to better communications networks, but the real reason for it is as a weather machine, or a WMD, Weapon of Mass Destruction, or whatever you want to call it. Our intelligence tells us that HAARP is funded by the US Navy and the US Air Force. Why would the military be involved? Plus there are identical machines in Sweden, Russia, Puerto Rico and another in Alaska. Our whole operation, as you know, is completely independent of any of the world's governments. We had to find out all of our information ourselves!'

'I have read about this,' said Robert, 'they ran a simulation with HAARP in 1997, calling the test Hurricane Sandy. There were even classified files stating that the simulation was in preparation for a real Hurricane Sandy, which would be manufactured when the weather conditions were correct, to create a super-storm. As of yet it hasn't happened, and speculation is rife that the storm will be unleashed during the US presidential elections as a means to distract the voters. That could happen in November 2012.'

'But there won't be a November 2012!'

'No... maybe! But if there is, it will be unlike anything seen in the world since Stonehenge was made.'

Chapter Seventeen

November 2011, Lincolnshire

The countryside was in the full throws of late autumn. All of the trees had shed their colourful leaves during high winds that had battered the country for the last few days. The clouds had been a continuous dark grey, which was delaying the early frosts. The clocks had changed a week ago, and so Coco and Art made the most of the daylight hours. All of their harvesting had been collected, pickled, frozen and preserved. They had easily doubled the produce they'd had since William had last visited. They had even made a second batch of ciders and perrys. The Brew House was full of barrels standing on the floor, and jars on the shelves. They found a third freezer, a tall, freestanding unit, which was what they had wanted as the other one in the garage was a chest freezer. This allowed them plenty of space to freeze any meals they made over winter, storing them in recycled plastic mushroom boxes, wrapped in cling film.

It had been a very pleasant autumn, as neither Coco nor Art had to go to a mundane job, spending hours away from home for a rubbish wage. Coco would spend all her time drawing, while Art cared for the produce they were growing. He made different sauces, jams and pickles, labelling them with Coco's hand-painted labels. He even made some small hampers, using baskets he had found in a charity shop, with a selection of the things he had made, to give to a few friends and neighbours. He even did one for William. He used a little sprig of autumn berries to decorate the front of the baskets, and wrote a handmade card, saying 'Happy Autumn, from all at Railway Cottage'. He made about 20, of which four were for neighbours within half a mile in each direction of the cottage. Coco helped every now and again, with the apples and forest fruits, but generally spent most of the precious few daylight hours working on her drawings. Art went fishing regularly, but could not work out why he could not catch the same amount of fish he had that day William had been over. He was catching them, but they were just a lot smaller than they had been. *Maybe it's the weather,* he thought, looking at the heavy clouds, and low mists regularly forming each evening.

'Why don't we have friends over, you know, do a huge chilli or something, jacket potatoes, that sort of thing. We have all this space, all this produce, we might as well. Sort of celebrate harvest, like people used to?'

'Yeah, we can do,' said Art.'We could do something in the meadow, and get some loud sounds going!'

'Oh wow, that would be really cool! People can pitch tents and park their cars in the meadow too. Ha, it would be like a mini festival,' Coco said as she did some of her drawing. Art was sat on her studio sofa, with Nicholson on his lap, licking ice cream out of Art's bowl. 'If it's too cold, there's the spare room, various sofas and The Den for people to stay over.'

'Be careful who you ask though, Cocs. I don't want any unsavouries here. Keep it small, ay? Just our proper friends?'

'Course, I wouldn't want our little paradise to get ruined or damaged!'

'I was thinking more along the lines that we could invite our closest friends, tell them not to bring anything, and we will supply everything. We have all the food, and the booze, so why don't we make it a sort of a "thanks-giving". You need to get a move on though, as the weather is set to get really cold soon.'

'Okay, I'll text everyone. Just the usual crowd, yeah?'

November 5th was on a Saturday night, and so on the Friday, Coco and Art, with the help of Pod and her eighteen-year-old daughter, Logan, got as much ready as they could. There would be a table in front of The Brew House to serve drinks from, and opposite it a table for food that was brought out of the kitchen, or from the homemade stone barbeque. Art had built it using reclaimed bricks, tiles and slates. It was based on a tall-chimney pizza oven, with a place for a grill above the coals. The enclosed sides funnelled up to a extractor chimney, ensuring the smoke went up the funnel. It had some amazing similarities to an early steam train. The formation of different bricks, both in colour and size, tiles both decorated and plain and layers of thin slates made a very impressive piece of garden furniture. It was not ostentatious in its size, but although it was big, it did not look out of place, if anything it complimented the cream cottage and The Brew House. At its very base, Art had made an iron grate, for the logs and coals to sit in, with a metal shelf next to the grill to stand pans or potatoes on. It also added heat to the patio. Whilst Art prepared the cooking facilities and bar, Coco, Pod and Logan wrapped potatoes in foil and checked on the three big pans on the cooker, one each of a chilli, basil and chicken-based tomato sauce and some roasted Mediterranean vegetables in a feta cream cheese sauce. Logan had spent most of the time sat on the floor, playing with Mahoney, though she did enjoy testing the hot caramel for the toffee apple crumble.

When Coco and Logan were finally left alone for five minutes, they whispered to each other.

'Have you brought it?' Coco whispered.

'Yeah, the band went to my house today and picked it up. I left it in our Wendy House for them!'

'Okay, well, best we don't let your mum know that bit. It's too expensive to be left about.'

'I know, but there was no other way to keep it a secret.'

'I really want to do this for her. Art has put it in the garage, down the side of the Astra.'

'No problem, ask Art to get it out for you once it's dark. She might notice if I disappear. You got your light?'

'Yeah, the boys said it would look brill if a spotlight came on, and there I'd appear, out of the dark! Joey has a spotlight lamp with a foot peddle, so I can just have it under my foot. It should work a treat.'

'And how is the song?' Coco continued to whisper, checking Pod wasn't near them.

'Wait and see!' smiled Logan.

The party had escalated in size, but they had managed to keep the numbers down. There would be about 30 people coming, though no one planned on staying over. However, they had all been told there was spare space, if anyone wanted to stay. The size had escalated as Coco's old flatmate was coming and bringing his band. They were going to play on a little homemade stage which would only be about five inches high, but as it was their first public appearance, it would be fine. *The greatest little outdoor stage, ever*, Art had thought as he made it.

Joey had asked Coco if he could perform, when she invited him to the party. She had always supported him, when he went from playing drums, to learning to play the guitar. They had gone through some very turbulent times together, moving from house to house, eventually settling into a little terraced cottage. They would regularly spend two or three days at a time, watching punk videos, or listening to all the different recordings Joey had of all of the bands he had played in. He had overcome some life-challenging situations with help and support from many of his friends and family, and was now a successful and happy man. She loved to hear his stories, like when he opened his first music shop in Camden during the late seventies, before it became the trendy tourist attraction it is today. She felt honoured that he was going to play his first gig with his new band, Ice Cream, in the meadow. It was a particularly momentous occasion, as not only was it Joey's first gig on guitar, but his musically brilliant brother would be singing.

Joey and Liam were brothers which was clearly obvious when you looked at them. They both had successful music shops, Joey sold musical instruments and Liam sold records. The brief time they had shared a shop, it was closed more often that it was open, as each would think the other had opened up, when in fact neither had. Eventually they went their separate ways, maintaining that brotherly love even through some typical sibling squabbling remained. Joey had got his nickname from Coco, and only the two of them knew the origins of the name.

Liam had not been in as many bands as his brother, but his skills as a lyricist had never gone unrecognised by Joey. Liam had a period of being completely addicted to computer games, so Joey took it upon himself to encourage Liam to swap the joystick for a pen and start writing again. They'd had many family squabbles over the years. It was seen as a big move by people who knew the two brothers, which was most of their home town, when everyone heard they had formed a band together. This was Joey's idea, as a distraction so Liam might kick his old habits. Joey would insist Liam wrote down everything he felt, both day and night. Liam was also to write if he woke up in the middle of the night to go for a pee. The intense concentration Liam put into his writing, gradually became the thing he thought about the most. Without knowing it, Joey had directed all of his brother's gaming attentions towards a more creative obsession.

'It doesn't matter what the addiction is, everyone has it,' Joey would say, reading through the brilliant words his brother would have recorded in a small notebook, in his neat handwriting. Liam could write lyrics to rival those of Liam Gallagher, who was his hero. He even had the same haircut, and the same sultry looks when singing, taking all of Liam's mannerisms but making them his own. He loved the fact they shared the same name. Coco would often wind Liam up, by saying his stage persona was identical to that of Ian McCulloch of Echo and the Bunnymen fame. Liam would retort with 'Mr Gallagher... not Ian...d'uh!'

The sun was turning the sky a soft peach colour as it set, with pale greens merging into pale blues, with lilacs following. Long, straight, bright orange clouds criss-crossed the sky which gradually dispersed as the high altitude winds blew through them. It was cold and Art could see his breath as he worked. The land around Railway Cottage had become open plan, with the protection of green leaves now becoming mulch on the damp ground. The cottage was surrounded by arable farmland, which had gradually gone from a fresh green, to a golden yellow, and finally to a muddy brown, as their crops grew, ripened, and then became a ploughed field once again. He could never work out why everything seemed so much sharper and clearer in winter, with summer always being hazy and fuzzy. *Different height of the sun in the sky,* he eventually concluded, after looking across the field next to the meadow, with crows circling a clump of trees in the distance. Art had been building the covered stage for the band, and had sunk two long posts into the ground, in the left corner of the meadow. He had held them in place with guide ropes, and stretched a tarpaulin over the top, to provide a sloping roof to protect the little stage and those on it. The back was tied to the meadow's fence, with pallets fitted neatly underneath. Art was not sure if the band would need electric, or if they were going to do it acoustically, but he laid an outdoor extension lead to the stage, just in case.

'Hellooooo Wembley!' he said, pretending to be a famous rock star on a massive stage, using his hammer as a microphone, with just an unimpressed Nicholson as the audience.

Art went to check the bonfire he had prepared. The wood was laid in a pile, raised off the ground to protect the turf beneath. He cut six lines in the grass to form a star shape in the turf, rolling the sods back, from the pointed centre of the circle, to the edge. The rolled turf acted as an edge to the fireplace, and he was satisfied that he would simply roll the turf back, once the fire was over. For the first time in many nights, the sky was clear for a change, and some of the stars were already shining, against the fading light of the day. Everything outside was now ready for the 'thanks-giving', with the exception of some of Coco's jam-jar candle holders, to illuminate the patio, The Brew House and on top of the fence at either end of the gate to the meadow. He walked to the end of the drive and lent over the gate, and looked up and down the lane. In one direction, the navy wave of night was already approaching from the east, enhanced by the tall trees overhanging the roadway. To the west, the last few colours of the day were melting away, and just for one piercing moment, the disappearing sun shone straight into Art's eyes, finding its way between the branches of the trees on the horizon, to strike him like a laser. He shut his eyes, turning away from the blinding light. When he opened his eyes, the sun had set just that much further that it was below the fall of land, and was gone for the day. As his eyes adjusted to the darkness that followed, he marvelled at the beauty in front of him. *People are too busy trying to recreate beauty not to see it all around them,* he thought. The fallow field before him, stretching out into the distance was silhouetted with trees. There was no sound, just rustling leaves as a small animal passed by Art in the undergrowth, and the distant rhythmical rumbling of a train going over the level crossing in town, which quickly faded away. *It seems a shame to cause so much noise here tomorrow night,* he thought, *wonder what all the wildlife will think of it?* Art knew of Joey and Liam from the stories Coco had told him. He liked the guys, they were extrovert, flamboyant and totally individual, and he felt good that he was able to offer them a place to play. He suspected their new band would be a cross between early punk and Beady Eye, but however it sounded, the one thing he knew, was that it would be loud. With no neighbours to upset, the boys would probably be putting it out in the red, pushing their equipment to the max. It should be a great evening, as everyone who was coming knew each other from previous parties. He called for Nicholson, and walked back into the house, locking the door securely.

The following evening, everywhere was ready. People had been told to turn up whenever they wanted, from about five o'clock onwards. Art had put some plastic cups in The Brew House, and lit the barbeque ready to start the potatoes off. He had also lit the fire, which first of all he'd had to build. He had always built fires and lit them immediately, as wildlife would take comfort in a pile of logs, and the thought of burning field mice and hedgehogs alive was not something he wanted to risk. At dusk he started the fire off in the middle of the meadow, in the circular fireplace he had cut into the ground. He left enough room for about ten cars to park down one side, around the edge, with the mini stage in the corner. The candles would be lit around the gate, on the patio and amongst the herb and rock gardens. The gentle breeze would then catch their flames, so shadows danced against themselves.

At lunchtime, Art had decided to take his hamper to William, and having rung him, he set off with Coco. They had never been to William's house, but with the cold weather, he had developed a chest infection, and was staying indoors until he was better. Art had invited him to the party, but as he had declined, Art made the effort to go see him. They drove towards Sleaford, and out onto Lincoln Heath as Coco thought out loud.

'Art, I've been thinking. Pod and I talked about this the other day, but I was wondering, what makes great men great?' Coco asked, flicking the Vs and giving the international hand gesture for 'wanker' as someone pulled out on their car.

'What do you mean?'

'Well, you know, Tesla, Einstein, Pythagoras, Plato... great men of thought and thinking. What makes them great? What sets them apart from shell-suit-wearing-Jeremy-Kyle-wanna-bes? What sets them apart from those who think self-sufficiency is a poor man's answer to survival?'

Just then, *Anarchy in the UK* blasted out, so Coco answered her phone. 'Hello... hi Pod... no worries, yeah, that's fine. The best ones are in boxes wrapped in paper in the garage... yeah, on top of the chest freezer... no, don't charge them. We have an agreement with Drayton, he'll drop manure off in exchange... Okay dude... yeah, you too. See you in a couple of hours tops! Okay, bye!'

'Everything okay?' asked Art.

'Yes, Drayton was passing and had called in on the off chance that we still had some apples. He's going to make toffee apples for the women and their kids at The Lodge.'

'Text Pod, tell her to give him a few of my hampers, they're in The Brew House on the racking.'

'Okay. It was handy finding him. At least we know most of our surplus apples are going to a good cause!' said Coco. Drayton got all of his building supplies off a nationwide company in Boston, which just so happened to be the same place where Art's father was a manager. They were good friends, and once they got onto the subject of Art and his homegrown produce, the connection was made where Railway Cottage would supply The Lodge with surplus fruit and veg, in exchange for building work and manure for the gardens. Although the soil was very fertile, it would not take long for all of the nutrients to be used up, and so Art fertilised the land before every crop was planted.

'So, what makes great men great?' Coco repeated, having sent her text to Pod. 'It must be a brain thing!'

'Yes, I guess it is,' said Art, who sometimes had difficulties with Coco's opinions on things, and would rarely offer an opinion, and instead opt to listen.

'I mean, these guys must be wired up differently, right? The way their minds work differently. Is it like a gift, to have foresight to think outside of the box?

'I don't know? Switch off the television and you won't need a box to think outside of!'

'What?'

'Your great men... I know Pythagoras and Plato didn't have a television, but what I'm saying is... well, they went in their own direction, they asked questions. It's like when you start pulling a thread on a jumper. Firstly, why would you want to unravel the jumper, you know what's going to happen, so why bother? Once you start, you can't stop until the whole jumper is unravelled in a big pile on your lap. Your great men, they asked themselves one small question, and as they thought about it, and researched, they discovered that first pull on the jumper was an enticement to reveal what was hidden!'

'Wow, that's a bit profound for you!' exclaimed Coco, delighted that Art obviously did listen to what she said. 'You do think about what I ramble on about then!' exclaimed Coco, totally taken aback.

'No, not at all, I just overheard you and Pod talking,' he replied, a massive smile on his face, 'I do listen to you, sweetheart, but sometimes I have difficulty in accepting. No, not accepting, more like understanding what you're saying. It's a bit far-fetched sometimes!'

'Sometimes people don't want to hear the truth, because they don't want their illusions destroyed,' Coco quoted. 'Friedrich Nietzsche said that!'

'Is he one of your great men?'

'Yes, I think so. He was German born in the late eighteen hundreds. He knew some philosophical stuff, but he also knew he was a bit before his time, and that he wouldn't be properly understood until long after his death. He was friends with the composer Wagner, but they fell out over the opera *Parsifal*, which Fred thought was too Christian!'

'Another friendship ruined by religion!'

'Um, I know. Bloody bible bashers. I wouldn't mind religion as much, if you knew all of the characters do or did exist. But they preach their bollocks, about make-believe deities. My religion is Tottenham, and my church is White Hart Lane! At least I know they exist, I can physically see them, hear them talk, move and probably fart. Anything that can fart is real... can God fart?' Art was laughing at Coco's outburst, one he had heard many times before, but it was one of the things he always agreed on.

'What do you think makes great men great?'

'They know a secret I guess. They know the meaning of life or which came first, the chicken or the egg! I don't know what it is, but they definitely all knew something the rest of us don't!'

'Yes, maybe!' They were nearly at William's house.

'Maybe they were more connected to the Universe than the rest of us. Maybe they knew that by thinking more, and having the ability to observe and question everything, they became more knowledgeable, which in turn allowed one question to lead to the next, and so on! You know... the Law of Attraction, and all that. Like attracts like, think good thoughts and good things happen. Think negative thoughts and you attract negative things. Einstein said "Everything is energy, and that is it!" I definitely think it's important to think and feel freely, and to be open-minded to everything I see. The one thing that has always stuck with me, Lydon, you know, John Lydon, Godfather of Punk, he once said "The written word is a lie". 1986 I think it was, in his tune *Rise* he did with PiL... It's always stuck with me, because anything written, or said, can be a lie. It's only if I see something, can I honestly say, yes that event happened because I saw it! And I don't mean stuff you see on TV. I mean things for real, in real time.'

'Why Miss Marple, are you saying you don't believe what the TV tells you?'

'What, the FOX-CBN-NBC-CNN-BBC!' laughed Coco.

'Who?'

'The news people! They should all have the same name! I don't know why they all have different names, they should all just be called Propaganda for the People! All the news is governed by the top people, the top nobs in charge of all the banking in the world. They only allow us mere mortals to hear about stuff that makes them look good, or better. Let's face it, if an independent company was able to report the news, it would show how chemtrails are poisoning us, that fluoride in America's water is a means of creating depopulation as it was a World War Two poison and that despite what everyone thinks, The Church is one of the most corrupt companies in the world. EVER!'

'I bet the Godfather of Punk farts!' laughed Art.

'You bet your talking arse he does!' They both could not stop laughing, as they pulled up outside William's house. Coco could always talk about things with Art, but he would never really offer his opinion, unlike the conversations Coco had with Pod. William was putting out fat balls and wild birdseed on his bird table, in front of a downstairs window.

'Hello, hello, hello!' William called out, waving a bag of peanuts at them. Come in, it's too cold...' he coughed, his rasping breath sounding painful.

'You alright Sir?' asked Art, walking over well-manicured lawns, past flowerbeds that were finished for the year. He did not call anyone else Sir, but liked to show William all the respect he could, considering the guy had given him one of the greatest gifts a fisherman would want.

'Yes, yes, it is too cold to be hanging about out here. It's going to be a harsh winter this year. Watch the animals, they will show you!'

'I have noticed that Coco's rabbit has already grown a thick coat, and he spends most of his time indoors,' said Art.

'Watch the birds, Art. The way they feed. Do you feed the wild birds at Railway Cottage?'

'Yes, I have several bird tables, and feeding stations hanging in the orchard. There's a table outside the art studio window, so Coco can watch them while she draws.'

'Good man, watch the birds!' he said quite sternly. 'Now then young lady, how are you?' he asked, turning to Coco. 'You both seem to be in high spirits, judging by the laughter I heard!'

'Hello William, how are you feeling?' Coco asked, holding the old man's hands and kissing him on his cheek.

'Don't get too close, you don't want my old-man-lurgy!'

'If it's good enough for you, William, it's good enough for me!'

'Bless you!' he looked at Coco and then to Art, before looking back at Coco. 'I'm in quarantine in there!' he said, nodding in the direction of the house. 'My tribe insist I keep my germs to myself and they won't visit until I am fully recovered!'

'Bless you right back,' Coco replied, linking her arm through William's, as they walked back to the house. 'Art has something for you!'

They sat in a large farmhouse kitchen, heated with a massive Aga. There was a little battery radio playing, but it was the only modern thing in the kitchen. The kettle sat on the Aga, and a giant old-fashioned juicer sat clamped to the end of the worktop. William poured some tea, and got out some Halloween biscuits he had made for his grandchildren, but because of his chest infection they had not been brought around to see him. The little pumpkins with orange icing and bat shapes with brown icing all sat in a tin on the large oak table, with a tea-stained tea pot brewing the tea.

'This is for you, William!' said Art, handing him his homemade hamper, consisting of homemade apple and honey sauce, orchard jam, basil and tomato sauce, a selection of nuts and some dried chillies. It was beautifully finished, with a sprig of berries on the front, and some straw lining the basket. William did not say anything, taking the gift with a nod. He poured out the teas, all in porcelain mugs with hunting scenes on them. Then he got up to get some milk and whilst his back was turned, Art and Coco looked at each other, in silence shrugging their shoulders, mouthing to each other 'Is he okay?' William had his back to them, getting milk out of a cold pantry, which caused a shiver to go down Coco's back.

'I am fine, you don't have to worry about me.' Art and Coco sat staring at the old man's back, wondering how he knew what they had been thinking. He sat back down at the head of the table, 'It's a really lovely gift, thank you very, very much!' They could see that William had watery eyes, and as he sniffed, he added a cough, trying to disguise his emotions with his illness, 'You are a great man, Art, and there aren't many great men around anymore!'

'We were just talking about great men, it was what we were laughing about,' said Coco, taking a bat biscuit.

'Great men, ay?' William repeated, a soft smile coming to his kind eyes.

'Yes, we were just saying, well I was, Art was just listening, but I was asking, what makes great men great?'

'Who do you mean, which men, Simon Cowell and that pip-squeak Beiber my daughters and grandkids keep talking about, worshipping the ground they walk on?'

'No, ha, the day I call them great would be the day I'd give up living. I meant Einstein, Nietzsche and Tesla!'

'Ah, Einstein, now he *was* a great man. He had honorary doctorates in philosophy, science and medicine, you know, and he was awarded the Nobel Prize in physics in 1921.'

'You see, definitely great, so why did he do what he did, when others don't have the brain power to even remember how to spell his name?' said Coco.

'You know a lot about him. Is he a hero of yours?' Art asked, hugging his mug to warm his hands.

'No, not really, I just thought he had something more about him. He had knowledgeable eyes. You felt comfortable in his presence, and knowing what a genius he was, you kind of felt you had the answers to the universe right at your fingertips, all you had to do was just ask him,' replied William, dunking a pumpkin into his tea.

'William?' asked Coco, looking at Art and then back to William, 'did you meet Albert?'

'Yes, 1955. January I think it was. About four months before he died.'

'Wow, that is *so* cool!' shrieked Coco, causing the big ginger tom cat staring at the birds from the warmth of the kitchen window to spook, and run out of the room, 'Sorry Hedges, or was that Benson? I can never tell them apart!'

'Benson!' William answered. 'Yes, a truly great man. I was only young, about thirteen. He was living in New Jersey by then, but had come to London for an award. He was in the science museum, just walking around. I knew who he was, as my father was interested in him, and we had a few of his books at home. Most of them had his picture on the back. Obviously I was too young to understand any of his work, but just by the expression on my father's face, I knew it was him.'

'That's really amazing. What a moment!'

'Yes, it was, but I didn't realise the significance at the time. He spoke to me like I was an adult, and the one thing I always remember him saying to me, was "the world is a dangerous place to live; not because of the people who are evil, but because of the people who don't do anything about it." Never more fitting than these days, ay?'

After they had chatted about William's meeting with Einstein, they watched all varieties of birds feeding from the treats William had left for them. Finches, tits, blackbirds and thrushes came and dined, and before they had noticed, a good hour had passed.

'So, are you all ready for your festival tonight?' William asked.

'I wouldn't call it a festival, just a few people listening to live music, drinking and dancing!'

'Outdoors?' asked William, knowing the answer.

'Yes, why?'

'Makes it a festival! They all have to start somewhere. Glastonbury still had the cows in the field, the first year that ran. Look at it now!'

'You should register, William, and come with us in 2013. It's a lay year in 2012, to rest the land. You should come, the atmosphere is amazing! The sounds, colours, smells and everyone is always so friendly. It's an amazing experience, though for someone who has met Einstein, maybe not so great.'

'I'll be in my seventies!' he chucked.

'Age is nothing but a number!' said Art, who had been sat quietly watching a robin see off a blackbird. *Such a small bird standing his ground against a bigger bird. Bloody bullying blackbird!* he thought.

'You are right, Art, you are as young as you feel. Having such excellent company that I have found in you two, has seen the years fall away. I feel forty years younger. You two have good spirits, you were meant to be together.'

'I often think that,' said Coco, looking over at Art, who had turned to wink at his girlfriend. Whenever Art smiled, Coco could feel her inners melt. He was such a good-looking man, but in ways she could not pinpoint. When he smiled, she could see into his very soul through his striking grey eyes. Sometimes, when he was angry or tired, they would go a very pale grey, making him look like a fierce 'man of the wilderness', with his long hair that sometimes went curly, and his neatly trimmed facial hair and goatie. 'You watching the birds?'

'Yes, watching the birds!'

'The ones with boobies or feathers?' joked Coco.

'Boobies of course, that one has red breasts!' he joked, winking this time at William.

William noticed the exchange, and smiled. 'How are your drawings coming along, Coco?'

'Really good, thanks. I find it easy for a few days to pass, and I've not picked up my pens. I sometimes wonder if I should be more focused.'

'It is good for you to take a break. You may think your drawings are the most important things to work on, but you mustn't neglect the land, your fruit and veg, the lake. Without them, you might find you don't have the right environment to nurture your inspirations, to do the drawings.'

'Good point, I might write myself a schedule!'

'I wouldn't bother. You will draw until the land needs you, and once you have tended to it, you will find your drawings exactly where you left them!'

'I have had a distraction recently, you might be able to help actually. Have you ever visited Temple Bruer? I had a weird experience there back in spring!'

'Ah, yes. I know it very well. What is the problem with it?'

Coco proceeded to explain about the woman with the shotgun and her Labrador, how she had tried to deter them from looking for the tower. She explained that when she had touched the tower, she had seen the symbols.

'Let me show you around my place. I know Railway Cottage very well, let me show you my farmhouse!' he replied, not bothering to answer Coco's question, 'I've lived here all of my life. The house is five hundred years old, stone built, and has had no extensions or modifications done to it. It is exactly how it was, when it was first built. Come on, I'll show you!'

They walked around the thatched, stone farmhouse. It was an unusual shape for Lincolnshire, as it was very long and low, more like the farmhouses in Somerset or Scotland. William needed to know they were the right people to be shown the farmhouse's secret. They walked from room to room, each very tidy and clean, with tasteful furniture that was neither too old nor too modern. Thick, warm curtains and carpets in rich burgundies and blues kept the place warm, though Coco felt that William probably did not use most of the house, as it was very big for one man.

'I know it is a bit big for just me, but having lived here for so long, and it has been paid off now, I can't see the point of selling it and downgrading,' he said, answering Coco's thought, which stunned her a little. *Coincidence!* she thought.

'Why should you leave? Where are the rules that state once you get older, you have to move into a rabbit hutch?'

'I'd be happy in Mahoney's house,' joked William, who had taken a shine to the big yellow rabbit.

'You're welcome anytime, William, just turn up on our doorstep,' Art said. 'You might be able to show me what I'm doing wrong, as I haven't been able to catch the big fish like we did that weekend.'

'No, you won't get many days like that, son. That was a one-off I guess. Let me get rid of this cold and I will pop by, if that is okay!'

They got to a door in the hall that led down to a cellar. Coco stopped in her tracks, just before William opened the door. He was smiling, as he saw the expression on her face.

'You alright?' asked Art, putting a long, reassuring arm around his girlfriend.

'William, that symbol on the door?'

'Yes?'

'What about it, Coc... oh!' Art exclaimed, once he had realised what Coco was looking at, and why William was smiling. The cellar door had a small piece of marquetry inlayed into the wood. Rather than sticking a wood veneer design onto the door, the symbol had been cut out of the surface and a thin slice of different coloured wood had been laid into the shallow indentation. A skilled craft to perfect, this example was quite clearly very old, and had been expertly done. The symbol was of a tower, and a pyramid, with the sun in-between the two, about six inches in size.

'Recognise it?' asked William.

'Yes!' Art and Coco replied together.

'That is my symbol!' said Coco, looking confused and worried. 'Why is it here?'

'Let me show you,' said William, with a youthful glint in his eye. 'You two will be warm enough, but I just need to get a coat to keep the cold off my chest!'

They went down some stone steps to the cellar, which had a low ceiling. It was brightly lit, with four or five bulbs on cords hung along the length of the room. It was the same size as the main building, with a coal bunker at one end, where coal would have been tipped from the drive into the cellar to be used at a later date. As the house was still fired by coal and wood, the coal shoot was totally full, prepared for winter. They walked along the flagstone floor, passing old sets of drawers and wardrobes used as storage and under a rack hanging from the ceiling filled with William's fishing rods. When they got to the end, William turned right, and stepped behind a wooden rowing boat. It was stood on its end, about a foot away from the wall. William stepped behind it, and disappeared. Art and Coco looked at each other, rooted to the spot.

'Come on kids. I've wanted to show someone this for years.'

Coco stepped forward and Art followed her behind the boat. They found themselves in a brick corridor, and William was shining a torch into the distance.

'Come on. It's quite dry and clean down here, you will be spider-free, I promise you Coco!'

Chapter Eighteen

November 2011, Manchester

Dylan loved Manchester. The music scene was fantastic and the football was pretty good provided you liked United or City. Good luck if you supported Liverpool or Everton, it was probably better to keep it to yourself. He would love to have a few days in the city every now and again, even if it was to just to see a few local bands. If he was lucky, there would be a derby game, when the whole city passionately got involved. A tense, nervous time for the supporters, but a brilliant weekend for the neutrals.

With all the work he had been taking on, and the stress it was starting to cause, Dylan was having trouble sleeping at night. Unlike the other members of the MBHK he was a single man, and wondered if he should find himself someone to be with. It was a really difficult decision to make. Selfishly, he did not want to be alone when the shit hit the fan, but likewise, was it really fair to hook up with someone, just so he had close company during and after the event? Whilst his research took up most of his time, he wondered how he might keep someone happy, with all the secret meetings he had to attend. It would certainly look suspicious. The other guys were alright, as they already had someone who had been with them since the beginning. Their partners understood that the land they had been given to develop was all for a 'bigger plan', and so the women tolerated it. But someone new would end up asking questions, cause rows and just generally upset the smooth running of his life.

He was in Manchester for a special trip, and had left his new pet rabbit with a friend. It had followed him all the way back to the farmhouse from the Stone Circle. Dylan had picked up the little thing, and it had sat on his shoulders some of the way. It followed Dylan around the farm for the duration of his stay, and he had no choice but to take it back to

London, as it had jumped unseen into the car whilst he had been saying his goodbyes. It showed itself to Dylan after about an hour of the journey, and so he kept it. He was worried how it might be whilst he was away, but his friend had texted to say it was quiet and happy to sit and watch TV and eat carrot sticks.

Although he would probably visit a few of his favourite clubs and venues, he did have a specific meeting to attend. That was to be held in some railway arches. Railway arches with a difference. It was a club he liked and as it was late afternoon it would be closed, the bar staff would be cleaning up, and one of the DJs might be running through one of his sets. 'R Cheers' was quite exclusive, not because it was fancy or selective, but purely because it was hard to find, and was off the usual beaten track for drunken clubbers. Walking past other lock-ups housed under the railway viaduct, which were mainly secondhand furniture stores and car body shops, he started to wonder if he had passed it. Just before he was about to turn around, he recognised the next wooden double door. It was hung straight and snugly in its frame, unlike the others which were hanging off their hinges. Above the door was a small chrome 'R', illuminated from behind by a purple light. He tried the doors and found the one on the right-hand side swung open smoothly. He walked past a ticket booth, and down a few steps. The arched roof and walls were all made from the brick of the railway bridge, highly varnished, separated by rows of purple spotlights mounted on the walls, pointing in various directions onto the curved ceiling. He walked along the corridor, past a cloakroom, and down four more steps. It was strange being here in the daytime. Normally there would be the latest electro house blasting out of speakers that could make your ears bleed. The dance floor would be full of people dancing quicker and quicker, as the beat sped up and got higher pitched, until it was so fast and high pitched the music would become one noise, with the audience probably taking a break, hands in the air, waiting... and then a massive beat would drop and the house would go crazy.

The decks were silent, with just a radio on in a backroom somewhere. At the bottom of the stairs, the room opened to include the next two neighbouring arches on either side, with the bar running the full length of the back wall. Brick pillars supported the high ceilings where walls had been removed, and each of the vaulted ceilings had the same purple spotlights complimenting the feminine curves of the building. It was always so deceptive coming here, as although the club was built across five arches, the other fronts were actually false, with poorly hung doors hiding secure brick walls. Along the end wall opposite the DJ booth stationary Waltzer cars had been used as seating, with a circular round table fixed into the middle. The Waltzer cars each had silver and mirrored designs painted on them, with purple neon lights running around the underneath and purple padded velvet seats. Sat at the end of the bar, was his meeting partner. He walked towards him, lit by purple spotlights hidden under the rim of the four-foot wide mahogany bar.

'Ah, Dylan, good to see you fella, how goes it?'

'Yeah, good man! All good,' he lied, sharing a personal handshake perfected over the years.

'D'ya wanna drink? Beer, tea, coke... fizzy not snorty!'

'A cup of tea, please mate, would be great. It's bloody cold out there!' replied Dylan, sitting on a wooden stool next to his friend, 'no sugar please dude, but get ya jaffa cakes out!'

They spent fifteen minutes catching up, discussing the newest names on the band scene in Manchester. Dylan dropped a few names he had heard on the London scene, and after the pleasantries they got down to business.

'I've got you a guy lined up. He's in London, so it should be easy to meet him if you need to. His name is Jeff Keiffson. Dutch. Very rich. He can get you one hundred thousand but it's going to cost you big time. He's going to get them in from Jamaica, as that's where his most reliable contact is for dealing with these amounts.'

'I don't mind where they're from, so long as they're the variety we talked about.'

'Yes, this guy is shit hot mate, as is his contact.'

'How much we talking?'

'Quarter mill!'

'Okay, half and half?'

'No, seventy-five per cent up front and twenty-five per cent on delivery.'

Dylan whistled, and did some quick sums in his head. He had a little saved, and could possible ask the MBHK for a few grand but the rest would have to come from the bank. *Fuck it. What do I care? I'll get the lot off the bank. It's not as though I will have to pay it back. They've been butt-fucking me for years, it's about time I did it back.*

'Okay, that's okay!' Dylan replied.

'You sure? This is not a guy to piss off! He has an excellent reputation because he stands for no shit!'

'No mate, it's well cool. I can do that no worries. I just need to organise the funds. What we talking? A week?'

'Not from Jamaica, dude. They don't come directly here. It will take about a month, give or take a day or two.'

'Wow, a month,' said Dylan, again doing some figures in his head. 'This guy isn't going to let me down is he? I haven't got time to waste starting all over again in a month's time if he fails me. We've been on this a month already.'

'Have I ever let you down, man?'

'No dude, you haven't. Okay, it's the best we've got so far, so let's do it. Cheers Manni, you are a star. Ya going to drop a bass line, what's the latest thing you're spinning?'

'Rinsing mate, rinsing!' Manni replied, doing fast, circular movements like a record going around.

'Alright, are they good?'

'Who?' replied Manni.

'Rin Singh!'

'You fucking southern monkey, "rinsing" is the term for a track a DJ plays all the time!' he explained, doing the circular motion with his finger again. 'Rinsing! Stick to your stick and stings, dude, leave the discs to the pros. How is Ed anyway?'

'I've not seen Ed in years! Why do you ask?' Dylan said, putting his guard straight up. The only recent connection Dylan had with Ed was through the MBHK'

'Oh, I must have got the wrong person. I thought I saw you in London back in May. Richmond underground?'

'Oh yeah, I forgot about that time. I bumped into him in China Town, and we were just going round to a friend of mine who'd built a new guitar. I dragged Ed along!' lied Dylan again. When he'd realised that Manni had spotted him, he knew he was going to have to bluff his way out of it, but some of the training they had at the MBHK covered how best to tackle a confrontation if they had to justify being seen going to or from a meeting. They had been repeatedly told to deny it as far as you could, but if at any point it sounded like they had definitely been seen, they were to admit it as best they could, making sure not to mention or involve anybody else in the cover-up fib. Manni put on the latest electro house tune, which gradually escalated to an ear-piercing high pitch, paused, and then dropped the heaviest reverberating bass line Dylan had ever heard. Stood dead-central in the empty club, the sound was much louder, as there was nothing for the acoustics to be absorbed by. When the bass dropped, Dylan could 'see' the beat, as the wooden floor absorbed the sound from the speakers, Dylan involuntarily moved with it. When the tune had finished, he actually had a faint buzzing in his ears.

'I thought clubs only went to one hundred and ten decibels. That was louder than a jet engine. My heart *had* to beat in time with it, as the force was so great, it couldn't beat against the sound. I could see the beat!'

'Rins...ing!' Manni shouted, leaping over the decks and dropping down to the floor. 'I'll give you Mr Keiffson's mobile. Ring him ASAP, arrange to give him the seventy-five per cent, and let me know how you get on with him!'

'Cheers Manni, love the new decor of the club by the way.'

'Glad you like it. I got a woman to do it. I think it has a softer, more lady friendly look.'

'Yeah, definitely. The Waltzers are ace. Who came up with the name R Cheers... Arches... it's brilliant!' They were both at the front door, and shook hands heartily.

'That would be telling. My magic market researcher came up with it, the whole look, after smoking shit loads of weed all night, and drinking home brewed cider!'

'Pot of thought!' punned Dylan, waving over his shoulder as he walked away, into the cold, crisp evening.

Chapter Nineteen

Molay Barn, Lincolnshire

Coco and Art followed William into the brick corridor. It was not as cold as they thought it might be, and was surprisingly dry and dust-free.

'Any scary movie you watch, you *scream* at the TV not to go into the dark, underground tunnel. What are we doing?' Coco whispered, as they went behind the upright boat.

'Come along, I can't wait to show you this!' called William's voice, with an echo from the arched, long corridor.

'How does he do that?' asked Coco, whispering to Art as she grabbed a bit of his fleece for security, 'know what we say when he's out of earshot?'

'I've got really good hearing, my dear, plus I raised two monstrous daughters, so I learnt to listen out for things. I guess I still have that touch,' he chuckled to himself as he shuffled along, with a big powerful torch in his hand.

They walked along the corridor for a few hundred feet, until they came to a small room, with the corridor continuing in the direction they were walking. There were two chairs, a little table, and an extension lead hanging from the ceiling in the corner. The chairs were very old, made from carved wood. The intricate design was of Celtic knot-work, but in the very centre of the design, on the headrest, was a clockwise rotating swastika. The chairs were beautiful, made from a deep red cherry wood, with tapestry cushion pads.

'Oh. My. God!' said Art, kneeling down to look at the carvings on the chairs. 'These are beautiful, William, they are simply... beautiful.' He touched the carving with his fingertips, feeling the grain of the wood, and the shapes that had been worked. The finish was smooth, eroded away over generations of time. 'Thank you for showing us them, they really are amazing. How long have you had them?'

'What, those old things? Oh, I don't know. They have been here as long as I can remember. Come on, let me show you my surprise. Coco, you will be particularly interested in this!' said William, dismissing Art's wonderment regarding the chairs, waiting for his friends to follow him on down the corridor.

'These chairs are fabulous. Why don't you put them in the house, William?' asked Coco.

'I thought about it, but to be honest, I just cannot be bothered with all the commotion that would go with it!'

'Why, whose are they?'

'Oh, they are mine, always have been!'

'Shine your torch on them please, William, I would like to look at them closely. The swastika on the headrest is so beautifully carved, with all the knot-work intertwined with its arms. It is one of the oldest symbols known to man, with cosmic symbolism. Many people get confused with the swastika adopted by The Third Reich. Their one is always anticlockwise, but people get easily confused.'

'Yes, yes. Come come,' said William impatiently, 'you can look at them another time, come come!' he hurried off continuing down the corridor, with the only light they had leading him forward.

'Oh, I thought the chairs were what you were showing us?'

'No, no, no... just wait and see. We need to get a trot on though, it is a bit of a walk. Have you time?'

The second half of the corridor was as dry and surprisingly cobweb-free as the first half. The floor was compacted flat earth, with a metal grill running down the entire centre. It was not apparent if its smoothness was due to many trampling feet, or because it had been constructed that way. Art and Coco had no choice but to follow him, or to be left in the dark alone. As they walked, they talked.

'What is this tunnel, William?' asked Art, taking up the rear with Coco in-between the two men as they walked in single file. 'Those chairs are amazing. This is all very surreal. Are you going to tell us where we're going?'

'What was that room used for?' asked Coco, not letting William answer the last few questions that Art had asked.

'All will be clear, it is only about half a mile, ten minutes or so!' replied William, picking up the pace a little. 'It will be well worth it, I promise. I just don't want to make you late for your festival!'

Coco chuckled to herself. It was true what William had said, that it was like a mini festival. She looked at her phone. She had no signal but looking at the clock she noticed there was still plenty of time. Pod and Logan were at home, dealing with Drayton and anyone else who turned up. There were still a few hours before any of their friends were due. *I wonder what William is going to show us? I can't even work out which direction we are going in. I wonder what that room was used for, and the chairs, they were beautiful* she thought.

'We are travelling towards the east,' said William, as if he had read Coco's thoughts again. 'I will tell you a story, but you have to promise me that you will keep it to yourselves. I consider us friends, you both have high morals and principles that I value, and so I would like you to share a part of my life I have not shared with anyone for fifty years.'

'AH!' squealed Coco, as William had stopped and turned round. He had shone the torch under his chin, so that this face became distorted and quite daunting, with his sunken eyes and shallow cheeks shadowed by the torch.

'Sorry my dear, I could not resist,' he laughed as Art joined in. Coco gave a half-hearted chuckle and it wasn't until Art had recognised that she had not been impressed with William's antics, that he put his strong arm around her. 'Please promise that you will not tell anyone of what I am about to show you? It is very important. Please?' he asked sincerely.

'Of course, you have our word!' said Art, as Coco nodded.

William turned around and carried on down the corridor. They passed through two more rooms, exactly like the first, but there were no more elaborate chairs, just empty rooms with an extension lead hanging in the corner and the metal grill running down the centre of the tunnel.

'As I told you, in the sixties I worked with Tarquin. Tarquin Philbert. When the green came off the boats at Boston, it was brought here, and stored. I had shown Tarquin this tunnel when he stayed with me that summer, and it was the perfect place to store anything you did not want found. Nobody knows about this, except of course Tarquin and my parents, who are both dead. It had remained a secret as I have been very choosy over whom I showed it to. The reason is that if this became public, the area would become flooded with tourists, sightseers and conspiracy theorists. To be honest, I am too old, and do not need all the crap that would go with it. I love the peace of my remote home. It is how it has always been.' They had been walking for a few minutes, and the corridor had not changed in appearance, suggesting it had been constructed by the same person or people. 'Do you know about weed, marijuana, cannabis, or whatever you like to call it?'

'Yes, I know a bit,' replied Coco walking behind William and in front of Art.

'Well, going back to the start, the use of hemp has been going on for five thousand years. It was one of the fundamental traditional herbs. As for the weed, no one has ever died from smoking it. In fact, you would need to smoke fifteen thousand pounds of it, in fifteen minutes to overdose. That would be a six-foot spliff the size of this corridor, so don't go trying to do it, it's impossible!' they all laughed. 'Moving forward to the American Colonial times, when it was *compulsory* to grow it. In 1906 the first restrictions were enforced, in the District of Columbia, and by 1911 it was the same in Jamaica.'

'How do you know all of this?' asked Art.

'Tarquin told me most of it, and I did a bit of research in the medical and horticultural journals at Oxford. It was the best place in the world, so much information, you just had to know where to look for it. Anyhow, two key men in America, Chester Rochester II and the Klifterson family both saw the advantages of using hemp in the building and paper industries. Rochester had wood mills, which was used to make paper pulp, and the Kliftersons had just invented a hideous man-made fibre. Funded by these men, the government made it illegal to grow hemp anymore.'

'I have always found it opens your mind, allows you to visualise things differently, and it is the single contribution to the effect I get with my drawings. I have an amazing imagination when I eat green brownies!' said Coco.

'Well, the Chinese, Shaman, Hopi and Sufi have all been fans of it, even William Shakespeare! They found pipes in his garden that had traces of THC in them!'

'I always said he didn't write all that stuff himself, he wasn't educated enough. He wouldn't even know what most of the words he was supposed to have written meant. That explains it all, if he was a stoner!' joked Art.

'Sonnet 76 "noted weed" and sonnet 27 "journey in my mind" are both references to weed!' continued William. 'And you could add Lewis Carole too! Who could possibly come up with Narnia and Alice in Wonderland without a little "opening of the mind" shall we say?'

'What about Harry Potter? Rowling said she sat in coffee shops writing the books as she was too poor to heat the house, so worked in a "coffee shop"…wonder *what* sort of coffee it was? Dutch perhaps?'

'No, not Rowling! Not buying that! Well, there's no scientific proof on the story writers, but yes, it would make perfect sense. Today, there are many non-profit making organisations and some political parties trying to get it legalised.'

'I have researched this bit. Cannabis oil has been proven to cure all sorts of illnesses, whilst cheaper than pharmaceutical drugs and with better results.'

'It has so many great uses, as an analgesic, a cure for gastrointestinal illnesses, induces hunger in chemotherapy and Aids patients and even for Glaucoma. It's the THC, or... now, let me see if I can remember it! THC stands for Tetr... Tetra... got it, Tetrahydrocannabinol,' he quickly recited the long word, laughing.

'I could never remember that!' laughed Coco.

'Well, here is the crunch. It is still illegal because the pharmaceutical industry would lose out on too much money. All those grants and charity money they get for the research into various diseases would be lost. But it is just crazy, if only we could cultivate cannabis and hemp together, it would increase the quality of so many lives and there's the trees and atmosphere that would benefit! It is fast growing and would stop the forestry depletion worldwide!'

'So the woodmen are probably against hemp growth too. They would also lose jobs and money!' added Art.

'Indeed, but just imagine, no work and lots and lots of unlimited weed! Paradise, right?'

'William,' said Coco, with a fake indignant voice, 'What a marvellous idea!'

'Right, we are here,' he replied, as they came to a dead end.

'This is it?'

'Not quite. One minute, let me check the way is clear!' William said, standing on a brick next to the blank wall. He reached into the corner of the corridor and found a round, wooden handle, which he pushed, and then turned. A locking mechanism echoed around the confined space accompanied by a sudden breath of cold fresh air. Stepping off the brick, he pushed it to one side with his foot, and prised the newly made door open with his fingers. 'I can't open this, Art, could you help please?'

Art opened the door, which was a lot lighter than he thought it would be. It was made of thin wooden panels, which had a cement surface, decorated to look like the rest of the corridor. As he swung it open, the dry atmosphere was replaced by a sharp, cold gust of air. The fresh air was damp, and smelt earthy. On the other side of the door, were a few very steep, high steps. At the top, just above head height, daylight shone through the bottom edge of the wall. William climbed the stairs with difficulty, but once at the top, he was stood in a very narrow passageway, big enough for about ten people, which branched off to his left and right. He peered through a round hole he had opened, by removing a small piece of stone carving. William grabbed a metal bar, secured into the base of the wall, and pulled.

'We have to be very quiet, in case there is someone on the outside. I have checked inside, and it is empty. Art, I don't have the strength to pull the bar, could you help please?'

Art pulled the bar and the whole wall section pivoted on a central axis, until it rested in a horizontal position, causing Art to step to one side, to allow for its length to swing half into the passageway. They crouched down and silently walked into a square, stone room.

'Oh, my... Fuck... Fuck!' said Coco, in a loud, excited whisper. 'FUCK!'

'Shhh!' said William, putting a finger up to his lips, as he went to the door and peered again, through a gap between the door and its ill-fitting frame. Art and Coco stood in the middle of the room, turning round taking in all the detail of the carved stone and sheer height of the room.

Chapter Twenty

November 2011, Lincolnshire

Coco and Art got back to the cottage at four, just as it was getting dark. Art got potatoes ready to put in his barbeque oven, and checked the fire he'd lit when he'd got home. Coco had gone into the house, to find Pod and Logan, taking with her three glasses of raspberry cider, Coco's favourite of the home brew flavours. Mahoney was asleep under the drawing board, and Nicholson was out with Art. The house was really warm and snug, as the cooker had been on for most of the afternoon. They caught up on the day's events whilst drinking the cold cider, Coco told Pod about William, omitting to mention the corridor, as requested and Pod explained how Drayton had called by and taken the rest of the apples. The first guests started to arrive just after six.

Joey and Liam turned up, with two other friends who were the bassist and drummer with Ice Cream, and unpacked their instruments on the little stage. It was just the right size for a four-piece. Once they had set up a few flashing lights, the homemade marquee looked quite special. Art had put six straw bales in front of the stage, so people had somewhere to sit throughout the evening. Jam-jar candle holders decorated the ground at the edge of the stage, and more candles had been sat on the top of the fence and in the stage's corners. Cars were parked on the opposite edge of the meadow, and the fire in the centre almost made the event look like a tribal gathering. By nearly eight o'clock, everyone had arrived. There was some serious drinking done, and everyone enjoyed the hot food on perfect jacket potatoes. The meal was that successful, everything got eaten, though enough room was left for the strong, homemade cider and apple toffee crumble.

Coco had managed to get a bit of time with Art, when he had walked down to the lake for some time to himself. They sat on the 'trunk bench' and chatted about their afternoon. William's corridor had run to the tower at Temple Bruer. They had walked from Molay Barn, near the village of Wellingore, underground to the tower. It had turned out that one of the walls of the tower had a double layer, with a cavity in-between. It had never been noticed, and presumably it was considered that the walls were just really thick. The stairs they had climbed had entered the wall cavity, and the pivoting door had been part of the internal wall of the tower. Once this was swung back in place, there was no visible join as it fit against a pair of stone carved pillars. Nobody knew of the passageway except for William, his parents and Tarquin. It ran in the opposite direction from William's house, to the village of Wellingore, and was the reason that the farmhouse had been built, as it was halfway from Temple Bruer to Wellingore. Art and Coco had not made the connection, as the village stood on the other side of a wood, and the roadway went in a different direction. The corridor had been built as the crow flies, from the tower to the village.

They had spent twenty minutes in silence marvelling at the detailed carved stone, studying some of the graffiti, trying to work out if it was old or recent, and craning their necks so they could look up into the rafters of the roof, three storeys up. The tower had smelt damp and cold, though there were no signs of a leaking roof. Coco had been beside herself, and could barely contain her excitement until they were back in the corridor. William had swung the door back into place, replaced the stone carved rose 'bung' and secured the corridor door by standing on the brick once again. Art used his weight to hold the door shut, whilst William twisted then pulled the handle, securing the secret once again. All the way back to William's house, Coco had talked nonstop. It was one of the greatest things she had ever experienced. She did not even stop to marvel at the chairs, as they were now insignificant compared to the tower.

William had explained that the marquetry symbol on the door to his cellar had always been there, but nobody had really mentioned it or taken much notice of it. He had researched the Knights and learnt that the symbol had cropped up as a tiny detailed engraving on some stones that had been found in Somerset and in different parts of the world at ancient sites. He knew the symbol on the door had some significance. It had taken him two years to find the entrance to the tunnel. He had excitedly gone to tell his parents, but they were unimpressed. Of course they had known about the tunnel as they were the ones who put the boat across the entrance in their cellar. William had proceeded to throw a fit, explaining he had been looking for it for two years. His parents had replied, 'If you don't ask, you don't get!' It was an important lesson for

William to learn, especially as he was still in his late teens. They made him sit at the kitchen table and made him promise not to show anyone. They had said that if anyone found out, they would lose their home, and even end up in jail. William had not believed them about the jail bit, but was warned off enough by his liberal parents (who never lied to him) to not tell anyone. He had felt comfortable enough to tell Tarquin, as after all, who had more secrets on who?

Coco had asked William if he had walked the other way along the corridor, towards the village. He replied that he had with Tarquin, but it had been quite creepy. It was only once he'd told his parents about what he had found that he realised what a gold mine he lived above. The obvious destination in the other direction was Wellingore, but when he got to that end of the corridor, there was just a blank wall, and despite spending hours searching, he'd never managed to find a handle or lever. Wellingore was set on the Old Viking Way, which ran through Lincolnshire from the Humber to Oakham. More importantly, it ran past Lincoln Cathedral and Byard Leap, both important Templar locations. William had deduced that there had probably been another Templar house in the village, which had since been destroyed, or the exit had been built over.

The most important thing William told Coco and Art was that the symbol Coco had seen when she had touched the tower was a symbol the Templars had used, as a code to show where an underground stream had run. William had access to some sensitive papers through his Oxford University Library account. They used the symbol so other Knights might recognise the all-important pure water that ran in springs underground, and only surfaced in a few locations. William went on to explain how the Knights had found a papyrus in Israel, showing where the stream ran. The importance of the find was significant, as the water was so pure and had great powers because of its purity. Crops would flourish, and animals were healthy with great stamina. On finding the papyrus the Knights spread all over Europe looking for the places where the spring surfaced, creating preceptories wherever they settled. Temple Bruer was one of their main locations. Whilst researching, William had wondered why the tower was still standing, and the rest of the houses and church had not survived. It was one of the questions that was still unanswered.

Chapter Twenty-one

The Stables Tavern, Camden, London

Rev was sat in a busy pub just off Camden High Street, the alternative clothing capital of London. It was mid week, so most of the people browsing in the shop windows were tourists. The weekends were always packed, with everyone and his mother visiting the locks, trendy bars and unusual clothes shops. Rev had been once before at the weekend, and he decided he preferred it when it was less busy. It was early evening and the bar was starting to fill up with evening drinkers, but there were still some shoppers finishing their teas after a long day of purchasing. He was extremely uncomfortable in the pub, as he was still struggling with his addiction. He could go a few weeks without a drink, but then he would have a spell of restlessness, nightmarish dreams, and just general crappiness. He would lay in bed thinking about how he had made such a wonderful life for himself with his girlfriend, their house and the fact he would have been a father. He would feel the burning anger slowly build inside him, until he wanted to run... run away as fast as he could to leave the memories behind. His only option was to run to the local and down just one shot, to calm his nerves but he would struggle to remind himself that he could handle 'just one'. It never worked out that way. Friends would reluctantly buy him a drink, as he manipulated them into thinking he was sober, and it was just a 'social tipple' before he went home. He would also lie to people, saying his rehabilitation was going really well. He would then leave the pub before he got too drunk, and would down a bottle of vodka at home if John was out. Sometimes when things got really bad, he would end up at the old squat. He would wake up cold and aching in the early hours of the morning, slumped on the stinking, filthy mustard coloured carpet, where it could take him up to ten minutes to try and work out if he had dreamt his attic flat, or if indeed this stinking hell hole on the seventh floor was still really his home. When John would ask him where he had been, he would lie again, saying he was with a friend playing snooker or cards.

This vicious circle would continue, as the following morning he would have huge bouts of remorse and guilt, knowing he had let himself down, John down and to an extent, his ex-girlfriend. He would sob uncontrollably when he thought about his amazing former girlfriend, thinking how she would be so upset with the state he had got himself into. He hated himself for lying to John, who had found the willpower to be three months clean. After a binge on the drink, he would be so disgusted with himself that he could control his anger for a few days or weeks, until his addiction reared its ugly head again. If he was kept busy, and John was around, it was much easier. He just did not have it in him to admit he still had a serious problem. He knew John would understand, probably forgive him for lying about the drinking and squatting, and more importantly John would offer him support and encouragement. He just needed to find the time and place to talk to John. The problem was, Rev was very good at hiding his feelings. There had been many times he had just wanted to scream 'HELP ME!', but it was always at a time when John was not around. Most often as not, it would be as he staggered home to the attic flat, dirty, smelly with rank breath and the feeling he had let himself down... again.

The situation he found himself in, sat in the upstairs room of The Stables Tavern was quite surreal. It was an important meeting, and so he had to remain sober. He also had to get the train back to Nottingham that night, as he did not have the funds to spend a night in a London hotel, and he did not fancy negotiating the underground pissed. Looking out of the window, he saw across the road the old stable blocks, where hundreds of horses used to be housed in a three-storey building, with ramps to the upper and lower levels. There were even some traders still wheeling their boxes on sack barrows to illegally parked vans. The road was busy in both directions. Taxis and buses crawled through the cold London night with the odd brave cyclist weaving through the traffic, or a motorbike streaking down the middle of the road. This end of Camden led into Chalk Farm which was a sought after area, unlike the Mornington Crescent end, around Kings Cross and Euston stations. The specialist shops with their colourful frontages, many with enlarged versions of their wares hung on the buildings, lay between the two ends of Camden High Street.

He had a soda water with lime, but had considered a hot chocolate, as it was cold outside. He opted for the lime drink, so people might think it was vodka, rather than Grandma's Horlicks. The room he was sat in had dark grey painted walls, and black painted wooden floor boards. There were sofas, mismatched chairs and a little stage at one end, situated between two double doors that led out to the closed sun terrace. On the stage was the biggest sofa he had ever seen, with a gold and black throw over it. A low wooden coffee table was in front of it but there was not much room for anything else on the stage. All of the furniture had throws and cushions on them, and different types of lamps on the tables. This was quite clearly a pub where people came to just sit and talk, or read a newspaper whilst they relaxed, not like the dumps he had frequented in Nottingham in the past. The Victorian building, with its high ceilings and etched glass windows seemed mismatched with the bohemian style interior.

A well-groomed man appeared at the top of the stairs, and walked towards Rev. The man's features changed as he walked through the room, with the lamplight casting various degrees of shadow. Rev could not make out if the man looked like pure evil, or Father Christmas's good-list checker. He was dressed in an expensive, well-fitting suit made out of a dark grey silk fabric which was collarless and had two rows of buttons down the front. The suit was complimented by a black shirt, with a steel blue tie. He had a mobile in one hand and carried a drink that looked similar to his own in the other. For some reason, this was not how Rev had imagined his boss to look.

'Mr Cheer?' he said, in a calm voice.

'Mr R Cheer!' Rev replied. It was the code by which they were to introduce themselves.

'Thank you for meeting with me here. It is as much time as I could spare to see you, so I am sorry you have had to travel so far. I shall give you the money for your travel before I leave.'

'Thanks... thank you... Sir,' Rev replied, not sure how he should address Mr Keiffson.

'I shall have to be very quick, as I could not find anywhere to park, and they just love to lift a Porsche around here. Bloody councils!' Jeff Keiffson exclaimed, with the hint of a Scandinavian accent, taking a sip of his drink. Rev was sat in the corner, looking over the room, and so Mr Keiffson sat beside him, so that they had a side to the table each. 'I learnt a long time ago, never to sit in a pub with your back to the room. You never know who might sneak up behind you. Now, how is the job? Are you happy with everything?'

'Umm, yes. Thanks. Everything is fine. You're going to fire me, aren't you?' replied Rev, hunching his shoulders over, and looking down at the table as he played with a frayed beer mat. He knew there was a reason he was asked to come to London. He'd be sacked and then so that he did not 'grass' on the business, he was going to be bumped off. *Fuck, John's never around when I need him!*

'No. I am not going to fire you Mr Rev. Please listen. You know what my business is, and I appreciate it that you just get on with the job. My driver, who I trust with my life, tells me you are consistent, reliable and have performed impeccably. In the line of business I do, I have to be very selective and cautious over who I have work for me. My business is reliant on its reputation, and my reputation is only as good as the people I rely on. I have other people running the same operation in various parts of the country, but I have chosen you for a special job that is very important to me. It's similar to what you've been doing, but it's one collection and one delivery. I'll pay you one thousand pounds to do it. You can still do the regular runs too, if you wish. Are you interested in my proposition?'

Rev sat there not believing his luck. It had been years since anyone had complimented him, excluding John, and so he was slightly shell-shocked and lost for words. He always seemed to mess things up because of his drinking. Why should this job be any different? It would just be a repeat of the countless other opportunities he had squandered. The long pause caused Mr Keiffson some concern.

'Mr Rev, please do not feel obliged to do this for me, I shall think no less of you. You have only been working for me two months.'

'No, Sir, it's not that,' Rev made a lightning decision, thinking the worse thing that could happen was that he would lose his job and would have to hitch home. He sat up straight and replied, 'Sir, I have a...' the words would not come easily. 'Sir...'

'Mr Rev, please forgive me, but my time is limited. Please, tell me what is wrong.'

'Mr Keiffson, I have a condition I sometimes find hard to control. I am worried with that sort of money, I would end up in a dark place again. I would love to do the job for you, but the money would just get squandered.'

'I see.' He got up and downed his drink. 'I must go before they tow my car again. If you would like a lift to Euston, I pass it on the way back to Chelsea. But I must go, either with or without you. I would rather you came with me, but the choice is yours.'

Fifteen minutes later they were heading for Euston station in the slow traffic. Sat in the cockpit of the Porsche, Rev suddenly felt very important. It had just struck him that this successful businessman liked the way he worked. Rev did not have the nerve to explain the reason he was good at his job, was because he just couldn't give a rat's arse about life anymore, and actually really did not give a shit if he got caught with five hundred grand's worth of super strength Mary Jane. The worse case scenario was that he would end up in prison for a billion years, which was no different to the life he was leading now. That was just like a prison. He was trapped, lived in a windowless cell, and had an unstable cellmate. He had a sudden thought, which he felt he should think through before he detailed it, but he had been put on the spot. Mr Keiffson had cut him short thankfully, with having to get the car, which had been a welcome distraction, giving him the time to analyse his plan.

'Please continue. You said about a condition. I hope it does not endanger my driver, van or imports?' he asked, somewhat sternly. Rev made a mental note not to piss this guy off, as he could imagine underneath this calm polite exterior, he was one hard nasty bastard. 'If it is cocaine or heroin I can help you maybe, but it would only be a loan.'

Rev knew what he should say, and how. 'Mr Keiffson, my name is Mr Rev... and I am an alcoholic!'

An hour later, Rev was on the train approaching Nottingham, and he opened a can of pop and some crisps he had bought at the station. He was smiling. His smile was on his face and in his heart, though his soul was still the dark, cold place it had been since this girlfriend had died. Today, Jess would have been happy for him. She might even have been proud of him. Today had been a good day.

The Attic Flat, Nottingham

John had just got back to the flat after another of his Narcotics Anonymous meetings. He was buzzing, really happy, which he had not felt in a long time. Not only had he been awarded an NA keyring that was handed out when people in recovery reached a milestone, but he had been the most successful with the plant. John already had his orange keyring for 30 days achieved, the green for 60 days, and had just been given his red keyring, signifying he had been clean for 90 days. It was a major achievement for him, and he had jokingly said that the group should all go out for a beer. This was laughed at by his fellow members, but frowned upon by the group counsellor. It had taken him a while to explain he had only been joking, but a short while later, he was jubilant again, as his plant had grown the most out of all of the others. The man who was responsible for organising the plants, had been particularly impressed with the whole group as all of the plants had flourished, growing thick waxy leaves filled with healing sap. He had used aloe vera before with NA groups, but none had grown like these ones. He could not decide if this group were better at growing plants than any other group, or was it a healthier bunch of plants? John's plant was the first to grow its own offsets, and the assistant had explained that once the offset was bigger, John was to remove the plant from the pot, take off the shoot, and re-pot it. He had even been given a book to borrow, so he had some pictures explaining the process. It sounded complicated, but John was determined to succeed, to be better than the others in his group. For once in his life, he planned to achieve something he had never thought possible.

Chapter Twenty-two

November 2011, Lincolnshire

Coco and Art walked back from the lake. They had debated whether to let people into the woodland and down to the water, but figured it would just cause problems and they felt as all of their friends had already seen the lake, there might not be such a curiosity about it. They collected drinks from The Brew House on the way past and Coco popped into the house to make sure Mahoney was locked in his hutch, to turn off all the lights and light a few candle lamps so people could see their way for the bathroom. She joined everyone in the meadow, as they stood around chatting and drinking. Art had carried a big box to the side of the stage and waited for Coco to come back from the house. She got everyone's attention.

'Hellooo, everyone. Just quickly, thanks so much for coming, hope you all have a good time. Joey, who used to be my housemate, I'm sure some of you will remember?' A ripple of laughter went around the group of friends as they remembered how things had been when Coco and Joey had house-shared, 'He's brought his band, Ice Cream. It's their first gig together and the first time in years that Liam is on the same stage as Joey.'

'Other than when I've had to drag him off a stage after a scrap!' interrupted Joey.

'And if he gets his fucking chords wrong again, someone else had better do it for me,' Liam heckled, 'so look out for him, he's my only brother!' Liam always had a brilliant way with words and much of the crowd did not get the joke he had made.

'So it's a big night,' Coco continued, 'drink shit loads, we have plenty! Just remember, while you're getting pissed, thank the orchard for producing such wicked fruit. Everything you've eaten or drank tonight we grew ourselves, except the chickens and cows, of course. Give us time, I'm sure it won't be long!'

'Just before you start, Joey,' interrupted Art, 'I have hampers here for everyone. They are only small, but... um, I made them myself. I made all of the stuff, there are jams, chutneys, preserves and sauces. They're all different. Please take one each, well, you know, if you live together just take one. I'm fond of you folk, but I'm not a charity!' Again, everyone laughed. Art was quite a shy person and when he had announced he had made hampers for everyone, there had been a loud, sincere 'Ah!' which had embarrassed him slightly. He was a thoughtful person and was not afraid to show it. This had always baffled Coco, because as a rule, Art did not like people, hence they lived as far away from the population as they could and yet he was able to show such affection and love.

'So folks, enjoy, don't forget your hampers, and here's... ICE CREAM!' shouted Coco, introducing the band.

'COCO... Coco!' shouted Liam, from the middle of the stage, his face lit by the band's lights. 'It's not "Ice Cream", it's "I Scream"'...1 ...2 ...3 ...4!'

The band went straight into the heaviest version of *That's Entertainment* by The Jam that anyone had ever heard. It was hard, fast and raw, with at first just Joey on guitar and Liam on vocals. A simple interpretation, probably helped by the fact the original track was done on just an acoustic. Liam had brilliant stage presence and an attitude that even Johnny Rotten would be jealous of. He spat the words out, in a manner that it had been intended to be sung. He had even managed to pick up a bit of Paul Weller's London accent. A fast heavy drum beat was added during the chorus, which everyone sang along to.

'What d'ya think of my big brother?' shouted Liam, as the track finished, holding out his arm in the direction of Joey, 'Fucking good, in'e?' They then went into a perfect rendition of The Who's epic track *My Generation*. Coco did not know who the drummer was, but he was very, very good. Joey had travelled Europe with his bands drumming, so anyone who became his drummer had very big shoes to fill.

By this time, everyone was well on their way. People danced little tribally dances with an arm in the air holding their drinks aloft, or pogoed in front of the stage. The heavy base lines and fast, deep drumming started to fill the air as everyone danced, absorbed in the moment. One of those moments, dancing like wild, free things... in winter woollies... in a field... in the middle of nowhere. One of those moments, drunk on pure cider... listening to a band who quite clearly were destined to go places. It was one of *those* moments. 'What d'ya think of my little brother?' Joey shouted mimicking what his brother had said moments earlier. He came level with Liam, bumping shoulders with him to use his microphone, 'Shit, ain't he!'

'This one's for Cocoooo!' shouted Liam, as they went straight into the next track, which was *The Cutter* by the 80s band Echo and the Bunnymen, as loud cheers went around the little crowd. Coco and Liam pointed at each other with outstretched arms, laughing!

The band was outstanding. They did a full set of covers, by bands like Killing Joke, The Ruts, and The Stone Roses and of course The Sex Pistols, but they had changed each one slightly, adding their own twist to each song. They inserted reggae beats and riffs, slowing it right down. Slow songs they made primitive, fast and loud. After half an hour, they came off the stage for a break to a welcoming audience. The boys were staggered by the response this small crowd of people gave them, most of whom they did not know. They explained that although they had a range of their own songs to play next, they wanted to be able to play some classics perfectly, before they could consider themselves ready for a public performance. They had been happy with the first part of their set, and so would play their own songs next. Coco handed them both big mugs of tea and the other two band members some cider.

'Let me introduce you guys,' she said, linking arms with Joey, as Liam and the other two band members, Steve and Jack followed. 'Sophie... Miriam, you both know Joey, this is Liam his brother. Steve the drummer. Jack the bassist. Guys, this is Miriam and Sophie, and this is Miriam's husband, Simon, who you probably know from the gigs in town?' The band nodded and shook hands with Simon and started to relax as they chatted with true music fans. Sophie got slightly bored and wandered over to talk with CT and Kay.

'Hiya, not seen you in ages,' said Sophie, kissing them on both cheeks, 'How was Egypt?' Sophie and Miriam both knew Coco through their college years and had been on many of the Saturday nights out clubbing with her and her work friends, which is when they became friends with CT and Kay.

'Egypt was amazing, really hot and very relaxing,' said Kay. 'Didn't you go to Italy with Miriam while we were out there?'

'Yeah, we had an amazing time. My God, there are some tasty guys out there, Kay. Sorry CT!' she laughed. 'Mirry... MIRIAM...' she shouted, 'Talking about Italy... Kay and CT were in Egypt at the same time!' she called to her friend who was still stood with her husband and the band.

'Hiya, how was it?' Miriam shouted back, 'Did Annie, Deano and Charlie enjoy it too?'

'Yeah, they couldn't make it tonight unfortunately. All working,' called back Kay holding a glass of fizzy water in her hand, 'we'll have a catch up later, some strange things happened!'

'Ha, we had strange things happen too!' replied Miriam, but due to the alcohol consumption and the emotions of the night, they didn't get round to talking about the events they had experienced and symbols they'd seen.

The evening carried on with everyone drinking plenty, chatting, singing and dancing. Most of the friends had met before, so nobody felt left out. The band played the second part of their set, which totally stunned everyone. The composition of the music and the balance of outstanding lyrics and a very tight production were far better than anyone had imaged. I Scream were certainly going to be big. They had another break before they did the third and last part of their set.

'Right... the last set is going to be different,' said Liam. 'You fuckers need to chill, sit down, and listen up!' Steve on drums counted in the band on his sticks and the audience stood looking at the stage.

To everyone's surprise, no one had noticed that Joey had changed his guitar to an acoustic, and the band went into a very slow acoustic version of The Foo Fighters' *Heroes*. Liam's voice and Joey's harmonies with the guitar had everyone battling emotions by the first chorus and gradually they all sat down on the straw bales in front of the stage. The bonfire behind them lit the scene with an orange glow as they listened. The band performed for another half an hour, doing their own songs and a few acoustic covers. The individuality of the melodies, rhythm and beats had been blended perfectly, to produce a sound that was totally unique. Their ability to go from a haunting, tear-jerking tune, to one that would make you jump up and dance like your life depended on it, but then back to a slow song, was amazing. As everyone sat, intoxicated by cider, intently listening to every note being played, they swayed, or tapped out the beat. Liam had the ability to write lyrics that everyone could relate to.

The sky was of the darkest black, sprinkled by bright stars, as the full moon lit the surrounding countryside, defining silhouettes with bright highlights. The darkness was not polluted by streetlights, though a few moon-grey kissed clouds floated across the expanse. With the combination of the brilliant music, the remoteness of the location and the closeness of friends, everybody's worries left them. They could think. They all drifted into their deepest thoughts, as they sat there in the meadow. None of them had debt, or a rubbish job, or a house needing repairs, or a car that needed renewing. The natural world around them was alive... alive and breathing, living and growing, doing what it did because that is what it was supposed to do. Coco looked around at the faces of all her friends. Their eyes were all sparkling with the candlelights reflecting off them, wrapped up in thick woolly clothes, making them look three times bigger. Simon had his arm around Miriam, CT was sat between Sophie and Kay who each rested their heads on his shoulder and other friends sat huddled together, totally encapsulated with the moment. Art had his arm around Coco, as they stood behind their friends, all watching 'I Scream'. The band stole their worries and gave them notes of contentment back.

'Ladies and gentlemen,' said Liam, as the band very quietly played a short intro, repeating a few notes over and over again. 'We have been I Scream. We hope you've had as great a time as we have. You've been a great audience and it's about time you did some work. Get up please,' he asked stretching out his arms and lifting them above his head. The intro was still going but nobody could quite recognise it. 'You're our backing singers, let's have it!'

Everyone brought their thoughts back down to the meadow and stood up. The intro was still on repeat, as Joey held the audience at the point of eruption while they worked out the tune, until eventually the band went into the song. As the melody became recognisable to everyone, there were several calls, 'There's Logan!' followed by clapping, as a spotlight shone on Pod's daughter and her cello, as the band went into Oasis' *The Masterplan*. The harmonious strings flowed around the meadow, complimenting Joey's acoustic and the heart-beating drumming.

Everybody sang together, looking round and smiling to one another, not wanting to out-sing Liam, who was stood up tall, with his mike a little higher than his mouth, so he had to sing upwards, just like his hero. His hands were behind his back and his eyes were closed behind round rimmed sunglasses as he put his all into it. The audience increased their vocals as the song built, with Logan supporting the band on her cello. Coco noticed that Pod had happy tears, clapping and laughing, watching her daughter's performance, totally spellbound by the music. *Definitely a surprise then! Don't think this was expected. Excellent,* Coco thought, smiling.

Emotions flowed freely on the faces of the audience, as they sang along, taking big breaths in-between lines so they might have a full lung of air to send back to the band. They had now all realised that the song was from Liam to Joey and it was probably the greatest gift he could have given him. Liam had every member of the crowd singing loudly back and it was noticed that even Joey had to use the back of his hand to wipe his eye. He turned away from the audience slightly embarrassed, despite having practised this song many times before, this time was different. He was totally choked that Liam was actually singing this to him and had a field of backing singers to help him.

The musicians switched to playing very quietly, Logan leaning into her cello, her eyes closed as her right arm passed across the front of her strings, leaning back slightly on the long, drawn-out notes. She looked towards her mum, for a reassuring gesture of some sort and when she saw Pod's face, they exchanged a wink and a smile. It was as if she had been playing with the band for years.

Liam's vocals became stronger and louder, as he held his head up to the mike and the crowd put their arms in the air, 'gig worshipping' this young man who sang with the passion and emotion of an opera singer. Liam opened his eyes for a moment and looked up at the moon as his pupils suddenly dilated from the sudden brightness of the light. He took in big gasps of air, in order to be able to do the final chorus with everything he had and everyone complimented him with their own harmonious vocals.

The crowd swayed together in a semicircle before the stage. From an outsider, it could almost look like cult worship, the crowd swaying and singing in a trance-like state. Even some of the men were having trouble trying not to show too much emotion, which was impossible once Joey came to stand next to his brother.

Didn't think Liam sang this one with Oasis? thought Coco.

Liam lovingly put his arm around his brother's neck and kissed him on the cheek, as they both sang the lyrics. They had travelled a very long, bumpy road over the years, but this is how it should be and how it was going to be. Expressing themselves, telling people about their lives through lyrics and tunes as musicians had done for generations. They were side by side, centre stage. Together.

Chapter Twenty-three

The Attic Flat, Nottingham

By the time Rev got back to the flat from the station, most people were letting off the last of their Bonfire night fireworks, and heading into town for the pubs and clubs. He got home to find John reading a plant book. They spent an hour or so discussing the plant's requirements, the plant's sunlight supply, the plant's offsets, *whatever they are,* thought Rev and the plant's optimum temperature. Rev listened as John babbled on, showing him certain pages from his book, and the little shoot that had grown off the plant. *That's what an offset is,* he thought. He had some amazing news for John, but would wait until he had calmed down after what had obviously been a very successful evening for both of them. John then proceeded to explain how good it felt to get his red keyring, for the 90th day he had been clean.

Rev occasionally drifted away, thinking about his own elation at what Mr Keiffson had offered him. He was not too sure how he was going to explain the full situation to John, as John did not know the full extent of the problems he was having with his addiction or the true nature of his job. His triumph today was more of a personal one, as only he knew the true relief he had felt when Mr Keiffson listened to his cry for help. By the time he'd been dropped off at the mainline Euston station with £50 in his pocket, he'd treated himself to a burger tea while he waited for his train. He bought a magazine about cars and some refreshments for on the train later. He had got on the train as it waited to start its journey and chose a window seat with a table, facing the direction he would be travelling in. He got off the train in Nottingham where on passing John's favourite pizza shop, which had a few tables in the window to sit at, he went in and ordered John's favourite pizza. He ordered it for about 11pm, and asked the staff to reserve the table nearest the kitchen, which they usually used, as a surprise for John. All the staff knew him, as virtually all of his benefits money now went on pizza, now that he had a bit of money having kicked the drugs.

John had finished talking about his keyring and plant, which Rev saw as a good time to tell John he had organised a surprise tea for him. John then went into happy fits, giving Rev some 'man hugs', and thanking him for such an amazing surprise.

'But how did you know I wanted to celebrate tonight, what with my plant and 90 days?'

'A good friend knows what you need, before you know it yourself!' he had smiled. His news could wait until tomorrow.

The Railway Cottage, Lincolnshire

In the morning, Art was up early as usual. As he walked down the stairs, being careful not to wake Coco, he stopped and looked at the faces framed on the stairs wall. All of his heroes. His unofficial family. It was the first time he had stopped to look at them for some time. Last night had been life changing. The band had been amazing and the emotion they had handed out through their songs was still filling his body, they had been that good. Dimebag Darrell sneered out from his frame, long hair dishevelled and wild. Art stared at the picture, looking into the guitarist's eye. *The power of music is so underrated* he thought, touching the picture. Little did he know how true that would turn out to be! He took a walk down to the lake, which was the first thing he did everyday, with Nicholson as his wingman. It was cold and there was a sharp nip in the air; his breath blew out in a vapour cloud as he breathed. He had wrapped up well, with a peaked woolly cap and two fleeces; one zipped up to his neck. He sat on the trunk bench and looked out over the still lake. The water reflected the white, cloudy sky as a mallard glided alone across the mirrored surface.

Walking back past the cottage and The Brew House, he noticed there were a dozen tents erected in the meadow. Most people had decided to stay over, after the success of the gigs, to continue the euphoria. Crows called to one another in the distance and he saw them pecking the farrowed field next to the meadow. As he stood looking at them he picked up the box of hampers. He thought about the pictures hanging on the stairs, as his friends slept in their tents. *Every man should have more than one family,* he thought, *A lucky man should experience something like last night, at least once in his life.* He went around and left one hamper beside each tent and

198

went back into the house to make as much tea as he could, knowing his friends would need the early morning warmer. As he walked past the little stage, he noticed there was an inch of water lying on the ground and yet the grass was not muddy and churned up. He wondered if it was spilt cider, but that would be impossible. There was too much of it. He walked over to it. The little stage was now empty, with the band having driven home late last night, taking all of their equipment with them. Steve and Jack were very lucky, as Joey and Liam did not drink anymore, so they always got a lift home after their gigs. Art smiled when he thought about singing along to *The Masterplan* and goosebumps shot up his spine, causing the hairs at the back of his neck to stand on end. Nicholson ran up to the water and started drinking it. *Can't be booze then*, thought Art. As the little dog lapped, small ripples ran around the taller grass blades that had broken the water's surface. Art witnessed the strangest thing. The surface of the puddle became a kaleidoscope of green and silver lines that shimmered and sparkled. Puzzled, Art watched the water for a little longer, and then studied the whole area. There was no obvious source and he wondered if he had cracked a water pipe when he had hammered the poles into the ground for the stage supports.

He went back to the cottage to make the tea. He would have to use his two camping stoves, the kettle and a few big pans. He could hear the radio as he walked into the dining room and saw Coco had started on the tea and was fully dressed. They hugged and chatted about what a good time it had been. Art had really enjoyed having people over and felt very privileged and grateful for the wonderful place he lived in, with all his friends safe over in the meadow. Coco recalled how brilliant it had been when Logan had joined in on the song. The hairs on the back of her neck all twitched and stood on end, as goosebumps ran down her arms. The previous night had been quite spiritual and tribal. The drum beat controlling everyone's tempo, how Liam had been god-like in his control of the crowd actions and how the melodies and rhythms of the songs had set every nerve alive.

'We should do this every year,' suggested Art, which shocked Coco as she had been concerned it had been too loud and too claustrophobic for him. She had longed to make the suggestion herself, but felt it would be better to see what Art said first.

'The Meadow's Festival,' she replied.

The Attic Flat, Nottingham

Rev woke first and got straight out of bed. He had planned to surprise John with another meal, and so nipped out to the supermarket a two minute walk away, and bought bacon and eggs with the few pounds he had left from Mr Keiffson's £50. He saw a little book in the clearance section, which although had a damaged cover, would be well received by John. At the checkout, he argued that the book was badly damaged and so should have its price reduced. He won the argument, and triumphantly rushed home. He started to cook on the one ring of the electric cooker that worked. He hoped the smell would wake John. The previous evening John had talked like a sixteen-year-old whizzing his tits off on speed, for nearly two hours about his plant and key ring, while they had their pizza. They had eaten John's favourite pizza, which had doner meat, pepperoni, spaghetti bolognaise sauce and spicy beef with a cheese stuffed crust on it, with garlic mushrooms and onion rings. The restaurant had even laid out a paper tablecloth, so the meal had significance to it. John kept talking about his evening, right up until he fell asleep. Rev was so happy for his friend, and for himself. He could only imagine how his news would make John feel.

Rev thought back over the conversation he'd had with Mr Keiffson last night in the Porsche. He had told his boss that he was a recovering alcoholic, and was still struggling with his demons. His boss had asked what had brought on the addiction, and Rev had explained about the loss of his girlfriend. After a long pause, Mr Keiffson had offered to pay him for the job with a different commodity, and had asked if he would prefer to be paid with something else he might need. A new television or a secondhand car perhaps. Rev had sat and thought. He asked Mr Keiffson if he would pay the deposit and the first month's rent on a new flat, for himself and his flatmate. Instantly his boss had agreed, asking for the details to be sent with his driver and he assured Rev that he could consider it done. For the rest of the journey, they chatted together, though Rev did most of the talking, as he was asked questions. Just as they had pulled up at Euston, he was handed his train fare home.

Mr Keiffson continued, 'I like you, Mr Rev. I believe everyone should be able to better themselves, if they work hard enough. I know our field of work is unconventional, but it is only the government that think what we do is wrong. You do know all you ever pick up for me is marijuana? I don't like running the harder stuff, those days are behind me. I've made my money, I now offer a service. There is a massive demand for good quality weed, and that is what I sell, with the odd special job like the one you'll be doing for me. This marijuana is the best. My customers are all artists or musicians, creative, interesting people. Celebrities. My marijuana helps the economy of this ungrateful country.' He paused as he mulled over his resentment for the laws concerning marijuana. 'It pains me, the amount of money my customers pay in taxes each year, on money that will improve the country's diabolical economy. They should get their drugs for free.'

'The seeds you are dealing with are for a very special customer, and the delivery address is very, very special. We are probably working for the greatest man in our industry. When my driver picks you up, he will take you to a shop to buy a suit. Nothing too flashy, just something neat. You must change in the car, and be smart when you make this delivery. Please show Mr Idol the upmost respect. We cannot fail this job, as a lot rides on it!'

Rev and John ate breakfast by lamp light, even though it was eleven in the morning and they thought about what they might do for the rest of the day. John got straight into his book after he had eaten and kept reading little extracts out to Rev, who tried to show some interest while he read the car magazine he had bought at Euston. Eventually there had been the first spell of silence since he had got back from London the previous night.

'I've been offered a job. Need to know what you think!'

'Really, you should have said. I've been blowing bubbles about my good news. What happened?'

'I met Mr Keiffson in London, you know, the guy I work for?' John nodded, as he closed his book to listen to his friend. 'It's one thousand pounds for one job that will take me about an hour.'

'How many years is the risk, if you get caught?' John asked, knowing straightaway that this was a job with severe risks.

'I dread to think. High double figures, at least. I don't know of anyone who has carried this much.'

'How much?'

'Five hundred grand's worth of Jamaican, a very special Jamaican seed, some skunk/hemp hybrid!'

'Fuck!' John said hoarsely, as he had trouble finding his voice. 'Are you freaking crazy?'

'Yes, but you've known that for years!'

'You started sniffing glue or something? It's nuked your brain.'

'Let me explain. Mr Keiffson complimented me saying how much he liked the way I work.'

'So one compliment and you're bending over to be arse-raped?'

'No… He's chosen me for a special job. A one-off.'

'Yeah, "one-off" 'cause everyone involved is gonna get caught!'

'No, honestly. I get picked up as usual, go out to a pick-up point on a flood barrier some place out on the Boston mud flats, take it to a house near Lincoln, that's it.'

'Oh!' said John, not being able to see what could possibly go wrong.

Chapter Twenty-four

December 2011, Cumbria

Victoria had been sat outside Durham station for over an hour. She'd had to keep the engine running, as it was so cold outside. She had sat and watched people getting dropped off and picked up. They had arrived in buses or taxis and left on motorbikes or cars. All manner of lives, going about their business. She had seen tears of happiness at a reunion and tears of sadness during departures. If it were not for who she was picking up, she would have gone home by now. During the time she had been sat, facing the station's entrance whilst avidly looking out for her friend, the car had acquired a half inch of snow. It had snowed on and off for the last few days of November and the first few days of December, but only that wet snow that disappears as soon as it hits the ground. It seemed that today would be the day it had decided to stick around, so Victoria was not looking forward to the usual hour drive back to Holy Island. If the snow kept up, even in her new 4x4 it could easily take an extra hour. She needed to keep an eye on the time because of the high tides that were due at the weekend.

She had drunk a hot chocolate from the station shop and eaten a packet of Minstrels, whilst occasionally putting the blowers on in the car, both for warmth and to clear the steamed up windscreen. She had been into the station to enquire how much more of a delay there would be. Apparently there were frozen signals just after York. She could only imagine the scene her friend would be making on the train and laughed. Phil, her drag queen friend, was coming to stay for a long weekend, *Might be a week, looking at this weather,* thought Victoria. There had been extra provisions brought to the island, as Elizabeth's father had rung her to say there was some serious weather heading her way and to stock up. He had even told her to use the emergency gold credit card and to overstock on everything from toilet roll to pasta. He had mentioned that a lot of unusual weather had been occurring recently, that was not being reported in England. Italy, where he was, had broken a few records, one in May when there had been some powerful waterspouts that had travelled considerably inland and in November Venice had flooded double the amount of the times it usually did.

Victoria pulled on a faux fur hat, did up her coat and went to see if the train was coming. It was due any minute, so she waited on the packed, exposed platform. The snow had started to settle on the edge, as the wind started to pick up, causing flurries of snow to dance and twist, mocking the passengers waiting for non-arriving trains. The people going north had no chance, as the snow was drifting heavily in the Scottish lowlands and no trains could get through. The public address system kept repeating a message advising travellers to use alternative transport, or to delay their travel if they could, but nobody seemed to want to believe the information as they all stayed on the cold, wet platform. The train from London appeared in the distance, its front thick with snow. It looked like a faithful St Bernard dog, safely getting travel weary adventurers back into civilization. Victoria was distracted by an argument in the ticket office. A distressed African gentleman was desperately trying to explain that he needed to get to Heathrow for a flight home. Obviously there was nothing the railway staff could do, but the gentleman's plight brought home just how susceptible people were to the weather. She started to wonder if she might be better in the security bubble of the big city, where bad weather never really affected life much. But out here... well, this was serious weather. The station was packed, as everyone going north tried to get on the newly arrived train, which was now terminating at Durham.

Her focus was brought back to the platform, as raised voices and shouting could be heard. She stood on tip-toe to see what was going on through the crowds, as did many of the people stood around her. The commotion got louder as it got nearer to the exit, until Victoria could see a 6-foot-4 cerise pink yeti mincing towards her. The yeti had fluffy, long pink fur, a white fluffy fur scarf and gloves. It was also wearing white fluffy snow boots. One of the station staff was wheeling two trunks the size of washing machines, whilst apologising to the yeti.

'Victoria, princess, look at you darling!' Phil shouted from about thirty foot away. Everyone turned to see who had shouted and followed Phil's gaze to see who he was greeting. Victoria wondered for a brief second whether to flee or fight. She told herself to grow one and ran towards Phil, praying she did not slip and reaching him in safety, gave her old friend a big hug. 'Darling, it's just madness, nothing works outside of London. Everyone says it, I have just never believed it. Young man, darling, we need those trunks in this young lady's car. I have a brown one for you if you can help?' The station worker did not know what that meant. This pink man was quite clearly loved by this lady, but they seemed such an odd pair and he certainly did not really fancy waiting to see what a pink yeti classed as 'a brown one'.

'Sir... Madame... Sir... I'm not suppose to do this. It's not my job. I have to get the post off the train... Sir... Madame.'

'Please can you help us? I know my friend never travels light. You wouldn't believe he's only staying for three nights,' Victoria laughed at the unbelieving look on the porter's face. 'Please, there is ten pounds in it if you can help.'

'We have big tips in London, young man. A fit, young thing like you would do well down there,' continued Phil, his features softening, as he stopped to look and take notice of the petrified worker. He had high cheekbones and large sultry eyes, with smooth olivey skin.

'My friend is just messing,' said Victoria, trying to prevent a scene, as another, older porter started to investigate what the blockage on the platform was. There were people everywhere, as it had just been announced that the north-bound train was not able to go any further due to the snow. 'There you go, the train isn't leaving now, so the mail will be fine for a moment. I'm just outside. Please?' Victoria took a £10 out of her own pocket and gave it to him.

Fifteen minutes later, they were in the car crawling out of Durham. 'Oh God, you don't think he'll do what I say and go seek his fortune in the big smoke do you?' laughed Phil, once Victoria had to explain that people in the north were not used to an alternative London Soho language. The traffic was horrific, as people left work early to get home before they got snowed in. Victoria did not really know what to expect, as she had never had to live anywhere where the weather could affect life and from what she had experienced so far, people took it very seriously. The journey had already taken twice as long as it should have.

'We have to get to the island before the tide comes in. If it comes in while we are halfway across, we'll get caught in it. This thing...' she banged on the steering wheel, 'is fantastic, but Elizabeth has warned me not to risk it, if we get there after three-thirty, we shouldn't try it! The causeway is a skating rink too, so I can only drive slowly. If you come off the road, you get stuck in the sand!'

'I've never stayed in a castle before!'

'You've never left London before!'

'Oh, I have darling, don't lie. I used to go see a man just off Swiss Cottage!'

'That's still London!' laughed Victoria, loving the old banter, and the reminder that some Londoners just can't get enough of the place. She started to feel a little homesick, as she thought about her job at the Victoria and Albert Museum, the little coffee shop around the corner, which did the richest hot chocolate, complete with fresh whipped cream, a flake, chocolate sprinkles and a real cherry. She missed her hedonistic friends and the fast pace of living in London.

'Tell me about the castle, darling. I have always said, every queen should have a castle!' Phil laughed.

For the rest of the arduous journey, they talked about the old times, the parties at her father's house, and the episode with Flynn. The weather had got worse. The snow was falling quickly, big flakes so heavy they fell straight down, covering the tracks on the tarmac that the car in front had just made. It had built up on the edges of the windscreen beyond the sweep of the wipers and the heater was on full. Phil had taken his fur coat off for the journey, but started to pester Victoria to pull over so he might put it on again. The countryside gradually transformed from a grey, bleak landscape, to a pristine white wonderland, *not so wonderful when you still have ten miles to go,* thought Victoria, as the expert 4x4 made no issue of the icy patches and drifting snow. The wind was coming from the east, over the sea, just as Elizabeth's father had said. She had to remain calm and not rush to beat the tide. It was not worth dangerous driving and then a deathly decision to cross the causeway when she knew she shouldn't. Over the months, she had learnt to recognise how far onto the sand flats the water had come, as to whether she needed to hurry up or not. So far, luckily, she had always got home safely.

She turned off the single carriageway A1 that had been crawling along at 30 miles an hour. The Great North road, as many around Holy Island still called it, would be impassable within two hours if the snow continued. The 4x4 dropped down between two gentle hills, to sea level, handling the conditions with confidence. With no other cars using the lane to the village, the snow was about an inch thick. They drove past the tourist car park, which was deserted and on into the village. She turned left towards the causeway, looking out to sea to see if she could work out what the water was doing. However, because of the snow and the fading light, the visibility was very poor. Nobody was out walking and the little shops had all closed early. Only the pub looked open, though it would be doubtful they would have many customers. Victoria drove the short way out of the village to the start of the causeway and stopped. The visibility was so bad, she could hardly make out the island. The purring engine and the blowing of the heater were the only sounds inside the car, highlighting the sound of silence outside. The snow was falling heavily, like flakes of gold as it passed through the car's headlights. Victoria and Phil leaned forward and peered through the windscreen. The start of the causeway disappeared and merged with the rocks and sand of the shallows. They did not know what to do. Victoria was a city girl at heart, and Phil, well he considered Swiss Cottage as travelling and it was only about three miles from his safety net that was Soho.

'You can go get your coat out of the boot now, if you like,' joked Victoria, 'and while you are out there, walk in front of the car to show me the way so I don't fall onto the sand!'

'Darling, I can do better than that! I didn't know what to pack, so I packed everything!'

An hour later, three sets of toes were stretched out in front of the massive range, which was set back into a stone, walk-in fireplace in the castle's kitchen. It had two ovens at each end, with an open coal grate in the centre. The small, round kitchen table had been pulled closer to the fire and Elizabeth had got out some thick blankets from the chest near the front door which she draped over the high-backed wooden chairs. Some soup had been in the slow cooker all day giving off a hearty smell. Elizabeth had put a CD on, selecting Vivaldi's *Four Seasons,* which had echoed around the castle when she had cranked it up a bit. Elizabeth had been watching the road from the music room, and when she had seen the car crawling towards the island, she had stoked the fires in the foyer and kitchen and put the kettle on the Aga for teas. The castle was lovely and toasty by the time they had slipped and slid up the ramp to the courtyard. Victoria and Phil had finally got back to Holy Island and sat in the kitchen while Elizabeth served up a homemade chicken and mushroom soup.

'You should have said,' Phil laughed, 'I have loads of shrooms at home, I could have contributed!'

Victoria had forgotten how every moment spent with Phil was an adventure or a laugh or an event. There was never a dull moment and considering his whole world was about a mile square, he could be very resourceful when he needed to be. He put his skills down to who he was as he'd had to fight his way out of some very compromising situations, growing up as he did, in the lifestyle which Victoria remembered all so well. They had managed to crawl along the causeway, with plenty of time before the tide came in, which was just as well, because it had taken ages. In one of his trunks, Phil had packed a full length bright orange parker. He had put it on, with his white fur scarf and hat and had done what Victoria had asked. He led the way and walked in front of the car until they could see the island. This had sheltered the causeway enough that the visibility was much clearer, so Phil had felt is was safe to get back in the car. For his first experience of the wilderness, he had taken 'Mother Nature on by her nipple tassels' and said 'she'll have to try harder to slow this old queen down!'

Two days later, Holy Island was on lock down. The snow had not stopped since the trip from Durham station, but they had plenty of food and fuel. Phil was having problems as he could not use his internet or text his friends. Every few hours he could be heard shouting from some far corner of the castle, wondering what Bambi, Juju and Mar, short for Marrow, were doing. They spent the days exploring the mini castle, looking at the old pictures, decorations and books, when Phil spent most of his time stooped over because of the low ceilings. He had decided not to wear his heels because his hair then brushed against light fittings and he got fed up with banging his head every time he walked through one of the stone doorways. He would spend ages wandering the crooked corridors and little stairways as the castle floors followed the contours of the rock it was built on. He admired the different bricks, flints and tiles that had been used to give different textures on the walls and floor. He marvelled at the tapestries, pieces of armoury and old furniture that was all in everyday use. He started to settle into castle life and the feeling of isolation started to allow him to open his mind and think about his life, his surroundings and how this trip might change his thoughts on life. Living in London as an infamous drag queen, almost reaching the heights of stardom was about as far as you could get from life on the island. He knew he was a star at Madame Jojos, the club he worked every Saturday night, but on the island, he was just 'Phil'.

'You know darlings, this place is just fabulous. I know I can spend hours looking at my shoe collection, but this is just so... it's... well darlings, it's a little piece of history, isn't it? said Phil. He sat on a sofa with a blanket over his knees, with Victoria laid beside him, with her legs across his lap. They were in one of their favourite rooms, though it was not an actual room. One of the corridors led to an opened-up area with a big fireplace, with a sofa facing it. They spent quite a bit of time there, reminiscing about the past and all the parties at Victoria's childhood home. It was a quiet part of the castle, with whitewashed walls in-between stone door frames and windows.

'I have a bit of a mission to do. Beth says there is a book somewhere that her Great, Great, Great, Great... I'm not sure how many "greats" he is, Great Grandpa Claudius had kept, about all the plants in the Walled Garden. Do you want to help me look for it?' asked Victoria.

'Oh, yes. We can pretend it's a treasure hunt. Do you think there are secret passages and doors we could get lost in? Mind you, with everything being "mini" here, I doubt I would fit into any secret passages and doors. Come darling, let us prepare!'

'Prepare? I was just going to get up and start looking!'

'Oh no darling, we should get dressed up. I haven't put my face on for two days and am beginning to think I won't remember how to do it.'

'Oh, Philly nooo, it will take you ages. Come on, go natural, let's start now! Where is Beth?'

'She's having a little nap with Hadrian. Bless them, he is such a cute-ums baby!'

'His name is Adrian, stop calling him Hadrian!' laughed Victoria, getting up from the sofa, leaving the warmth of Phil's lap.

'Why? Hadrian sounds so much better. Especially as the little mite lives in a castle! Who would call a baby "Adrian" when Hadrian is so much grander?'

'Shhh, he is named after Beth's brother who died when he was a baby.'

'Good enough reason not to call him Adrian then, 'Yes son, you're named after a dead baby, but don't worry, it's not a hereditary thing!'

'Phil, Shhh!'

'It's true though darling. It's one name up from Flynn!'

'PHILLIP D'ARSE, I cannot believe you just said that! We don't bring up the "Flynn" thing. We have talked about it a lot, but decided that it was in the past and it was best left there. Did you know he got two years?'

'Oh my giddy...!' Phil said, 'Did he really? That's terrible. He should have got more!'

For the next few hours, Victoria searched for the plant book and Phil searched for secret passageways. They looked out of the windows, first at a view of the sea and then of the causeway leading to the little village.

'What's that over there?' pointed Phil.

'That's the old monastery. Monks sell wine from the village, but the monastery is just a ruin now.'

'Can we go have a look, sweetie? Pwease?' he asked, playing with a bit of Victoria's hair.

'How? Look at the causeway. You won't be going home if it doesn't clear up a bit!'

'I'm not sure I want to go home. Wonder what the retirement age is, in the drag industry. I mean darling, how much longer do you think I should carry on performing?'

Victoria gave him a peck on the cheek. 'Philly, your life is one big performance. The day you give it up will be the day you're six foot underground!'

'DARLING!' he shrieked in shock, 'do I look like worm food. Oh no, I don't want to be in a damp, cold box, not even if it was covered in sequins and I was wearing a vintage Westwood!'

'Vintage Westwood?' questioned Victoria, thinking of a pimped out coffin. *Very fitting though, Philly in a pimped coffin with neons and a cocktail maker,* she thought to herself, smiling.

'Not Tim darling, Vivian!' he said theatrically.

Chapter Twenty-five

The Attic Flat, Nottingham

Rev was sat with Mr Keiffson's driver, looking out over the North Sea. They were parked on the raised levy that protected the countryside from any floods. It was sleeting and the horizon merged seamlessly where the grey sky joined a grey sea. It was a wild, remote place and yet it was just a few miles from a bustling market town. Rev imagined how nice it would be here in the summer, with long, coarse grasses and wildflowers. Maybe he would bring John here, *the poor sod never gets out of the city,* he thought, watching sea birds diving into the frothing waves. There was nobody else about, despite it being a bit of a tourist area, with the Pilgrim memorial nearby, plus a large nature reserve. The clouds were racing across the sky and the wind whistled outside the car. They could hear the birds calling and the wind whipping through the grasses. A thin layer of sand had started to cover the windscreen when a crisp packet had got stuck under the wiper arm. Mike, the driver, braved the elements and opening the car door, he grabbed the packet and got back in the car.

'You hungry?' Rev had asked. They did not talk much, but since Rev had met Mr Keiffson, there was now a mutual respect, as each now knew that the other man was highly considered by their boss.

'No. Why?' Mike replied, in a strong East London accent.

'The crisp packet?'

'The crisp packet?' Mike repeated, a little puzzled until he realised that Rev was trying to break the ice a little.

'Yeah. The crisp packet!' Rev said again, turning slightly to face Mike.

'Yeah, I am. Want one?' he said, trying to be serious, as he offered Rev the empty bag. There was a moment's silence, as both men wondered if his colleague knew that they were each messing about. Mike's face started to twitch, and a smile appeared around his eyes, as he tried to contain the laughter, 'No. No, mate. You see, there is a nature reserve around here somewhere and some delinquent motherfucker has littered. Littering is not good.'

'No, you're right,' replied Rev, turning back to look out of the windscreen again. He was quite shocked, that for a man who had probably seen some pretty nasty stuff, he clearly cared for his environment. Mike was of average build, had average looks and was the sort of guy who would blend into a crowd inconspicuously. There were the fleeting signs of tattoos on his arms and neck, though his quality clothes covered most of them. The bits that Rev had seen were outstanding. Most tattoos he had seen before were a faded black, sometimes even a blue colour, but Mike's were of rich intense colours and delicate fine lines. 'Can I ask you Mike? Can I see your tattoos please?'

'What? *all* of them?'

'Well, I don't know. Just the ones on your arm. Why, how many have you got?'

'Just the one!'

'So why ask which one I want to see?' asked Rev, a little confused as he started to wonder if Mike was being funny with him.

'I've got just the one that covers my whole body,' he laughed. 'Fag?'

'What?' said Rev shocked, quickly turning to look at Mike, wondering how badly he would come off, if he ended up socking Mike in his southern Nancy-boy mouth. He swung around in his chair and was about to repeat his question and raise his arm with a clenched fist, when he saw Mike holding out a packet of cigarettes. 'Oh... no... thanks,' he laughed. 'I thought you had called me a...

'I know, that's why I did it, to see what your reaction would be. You were going to smack me, weren't you?'

'I was undecided. I was trying to figure out how much it would hurt when I hit you!'

'Don't you mean how much you would hurt me?'

'No, because I figured if I did land one on you, you would probably kill me.'

'You keep thinking that, son, because you're dead right!' Mike had replied, as he turned up the heater. 'Kit Kat?'

'Yeah, thanks. Thanks Mike... Thank you!'

'It's only a Kit Kat, save the thanks for when I get you away from chasing police cars!'

'No, I meant thanks... you know... Thank you for driving me,' said Rev, having realised that this man was Mr Keiffson's driver, so therefore he was probably the best there was, which was reassuring as they were about to collect 100,000 special hybrid marijuana seeds, Jamaica's finest, which any copper in the land would love to bust him for. 'Is that the boat?'

A red and white trawler could just about be seen coming into view. Rev knew what he had to do. There was a dyke run-off pipe housed in a square concrete block, which stood in deep water. The trawler would pass as close as he could, and Rev was to use a big fishing net to catch a box thrown from the boat. The waterproof polystyrene box would have been packed so the goods inside had no chance of getting wet or damaged. The time for the drop had been specifically chosen as the tide was on the way in and so if Rev did miss the catch, the box would float inland, and not out to sea. Rev sat straightening his new suit. It was dark grey and collarless, like the one Mr Keiffson had worn, but probably the tenth in price. Mike had gone to the only department store in Boston and picked out a few suitable choices. Whilst Rev tried them on, Mike pinched three silk ties and two silk handkerchiefs. *Robbing corporate fuckers,* he thought, *It's all over priced anyway!* and would have continued on his pinching spree, if it was not for the fact Rev had picked the suit he wanted. When they got back in the car, Mike took the pilfered items out of his coat. 'Here, pick one of each!' As he decided, Rev asked him why he had stolen them, when Mr Keiffson had given him an unlimited budget. Mike had explained that he sometimes had the urge to be Robin Hood, but *his* Robin Hood did not steal from the rich to give to the poor, he stole what the poor were entitled to, when they had just spent £200 on a suit!

An hour later, they were driving along the A17. They looked like normal businessmen, driving along in their three-year-old dark grey Audi A4, with a briefcase on the back seat filled with small bags of seeds. After they had picked up the parcel, which had been far easier than they had thought, they had opened the box and emptied the contents into the case. The trawler had passed the concrete pipe housing just a few feet away, and so the fisherman had thrown the box onto the land. They had unscrewed the fishing net so it easily fit in the boot and had torn open the box to inspect the seeds. They were all neatly in their bags, with a bit of air in each bag, which acted as some form of protection from being crushed. The car came to a slow crawl as they approached the big roundabout at Sleaford. It was then that Rev brought up the subject again about tattoos. Mike pulled his sleeve up a little, to reveal his artwork, which Rev was in awe of. The tattoo was part of a 'body suit' which covered every bit of Mike's skin, except his hands, and from his neck up. The detail on his left arm was insane, with miniature portraits of his favourite musicians almost looking 3D, but Rev only recognised Jimi Hendrix and John Lennon out of all the faces looking out at him. The portraits were only slightly bigger than a fifty pence piece but the detail that had gone into the work was mesmerising.

'Wow, they're amazing. And your whole body is like that?'

'Yes, yes it is. The theme is my favourite music. If ever we get the chance, I'll show you. Do you have any?' he asked as the traffic started to move forward.

'No, but I want one. I thought I would have a portrait of my ex-girlfriend, so I might actually be able to move on. It's been years, but the drink won't let me forget!'

'You a drinker?' asked Mike, which surprised Rev. He had felt sure Mr Keiffson would have said something.

'Yes. I am... I'm... I'm an alcoholic.'

'Is that why your girlfriend left you? You should move on mate, there are plen...' Mike was cut short.

'She died. She was pregnant, and she died.'

'Oh!' Mike did not know what to say. He had dealt with death many times and nearly met his own a few times, but he had no fear of it.

'Sorry. I should have said something!'

'Why? It's none of my business.'

It was the Audi's turn at the roundabout and Mike pulled straight out into a space, gunning the engine so the car powered forward at an alarming rate. *Jeez...* thought Rev as he clung onto the handle on the door as Mike brought the big car quickly around the roundabout, *this car is more than what it would appear to be!* thought Rev. They continued heading towards Newark, until they turned north towards Lincoln, where a road sign listed Wellingore. The roads were very wet, as the sleet had continued, so Mike slowed right down. It was all well and good that the car had unparalleled acceleration, but he had to remember the precious cargo he was carrying. He had regretted the display of advanced driving he had done around the roundabout as he could have drawn attention to the car, but he just needed to vent off some of his anger after he had wrongly assumed Rev had lost his girlfriend because of his drinking. Mike also wanted to demonstrate to Rev what his own capabilities were behind the wheel, in the hope it might show Rev that he was very safe being driven around under his care. *I owe this boy one,* thought Mike, *you wanker, putting your foot in it like that. I'll look after the poor bugger as best as I can.*

'Is your tattooist in London?' Rev asked, 'I bet he costs a packet!'

'He's eighty-five pounds an hour. I had about 150 hours with him,'

'Jesus Christ… your skin is worth…' Rev had trouble with the sum.

'Thirteen grand!' Mike said, who also had trouble with sums, but he knew how much had gone out of his bank account for it, even though he personally had only had to pay about ten per cent of it. 'Do you want me to put a word in for you? He has a five-month waiting list, but we get special appointments and rates. He's normally a hundred and twenty quid an hour!'

'I'm in the wrong job,' said Rev, feeling a little despondent.

'Son, if you want a tattoo by Louis Lou, you are in *exactly* the right job!'

Chapter Twenty-six

Holy Island, Cumbria

Victoria and Phil continued their search for the plant diary, but they kept getting distracted by things they found. They did not look in Mr and Mrs Claudius's room, it just did not feel right. As Elizabeth's parents were away a lot of the year, they always insisted that anyone could stay, so long as they respected the place, but no one was to stay in their room. The snow continued to fall outside, shrouding the castle in a cottonwool cover. Even the seagulls were not brave enough to venture out. As the day drew on and got darker, little orange lights could be seen where the village was. The castle stood solid, as it had done for generations as the elements blasted the outer walls. The waves on the sea were small, but very long and frequent. Their foaming crests skimmed over the sandy surface of the bay, chasing each other to the shore. Small peaks of snow collected on the windowsills as the snow storm entered its relentless second day. The cold grey, blues and purples outside were a chilling contrast to the warm oranges and reds on the inside of the castle, with lamps lighting alcoves of red brick and the little nooks and crannies made from ochre-coloured stone that were in every room.

The castle had about 15 rooms and each had chests, cupboards and shelves to investigate. On their search, Phil and Victoria found old board games, jigsaws and things like skittles, hula hoops and skipping ropes. There were family photo albums, sweet tins full of odd buttons and some really old, rare items. Next to an aging, scientific ink drawing of some magnificent blue lillies surrounded with Egyptian hieroglyphs, in a grand wooden frame, Phil investigated a tall slim cupboard. They found some worn, red leather-bound boxes, which contained some clay pipes laid on discoloured white silk. He found some fur coats, which he immediately tried on. None of them fitted, much to his dismay. There was a small silver trinket box on a shelf in the cupboard, above the rail the coats hung from, containing silver and jewelled hat pins, and cardboard boxes on the bottom shelf full of beautiful, glass Christmas baubles and 1960s decorations. He took one of the hat pins out. It was a silver Art Nouveau designed pin, with swirling vines carved into the flat head, dotted with diamonds.

'Oh darling, how scrummy is this?'

'Surely they can't be real diamonds or silver for that matter?' asked Victoria, coming over to see what he had found, 'God, it's beautiful.'

'But, oh sweetie, Queen Philly would look so pretty in this. Can I have it, pwease?' he asked fluttering his eye lashes.

'Of course you bloody can't. We are both guests here!'

'But it was rammed in the back of this cupboard, no one will even know it's missing!' Phil had had to fight for everything that was good in his life. If he wanted something, he always got it. During the early years in the eighties he had stolen, prostituted himself and pimped his own friends out to get what he wanted. He earned good money at the club, but sometimes his old ways would surface.

'No Phil. Ask Beth though, she'd probably give it to you.'

'Okay, I'm sorry. Let's look for that flaming book.' As he stood up, he stubbed his socked toes on the corner of the cupboard with such force, he knocked it causing something to fall from the top. Being the drama queen that he was, he yelped and cried as he hobbled around on one foot, dramatically throwing himself on the sofa, in a fake movie star faint. An actual tear ran down his face.

Victoria rushed over to him, picking a slim black book up from the floor and put it on the sofa arm. She would deal with Phil first and then put the book back. She lent and gave Phil a big hug. He had the lowest pain threshold of anyone she had ever met. She hugged his tear-soaked face against her chest, cradling his head and stroking his hair. His mother had died at a very young age and so any maternal affection was always greatly appreciated. They had discussed endlessly if that had been one of the reasons he had taken the career path he had. He spent most of the eighties searching for something as a replacement for his mother, but he never found it. No matter which parties he went to, which drugs or drinks (or any combination of) he took or which men he used, abused or loved, he could never find that unconditional comfort that a mother will always have for their child. He had no interest in woman and had known from an early age he was gay, but it was not until the nineties that he realised just *how* gay he was. It was one of the fundamental reasons their friendship had lasted so strongly for such a long time.

The sobbing gradually subsided and the sniffs became less regular but Victoria carried on hugging her friend, sitting on the arm of the sofa. Phil went to get a tissue he always kept up his sleeve, 'Always handy for the little drips,' he would always say, and knocked the book Victoria had picked up from the floor. As he blew his nose, sniffing and wiping his eyes, he suddenly stopped everything and looked at Victoria.

'Look what we've found!' he said smiling, with all signs of the drama gone.

Chapter Twenty-seven

Molay Barn, Lincolnshire

Just before Mike drove into Wellingore, he turned right towards a long, low farmhouse. They were in the middle of nowhere, with nothing to see except trees and fields. Everything looked dirty as the sleet formed slush on the road. The concoction of road dust, diesel fumes and oil particles splashed onto sickly looking hedgerows and grass verges. Mike had run through what Rev had to do. He was to knock, go in and follow the man to wherever he wanted the case to be left. This was one of Mr Keiffson's most valued advisors and so it had to go without a hitch. The powerful car wound around the country lane and turned into the drive at Molay Barn.

'Right, I'll wait here. Be as quick as you can. But don't rush him. In and out! Okay?'

'Okay,' replied Rev, surprised by how nervous he felt. Up until this job he had not really considered the consequences of what might happen if he ever got caught. Since meeting Mr Keiffson in Camden, he had started to think of himself in a different way and had started to feel the value of life again. It frightened him, as he didn't want to stop remembering Jess, but knew if he was to get on and be something, he was going to have to move on. He also realised he was going to have to control his thoughts and learn to balance his grieving with his everyday life. This is what he had always found so hard, facing up to the reality of getting on, without Jess, which always led to him looking for the answers at the bottom of a bottle.

'You can do this. Remember his name is Mr Idol... or SIR!' called Mike, as Rev got out got the car with the briefcase.

The stone cottage was long and old, with bare rambling roses climbing over the open porch. The lawns were immaculate, even though there were a few patches of icy sleet starting to settle. Anyone looking onto the scene would think Mr Idol was being visited by a salesman, though why would a salesman need a driver? Mr Idol opened the door before Rev had had a chance to knock. He was not what he had expected and appeared to be about seventy years old, with a weathered face and piercing blue eyes. At this point, Rev's heart was racing, his palms had gone sweaty and he thought he needed to go to the toilet. *Fuck sake, man up* he thought. *This is just a doddery old man, not the drug baron I was expecting. I can do this.* If he had known who Mr Idol really was, behind the façade of a little old man, Rev would have crapped himself in disbelief.

'Good afternoon Sir, I am Mr Rev. I have some paperwork for you to sign,' he said, gulping loudly afterwards. Mike had told him what to say, in case Mr Idol had any visitors. He was not expecting anyone else at the house, as Mike had said that Mr Idol would have made every effort to ensure no one was at the house with him, but there was no way of knowing if someone might just pop by.

'Good afternoon, son. Come in, come in out of the cold,' he said, smiling, pushing some boots and shoes out of the way with his foot. 'We will take the case to where I want you to store it.'

When Rev saw Mr Idol move the boots and shoes, he wondered if he should take his shoes off, as the old man was in slippers. But then if he did that, he would be in just his socks, which were full of holes and smelt a little. Laundry was never a very high priority. *Shoes on, shoes off...shoes on, shoes off,* he thought as he closed the door behind him and stalled for time. He then gave Mike a small nod. The door got stuck and he noticed the doormat was stuck in the door frame. *Wipe my shoes!* he thought. He followed Mr Idol as he shuffled down the long hall, to a door.

'We need to go down here I am afraid. It will take about fifteen minutes round trip.'

'Fifteen minutes in a cupboard? Is it fuc... Narnia?' asked Rev, instantly remembering he was supposed to be very respectful, but the appearance of Mr Idol had shaken him a little and so his guard had dropped. He still had Jess on his mind too, from talking about her with Mike, so he wasn't particularly focused. He also found he had forgotten most of what Mr Keiffson had said.

'Narnia? Yes son, it is a little!' laughed William, as he realised the young man only saw a cupboard, whereas he knew it was the door to the cellar.

'Nice marquetry work,' Rev replied, as Mr Idol unlocked the door, thinking that a compliment might override his near expletive, 'I used to do that. My granddad showed me,' he continued but then thought that maybe being too over-familiar could go against him.

'Thank you, yes, it's been there years, since the house was built. What scenes did you do?' William asked, as he opened the door and started on his way to the corridor behind the boat.

'Oh, I did a rose, a castle, all sorts.'

Rev began to wonder where he was being taken, as this was not how he imagined drug smuggling to be. He was following an old man down an underground tunnel, to God knows what. A sudden thought crossed his mind. *What if the house had been ambushed and the real Mr Idol was dead somewhere, probably somewhere in this tunnel. This Mr Idol might be a decoy. Fuck, it's like every horror and gangster film rolled into one! That would make sense. This old guy was never a drug smuggler, the whole thing could be a set up between two big drug cartels. What if he got mugged? This old boy might even be a copper! Oh FUCK FUCK FUCK!* he screamed inside his head, *how could I be so fuckingly dick-twattingly stupid?*

'Here we are, son,' said William, as they came to a small room, with two old chairs and an extension cable hanging from the ceiling. 'Stand on the chairs please, near that cable.'

'On the chairs? They look old, I wouldn't want to break them, I have my shoes on!' said Rev quickly, which was the only thing he could think of to say, to stall a bit of time. Up until recently, he would have got onto the chairs and hung himself for the old man. Now he had reservations. He had things he needed to do. He wanted to get that new flat with the money from this job. John would have lots of windows to choose from for his plants. He wanted to get a tattoo in memory of his beautiful Jess, *on my arm, so I can see her all of the time. And I guess so she can see everything I do!*

The old man had taken the case out of Rev's hand. 'Watch your suit, don't snag it on one of the chairs, it looks new.' Rev climbed onto the chairs. 'Now, pull the cable. It's not just a power line. Go on, it will be okay. Just watch the door as it op…' Mr Idol did not have time to finish, as Rev had tugged on the cable and a hatch popped open in the ceiling. 'Open that please.' The hinges to the door were quite stiff causing Rev to wobble a bit on his chair. *There is still time for an ambush,* he thought. 'Now, put your hand in there and feel for a handle. You need to push, then twist it. It might be a little stiff, it's not been used in years.'

Rev was dubious about putting his hand in a small dark space in the top corner of this underground room, in the middle of Lincolnshire. *John… this is for your plant!* he thought, knowing he had to do this, if he wanted paying. *What if I put my hand in there and a vice clamps shut on it. OH GOD, I'm going to bleed to death down here, hanging from the ceiling. Jess,*

I love you!

The wall on the right of the exit tunnel sprung open a few inches. Mr Idol shuffled over to it and pushed it open more. As Rev got off the chair, he saw that the room they were standing in was only a quarter of its actual size and it was in fact the corner of a much larger room which ran parallel to the tunnel. They went in relying on the big torch Mr Idol was carrying. He switched on a light and the room became flooded with fluorescent tubing. Rev could not believe what he could see. The foil lined room had lots of different sets of lights hanging from the ceiling, extractor fans and a sink. In four rows down the centre, were empty metal tanks with hose pipe tubing linking them together.

'Cool or what?' asked Mr Idol, with a huge smile on his face.

'My God. Is this what I think it is?'

'Nuclear bunker? Or Narnia perhaps?'

'A growing room,' said Rev in total shock at what he was seeing.

'It is, son. Built it in the sixties. I have two more!'

'You have two more?' repeated Rev.

'Yes, two more, exactly the same. Do you grow?'

'No, I have friends who have had some success, but that is two plants in a converted wardrobe. My housemate John has just started growing aloe vera plants. We live in a place with not many windows, so he is struggling a little. You must have room here for forty plants?'

'One hundred and twenty, don't forget the other two rooms. Stick the case on the bench, I will get some storage jars for the seeds. This room is airtight and watertight, but Mr Keiffson said this was a very important job, so we will take every precaution.'

He instructed Rev to get some large glass jars with rubber clamped lids. They needed ten of the large jars to secure all of the seeds which were then placed on purpose-built shelves. Mr Idol stood back and looked at the jars on the long, floor-to-ceiling shelves. He turned and looked around the room, doing a complete turn, to face the jars again.

'I used to import most of the weed in England during the sixties and seventies you know... well, until the industry needed a professional to organise it. That's when we started cross-breeding varieties to produce a super skunk. I couldn't keep up with the demand. I got all of these old lights from abroad. They didn't make them over here back then.'

'It's the perfect set up though. Because it's underground, there would be no heat traces if the police swept the area by helicopter, you're miles from anywhere, so long as no one saw you bringing stuff in or out and there weren't too many people coming and going. It would be foolproof. Genius!'

'Thank you. It was. It has never been found. You are the first person to see it in forty years. I trust you understand the severity of the consequences if you mention it to anyone.' The sternness in Mr Idol's voice put shivers down Rev's spine. He had used a tone he had not heard the old man use. 'Mr Keiffson knows me very well. One phone call is all it would take. Do I make myself perfectly understood?'

'Yes Sir. Of course. Mr Keiffson briefed me in person for this job. He specified the relevance for totally anonymity. You have my word.'

They left the jars on the shelf and turned out the light. Rev got back on the chair and turned then pulled the handle, as Mr Idol leant on the door so the mechanisms connected. The concealed door could not be seen at all, as its two edges made up the corner of the room and the corner wall to the corridor. It was completely hidden and sealed tight. They moved the chairs so they looked like they had randomly been placed and made sure the little door covering the lever was firmly closed. It snapped shut with a click.

'It's just magnets... that lock!' Mr Idol said, pointing. 'The cord is an extension lead, but it lies in a pulley, so when you pull it, it pulls the magnet away, causing the little spring in the door to open it away from the ceiling. Clever, ay?'

'Yes, it is. Very simple,' replied Rev, as he followed Mr Idol back to the main house.

'I did a degree in structural engineering. Those rooms were my final project. You know modern kitchen cupboards, the ones you push and they slide open?'

'Yes, I know them. Expensive kitchens I would imagine?'

'Yes, they sometimes are. Well, my room and the hidden door and the door with the magnet... they are where the idea for those cupboard doors came from!' he laughed.

On the way back to the attic flat, Mike and Rev talked about the delivery. Mike had considered going to the house, as Rev had been gone half an hour. He was just about to deal with a potential problem, as he knew if the delivery had been leaked by anyone, Mr Idol might be in danger. What Rev did not know, was that Mike was there to protect the old man for this job. If he had to save just one of them, the old man would have come first. Of course Mike would have done all he could for the young lad, but Mr Keiffson had clearly stated that Mr Idol was the priority. They drove back into civilization, through Grantham onto the A52 and into Nottingham. They parked in the usual spot just down the road from the attic flat, where Mike handed Rev a piece of paper.

'You're booked in at Lou's N Up, the tattoo shop owned by Louis Lou. Don't fuck it up. The appointment is the first one available, in mid-December.'

'What do you mean? Thank you, but I can't afford to have work by him. I know I have a lot of money coming for this job, but I need that for something. Talking of which, these are the papers for Mr Keiffson. He told me to give them to you,' replied Rev, pulling some crumpled papers out of his old jacket, which he had shoved into the department store's bag.

'Thanks, I'll see he gets them. Make sure you turn up at the tattoo shop. I spoke with Mr Keiffson while you were with Mr Idol. He said to set you up with a tab, so you can get the memorial tattoo of your girlfriend. It will be about a grand but will cost you nothing. Mr Keiffson told me to tell you it's a bonus, as you don't like cash, we've set this up for you.'

'I do like cash, I love it, but I always end up binge...

'I know,' said Mike, looking sympathetically at Rev. 'We will say "you don't like cash." It sounds so much better than "please don't give me cash because I will blow it all down the boozer." So, as I was saying, all you need to do is turn up on time, with the picture you want to have as your artwork. It doesn't matter if you use lots of pictures or just the one and it doesn't matter if they are damaged. At Lou's N Up, they draw everything freehand. That appointment we've made for you is just for the drawing to be booked in and for them to size the area you're having it on. They've all studied the human body down there, as well as having art degrees, so your design will be drawn to fit you perfectly, using your own muscles and bones as points of reference for placing the tattoo. When you're there, book your second appointment, making sure you say that Mr Keiffson has asked me to book in with you as soon as possible. That will get you one of our appointments. Okay?'

'Thank you. I can't believe that something so great is going to happen. This tattoo I'm having I hope will help me get over Jess. I don't want to be a disgrace anymore.'

'You're not a disgrace, Rev. You've had things to deal with that no human should ever have to deal with. Mr Keiffson lost his wife twenty years ago. He was where you are. Take the opportunity that's being handed to you on a plate, son. Offers like these never come around twice. Seize the moment.'

'I will and you will give those papers to Mr Keiffson for me? I have no way to thank Mr Keiffson. Will you tel...

'I'll give him your papers,' interrupted Mike, 'I'll see him later, but I won't thank him for you. He won't want your thanks. He'll just want your loyalty and professionalism.'

Mike drove off, leaving Rev stood on the pavement in the cold sleet, with his old clothes in a bag. He felt completely different. He felt 'like someone.' He felt how he did on the drive home from work back to Jess. He could feel hope and a consciousness inside his body, as if little parts of him were starting to wake up. He had tingling sensations in his veins and for the first time in a very long time, he realised he did have the power within himself to beat his demons. This time they were going to be obliterated.

Chapter Twenty-eight

Holy Island, Cumbria

Four days after getting to Holy Island, Phil was snowed in. It had snowed for the first two days of his trip and although the skies were now a translucent blue with not a cloud in sight, the causeway was a few inches of ice and totally impassable. The landlord of the village pub had rung the castle to make sure they were alright. He told Elizabeth that the village was completely cut off, as rescue vehicles had not even reached the A1 due to the amount of snow. One of the worse winter storms the area had suffered, it had broken all previous records, with snowdrifts reaching six feet in height. It had affected most of the country, especially the eastern coast, though by Lincolnshire there were only inches of snow.

After the 'toe-stubbing' incident Phil, Beth and Victoria had taken turns to look through the notebook. It had been started in 1751, by Great, Great, Great Grandpa Claudius who, as it turned out, was a bit of an artist. Each chapter was a catalogue of what plants had been imported from which country, with pages dated and full of beautiful ink drawings. There was also a section at the back, which Phil had been the first to notice. Here, the plants and their healing or health qualities were listed and it seemed that Great Grandpa Claudius had mainly concentrated on plants that were considered today to be popular homeopathic remedies. None of them could understand how these plants had been picked, without today's knowledge of what they did. Beside each entry, there was a number and a letter. They could not work out what they were in reference to, but continued to study the book. *Ancient Plantlore* thought Victoria, *reminds me of the* Voynich Manuscript *with all of its really old botanical drawings and cryptic content that cryptologists had still not cracked.*

As the days went on, it was getting harder to entertain themselves. They had played all of the board games, done a few of the puzzles and spent long lazy afternoons over a few bottles of wine. Phil had decided to learn a musical instrument from the music room, which was proving frustrating as he had no tutor, nor any simple book on how to learn. He could be heard killing a violin or blasting some random trumpet noises, but could play *Chop Sticks* like a pro on the piano. By the fifth day, they sat in the kitchen, toasting crumpets over the open coals of the Aga, deciding what to do for the day. Phil had rung London on the landline, which thankfully was protected from the elements, as were the electricity cables. He had explained that he might not make his Saturday night slot, which had been filled by a friend, but the club was not sure about another weekend. They did not believe that anyone in this day and age could get snowed in. Get the AA out, they had suggested. After a few more phone calls, Phil had persuaded his friends Bambi and Juju to cover for him, giving him another nine days in which to wait for the snow and ice to melt. He chatted about his friends as he spread lavender jelly and rose blossom honey, made from the herbs and plants in the Walled Garden, on his crumpets, and finished a pot of tea. Baby Adrian was about to have a mid-morning nap and while Elizabeth put him in his room, Victoria and Phil tried to think of something to do. They decided to play hide and seek. The limits of the game were anywhere inside the castle, excluding Adrian's and Elizabeth's parents' bedroom. Elizabeth watched the kitchen clock until two minutes had passed. She had suggested she should be the seeker, as she knew the layout better than the other two.

One minute later, Elizabeth had found Phil. He had tried to be smart by standing behind one of the huge stone pillars in the foyer, just outside the kitchen door. He moved around it as Elizabeth had approached, trying not to be heard as he held in childish giggles. What he had not noticed was a mirror behind him, quite surprisingly for someone who spent most of his time in front of one. Together they searched the rest of the rooms. Twenty minutes later, there was still no sign of Victoria. Phil started to get bored but Elizabeth kept thinking of different places they had missed, but all their searching was fruitless. They found themselves back in the hall, looking out of the window at the sea. Icicles on the windows were starting to melt, indicating the thaw had begun. Across the sky, Phil noticed long white clouds criss-crossing the clear blue sky. Some were quite narrow and dense in colour, whereas others were starting to spread out. He started to puzzle over it, as it was something he had never noticed in the sky before and pointed them out to Elizabeth. She noticed that aeroplanes were leaving the trails when she had seen two silver glints as the sun reflected off the planes. They discussed that it would be impossible for the planes to be on fire, but why would they be leaving such a mess behind them?

They finally decided to start their search for Victoria again and by being more methodical in their search, they were sure they were going to find her. They started in the foyer and kitchen, checking every possible place a slim person might hide.

'Kitchen clear,' called Victoria from the pantry, a room just off the kitchen. She walked back into the foyer and saw Phil looking up the chimney of the huge stone fireplace. Above him, there was the map with clock handles on it, which was attached to the weathervane.

'I know where she is!' said Elizabeth, running down the corridor leading to the rest of the castle. Phil followed her, until she came to a little flight of curving steps, which lead down to a door that was slightly ajar. A light shone around the gap. 'This goes down to the cellar. I bet she's freezing if she's down here,' she said, descending into the cold basement. 'Vic... Vic... you down here? You've won, I found Phil about forty minutes ago!'

'I'm here!' a muffled voice called.

The light cast shadows on the boxes and chests but there was no sign of Victoria. They eventually found her, after she had to call out to them again, emerging from behind the rack of wine, through the hidden gap.

'You'll never guess what I've found?' said Victoria, with several small boxes in her hand. 'I know what those references in the back of the plant notebook are. Look, the letters are on these drawers and these boxes have numbers on them. This is where Great Grandpa Claudius stored the seeds from his plants. I can't see properly because it's dark, but there are hundreds of drawers filled with boxes.'

Chapter Twenty-nine

December 2011, London

Although it was mid-December, crocuses and snowdrops were already a colourful carpet around mature trees at Kew Gardens, flowering two or three months earlier than they should. There was also a subtle shade of light green amidst the trees, as they started to bud. Never in recorded history had the weather gone from heavy snow and freezing temperatures, to a week of clear blue skies and high temperatures. An emergency meeting had been called by the MBHK. As the five members sat chatting on the gantry, the sun shone so brightly, they were down to their T-shirts. It was now warm enough to leave hats and scarves at home, and yet Robert had been snowed in for the last few days, as had Rik. The weathermen had not forecast the unusual rise in temperatures, and the MBHK members had been called to discuss the phenomenon.

Dave from the Final Decisions Committee eventually turned up, with his latest statistics. He got straight down to business, as they always did when meeting at Kew. 'Good afternoon gentleman, I hope it's not too uncomfortable up here. Being in a humid greenhouse is probably not the best place to meet, with the sun adding to the heat. On behalf of the committee I apologise.' There were a few pleasantries before he carried on.

'The unusual weather we are having is the tip of the iceberg I'm afraid. The governments of the world have started to prepare for December 2012 in a year's time, and one of the things they have done is to turn HAARP right up. The electromagnetic forces caused by HAARP are affecting migrating animals, and they are dying in their thousands. Flocks of birds are falling out of the sky dead, and fish are being washed ashore in their thousands. On our own shores, thousands of dead starfish have been washed up in Lincolnshire. None of the media is covering these events, as you remember me telling you, just seven companies own the world's media, but the independent social network sites are full of the stories. People are starting to ask questions, and luckily for us, most of our festivallers have been noted to be showing an interest. There are a few who are not on the internet, so they are being posted articles and adverts in order to try and prompt them.'

'These social sites are also discovering new, detailed information about chemtrails, and a few of the brighter thinkers have started to question the connection between the trails, the weather and the animal deaths. In accordance with our research, they are on the right path, and they are coming up with correct assumptions, but... Dave gave a pause, as he was about to deliver his bombshell 'but... it goes much further than this I'm afraid. The worldwide weather has gone berserk. Again, the mainstream media is avoiding it, so the general population is totally oblivious to what is really going on. Again, the alternative news channels are getting a fabulous response from the people who are paying attention.'

'What has the MBHK deduced from this?' asked Robert, sweeping his hand through his hair in the increasing heat.

'We've had a hand in this development. We are working under a different name alongside these sources ensuring these critical thinkers are getting the correct information. We have to keep a low profile, as some of the social networks have started to block some of the posts we have been advising on. Obviously as you guys know, that is because we're working against the government, who are now getting a little tetchy that we are nearing the truth. For our sakes, we won't give the whole game away; just ask a few questions to get people thinking.'

'Is it working?' asked Rik.

'Yes, unquestionably! Some are even connecting the HAARP frequencies with the disastrous weather. Some of the pages on social network sites are pairing up too. It is amazing how quickly it is developing. All of it is available on the internet, and people are starting to wake up. Now, getting back to what I have to tell you. Initially, the rising temperatures were due to the alignment, but this extreme weather is being brought on by HAARP, unquestionably. The droughts in Australia and the American mid-west, the floods in Indonesia and Europe, the forest fires in Australia and America are all results of HAARP being used to try and reduce the planetary temperatures. They are turning it up and using it more, trying to fight against conditions being created by the latter stages of the alignment.'

'Latter stages?' asked Rik, 'I thought we still had over six months till June?'

'We do, which is like a nanosecond in universal terms! The events are starting to happen already, but the world's governments being who they are, are trying to stop the unstoppable.'

'So all they are doing is making matters worse, rather than just leaving well alone?'

'Basically, but this is to be expected, and we did predict it. They do not have the extra knowledge about the symbols we have found at the farm, connected together by the plaque and the parts of the symbol found around the world. The world's governments do not have the translated ancient documents that we have, detailing the ancient wisdom of *Vibration Levitation*. There are so many soundwaves we can't hear, and yet ancient documents show that sound can be used to move objects!' Dave stopped to let the information sink in. 'There *are* soundwaves, vibrations and frequencies that can do this... think of a glass shattering with a high-pitched sound. Think of X-rays or ultraviolet. These are colour spectrums our natural eye cannot see. It's the same with soundwaves! They're all still thinking of a global catastrophe, the 2012 Doomsday Prophecies and all that horseshit, not the universal one we are aware of. This is why so much is being connected together on the internet. If the governments had not intervened, fiddling with magnetic pulses and radiowaves, the mass animal deaths would not have occurred. If they had just left it to do what it would inevitably do, only the warmer temperatures would have been noticed. The governments are panicking, thinking they can slow the process down, and have started to spray the skies more. They think that after messing with the atmosphere and weather for so long, they will still be able to reverse the process. This is not possible, as they have started one thing, and are trying to end something else which they have no control over.'

'Before we talk about that, why don't we just tell the government all the additional information we have? asked Rik.

'We have done. Those bureaucratic half-wits have their heads so far up their own arses, they weren't interested. Many independent historians and scientists have tried to tell of their discoveries. But because their ideas don't fit the general known information, they were ridiculed, discredited and never worked in their chosen fields again. There was Graham Hancock who explained about a lost third party civilisation; Robert M Schoch discussed a catastrophe that altered the course of human civilization, and Virginia Steen. Now she was exceptional. She proved she had found stone tools two hundred and fifty thousand years old. That was in 1966, around the time our discoveries were escalating.'

'What about the public, all those people who are going to die? If we share with the authorities, we might be able to save more people,' continued Dylan.

'The alignment is unstoppable. It is going to happen, and take most of the population with it. What would happen if we divulged too much information and the safety and secrecy of the site was compromised?' replied Dave, understanding Dylan's line of thought. 'Now, I need to know how your departments are going. Please keep it brief, just the basics. Dylan?'

'Okay, well, the site is totally prepared, and the equipment we will need, such as platinum-plated jack plugs, industrial sized converters and the loudest bass speakers, are already at the farm in storage. All of the audio equipment has had to be designed from scratch, to cope with the energy surge that will set off the site's protection. We have a lot of equipment being delivered over the next few weeks. They are due to put some special stakes into the ground too. These are of a copper compound, which will accelerate and enhance the Vibration Levitation of the music and crowd's response, sending the energy produced down into the ground. The specially designed speakers are on their way too, four artic lorries full of them. The size and scale of the site's preparation is phenomenal! I think in total the equipment comes to just over four million pounds, which is under budget, but does not include the fence and the survival equipment. Uncle Sam?'

'Well, we are up to budget on the fence. We are using the usual super fence, which is six million pounds. It has been modified, with the outer side protected in a rubber compound, and the inner side with a metal one. Also, there are a few properties on the site, the farm for one, which will have untreated fence around them. For this festival we will be using some specially made copper alloy stakes, which have to be put in the ground at such an angle, that they all point to the ground beneath the pyramid stage and well in the centre of the original Sacred Stones. Their angle will meet up with Dylan's stakes focusing the energy to a precise spot. It's taken twelve years to work out what needed to be done, but the simulation shows that when the energy from the stage transfers to the ground, which powers the reaction, the fence will act as an outer boundary, containing the energy to the site. This had to be done so the pulse for the viral text will also be strong enough. If we lose any of the energy, it could affect how much power we have for the communications and the reaction,' explained Uncle Sam, looking over to Rik as a prompt for his information.

'Hello. All of the survival equipment is already in warehouses in Bristol. The survival packs have everything someone might need. Maps, wind-up torches, a 42-bit army knife and foil body suits. There are also survival guides with basic "what to eat, what to avoid" information, basic orienteering skills, basic first aid. There was only so much we could include. We even reduced the print and have provided small magnifying glasses. We have scrapped the "spare battery" idea for phones. We knew from Robert's research that although mobile phones will definitely not work, people could have still used them to look at their photographs, texts from loved ones and such – making them just a devise to keep morale up, you know, a reason to carry on. However, it would be a waste of time with no means to recharge them, and as morale boosters, they would only last a few days tops. People will be determined to get home in the first few days, but by about day three, when the enormity of the task is realised, that's when problems are really going to start, and coincidently it would be the same time the batteries died. Therefore it has been a rejected idea. There will be no mobile phones working at all, after the event.'

'The all-terrain vehicles have been a bloody nightmare. It is very difficult to acquire that many, without being questioned. The only way we could get our hands on them was through the MoD. We used a back door into the MoD computers, by-passing request forms, security checks and authorisation procedures. We got them anyway, and no one has suspected anything yet. They are stored in a field at the farm, under camouflage. They are fitted with solar panels, and a wind-up mechanism. They will be very slow to drive, as they will be reliant on human power if the sun isn't charging the panels. Each vehicle has cost just under one hundred and twenty-five thousand pounds each to modify. They will also be used as storage for survival equipment that we want to be saved during the event, until they are needed to move people about. Mr Lizard?'

'Prepare for the ultimate festival to end all festivals! As you know, we couldn't get shit loads of bands in, and all of their crews. We have therefore invited about a hundred musicians who will play various sets throughout the weekend, with different artists. We have increased the number of people who will be playing here by using holograms of deceased stars. The main event will start at midday on June 21st, building the vibe and energy up to a grand finale, which will see fifty of the world's best artists share the stage, to all play together plus perform various solos. And yeah, it's going to be bloody loud! There will be a full orchestra and choir, so any brass or wind section of a tune will be magically enhanced.'

'What will be the "last song" as it were?' asked Rik, imagining Robert Plant and Sid Vicious on a stage together. *That's never going to work,* he thought.

'We are working with a few tracks as the final song. We have to consider the speed of the song, and its length. It will need to be over five minutes long, known to everyone...' joined in Dylan.

'Not *Stairway to Heaven*, surely?' joked Rik, thinking about the title rather than the song.

'It's one that has been considered, along with Pink Floyd's *Comfortably Numb*, but neither of those created enough energy or sustained strength. The tune we need is going to have to be a whopper!' said Ed.

'Not *Let it Be*? butted in Rik again, *Hey Jude?*

'No Rik. It has not been chosen yet, but we are down to about seven but more keep being suggested. As I was saying, throughout the day various different combinations of artists will do an hour set that has been carefully formulated to increase the excitement of the crowd. The really big stars will appear throughout the day, to keep everyone buzzing. Imagine if you will, having a brilliant rock song banging out, with solos from Slash or Lynott. The event is going to be enormous. Also, throughout the site, there will be hundreds of booths, where people can go and chat to cyber musicians.'

'How will those works?' asked Rik.

'Everyone has been allocated a ticket number which they type into one of the booths. We've been checking their social network pages and phones so we were able to work out who likes who. The machines will be programmed so people simply type in their number, and a selection of celebs they like will appear. They can then talk to them, and they will answer back. There will also be stage simulation games too, like Fans Play with Bands, where they can pretend to be on stage playing with a hologram band. This will work in the same way where they type in their number, choose a band and instrument and they play it. They can even pick a particular gig with some of the bigger bands, for example, drumming with Nirvana at Reading. The program will even have the musicians mock the participant if they make a mistake playing. These machines cost a fortune, but as money is not going to exist soon, there will be no bills to pay. They will be set up in the tents and marquees that usually hold other stages, but for this festival there will only be actual music played on the Pyramid Stage.'

'It all sounds fantastic,' said Dave, 'it really does. If only the following event wasn't so horrific. I take it all of your teams are confident everything will work?' he asked, as everyone nodded back to him. 'Robert, what do you have for us?'

'The military is increasing the chemtrails, with the idea that the build up of barium will protect the planet. What they are actually

234

doing, is ensuring that the heat from the sun will be intensified by their chemicals. Although it is highly flammable and explosive, they do not believe anyone has the energy to create the power that could cause the chemicals to ignite. The thing is we all know different! As the alignment happens, there will be a point where the sun will act like a laser, which, as it passes through the outer atmosphere and then the ionosphere, will cause the barium to explode. Due to the extensive spraying, it will take about ninety seconds for the whole planet to be surrounded by a blazing sky. A few places like the Pacific Ocean, the poles, some of Siberia, the Sahara, the Himalayas and the centre of Australia will survive. These places have been sprayed in the past, but not heavily. The governments at the moment are concentrating on trying to "protect" the populated areas, when in fact they are increasing the amount of damage that will be done. When the heat impacts the earth, it will reflect back without causing too much damage to the ground itself. Geologists have studied rocks from five thousand, ten thousand and fifteen thousand years ago and there is no damage. The scientists believe that when the heat passes into our atmosphere it will weaken as it mixes with the oxygen. The oxygen levels on the very surface of the ground are extremely high, therefore diluting the intensity of the heat. This is how trees, plants and grasses will not be burnt. We think there will be an intense oxygen shield of about a foot around any vegetation. Basically, we will be left with plants, animals and birds that took shelter in trees or bushes, which most will because of their natural instincts. Roads and rails will remain, though probably damaged, everything else will be gone. No buildings, bridges or vehicles. And… um… no people.'

There was silence for several minutes. Every time it was pointed out that most of the population was going to die, it always really struck home. They often thought about it, but hearing it just brought it home. Dylan was pleased to hear his seeds would be safe. They would be vital for the survival of the people who would be left. He'd had a text saying 'Your ladies are safe in bed,' so he knew where they were, he knew they were stored in England as arranged. They would stay there, as the flat, warm fertile soils of Lincolnshire would be perfect to grow them. He had paid the rest of the money, and got the final text saying 'Ladies' housekeeping received with kind regards', which was code to say the money had cleared, and business with Mr Keiffson was complete. These seeds were going to produce the raw fibre to build everything they were going to need. Hemp was back in favour… only *these* hemp seeds had a very special attribute.

'I got a question!'

'Go on, Dylan, what is it?' replied Dave.

'We are basically grooming the festivallers who come to our attention by their internet activities?'

'Correct, go on!'

'If one of our festivallers doesn't have the net... how do we know who to contact through the post? I know once you've found them, you send them a questionnaire or whatever. But how do you know where they are?'

'The percentage of people without regular internet access is such a small amount of households, so we are basically sending fliers out to every address in the country!'

'ALL of them?' asked Dylan.

'Yes, all of them!' said Dave, wondering where Dylan was going with this.

'What about homeless Joe Bloggs on a park bench? Does he even exist to us? No internet, no address to post stuff out to him. How does he get to find out about the event?'

'He won't.'

'So we are going to fry one of our own?' mocked Dylan. 'What happened if fifty per cent of the festivallers were homeless. There wouldn't be enough energy generated at the site?'

'Well, we already have ninety-eight per cent of the people, so that scenario isn't going to happen. If it were, we would have devised a different plan. Okay?' asked Dave, still liking Dylan even though he could be a bit of a pain. 'Right, looks like we are all on track. There is no way I can emphasis just how hit and miss this all is. We have done all we can, and we are very confident...'

'I got a question!'

'Dylan... okay, what is it this time?'

'Well, after the event, isn't there going to be mass panic when people are told what has happened beyond the site? It's going to be pandemonium!'

'Um, well, there will be something in the drinks!' said Dave sheepishly.

'What?' Everyone turned to look at Dave.

'After the final tune, they will all be exhausted. Their energy will be totally spent through the connection they will have had with the Earth. All of the drinks sold on the day will have a herbal combination of a strong sleeping remedy. Once people fall asleep, they will stay asleep until the herbs wear off. The ingredients and recipes were found in a recently decoded manuscript from possibly the sixteenth century. The *Voynich Manuscript* was created by the Templars to keep secret their medicinal recipes. It's a totally harmless drug, one hundred per cent natural. In order to have people wake up over time rather than all at once, some of the drinks have more of it than others. For example, vodka drinkers may wake first, then the ones who drank shit loads of vodka, then say the cider drinkers, then the ones who drank lots of cider... and so on. Once they wake up, they will be talked to, processed, and sent on their way.'

'As simple as that, ay?' asked Rik.

'That's it. Out of the hundreds of plans we have studied, this is the only way we can save the ones that are suppose to be saved!' concluded Dave.

Chapter Thirty

The Attic Flat, Nottingham

It was just a few weeks before Christmas when Rev and John packed up their few possessions and moved into their new flat. Mr Keiffson had done all that he had promised. The deposit and first month's rent had been paid, so they had a month to save for the next rent payment. A friend with a trailer helped them, though getting their things into the new flat was arduous. The front door opened into a black granite kitchen, with sunken spotlights and beechwood cupboard doors. It was part furnished, with a cooker, fridge and washing machine, all brand new. They had laughed to themselves when they realised they would not have to worry about things going off anymore, nor in summer would they have to stand milk in a sink of cold water. The open plan flat was very small and narrow. The kitchen led to a small dining area, big enough for a round table and two chairs positioned under a spiral staircase. At the furthest wall, under a big window there was a sofa and just about enough room for their old leather sofa. They had decided to keep it as a reminder of harder times. It was good to have a reality check from time to time. The hardest part of moving in was getting their beds up the single-person width staircase, until John realised that the landing wall was actually a glass door and could be opened and folded back, creating a bigger space. Rev took the bedroom over the kitchen, with a window overlooking the balcony which went around the underground car park. John had the room over the lounge with a view overlooking a green park, with a small river running through it. There were trees and plants, with ducks on the water. They each spent considerable time just looking at their views.

The block of flats was a converted Victorian shoe factory in Grantham. It had a gym for the residents, secure parking for those with a car and an intercom entry system. Although being in a quiet part of town, they were just a few minute's walk to the high street. The flats had been tastefully decorated, with a lot of the bare brick left exposed and the walls were painted a standard magnolia colour. All of the metalwork, including the balcony, staircases and window frames were all painted black, which complimented the Victorian stonework.

Rev had kept it a secret from John, until the day before they were due to move, when they had gone to the council to change their address for their benefit claims. John was still claiming sick-benefit, as due to his drug dependency he was unfit for work whilst Rev was on unemployment benefit. He knew he was running a risk, but if he was seen in the car or van with Mike, he was going to say he was just with a friend. No one would know he was working. They would each receive something towards their rent reducing the need to save as much each month for the flat. They had an emotional 'man-moment', reminiscing about the squat, the times in the windowless attic flat and how proud they were, that despite everything, they had come so far. It was the satisfaction of having achieved it themselves that they were so emotional. By supporting each other through their highs and lows they had come through to the other side. Obviously they were fully aware that their demons could come back and haunt them at any time, but they had to stay strong and focused. Since meeting Mr Keiffson and landing the seed job, Rev had not had a drink. He had something to live for. He was due to have his tattoo done too and the thought of it was keeping him on an even keel and off the drink.

The first night in their new flat, John had cooked full English breakfasts. It was the one meal they had not been able to cook for themselves in years. They bought the best quality smoked bacon and beef and cracked pepper sausages, eggs, mushrooms, tinned tomatoes and fresh tomatoes for grilling, hash browns, beans and an unsliced loaf. It did not matter that it was the wrong end of the day; they did not follow the usual rules laid down by society. After all, they'd had a menu of chocolate for nearly ten days in the squat once, so breakfast at tea time was not that unusual. They bought three different flavoured squashes, cereals, milk for breakfast and everything for a chicken roast dinner for the following evening. Whilst at the attic flat they didn't do much washing but instead bagged it all up. Now they had a washing machine of their own, so all of the dirty laundry could be done. New, clean sheets for a new, clean, bright flat! All for a fresh new start. Rev had even bought some conditioner to put in the washing machine, rather than cheap priced washing-up liquid which he usually had to use discretely at the launderette. They had always struggled to buy washing power as it was so expensive and so used the next best thing. Rev had chosen Grantham as he wanted to get out of the big city, away from its temptations and somewhere that would help John to stay on the straight and narrow. He had seen a picture of the flat when he had passed an estate agent once, when Mike had driven a detour through the town to show Rev where the tattoo shop was. Rev knew they couldn't stay in the attic flat for much longer. It had served its purpose and was just one of the first steps on their ladder to success.

After their full English they had started to do their washing. John had already put his plant on the kitchen windowsill, next to the front door. It had doubled in size in just a short time and was in desperate need for repotting, as some of its roots were poking out of the bottom of its pot. Rev had asked how he had got it to grow so quickly but John would not divulge his secret. They had talked as they had sorted all the washing out on the kitchen floor into piles culminating in about four loads which would get everything they owned washed. By midnight the last load went in. They had sat listening to a little radio that Rev had bought, drinking juice and dunking jaffa cakes in tea. It was the simplest night in but to them, it was security, warmth and happiness. It was the best night they'd had in a very long time.

Once the last load was washed it was nearly two in the morning. They were going to stretch their first night out for as long as they could, hence the reason they thought of doing all the washing. The one thing they had not thought about was how they were going to dry everything. If they had just done one load it would have dried on the radiators and although it was warm outside, which was crazy for December, they had nowhere to attach the washing line. Instead John started to hunt around for some string or wire. He planned to erect washing lines from the spiral staircase with the other end attached to curtain poles. He found some old speaker wires at the bottom of one of their unpacked boxes and set to work tying his invention together. Rev had the premonition that the weight of the washing would pull the curtain pole off the wall and so they decided to tie it to the window catch instead but would only hang lighter things on the line. Everything else was laid over doors and cupboard doors. By the time they had finished the little flat looked like a Chinese sweat shop. They'd had a brilliant first night. Content, warm and clean they went to bed. Five minutes after saying good night, John called out to Rev.

'Rev... Rev... REV...!'

'What, you okay mate?' called back Rev.

'Thanks. Thanks mate... for the flat... for tonight... you know!'

'I know dude, it's okay. Thank you too. You inspired me to sort my mess of a life out. Thank you, you're a star. If it wasn't for you, we'd still be in the attic flat.'

'But you inspired me dude… I want to get a job! Work… like you do. We can stop the benefits then. Do it all properly.'

'We will, mate. One step at a time! One step…!' tailed off Rev, as he fell into a deep, contented sleep.

Chapter Thirty-one

Christmas Day 2011, Lincolnshire

By the time Coco had woken up, Art was already down at the lake fishing. Coco's mother was abroad over Christmas so the festive season was being spent by the lake. Nicholson was investigating in the undergrowth, sniffing out rabbits and foxes. Mahoney was in the house, so it was safe to sniff for rabbits. It was understood by Art and Coco that Nicholson knew Mahoney was an 'untouchable' rabbit, as he would never rabbit hunt when Mahoney was about. Art had his camera with him and while his rods lay in their rests, he took a few pictures. It was going to be another glorious day. He had been fishing on the lake everyday for the last two weeks. He had some success with the big fish, but nothing like the day he had fished with William. He was hoping that when William popped over later, he would ask him what his secret was. He took pictures from the furthest side of the lake, facing the cottage and the rising sun. In-between the trees, just before the sun rose over the horizon, Art got a fabulous picture of flaming orange tinted, dark plum coloured clouds against a watery, almost colourless sky. He stood and watched, sungazing. He frequently stood squarely, barefooted on the soft mulch by the side of the lake, facing the sun as it rose. The orange tints brightened, until the sun burst into view. Art felt the power electrify his senses. Bright neon orange light filled the horizon as he squinted slightly against the life giving rays, staying focused on the sun. A few minutes later once he was accustomed to the brightness, he noticed how the underneath of the clouds turned a bright crimson, with peach coloured tops. He took more pictures, with a black silhouette of leafless trees in the midground and the reflection of the colours of the sky on the still water's surface. He could sungaze for up to fifteen minutes, having practised on cloudless days for the last year.

He saw Coco waving from the other side of the lake, with something shiny in her hands. He walked around to meet her, tripping over brambles and stubbing his foot on hidden tree roots. It was so peaceful, with just the sound of Nicholson panting beside him and the rustle of resting vegetation. He thought of all the homes around the country in total chaos, as children got up to open presents, people prepared breakfast for the entire family and turkeys going into the oven. He saw a robin sat on a bramble by the water's edge and focused his camera to take the shot. He had to zoom in, as he did not want to get closer to the bird and scare it off. As he took the picture, a dark shadow had passed through the water, which he managed to capture in his photograph. Slightly startled, he viewed the digitally stored picture and to his surprise, he saw the shadow quite clearly. It was a massive pike, easily over 40 pounds. It was an absolute monster. Art stood looking at his lake for a few more minutes, until Coco called him again.

They sat on the opposite side of the lake, looking out over the water towards the house and ate crispy bacon, sausage, mushroom and tomato rolls all wrapped in foil. The perfect breakfast, while all around was bedlam! Coco had brought a great big flask of tea, so they sat there until the sun appeared over the trees in front of them. The colours changed, from olives and purples to browns and greens. The weather was so warm for the time of year it had brought out huge patches of undisturbed early snowdrops. Their colour changed as the sun rose; white patches with a gentle pink glow, as the sun kissed their delicate petals. The robin appeared again hoping for any scraps of bread or bacon, hopping from branch to bramble, reminding Art to show Coco the photograph.

A powerful sports car could be heard coming up the lane, at a slower pace than it might usually have been driven at. As the engine noise got louder, Coco walked back to the house. She was expecting her son, who was staying for a night or two. He was a club promoter and spent a lot of time abroad. He had visited Railway Cottage a few times, but his business was quite new and far busier than he thought it would be. He had flown in from Miami where he rented a flat as it worked out cheaper than hotels. It was nothing flashy, just like the one he had in Ibiza and Ayia Napa. One bedroom, questionable neighbours and well away from the trendy clubs that G'orgie promoted. He created his club name from his own and had originally been named after Coco's grandfather, George. His whole lifestyle sounded far grander than it was. He had never set out to make a fortune, just to make something of himself and enjoy his life. The last two years had been serious hard work. He knew he had to appear successful in order to gain the trust of his clients. He borrowed money to buy a decent car and a few decent outfits he could interchange, all to impress people who he never really understood, nor particularly liked. He loved promoting the music and the club life, but most of the people he could do without. In the beginning, when all he had was a sports car and smart clothes, he ate cold beans from the can and would often have to pick mould off bread before he could toast it. There was no champagne and bling in the beginning. He now ate healthily, regularly cycled, jogged and swam and had started to live the life he had dreamed of.

Molay Barn, Lincolnshire

William woke at his usual time but to the unusual din of small children and a bossy woman. His two daughters were over for the holidays. They looked after him and did odd jobs, but he knew they were only doing the bare essentials to maintain a basic contact with him. He had never spoilt them when they were growing up and it had hit them all hard when their mother had died a few years back. Each Christmas they would all stay over one or two nights, doing their family duties before leaving his home in not quite the same neatly ordered place it was for the rest of the year. He also knew that their begrudging kindness was a by-product of all the rows they'd had about the lake. William often thought how angry they would be when they eventually found out what he had done. He let them fuss around him, clearly missing the point that he looked after himself all year, so was perfectly capable of cooking his own breakfast. He sat at the table, watching them multi-task. His porridge was being stirred so it was neither too runny or too thick, crumpets were being toasted and bacon was turned under the grill. *They are damned if they do and damned if they don't!* he thought *if they fuss over me, it is just for my money, if they never visit, it is because they aren't being two-faced by pretending to care. Boy, are they in for a shock!*

After breakfast he would go and shower so that by the time he was back downstairs the bombsite that had been the kitchen would be tidy again, with everyone waiting in the family lounge. William had always chopped his own tree to decorate, but the recent decline in his physical health meant he had to get a friend to go with him. If it was not for his grandchildren he probably would not pick such a big tree, but instead might consider something more modest. He religiously always picked the one that was a classic shaped tree, with branches all the way to the very top with a maximum height of seven feet, which was the height of his ceiling. He would allocate the day just before his family arrived to get all of the decorations out. The local villagers always thought highly of William and loved the way he went to all the trouble of decorating Molay Barn for just three or four days. How Christmas had become a four-month fiasco was beyond him. However, William would dutifully go through the same process each year. He had also noticed how quickly the process seemed to come around each year.

Down in the cellar, near the upended rowing boat he would get out the tree and room decorations, ornaments, outdoor lights and a little wooden nativity which he had carved out of balsa wood and painted. It would take a whole day, but when it was for grandchildren, the limit was endless.

Isaac Newton House, Lincolnshire

Rev and John celebrated for the first time in years. They were not thinking about the regular Christmas that the majority of the population would be having but instead had decided to be thankful for their current circumstances. They had done their biggest food shop ever, with everything actually being paid for... with cash. As they had walked around the supermarket with a basket each, they selected bags of nuts, fresh fruit and vegetables, a turkey crown, some little sausages and streaky bacon from the deli counter, as John wanted to make pigs-in-blankets, and lots of treats. They also bought a cheap set of fairy lights, one tree decoration and three bushy tinsel strands that were supposed to represent Christmas tree branches.

They had bumped into John's mentor from the Narcotics Anonymous group, who also lived in Grantham. Joey was food shopping with his brother. John invited him around for a cuppa over the holiday season and said he would definitely call around. John had been buzzing after the chat and added to his basket a range of fresh juices that were on offer, some extra orange and lemon jelly slices and a family sized bag of Twiglets. He also bought some flavoured hot chocolate, some marshmallows, cream in a can and mini flakes. Their Christmas food shop came to just under £35, which was an astronomical amount of money for them to spend, but they had a lot to be thankful for, so it was justified. They both still had their benefits, but in the New Year, once Rev had had a chat with his boss, he was going to come off benefits. It was the final piece of the puzzle, from pulling himself out of the gutter, to supporting himself and John with a nice flat.

Whilst in the supermarket, they bought some plastic cups as they only had two at the flat, budget priced cutlery, two plates and glasses, so if people did call, they had extra drinking vessels. They were astonished as they watched other shoppers pay hundreds of pounds for their bursting trolleys full of stuff. *Bet most of that gets thrown out* thought John, as he waited to be served. The bored checkout girl tried to make small talk, but it was quite clear that she was not feeling the Christmas spirit! As they paid, John saw someone else he knew. Rev began to think that Grantham was not going to be the quiet town he had hoped for, as in the last twenty minutes John had bumped into two people he knew.

'Miss Kain, hello. I'm John; you visited our group and gave us aloe vera plants. I am the one whose plant has already grown babies, I mean um, offsets. I have repotted it and now have five plants,' he explained, talking quickly with the excitement of being able to talk to someone who knew about plants, which was his new passion.

'Oh hello, John, that's great news. How are they doing?' replied Coco as she shopped with Art.

'They are really well thanks. They're on the kitchen windowsill, but are getting a bit big so I'll have to move them,' he replied, looking at the tall, long-haired man stood with Miss Kain.

'Oh, this is Art, my partner,' said Coco, 'and Art, this is John. His plant we gave him is doing better than ours at home!'

'Alright man?' asked Art, nodding his head. He hated supermarkets. He resented the prices, the crowds and the need and the pressure at Christmas time for people to buy one of everything, literally. Coco and Art were just getting their monthly meat stock for the freezer, dairy products and a bag full of treats.

'Hello,' replied John, 'Miss Kain, did you say my plant is doing better than yours... but you're the professional, I'm just learning!' he chatted, beaming with delight at the thought of his newly pointed-out success.

'Yes, John, yours is much better than ours. What's your secret?'

'I don't have a secret; I just did what you told us. I water them, keep them in sunlight and turn them when they are leaning too far to the sun...'

'And you talk to them for bloody hours!' Rev butted in.

'Yeah, I um... talk... to them,' he said, slightly embarrassed. 'This is Rev, my flatmate. He goes to the AA meetings, but they aren't doing plants at the moment.'

'Just as well, they'd be no room for mine too; it's like a greenhouse in our kitchen!' They all laughed.

'You talk to them? Wow, maybe you could come and talk to ours some time?' replied Coco, with a look of horror from Art, when he realised that meant more people mooching around his home.

'Yeah, that would be great, Wow, thank you.'

'What do you talk to them about, if you don't mind me asking?'

'I talk about everything... my addiction... all the shit things that have happened. I... well, I guess I offload on them. I tell them how I feel, whether I'm happy or not. My plant was like an extension of my councillor Joey Paddock, I mean Mr Paddock. I talk to them like they are Mr Paddock!' John confessed, pleased he had told someone at last.

'Is Mr Paddock, Joey Paddock, your mentor. We know him, don't we, Art?' said Coco. 'He's an amazing man; he used to be my housemate. Brilliant musician too!'

'You know him? He was in here a few moments ago, with his brother maybe? A guy who looks just like him?'

'Liam? Did they look identical but with a few year's age difference?' she asked as John nodded, 'Yeah that's his brother, fantastic musician too!'

Coco had given her mobile number to John and they had all parted company. Art showed his displeasure at the thought of strangers at the house as Coco tried to explain her thoughts.

'He has had a really bad time. That night I went to give a short talk about the plants, they each had to introduce themselves for a few minutes. He was the only one who I thought had... well... a drive, energy! He was so excited about the plants and at the end I chatted to him for a minute. He told me what had happened to him, how he had ended up on class As. He used to earn over thirty grand a year, until he was set up by the bosses. Fucking fat-cats! He ended up in prison, for something he didn't do and lost everything. There was proof he was innocent, but the rich bastards pulled rank and got a shit-hot lawyer to bury him. Then his girlfriend went off with the boss's son while John was in jail, and then his parents died in a car crash on the way back from visiting him.'

The story made Art see John in a whole new way. He felt bad that he had judged him in the wrong way, which Art never did. He always took people as he found them and had liked John. It was nothing to do with him attending the NA meetings; he had just allowed his perceptions to cloud his judgement.

'Fucking hell, poor bastard. Wait here a mo!' Art pulled the car up on the 'drop-off' parking bay and ran back into the supermarket. Coco had no idea what he was doing, but was used to his mysticisms. He came back a few minutes later, slightly out of breath.

'What did you forget?' Coco asked.

'My manners!' replied Art. They had driven back to Railway Cottage relieved that the food shop was done. They had only done their regular monthly shop, adding a few extras in case friends called, but they could not work out why everyone else went berserk buying mountains of food, when the shops were only closed for one day.

Christmas day for John and Rev was a huge milestone. They listened to the little radio, admired the tree-like tinsel wound around the staircase and laughed at the aloe vera plant with a bauble hanging from it. They sat eating junk food, drinking tea and fresh juices bought as a treat, and played card games. John had given Rev one of his plants as a Christmas gift and Rev had bought John a brand new book, titled *The Year Round Gardener*, which explained with beautiful drawings and photographs what should be done each month, including a big section on houseplants. John had been beside himself and started to read it out aloud to his plants. Their gifts had been simple, but personal, which made them the greatest kind of gifts to receive.

The one thing neither of them thought about was their addictions. John was in the land of plants and was very safe, away from the dark places that sometimes occupied his thoughts. Rev had struggled a few times, but had resisted any drink. It had been hard walking around the supermarket, seeing all the trolleys with crates of beer and boxes of wine. He had looked in his own basket and nearly started to think how pathetic it was. Just as he could feel himself sliding down a slick surface to the open mouth of his demon, which was calling him, taunting him, John had appeared with baubles on his ears and tinsel around his neck. Rev had immediately snapped out of his trance and once back in the land of the shoppers, he managed to pick himself up. John had saved him, once again. He had even managed to walk past pallets piled high with cheap trays of beer, but although he was smiling at his power to resist, he knew his addiction could call on him at anytime. But *he'd* won this time. He was due to have his tattoo in the New Year and could not wait. He was sure that the memorial tattoo of Jess would help him get over drink even more.

Just as it started to get dark, the intercom buzzed and Mr Paddock called around. He was just passing on his way to see his brother, Liam, and so had called in for a cuppa like he had promised. John was over the moon and showed off his plants and new book. They chatted about their day, drinking tea and dunking chocolate-coated Christmas biscuits as the radio played festive and retro songs. When The Clash came on, Mr Paddock used his hands and feet to drum along to it, slapping his leg instead of his cymbals and a fat tube of cheesy footballs with a rubber lid as part of his tabletop drum set. With *London Calling* them, John and Rev sang along, both jumping up and pogoing around the tiny lounge. The following song was The Prodigy's *Run with the Wolves*, which was acted out just as energetically. They sat back down, exhausted, but full of spirit, their own home-brewed spirit.

Mr Paddock had time for one more cup of tea before he had to go and tucked into Twiglets and lemon and orange jelly slices.

'This is for you, Mr Paddock,' said John, holding one of his plants. 'Today has been the best Christmas I can remember. I grew this myself, you know from one of Miss Kain's plants!'

'Coco's aloe vera! Wow, it's amazing. Yours are doing so well. You should ask people you know for cuttings of their plants and grow them. I have a plant that has long dangling bits with mini plants on it. I'll bring you some cuttings. Let's look in that book to see what it's called, and how much of it you need to grow babies.'

'Offsets!' corrected John.

'Off-what?'

'They produce *offsets*, not babies!' John laughed when he saw the bemused look on Mr Paddock's face.

They spent ten minutes working out that spider plants were easy to propagate. Mr Paddock said he would drop off the cuttings in the week. They continued to chat about Coco and her plants, with Mr Paddock telling them all about Railway Cottage.

'It's a very special place. We played there for Bonfire Night and it was really intense, almost spiritual I suppose.'

'Miss Kain's partner, Art, he ran back into the supermarket when we saw you last week and he invited us to go fish there for New Year's Eve. He said it was a lovely quiet place, especially when... now, how did he put it... "especially when the two hells of drink and drugs offer the best parties on New Year's!" ' he quoted.

'Art is a very good man. He doesn't like many people, so you're privileged if he has offered you a day's fishing. His lake is, well, it's heaven. Now then guys, I must go. Make sure you go to the right party for New Year's... you have heaven or hell to choose from!'

The Railway Cottage, Lincolnshire

William had managed to escape from the bedlam of Molay Barn for an hour and drove over to see Art and Coco. He knew Art would be fishing and could not think of a better way to spend a Christmas afternoon than by the lake. He had a little gift he wanted to give Coco too. He had bought thoughtful gifts for all of his family and in return he got the usual socks, a new dressing gown, slippers and smellies. They had also bought him a joint gift, which had not only surprised him, but had also put a smile on his face. They had bought him a two-night stay at an old inn by the sea in Cumbria, for him and a friend. He could fish off the beach, or walk the dunes, or even visit the old monastery ruins. It was a lovely gift and he had been genuinely grateful. He had visited Holy Island many times in the '70s as the owner, Mr Claudius, occasionally had some unusual plants grown in his Walled Garden, which William would go and check out with Tarquin. As the country's premier hemp-cannabis experts, anyone in the know would call on their expertise, in the hope they had grown a new super strength plant, or one with strong hallucinogenic and healing qualities.

William was touched that his daughters had remembered his stories of how he would visit the little castle reached by a causeway. Obviously he always omitted the fact that he was in the weed industry, but instead chose to tell them he used to work for the Horticultural Society, before he invented magnetic locks. He would stay at the castle for a few nights, checking the new plants and seed collection. In the cellar, behind a rack of wine, was the most comprehensive herbal remedy seed collection in the country. Tarquin had insisted that every crop of seeds should be catalogued and a few saved. It was impossible to know how good a plant will be and so by keeping some seeds, those plants that were good, could be grown to order. Mr Claudius had taken on the role that one of his ancient relatives had started, when he had travelled around the Middle East, the Far East and Europe bringing in opium poppy seeds, ancient medicinal plants, Marijuana and anything else that had sounded interesting. He brought back some fantastic authentic furniture too, all stuffed with seeds. William had lost touch with his old friend from the island once he started a family, so this gift would be a brilliant way to arrange a catch up, all be it a 40-year catch-up!

As William pulled up at Railway Cottage, he noticed that G'orgie was visiting too. He liked the boy, who although was only in his early twenties, was shaping up to be a fine young man. A bit scatty at times with some crazy schemes that would be talked about in depth, but never actually came to fruition. He had met him twice and each time noticed how the boy was maturing, filling out and becoming a man. He was a credit to Coco, who had brought him up on her own, whilst studying for her Master's Degree and holding down a full time job. William smiled as he thought of Coco and how she had worked so hard, knowing what she wanted and here it all was, exactly as she had hoped. He called into the house before walking down to the lake, noticing the fish and rabbit amulet hanging on the 'Lake' and 'House' hook. The light was starting to fade, but it was still unusually warm. He called into the house to see Coco and G'orgie, handing Coco a slim present, in gold paper and black ribbon. He smiled at her reaction, when she saw what he had given her. It was a signed copy of one of Einstein's books. After he had received a big hug, he set off for the lake. He noticed the snowdrops starting to close their petals as the sun stopped feeding them and the bright green shoots of other bulbs starting to push their way through the ground. *You're too early, ladies* he thought as he passed daffodil shoots and blooming crocuses. He knelt down and looked at them. *You guys are going to freeze. That week of cold weather wasn't winter and this isn't spring.* He remained knelt beside them wondering what effect this wayward weather was going to have on trees and crops. *If everything flowers now, the cold that is to come is going to kill off plants. Oh dear, things are not looking good for next year!*

Holy Island, Cumbria

Christmas on Holy Island was traditional as always. Victoria and Elizabeth had put the thought of the seed find to the back of their minds, though it had taken a few days for the excitement to settle. Phil had returned to London a few days after the find, but had insisted he was kept informed of anything else they discovered. As Christmas had arrived, the weather was warm and sunny and no explanation had been offered by the weather people. Inside the castle, huge hearth decorations like the ones department stores used, hung in the foyer and around the huge fireplace. The tree by the front door was ten feet tall and about the same size around its lower branches. Gold, red and silver baubles and ornaments hung off its long branches and presents were piled up beneath it. As the weather had been so bad, Elizabeth's parents had decided to stay with friends in Austria skiing. The tree had been brought up to the castle by the same guys who delivered the wood stock. They even erected it in a giant old vice, which could support such a tall, heavy tree.

They had a kipper and scrambled egg breakfast, with alcoholic Bucks Fizz. They exchanged presents, drank a few bottles of wine and entertained a few of the villagers as they made a pleasant walk out to the island before their lunches, just to say Happy Christmas. Elizabeth explained it was a tradition that had stemmed from when one of her relatives had spent one Christmas alone at the castle. Throughout Christmas Day, the entire village called around at some point to check he was alright. By the end of the day, everyone had ensured no one was alone on Christmas Day. The tradition continued from then. Elizabeth made sure there were warm mince pies and mulled wine for their visitors. Nobody stayed long, just long enough to say 'Happy Christmas' and to collect a warm mince pie and a plastic cup of mulled wine for the walk back to the mainland. The tradition was a sign of a community that cared. There had been some years where the weather had been too bad, but someone always called, whether they were in snow shoes, on skies, or like Mr Pendleton, who had put his daughter's driving pony to an old sledge he had borrowed and driven out to the island. He had even put bells on the sledge, with lanterns on the front. It could not get any more traditional than that.

As the morning continued, Elizabeth and Victoria listened to Christmas songs, looked at the things they had been given, and talked about Christmases past, which had been fun. Elizabeth talked about huge family affairs, with up to twenty people sitting down to lunch at the castle, whereas Victoria talked about long, liquid lunches, hours of shopping on Regent Street and evenings in tastefully decorated wine bars, with woman dressed in their favourite cocktail dresses and classically accessorised shift dresses, who had come straight from offices. She remembered boozy works parties, which unfortunately involved Flynn. They had both found it was getting easier and his memory was starting to fade. They lived happily in the castle but the scars Flynn had caused were not quite healed enough for either of them to think about finding someone new. They watched Addi marvel at all of the bright fairylights and shiny paper and talked about all of the boxes of seeds they had found. Elizabeth had told her father what she'd found and he'd said he had no idea they were there. Elizabeth had been happy with that statement, except her father had warned her to leave them where they were till he got back home. 'They might be poisonous', and she was 'not to touch them under any circumstances,' he had warned. The severity of his comments had startled her a little. However, he was delighted that the plant notebook had been found again.

Dorset

Rik had tried to make his family's Christmas as normal as possible, which was really difficult as he was the only member of the family who knew it could well be the last. He had got up early, and fed all the animals and put the two horses in the field for the day. He took a long walk around his property, making a mental note of jobs that needed to be done. Everything seemed to be in order. The lazy river fed by the pure water stream that ran through the back garden looked crystal clear as it ran towards the sea at Poole. Everything seemed to look fresh and bright, with deep blue skies crowning what could only be described as a spring garden. He noticed tiny buds forming on the bushes, snowdrops and crocuses were in full flower on the riverbank, and daffodils were already appearing around the base of tall trees. *It's like March,* he thought. He walked over to check his well. He'd had a call from Dave from the FDC, to say it was confirmed that it was his well that was connected to the pure water spring, so his family and the property would definitely be safe. It had been questionable for a long time, as the water from the river had diluted the tests until they had been able to get a sample from deep in the ground. Rik had thought that it was part of the pure spring, as his land looked so much healthier than the surrounding countryside. Dave had also confirmed that the well on Rik's land was connected to the stream, and should have a marker on it somewhere.

They had sat down to a big family breakfast, opened presents and watched the DVDs they had bought each other. Their lunch had been fantastic, with a few glasses of wine and the boys had beers. They spent an hour outside tending to their horses, and put the animals away as it started to get dark. To the east, stars started to shine against a dark purple background, but to the west, the setting sun was a burning orange, with bright pink and purple clouds set against a light blue and green sky. Bright orange, long straight clouds criss-crossed the sky, in various stages of dispersal.

'God, look at that, it's beautiful out here tonight!'

'Dad says those clouds are pollution, God had nothing to do with them!' conversed the twins.

All around the country, everybody got on with their days, some loving it, some detesting it. Sophie went round to have a few beers with Miriam, Simon and the family. Every Christmas, Simon made a fabulous raspberry trifle, always leaving a portion for Sophie. Kay went to her mother's country manor house for a huge family celebration, CT sat at home, having invited his father and his little terrier dog to spend the day watching the sports channels. Charlie had not woken in his own bed, and only just made it to his parents' home after paying treble for a taxi fare, wishing he'd had time for a shower. Annie had driven down to her mother in High Wycombe. They had gone to a local pub that was serving three-course, expensive Christmas dinners. Annie and her mother had decided it would make a nice change, rather than going abroad to Florida or the south of France.

Dylan spent his day alone recording some new tunes in his studio. Peter, the little rabbit would sit in a soft fabric cat house in the corner of the room, following Dylan about if he went out of eyesight. Ed spent Christmas day with his sick sister in hospital. She had been in a coma for just over a year, so this was in fact his second Christmas in hospital. He spent most of his spare time with her, reading magazine articles and playing her his latest mixes. Robert and Uncle Sam each had to endure their partner's families, driving around dropping off presents, and filling the car up with more crap they would never use. Except the socks... *Surely men need more than socks in their lives,* they both thought, thinking of all the money they had handed over to buy expensive, thoughtful gifts, just to receive socks. They both knew it was about the giving, not the receiving. They just both wished they could receive something other than... socks. Mr Keiffson always spent Christmas in Sweden. He had family there, and would go rally driving through snow covered pine forests, and skinny-dip in hot springs whilst sipping cold beers. It was the one time of year he overindulged, switched off from work and enjoyed his undoubted success. Drayton sat in his large stone house with Lynnie and Lena. It was the usual, where Lena would arrive home in the early hours of the morning, then refuse to get up until late afternoon. By then Drayton and Lynnie would have exchanged presents, had their lunches, and would be curled up together watching the 50-inch flatscreen in the family room. Lena would proceed to moan and complain that they could have waited for her, or at least woken her. Her dinner would be heated in the microwave and her presents were never right. Over the years, they had learnt to switch off to Lena's Christmas tantrums, and instead got as drunk as they could, enjoying each other's company.

Chapter Thirty-two

New Years Eve, 2011, Lincolnshire

Art loved New Year's Eve. Not for the parties, or an excuse to drink to excess. It was for the simple fact it was a full year before the trauma of Christmas came around again. This Christmas had passed by quite peacefully, as they had stayed at the cottage fishing, drawing and gardening. He was looking forward to guests coming for a day by the lake and wondered if he had done the right thing by inviting John and his flatmate, Rev. He did not know them, he knew nothing about them, but he had felt it was the right thing to do.

The weather had made a turn for the worse and as hot as Christmas had been, within three days it had dropped to below freezing, dropping well below at night. He stood setting up his rods noticing that the small bays around the lake had a thin layer of ice over the undisturbed water. Crystallised frost hung on every branch and grass blade, making the countryside look like it had been dusted with icing sugar. The ground was rock hard below a pale blue sky, where the sun was just rising above the horizon like a white disc as it tried to fight through the low cloud. The robin called by, causing ice crystals to fall from branches as it landed. The delicate particles drifted and danced as they fell in the still air, adding to thick frost on the ground. The small bird hopped from branch to branch, chattering and fluttering its wings. *Wish I knew the language of the birds* he thought. It suddenly flew off, as a dark shadow reflected from the lake's surface. Art looked up and saw a buzzard, circling directly above the trees surrounding the water. He watched as it glided and soared, but could not believe it when it swooped down to skim the water before climbing above the trees. It did this a few times, which allowed Art to get his camera and take a picture. As he focused on the centre of the lake, watching as the bird descended, it changed course slightly, so as he took the shot it was flying towards him at an angle, capturing both its front and side. The photograph was fantastic, perfectly in focus, so all of the spray from the water and the bird's feathers were clearly defined.

Art had been working hard on his book. He had drawn watercolour pictures of the lake throughout the year, noticing the change in the seasons. He had recorded all of the fish he had caught, the weather and drawn plants and flowers as he noticed them develop. He had also taken lots of photographs of the dramatic sunrises and sets. The main thing he had noticed was that no matter what the weather did, the plants at the lake always looked healthy and fresh. There had been some extreme weather worldwide, not just in Lincolnshire, with strange temperatures at the wrong time of year. Art noticed in his photographs that the lake's water level never changed. He wondered if there was a leak somewhere, which would also account for the large puddle of water that was still in the corner of the meadow. *I'll mention it to William,* he thought, as the robin came back to sprinkle some more 'fairy dust frost'. He still had the camera in his hand and so took several pictures of the robin. He got a prizewinning picture just as the bird landed on a branch, with its wings splayed out, as frost formed a puff cloud of crystal. As with the buzzard, the clarity of the picture was perfect. Art could not believe his luck. Maybe the wildlife was getting used to him silently standing, watching the water. *Remember to watch the birds,* he heard William saying, thinking back to the day they had been shown the tunnel to Temple Bruer.

By lunchtime William and John were setting up a rod each. Rev was playing with Nicholson. There had been an awkward moment between William and Rev when they recognised each other from the seed delivery to Molay Barn, but as Art was talking to John about the lake, no one had noticed.

'Hello son, I hope all is well?' William asked Rev, as the kindness in his eyes was lost for a moment.

'Hello Sir, yes, everything is good thank you. That's John, my housemate,' he said pointing. 'He's the one I told you about who has just started to grow plants. One of Miss Kain's plants, and he now has a spider plant that his mentor gave him.' Rev had decided to ignore the stern stare he had received from Mr Idol, because he did not want to feel threatened by the strange, old man. Mr Keiffson trusted him and so for that reason alone, he was as good as his word. He did not need some gentle persuasion from the old guy. He felt that this afternoon would help Mr Idol realise that he could be trusted and so did not feel threatened by 'that look'. They tied traces and prepared their rods while Art talked to William about the strange things that had been happening. He mentioned the puddle in the meadow, the huge shadow he had seen in the water of a massive fish and finally how the nature around the lake seemed so healthy compared to the local land. William listened to everything Art had to say and put down his rod. He stood by the water looking across to the other side, squinting as he looked.

'You see that bit of land that sticks out and has a big boulder on it?'

'Yes, I see it!'

'You ever properly looked at it?'

'No, not specially.'

'When you get the chance, go and have a good look at it!'

'What am I looking for?' Art asked, puzzled as to how that could be the answer to all of his questions.

'You'll know it when you see it! Don't worry about the puddle in the meadow. The lake level is the same. It's probably just rainwater in the meadow!'

'That's the problem... it hasn't rained. I could understand the meadow flooding, but again, there had been no rain. The night we had the live band play was bone dry, and it definitely wasn't spilt cider. Nicholson taste-tested it!'

'You say that when you had the live music here the water appeared?' asked William, trying not to sound as interested as he was. 'I know you said it was a good night, but I thought you meant it was wild and mischievous. Why was it such a good night, son?'

'The band was great, really good. It was an emotional time for them as it was Joey's and Liam's first live gig together since they were kids. And Coco's friend Pod, her daughter did a guest set on her cello that had everyone in floods. It was just a *really* emotional night!' he said.

'What song did they play? The one when Pod's daughter played?'

'Why, what are you thinking?' asked Art, not knowing the significance of what he was about to say.

'Well, son,' stalled William, as he tried to think of something to say, 'I thought I might listen to the track, um... to try and see how it makes me feel,' he lied, 'though I know it's not the same as hearing it live with your friends in your own meadow!' William knew that the puddle in the field at Railway Cottage was a result of the pure spring rising to the surface, brought to life by the emotion and sounds of the mini concert. He would have to tell Dylan.

The House of Rock, London

Dylan was sat at home eating marmite on toast with Peter the rabbit munching on the wholemeal crusts he was fed, when he received a phone call. There had been a few, all from one unknown number. At first it had worried him a little bit, but after the last few meetings with Dave of the FDC, the calls were not so problematic. Dylan had received that many of them, he now had a process by which he tried to solve the problem he had been given.

'*The Masterplan*, Oasis. Mr Lizard has also been informed. You have three days, thank you, good luck!'

He lived in a converted old cotton factory in Islington, North London, where each of the three floors had been made into a huge, open-plan flat, complete with the original supporting decorative iron pillars. Each wall had big windows all the way along, made from the original metal squared panes. Dylan's flat also had huge, modern, Victorian skylights so sunlight flooded the enormous room all day long. The light came in from all directions, and Dylan would often sit in the middle of the room in a big leather chair, a guitar on his lap jamming as he watched the sun or moon circle the room. The bare-brick walls were covered in framed gig posters, gold discs and framed band merchandise. In one corner was his small recording studio, lined with racks of vinyl. His drums were set up in the centre of the room, and a selection of guitars hung around the walls, one in-between each window. There was an electric gate system and enough room for three cars outside, but up in his modest penthouse, he was the happiest he had been in a long time. There was the apocalyptic event quickly approaching, but his time in the penthouse with Peter had been productive and harmonious and he was too busy to have time to think about life after the Summer Solstice. He had planned and organised packing all of his stuff up in May, and storing it at Rik's homestead for safety.

He often sat up on his roof terrace, which he'd had reinforced so he could grow large trees in heavy pots, and sit on his wooden steamer chair, sipping a beer and playing his guitar through his headphones. He'd been able to buy the terrace with the money he won from the competition, and even had a greenhouse, potting shed and water tap so he could tend to his plants. It was all very low maintenance and easy to care for and the plants came year after year, increasing in size and intertwining themselves together. His mother popped by in spring to spend a week tidying the plants, and she would prune and stake things for the following year. He always made sure he didn't have anything growing in his greenhouse when she came, as there were certain plants grown in it that he did not want her to see! He'd also had to add a glass fence all the way around the roof edge when he had brought Peter home, as he did not want the little rabbit to fall off the edge, but did not want his views of the city to be spoilt. He had therefore chosen a green-smoked, toughened glass screen and also put a large deep peat-pit hidden in one of the corners for Peter to dig in, sheltered by a large, purple flowering hebe. There was a bench and table facing south with heavy beams supporting flowering, climbing plants where he would entertain friends with a barbecue and music played out of stone shaped outdoor speakers. He would sit with friends until the early hours of the morning, sometimes until the Sunday morning sun came up, talking about music and listening to new tracks. The sound of the city would vary, depending on the weather and time of day. He loved to stand in the corner overlooking the centre of London, in an old red phone box he had bought, protected from the rain as he watched everyone dashing about, getting wet. It made him feel like a Bond villain, or an extra in a Batman film, but he loved the isolation, watching the distorted lights through rain drips on the windows, listening to the patter noise of the rain and taxi brakes mixed in with police sirens and car horns.

As with every other song he had previously tested in the system, he fed *The Masterplan* into his computer, where a program was constantly running and analysing each song he entered. It had been sent to him by the IT guys at MBHK who would also be checking it. They had been doing this for nine months, looking for the best track list for the main event. Each song that was investigated, was judged for a series of criteria: the amount of energy from a crowd it might produce, the quality and power of the bass and drums, its popularity, the length of the track and finally whether it had the minerals needed to be 'The One' as Ed would say. It had always made him laugh. Dylan knew this one was not long enough to be the final song, but it would certainly be a contender for the show. They had run through so many songs; Bob Marley's *One Love*, Thin Lizzy's *The Boys Are Back In Town*, Deep Purple's *Smoke Over Water* and Guns and Roses' *Welcome to the Jungle*. He got goosebumps when he thought of the possible combinations of artists that might end up performing each song. It had not been difficult to book the musicians they had wanted, as the event had been billed as a charity event, and all that had been contacted were eager to play with holograms of their own deceased heroes.

MBHK Headquarters, England

'Gentlemen, sorry for this emergency meeting, but something has been brought to our attention which you must all hear about,' said Dave, over a secure telephone line linked to five other phones. He proceeded with his conference call. As important researchers and heads of their departments for the MBHK, Ed, Rik, Uncle Sam, Robert and Dylan all listened. 'We received a phone call an hour or so ago, to say the spring at one location has responded to human interaction. This is a very positive piece of information and proves we were thinking along the right lines. As you will all have noticed, the alignment is coming to its final stages, hence the erratic weather and general increased temperatures, which is another reason why the spring has responded. At one property in Lincolnshire, on the fifth of November, there was a live band which played to a small group of friends. It was a massively important event for all those who were there, and one particular song had roused really strong emotions. The owner of the property says there is a puddle of water where the stage was, and it is unexplained. However, we know that this property is directly over the pure water spring and a lake nearby is also fed by the spring. Our source says he has witnessed the unexplained puddle for himself, though the lake level has not risen. Gentlemen... everything we have prepared for over the last twenty-five years is about to be tested. From the event in Lincolnshire, it is quite apparent that the event in Somerset has a very good chance of being a success.' Dave waited, but there were no questions, just the buzz of static on the five phone lines.

'People... since 1600 when the MBHK was first formed, we have been working to this time. Our ancestor's time was very different from ours, but with the increase in technology over the last twenty years our job has been made a little easier. Please start to back up all of your files on portable hard drives, and download absolutely everything to the secondary main computer, or SMC. Just to remind you, as the SMC and the main computer are protected deep underground, they will not be affected by the heat and incineration. Although there will be no power to run them after the event, they will be safe until the survivors work out how to produce power from the wind, sun or water. Obviously there will be no satellites, so no internet, but the hard drive will work with power. The SMC is the only part of electrical equipment that is not connected to the internet and everything that is downloaded to it will be transferred over each night from the main computer, basically locking it in, safe from anything. Remember, we don't know when the satellites will be taken down.'

'As it is getting so close to the time, we at MBHK Headquarters feel it is also time we give you a full explanation, as to how we originally formed. There are only six months left, but please, remember this has to remain top secret, and can never be repeated.' Dave went to each listener independently, for a brief chat and confirmation of the severity of what he was about to say.

'We were formed after a secret that had been guarded by the Templars was discovered. Just before the 1600s, the same script that the Knights found at the start of the century was rediscovered in what is modern day Israel. Nostradamus had drawn a secret notebook too, translating the original copy which the Knights guarded. Isaac Newton was in on it too. He helped the early members of the MBHK find the derelict preceptories, indicating where the pure water spring flowed. The "Man Being Human Kind" foundation was formed in Florence. It held its headquarters there until recently, but back then Florence had the greatest minds that had ever existed in the modern world. They had met there regularly during the Italian Renaissance. Da Vinci had been one of the key theorists of the time, and the MBHK Foundation studied his notes on maths, science and the cosmos. He in turn had studied Ancient Greece and Rome. The Templars also compiled a book on herbal remedies, which actually corresponds with a seed collection in Cumbria. With the information we got from the history of the Templars, by studying the locations of their preceptories and the works of the High Italian Renaissance super minds, we started to deduce what the Templars had started working on. With the development of the internet, we could collate our information far quicker, and from all over the world. The symbols that were found were the greatest missing piece of the puzzle, and it was only once the Mayan Calendar was discovered and deciphered that all the other symbols made sense. Following in the path of the Templars, the MBHK were able to track the pure water spring, and quickly found that the symbol appeared wherever the spring surfaced. I guess you can consider yourselves Contemporary Knights of the Templar!'

'Please, if you have any questions please book a slot to have a personal call. I wanted to keep this brief so as not to disrupt your New Year's Eve. If anyone missed any of this conference call, hang back at the end and I will go over anything that was missed. Good luck gentlemen, and have a Happy New Year.'

The Railway Cottage, Lincolnshire

As the final hours of 2011 passed, Art, William and John fished. Rev wondered around the lake, taking in its beauty, comparing his new life with how destitute life had been on the seventh floor squat. He had nature all around him, fresh water harbouring fish and plants. Birds flew amongst the trees, winter flowers and berries added a splash of colour and the fresh air was cold and sharp in his lungs. He sat on his own, a little way away from the others and simply watched… watched all that was in front of him. A little Robin flew down and sat on a low branch, chirping and chattering as it hopped from branch to branch. It came so close to Rev that he could have reached out to touch it. He remained perfectly still and smiled as the bird continued to sing and dance. It startled and flew away when there was a sudden splash and shout from John.

'Help me, please. I don't know what I'm doing and I think I've hooked Jaws!' Rev heard a familiar voice echo across the lake. The splashing increased followed by John's expletives.

Art helped to bring the fish in. He gave advice as John acted on his instructions. 'William, he's not kidding. It's huge!' Art exclaimed. They had been catching some big pike all day and both William and Art had hoped that the massive shadow from the photograph might still be about. Art had been slightly miffed, as he only seemed to get the bigger fish whenever William was around. Rev sat and watched as the three of them reeled the fish in. It was quite comical, as William and Art were obviously accomplished fisherman and yet John who had never fished in his life had hooked a whale. Art held a landing net, which he quickly threw to the ground in order to pick up a much bigger one. William was demonstrating with his 'air' fishing rod, as John watched his actions and copied him. After a good ten minutes, the lake fell silent and the surface of the water settled back into its mill pond stillness. Rev stood up so he might see what Art and Mr Idol were doing.

John's pike was absolutely massive. Art was sat astride it, with his fingers in its gills, and a pair of forceps in its throat as he unhooked it. The fish wriggled and fought its long silvery, green body, as it tried to catch Art on his back with its tail. William was standing by with the scales as John took a step back. He crouched down to watch as Art expertly released the fish, taking care not to get bitten or cut by the predator. Just as the serenity of the lake had recovered from the commotion, whoops and cries echoed around the lake and much of the surrounding countryside. Rev jumped up and ran around to his friend and the commotion, wondering if there had been an accident. He ran into the clearing of the trees to see

Art stood next to the trunk bench, with John standing upon it. Due to their height difference, John needed some elevation to help hold the fish in the weighing scales with Art. They were each holding a short arm of the scales, as William tried to work out how heavy the fish was.

'Yes... yes... son, it's a record beater... forty-seven pounds and six ounces. It might be a world record, Son!' called William, as his excited tones echoed and amplified around the woodland. 'Right, let's get a picture. It's still a bit feisty, you two hold it and I will take the picture!'

'I'll take the picture for you. You should all be in it!' called Rev, as he picked up the camera. 'John would never have caught it, if it hadn't been for you, Mr Idol. You should get the credit too!' This was the opportunity Rev had wanted, and once they were all in place, he took the picture.

An hour later, they were all sat around the dining table in the cottage. It was dark outside and ice crystals had started to form on the outside of the windows. Coco listened to their excited chatter as she made hot drinks. They all sat and discussed the afternoon and she thought how unusual a bunch they were. A revered old man, a nature-loving ecologist, an ex-drug user and a reformed alcoholic, and yet they were all bonding over one of man's most primitive forms of survival. Art got out his book to show how the lake had changed throughout the year, answering John's eager questions. William marvelled at the beautifully articulate drawings and poetic words that described the scenes. Rev played with Mahoney and helped Coco in the narrow kitchen. She was really glad that Art had asked them over. It must be such a contrast from their previous lives. She was pleased she was able to offer the opportunity to embrace the nature that ruled her way of life. She came up with a brilliant plan.

The Apricot Mews

In London, Mike spent his New Year's Eve driving Mr Keiffson to various parties. The gritters had been out, as the temperatures plummeted. They drove past groups of girls scantily clad in sparkly dresses, staggering about on the icy pavements, not being helped by their drunken states and high heels. They passed party revellers going from bar to pub, to club, in fancy dress or premature party popper streamers and silly string. *City's gone mad!* thought Mike, breaking suddenly as a woman stepped out in front of him. He dropped Mr Keiffson off at an exclusive Gentlemen's club

263

and picked him up again an hour later, with a young lady upon his arm. Extremely slender, well-groomed and dripping in expensive jewellery, she was either an heiress or a high-end escort girl. He couldn't decide. One thing for sure, she was very drunk.

They drove around London, stopping for cocktails at Claridges in Mayfair, champagne at Chinawhite and supper at The Ivy. Each time, Mike would drop his boss off with one girl, to pick him up later with a different one. Mike could understand what they all saw in Mr Keiffson. Handsome, wealthy and successful, *How fickle some people can be,* he thought. As he waited in the fully-loaded, top of the range Lexus, Mr Keiffson's business car, he thought about his own life. He saw himself somewhere in-between his boss and one of his runners, Rev. *That poor dude has had it rough,* he thought, *I wonder who hands out the good cards and the bad ones? Your life will be shit...your life will be fulfilled... your life won't be worth living really...you will have everything you want! Who decides?* Mike liked Rev, he had a kind nature, seemed like a passive man, probably more from acceptance of his circumstances rather than being at peace with the world. Rev had even given him a plant grown by his housemate John. Apparently their place was overrun with plants so they were giving them away. He even had one for Mr Keiffson, who had been quite touched when Mike had given it to him.

Mike was happy that he had made the right judgment about Rev, booking him into the tattoo studio with Louis Lou. Having the memorial tattoo would certainly help the poor guy; it might even allow him to move on a little. The shop had studied the pictures Rev had taken in and allocated him an artist. Together they had spent an hour discussing all of the different design ideas and positions he could have the work done. They had made him cups of tea, listened to his story and eventually produced a fabulous drawing. Jess would be framed by roses and each year that passed, he would add another flower. As only three years had passed, leaves and vines would be used as a border, until the roses were laid around her each year. Louis Lou had rung Mike to let him know what the overall cost would be and Mike confirmed for the work to be done. Rev would have his first sitting in January.

The House of Rock, Islington

A few miles away from Mike sat in the Lexus, Dylan was in North London having a house party. Peter had been locked in his hutch, and various members of the music industry and musicians drank, smoked and listened to the latest white labels. They took turns to play instruments together, jamming different genres from reggae to thrash metal. As always, Dylan recorded everything that was played, as it was times like these when miracles were sometimes created. The clashing of creative minds, alcohol and drug stimulation mixed in a heady cocktail of New Year celebrations and anticipation for the forthcoming year could often produce some great riffs and beats.

Dylan had mixed emotions about the party. He had nearly decided not to bother, and to instead sit in on his own. But it was the last New Year's Eve for many. It would certainly be the last New Year's Eve as they knew it, and so he'd decided to throw the best party he could. Members of Coldplay, Muse and the Artic Monkeys popped by throughout the night, taking turns to play together. The greatest moment had been when the biggest names in music performed a medley of Oasis, Stone Roses and their own music. There had been a few fumbled notes and cries of laughter as they got the odd note wrong, but their collective talents produced the best twenty minutes of music most of the country would ever hear. Noel Gallagher arrived an hour after Liam had left, which was a close shave considering the bitter feud that was still going on between the Mancunians. The funniest moment was when Russell Brand had popped in with some of his new material. Russell had performed a stand-up set, having the whole room in fits of laughter as he performed one of his parody songs with some of the musicians present. Dylan made a mental note to ask Russell to do a stand-up set before the start of the main show.

A pub crawl, Grantham

In Lincolnshire, in a historical market town, Kay had organised a New Year's works outing. It would be a classical night out, starting at the local Wetherspoons, before going on to the other pubs with loud music and extravagant lighting rigs. As usual, they would end up in the old church that had been converted into a club. It had a younger cliental, but that did not matter. It was cool and airy, with a high vaulted ceiling and the drinks were cheap. They had pre-ordered tickets for the New Year's party at the club, though as they knew all of the staff, they would have got in anyway. The evening would start out civilised, until the drink started to take effect. The friends would start to talk loudly, laughing and mimicking events they were describing. As the evening wore on, their emotions would become less guarded.

Everybody turned up. Miriam and Sophie came with Annie. CT turned up with Deano, as they had shared a taxi into town together and Charlie turned up with an elegant young lady, who just so happened was not the one he had left in bed on Christmas Day morning. They had decided to get dressed up for the night, though in past years they had worn fancy dress. The men were to wear suits, and the ladies were to wear cocktail dresses. The evening proceeded as all the previous ones had, with dancing, singing and drinking. Friends joined the group, whilst others left, and they bumped into old colleagues with hugs aplenty and hearty welcomes. Their time together was always uncomplicated, happy and memorable.

Annie and Sophie spent a lot of the evening chatting, as they hadn't spoken much since the summer. They got onto talking about their holidays to Egypt and Italy. They had holidayed together in the past, and this had been the first summer they had travelled to different locations.

'Pompeii was fantastic!' Sophie shouted over the music to Annie, 'really spiritual!'

'I've been before, it was amazing. What surprised me was they still built a modern town nearby. That volcano could go off at any minute!'

'I know. Crazy or what!'

'Petra was awesome, really tiring day, but it was fantastic!' replied Annie, stepping aside to let someone squeeze past her.

'Did you see Indiana?' laughed Sophie.

'No, lots of hot rocks and donkeys!'

'Sounds like a porn film,' laughed Sophie again.

'I had a funny turn at Petra. Went all dizzy and started seeing things,' Annie said, not too sure on how much she should mention.

'What sort of funny turn? Miriam had a weird moment at Pompeii. Started talking in tongues and seeing things!'

'No way! So did I at Petra! I saw all sorts of crazy things. So did Charlie and CT! We've not talked about it much because now we're home it seems daft! Ask Deano about his snow globe I bought him! DEANO!' shouted Annie, waving the very drunk Deano over to them. He had two bottles of some fruity alcoholic drink in his hands, and even though he tripped up the step to where Annie and Sophie were, he did not spill a drop. 'Tell Sophie about your snow globe!'

'Yeah, Annie got a snow globe!' slurred Deano, as he had trouble focusing on the two girls.

'Deanooo, tell her about what it was of!'

'It was a globe... full of snow!' he laughed, distracted as the Kings of Leon came on. He tripped back down the stairs as his 'sex was on fire' and started to dance in a way only he could, and nobody else thought they ever should.

'When I bought it, it had a little model of Petra in it, but when I got back to the hotel, it had broken into a pyramid... well, I'd dropped it but hadn't thought I'd damaged it. When I gave it to Deano the three broken bits of Petra had made a rough pyramid!'

'A pyramid? But Miriam keeps seeing a pyramid shape. She even has photographs of a drawing she was 'told' to look at, by someone only she could see!'

'Holy Moses!' Annie said, listening to Sophie but looking over at the little stage at the back of the dance floor. Deano was gyrating around the pole encouraged by a small audience. The conversation was never finished, lost in the comical moment of Deano's antics and the copious amounts of alcohol. They were promptly asked to leave by two very hefty bouncers, and as always, they all went to the next pub together, as they never left a man behind.

Holy Island, Cumbria

In-between Christmas and New Year, Elizabeth and Victoria had been far too intrigued to not investigate the drawers of seeds and the plant diary. They had worked out that the listing in the back of the book referred to the drawer numbers. They had checked their theory out a few times, and found each time the seeds that they had chosen to look for, were exactly where the book said they would be. There were hundreds of entries, each with a date, name and in some cases a Latin name, all with a drawer reference. Elizabeth could not understand why her father had been so sharp when she had mentioned their find, nor could she work out why she had not known about the seed collection in the first place. Her parents were due back in the middle of January to attend a friend's wedding, before travelling to Mexico for a few weeks. Victoria and Elizabeth had decided to ask about the seeds then.

For New Year's Eve, they had decided to have a dinner party and to use the castle to its full potential. They had each invited a few friends. Elizabeth's were all quite local but Victoria's were all travelling up from London. It had been decided though, that there was enough room for everyone to stay for the night. They made huge fires in all of the hearths, laid the table out in the dinning room with the best crockery, glasses and cutlery they could find and ensured the meal was perfect. As their friends arrived, they sat around the fire in the cosy lounge, drinking wine and spirits. It was bitterly cold outside, and the causeway had been treacherous to navigate. Victoria had to drive over to the mainland and pick up some friends who were too concerned to make the drive in their little city run-around. The powerful 4x4 had come in handy once again.

The evening went exactly as planned. They had their meal at the long, oak dining table, lit with grand, silver candelabra. Chatter and laughter mixed with the sound of silver cutlery on porcelain plates and fine crystal 'tinged' whenever it was carelessly touched with a knife or folk. Whilst the fire gave a golden glow and its heat kept the room warm and snug, the howling, frostbitten winds wrapped around the castle and the little island. A rare ice storm was forming, where absolutely everything the rain fell on, turned to ice. The more rain that fell, the thicker the ice would become. By the time midnight came and the friends decided to go out to watch any fireworks from the mainland, the courtyard was a sheer ice rink. The top of the wall had an inch of ice and icicles hung down from the overhanging brick lip. The purple and grey landscape of rocks around the castle glistened as if made of diamond studded glass, as the moon reflected off some of the surfaces whenever it got the chance to shine through the clouds. It was eerily quiet, as anything that could have moved in the abating winds was frozen solid. Over on the mainland, the little village looked like it was made of sugar, as the monastery stood forlornly and ghostly when the lunar spotlight was switched on and off. Everyone was mesmerised by the remote beauty of the scenery, which became enhanced as the pub in the village let off some fairly impressive fireworks at the stroke of 12. The church bells rang out and the sound of distant cheers and renditions of *Old Lang Syne* drifted across the almost frozen expanse of water to the island. Each firework exploded into a million tiny, coloured stars reflecting off the icy surroundings. The countryside looked like it was under attack from a giant disco-ball as the dancing stars enraged the sky before disappearing.

Victoria's friends from London were very impressed, as they were used to thousands of people all crammed into Trafalgar Square, surrounded by red buses and black cabs permanently queuing around the London hot-spot. Street vendors would be selling flags and whistles, hot chestnuts and hot dogs. A heavy police presence was always felt, as the drunken crowd tried to mount the massive lions around the fountain. Riot vans and mounted police would be on hand to sort any trouble, as revellers battled with the cold and overindulging in festive spirits. The atmosphere at Holy Island could not be any further removed from the chaos and madness of the centre of London.

Around the world, as the earth spun from December to January, people celebrated in different ways. From carnivals in Brazil, massive firework displays in Australia and the big ball dropping in Times Square in New York, many of the world's cultures celebrated the end of the old year and the beginning of the New Year. The civilized world partied and drank, all except for a few. There were a few who knew it was the last year. Future celebrations would be thankful for a good harvest, celebrating the survival of a harsh winter or the completion of a new building. Things were going to be very different and most of the population of the world wouldn't know what was happening.

Chapter Thirty-three

January 2012, Lincolnshire

The big day Rev had been waiting for had finally come. He was due at Lou's N Up at 11 in the morning for the start of his tattoo and had followed the procedure he had been advised to take. His artist DD, short for Dragonfly Day had told him to rest well the night before and to eat a good breakfast and to take in plenty of fluids. It had been explained if the body was harmonious, the stress of the tattoo would be far less painful. DD had explained that the pain would vary depending on whereabouts on his body the work was to be done and how refreshed and relaxed he was. Rev had eventually chosen the left-hand side of his chest, above his heart. The roses would eventually come down his arm and around his shoulder. DD had warned that it was a painful area to choose, to which Rev had replied 'Not as painful as every day I have suffered without Jess!' DD knew that this tattoo would mean the world to his client, which helped him focus on the design and drawing.

The tattoo studio was a huge 1940s three-storey building, with glass windows extending up to the first floor on a narrow pedestrianised street in the old part of Grantham, near the Angel and Royal Hotel. It had been a clothes shop, but Louis Lou had bought it as soon as it became available. The building had many original shop features, with curved ground floor windows leading to the shop door set back from the street. The first floor above was supported by two decorative, cast iron pillars that stood level with the shop front and the same decorations framed the metal window frames. A delicate flow of flowers and vines, synonymous with the Art Nouveau style, were evident in all of the building's details, which had lovingly been restored. In each of the curved windows there was a tattooist's workstation, comprising of a state-of-the-art, black leather tattoo chair, various lamps and rests, an artist's swivel stool and a stainless steel surgical trolley on lockable wheels. A track ran around the top of the windows where a black plastic curtain could be pulled around, to make the space more private. Whilst he waited for the shop to open, Rev noticed how immaculately pristine and tidy it was. Each workspace had a glass shelf unit displaying a full set of inks neatly laid in colour order, with the shelves below storing glass jars of ink caps, disposable razors and wooden dental spatulas.

The decor was black, white or chrome accented with various blue and green tiles around the sinks. Some vintage Victorian tiles had also been interspaced with contemporary ones, each with rich complimentary colours. As Rev peered through the glass door, he could see a wide, wooden sweeping staircase in the centre of the room, with a tall reception desk on the left by the bottom step and a seated area to the right. Three large, expensive black leather sofas sat around a smoked glass table with some magazines neatly splayed out on it. A tall reading lamp stood in the corner, one-off framed drawings by the artists hung on the walls and some big plants stood in huge black ceramic pots separating the stairs from the waiting area.

It was very cold and Rev started to wonder if he had got the wrong time. It was nearly 11 and the shop was still closed. He dug his gloved hands deeper into the pockets of his jacket and stomped his feet, watching snug and smug people drinking tea in the very old Angel and Royal Hotel. He turned back to the tattoo shop and saw certificates mounted on the wall behind the reception, a drawing board with a lightbox and a small kitchen area at the back of the shop. Everything about the shop cried 'classy'. Every surface gleamed; even the wooden floor of the reception and waiting area. The tiled floor of the workspaces was clean enough to eat your dinner from. A wall of frosted glass bricks segregated the tattooing area from the rest of the shop, with a frosted glass door decorated with a large clear glass Chinese dragon tattoo design. It was not how he had imagined the tattoo studio to be. He had expected laminated pages of tattoo designs blue-tacked to the walls, and a scary black and red interior. Not this... the nearest thing he had seen to someone's front room.

At exactly 11 o'clock, a tall, slim girl in a short, tartan pink dress and tall, bright pink tartan Dr Martin boots turned up and made her apologises for keeping him waiting. He sat and waited on the edge of one of the sofas, flipping through one of the magazines, occasionally watching the girl as she busied about with her chores. The shop had a strong smell of Dettol and a hint of rose due to the products used to deep-clean every surface of the shop at the end of each day. She busied about, making him a cup of tea, turning on some heavy rock music and preparing the workspace for his tattoo. He marvelled at how efficient she was, wearing latex gloves to wrap the left-hand side of the chair with cling film. She then rolled out a wide paper towel to cover the back and seat of the chair and set up a tray with ink pots, a plastic cup of water and some black latex gloves.

'Would you like the blinds pulled, or are you happy to have the public walking by watch you?' she called over the music, popping her head around the dragon-designed door.

'I don't mind. What do people usually do?' he replied.

'Well, it varies. This is your first tattoo isn't it?'

'Yes, bit nervous really.'

'It's up to you. See how you go and if you want them shut, just ask. There can be quite a crowd out there sometimes when people stop to watch a really good piece being done.'

'If I start crying like a baby, maybe I will have them closed!'

'It's not that bad. A bit like scratching severe sunburn. That's the best way to describe it,' she smiled.

'No, I mean... I mean I might be a bit emotional!' Rev said, looking slightly embarrassed.

'Oh, sorry... wrong end of the stick... really sorry. Let me know anyway!'

An hour later, the receptionist was pulling the curtain across the window on Rev's request. DD had stopped work for a moment, as he changed his tattoo gun for a different needle type, allowing Rev time to compose himself. The outline of the design had been lightly tattooed in a grey shade, so DD had all of his guidelines in place, ready to work. With the help of Katie, the receptionist, he had got Rev to stand perfectly straight, with his arms hung naturally by his sides as he looked straight ahead. It had been explained that he had to stand as true as possible, so the carbon design of his tattoo could be placed exactly right. A muscle tensed wrongly would distort the placing of the tattoo carbon. DD had put the faint image of Jess on his chest, with three roses around the bottom and vines and rose buds framing her portrait. There were eleven rose buds; one for each of the years Rev had known Jess, which completed a beautiful border around her portrait. The work in its primary stages already looked just like Jess, which had caused Rev to get a little emotional. Katie, the receptionist, brought him another cup of tea and offered him a lollipop to suck on.

As DD worked with his tattoo gun in his left hand, he used his right hand to pull Rev's skin tight. He worked quickly, constantly referring to the drawing laid on Rev's ribs. As he worked, Rev watched the image appear before him and smiled. This was definitely the right thing to do. He thought back to when DD had asked a few questions as he had filled out a consent form. He had proudly answered 'No' when asked if he'd 'had a drink?' Rev paid careful attention as DD expertly worked. He had used a wooden spatula to put Vaseline on the back of his right hand, ready for when he needed it. DD had explained as he worked, that the Vaseline stopped the wiped away ink from staining the skin. He expertly used the gun, powering it with a foot peddle. He worked in a flowing manner, leaning over Rev for a perfect view, starting the gun up each time he dipped the needle into the little pot of 'light grey-shade' and stopping it after the ink had been applied. He repeated this until he had all the lines and shades in he needed for the first sitting. DD left the room when he had finished and Katie then came in and put some more gloves on. She got a mirror for him to look at the work. It was too much for Rev and he broke down sobbing. Katie stood with him for a while, putting a hand on his arm and handing him a tissue. She stayed with him as he told her the story about Jess, and dutifully Katie listened as she wiped over the work with a mild soap and water solution. She then applied a thin layer of Vaseline and stuck down cling-film over the design to keep it clean.

Before he left the shop, he was given a guide on how to look after the tattoo. DD explained that the first sitting was to just get basic outline and shades in. The next sitting he would complete the portrait and the final sitting he would touch any bits and add the very black shadows and white highlights. Rev had wanted it to be finished in one day, but DD explained the work had to be built in stages, so he could look at it with fresh eyes each time, to make the necessary additions correctly. It was one of Louis Lou's strict rules, as no work was ever to be rushed at Lou's N Up. DD also explained that the photographs that had been taken at regular intervals throughout the work would be put onto a CD for him to take home, so he could see how the portrait developed. By the time Rev left the shop, it was well past lunch time. Louis Lou was working in the other window, on a huge design on someone's back and a large crowd outside had formed to watch him work. He wore silk, dark grey trousers and a white, collarless Chinese shirt. *Not your average tattooist!* Rev thought, *but then again, his work is way above average!*

As Rev stood waiting to make his next appointment, people came and went. Upstairs there was a tattoo removal service run by DD's wife and a beautician offering manicures, facials and massage which was run by Louis Lou's wife. There were a further four tattooists in the studios on the other floors, each having been strictly vetted by Louis Lou. He would only employ someone if he felt their work was good enough to be on his own skin. Part of their interview was to tattoo him. He therefore had a full sleeve of beautiful flowers, each by a different, accomplished artist. If he was in a particularly awkward mood, he would ask the interviewee to design a cover up for a botched tattoo he had done himself on his ankle bone. It was one of the toughest places to work on but it was set as a test of creativity and stamina, not artistic skills. He never had the botched tattoo covered, it was all just a mind game to try and work out the artist. Katie was kept constantly busy, as she cleaned up after DD, passed things for Louis Lou and advised customers with their design ideas.

Once he had booked his next appointment, Katie helped Rev on with his coat. She had booked him in four week's time. It was explained that the minimal time was a month, to allow the skin to heal before the next session. As he left the shop, a tall Oriental security guard in an authentic blue and green Samurai outfit acted like a club bouncer, checking who was coming in the shop and making sure customers could leave through the crowd. He opened the door for Rev, performed a quick little martial art movement and bowed. Some of the crowd clapped at the performance, as he resumed his position as doorman. The bouncer ensured none of the public came too close to the window and anyone making a noise or touching the window would be asked to move on.

As Rev made his way home, he kept putting his right hand up to his chest and smiling. Jess would be with him always from now on, just where she should be, over his heart. He was ecstatic about the design and all that it stood for. His experience at Lou's N Up had been almost enlightening. The atmosphere, the confidence and professionalism of the staff and even to a point the doorman, had all contributed to an amazingly emotional experience. He had often thought about having a tattoo, but he could never think long enough about it, because of his alcoholism, to make a decision. As soon as he had managed to sort himself out, he'd had the idea to have Jess done. It was strange in a way, a vicious circle. He drank to drown the nightmares he harboured in his dark side and yet it was only once he stopped drowning them, did he have the foresight and focus to think about how to cure them for good. If he hadn't stopped drinking, he would never have thought of the idea that he came up with. *The evils of drink doth cometh twice!* he thought, amazing himself at the creativity of his thoughts.

Holy Island, Cumbria

On New Year's Day, William had received the most surprising phone call. He instantly recognised the voice and had to quickly sit down. He could not believe who he was talking to after 40 years. They chatted as if they were still in their twenties until the talk of grandchildren brought them back to reality.

'Yes, I'm a Grand Pappi at last. Elizabeth had a little boy, Adrian, in June last year!' said Mr Claudius, from the island.

'Well well old man, the castle must feel vitalised, energised!' replied William.

'I wouldn't know. We spent a few weeks at home until Elizabeth was settled in, but she has a friend staying with her, so we carried on touring. Austria was fabulous, you should go, old man, before you are too rickety!'

'I'm long past Austria, already way past rickety!' William mocked.

They continued with their banter until they had arranged for William to visit Holy Island. Mr Claudius would be retuning home from a trip to Mexico in a few week's time. William had lied to his daughters that he was going to use his holiday voucher for two, when he had really given it to Art and Coco. He would instead use the holiday to the inn as a cover-up to go and visit Holy Island. What William could not work out was why his old friend had been so keen for him to visit as quickly as he could, considering they had not spoken to each other for decades. William knew a visit to the island would be extremely beneficial right now, with the Summer Solstice fast approaching, but could not understand why there had been such anguish in Ivan's voice. All of the seeds would be quite safe in the cellar. The plant diary was a perfect cover for the true identity of each seed. Perhaps the book had been lost, or Elizabeth's friend had found the seed drawers?

Two weeks later he was driving up the Great North Road through Cumbria. The landscape became more and more remote, until he turned off between a few small hills and dropped down to sea level. Out in the distance was the little ochre-coloured castle on top of its perilous perch, with an azure sea reflecting the deep blue of the sky. It was a perfect blue sky. *Perfect*, William thought. *I can't remember the last time I saw a perfect blue sky. I guess they don't need to spray out here as there isn't much to protect or destroy, depending on which story you believe!* he considered. Seagulls floated in the gentle breeze screeching and shouting to one another. He drove on past the tourist car park, which was virtually empty. At the crossroads he turned left towards the causeway, and stopped outside the little inn where his daughters had bought him the mini break. *Nice place, open log fires, and no fruit machines!* he thought, looking through the small leaded windows, *Art and Coco will like it in there!* He drove on and checked the time. Ivan Claudius had told him the best time to get there because of the tides and he was virtually spot-on.

Later in the afternoon, Ivan Claudius had suggested the girls should go shopping in Durham for the following day. They could take the gold card and treat themselves. That way the two old men could talk about old times in peace. Elizabeth, Victoria and Mary, Elizabeth's mother, were quite happy to go and shop, knowing the two old friends had a lot to catch up on. None of them knew the true origin of their friendship and they did not need to know. With everyone out for the day William and Ivan could check out the seed store. It had been a joyous reunion when Ivan and Mary had seen their daughter after such a long break away. Ivan asked how the business was doing and Elizabeth said the hotels were always full and doing really well. Mary tended to Adrian, loving the feeling a new baby brought to the family home. Adrian was her first grandchild and she became very close to him. The mutual bond was quite obvious. William also enjoyed the giggles of the child and would spend ages pulling silly faces and making daft noises to which the boy would gleefully respond. At nearly seven months old, he was forming his own character and personality. He was a happy child and although two of the people staying at the castle were not related, they all felt like a family.

Ivan and William waved off the 4x4, as Victoria drove off the island onto the causeway. They had been wasting time with getting ready and nearly missed the crossing before the tide started to come in. Ivan had suggested they should make a day of it and booked them into the best hotel in Durham for the night. This gave plenty of time to sort out the seeds.

'Okay Ivan, spill the beans old man!' William had said, as they walked back up the ramp to the courtyard. They stood looking out over the sea in silence, remembering some of their little rowing boat trips to and from trawlers anchored just off the sandbanks. Their connection with the MBHK had lasted for most of their lifetime, and although there had been years of non-contact, they picked up their friendship where they had left off. The periwinkle blue sky and forget-me-knot blue sea could quite easily have been mistaken for the Mediterranean, if the weather had not been so cold and sharp. 'Elizabeth has found the seed collection, that's the main problem. The diary went missing years ago. I was concerned that should the seeds be found, there was no back-up to disguise what they might be. Now, strangely, the diary and seeds were both found by Victoria, the girl who is staying with Elizabeth.'

'Oh! Oh dear! Why didn't you just move them somewhere off the island? Put them in one of the disused rooms at one of your inns?'

'William, do you have any idea how many seeds we had collected. There were already the 700,000 from my ancestors and we managed to catalogue about 300,000. Would you risk moving them, knowing half are super strength marijuana seeds?' replied Ivan watching gentle waves break over the sand flats, as the tide started to come in. Within twenty minutes it would be a few feet deep and the island would be cut off once again.

'Good point. Isn't there somewhere else in the castle you could have stored them?'

'Well, that's what I considered, but the seed store is twenty feet long and five feet high. Each drawer is full of seed. There isn't anywhere big enough, which is why I have left them where they are and rung you. How's our dear friend Tarquin?'

'I've not heard from him for a few years. You know he dabbled in politics for a bit in 1997 and has been in all sorts of films, music videos and the such. He was on the bill at Sonisphere Festival at Knebworth a while ago!' laughed William, remembering some of the antics they had all got up to in their past.

'He was a good man. The creativity of this country owes him so much. It's such a shame he isn't more widely recognised for his contribution to the development of this green, very green, and pleasant land.' Laughing, they walked back into the castle, bolting the front door firmly behind them. The secret in the cellar had been there for years. It was a plan William had formed. Back when he first discovered the tunnel in his parents' home, William had constantly wondered what he could do with such a secure, secret place. During their university days, he and Tarquin had devised the scheme whereby they imported goods via Boston port, and stored them underground. They had bumped into Ivan on the party scene in the north and the plan was formulated. Ivan had explained about the Walled Garden, and how for generations seeds were harvested and stored. He told William and Tarquin that an ancient notebook written by a group that stemmed from the 1300s Templars, *The Voynich Manuscript*, listed vital plants that needed to be preserved, as the Knights knew they would be needed at some point.

The connection with the Knights and Holy Island was not written in the history books, as the Templars' secret preceptories had always remained a secret. The name of the island itself was a bit of a clue. From the Holy Land to Holy Island! For 400 years, starting with Great Grandfather Claudius who had introduced himself to the MBHK during a trip to Egypt in the seventeenth century, a long and beneficial partnership had been formed. Grandfather Claudius travelled extensively around the Middle East and Egypt buying items for his new castle, just at the same time that the MBHK was forming, to carry on the great work of the Templars. With the information the MBHK had rediscovered, it had become a monumental task to cultivate and preserve all the plants needed should a global catastrophe occur, which the Templars had discovered was an eventual probability. An interesting paragraph had been translated from the notebook, stating that although no harm would ever come to the plants, flowers or trees, 'caution would go rewarded'.

William and Ivan would store their own seeds at the castle among the flower seeds. Once Ivan became heir to the castle, he filled the drawers with marijuana and herbalistic seeds from all around the world, brought in by small boat to the island, and seeds harvested from the collection in the Walled Garden. When Tarquin had gone into the big league, the seeds remained safely stored, as it was too risky a job to move them all and Tarquin had decided to carry on importing, rather than growing. William had never forgotten about them and knew the 'Plantlore' diary at the castle listed exactly what had been collected. It had just been a matter of choosing a time to collect. As the Summer Solstice had gotten closer, he had wanted to try and move them to Lincolnshire. There was still the ancient family connection from Great Grandfather Claudius and the MBHK. After the Summer Solstice, William knew all medicine would have to be grown, so a comprehensive seed collection was needed. The growing environment was too harsh in Cumbria for them and they could keep Mr Keiffson's seeds company. He had just been unsure how to contact his old friend, Ivan. He did not want to contact him too soon, for fear the secret would be leaked, but he could not leave it too late, as the seeds had to be stored somewhere watertight and underground.

When Ivan had rung him, he knew he had to implement the final stage of his plan. This was exactly what Ivan had wanted, to get the seeds finally off the island. He knew Elizabeth and her intelligent friend had found the store and there was also little Adrian to think of. Although no one knew about the seeds, if they were discovered it would tear his happy family apart and it was a risk he was not prepared to take. The two old men had mutually decided to get the seeds down to Molay Barn as soon as possible.

'Which bottle was it hidden in, I can't remember?' asked Ivan as they descended into the cellar to look for hidden pages of the Plantlore diary, which 45 years earlier they had stored away for safety.

'Oh come on Ivan, think about it.'

'Yes, I can think of a few... oh come on, entertain me old man, it's been a while!'

'Fourth row down, twentieth bottle across. 4:20!' laughed William, putting his arm around his old friend, as they walked to the back of the cellar and through the gap in the racking.

'Of course! 4:20! What else could it possibly be?'

They found the empty bottle in the rack, protected by the dark shadows not dissolved by the small light in the cellar. The metal pillar to the weathervane also helped to disguise the bottle with no cork. William pulled out several sheets of rolled up paper. They were yellowed with age and dusty. A small spider swung back to the rack on a thread of web while the two old men started to study what seeds they had collected. The list brought back many memories. Some were good and a few were bad. There had been the odd time they had nearly got caught and the times when the weather had been so bad they had nearly lost the rowing boat and its contents. There had been many contingency plans for moving the seeds to Lincolnshire and they chose the simplest, least complicated plan. They had decided that the best idea would be to transport the seeds to Molay Barn in cases of glass bottles disguised as 'Holy Castle Red'. One or two actual bottles of wine travelling in each case. The bottles with seeds in would be partially wrapped in decorative tissue. If in a very rare chance a case was opened and inspected, it was hoped it would just look like 12 bottles of wine and nobody would bother to unwrap the covered bottles. It was a simple theory and knowing only too well how other people's minds worked, William was confident that the disguise would be enough to fool anyone.

Ivan had got everything they had needed ready. Cases of empty wine bottles stood among the other boxes in the cellar. He had also had some thin slithers of cork made, which were glued inside the foil wraps that would seal the bottles. Each variety of seed was kept in a small plastic bag which was then folded neatly and poked into the bottles. As they got to work, they made sure each seed packet was clearly marked. The flower seeds were to travel in little boxes. The task ahead of them was enormous. They knew they would have to work right through the night, but had covered themselves by telling the shopping family that they were going to go night sea fishing. They had wondered about the feasibility of their plan, but decided it was the best one. With the rooms of the castle upstairs being undisturbed, no suspicion would be aroused. At least with this plan, there would be no real evidence of their activities except for some newly delivered boxes of wine, should they be discovered before they were moved off the island.

After 36 hours of work, stimulated by energy drinks, Ivan put the last lid on the last bottle and sealed it with a foil wrap secured by a small handheld machine that heated the thin layer of glue on the underside of the foil, gluing it lightly in place. Their work was done. It had seemed like a crazy idea when they were halfway through and had both doubted if they were doing the right thing. William was most insistent that they pushed on through to get the job done. He had already approached Mr Keiffson about transporting the bottled seeds, specifically asking for Rev. He had not let on that he had met the young man at the lake, but instead chose to say he had liked the boy when he had dropped off the Jamaican seeds. William knew that a job like this would pay well and thought Rev deserved the chance to earn it. Mr Keiffson had said the job would be done within a week.

Molay Barn, Lincolnshire

William came off the phone to his friend, Ivan Claudius, a few days after he had come back from his trip to Cumbria. He had rung his daughters telling them what a great time he had. Ivan had said the van with the wine would arrive just after lunch. Two men had turned up and lifted the boxes out of the cellar and onto the van. It had taken them an hour as it was a long way from the wine rack to the top of the ramp where the van was parked. The small vehicle with false plates had been driven by Mike with Rev sat beside him. They even wore shirts that matched the signwriting on the outside of the van. William had been very specific that nothing could go wrong with this job and Mr Keiffson had excelled in the execution of the task. Rev had accepted the position as soon as he was offered it. Although he was now more aware of the risks and dangers involved, he had one more thing he wanted to do before getting himself a proper job.

Coco had offered John the chance to grow his plants at Railway Cottage. She would check on them for him and he was invited to visit whenever he wanted to, to tend to his business. She had offered him the potting shed as somewhere he could grow them, until they could find a way to put a greenhouse up in the corner of the meadow. John had been over the moon, but also full of despair, as there was no way he would ever be able to afford a greenhouse. Rev wanted to do this one last job, so he could be paid in greenhouses. He hoped that this would allow John the chance to develop his own business and the idea had been cleared with Coco, who had to do a little persuading on Art. He did not like the idea of someone constantly calling at the cottage. 'It's bad enough the beehive people and Apple Society being here!' he had protested. Coco had gone on to explain John would come and go unnoticed, just to tend to his plants and would always call when he was visiting. He agreed to the plan after she had mentioned that once John had greenhouses, they would also grow things in them, increasing their output and variety of things they could produce. Art liked the idea of growing herbs and exotic plants for his sauces. The deal was settled. Mr Keiffson would pay Rev in greenhouses as specified by Miss Coco Kain, the lady who grew the plants for the NA group. He liked the idea, ironic as it was.

Chapter Thirty-four

April 2012, Lincolnshire

Drayton finished wiring the final light switch into the wall and stood back to admire his work. He had been working at Railway Cottage for nearly three weeks and could not help but notice how fantastic all of the orchard and plants looked. His own rose bushes were still looking rather sick, except for a solitary yellow rose bush near the kiddie's outdoor water fountain. Art and his father had asked for him to build two greenhouses, each 20 feet long and 12 feet wide. They had all worked together, laying the concrete footings and building with reclaimed wood, which was used to make the panes and they glazed it themselves. John helped by passing things and clearing up, making teas and holding the structure during times of instability. It had been very warm and dry, after a long cold winter. Since the end of February, the weather forecasters had predicted a hot spring but had given no explanation as to why.

After Rev and Mike had delivered the seeds to Molay Barn, with only Rev being allowed to go down into the cellar, Mr Keiffson had contacted William about the payment for the greenhouses. Art had been in contact with his father's friend, Drayton the builder, when an advance had arrived in the post for the building materials. An account had been opened so all of the necessary materials could be purchased and delivered to Railway Cottage. As all the lorry loads of cement, wood and glass had been delivered, Art had become quite distressed. The tyres cut up the grass and one lorry nearly took Coco's decorative drive wall out, as he turned too sharply into the narrow gateway. He admired the way the drivers negotiated the tight turns and knew in the long run the grass would grow back and he would have some spectacular greenhouses. They had decided to put them on the side of the meadow away from the road. That side was in full sun for most of the day. Art also mentioned the puddle that had mysteriously appeared and then disappeared, so the front left of the meadow was avoided, just in case.

The Victorian-style greenhouses had brick footings and low walls, painted the same cream as the house and the wooden window frames were left natural and simply varnished. Along the length of the greenhouses was a raised seedbed down the centre, with a long bench to stand seed trays or pots on down the sides. Coco had insisted that a flowerbed should run along the length of each house on the outside, helping the new structures to blend into the ambience of the small homestead. As the weather had been so kind to them, the work ran smoothly. Art had trouble coping with so many people coming and going, so he would take himself off for a walk around the lake. He took the chance to wander around to the boulder that William had suggested he investigated. Nicholson accompanied him as they walked along the path through early bluebell patches. The deep purple flowers complimented their green leaves, springing up where the sun managed to filter through the trees. The whole woodland was coming alive. Everything seemed so vibrant and luscious. The blossoms in the orchard were as bright and colourful as ever. He had spent quite a few afternoons with Coco in the hammock, drinking homebrewed cider chatting about things that needed to be done. The building of the greenhouses was a little more than they had ever planned for the meadow. They both wondered if it was the right thing to do. Having someone else's greenhouses on your land might prove troublesome, but Coco had been adamant to everyone involved, that if for any reason the scheme did not work, they were to sit down and try to solve the issues. It was also a favour for William, who had supported the idea for John to grow his plants at Railway Cottage. As he had given them the lake, they could not really deny his requests. Art felt slightly trapped, but as Coco kept reminding him, they could also use some of the long benches to stand pots of seeds on, without interrupting John's plant growing.

As Art walked around to the boulder, he noticed an increase of birdlife on the water. All over winter there had been a pair of moorhens, but now he noticed a few other ducks, four swans and a couple of geese. *Bloody things!* he thought, knowing they might disturb his peaceful fishing sessions. The tree tops were full of pigeons and he could hear a cuckoo calling and a woodpecker chiselling at a tree trunk. There even seemed to be an increase in the chicken population, as several birds had migrated over from the freerange chicken farm beyond the fields, behind the cottage. *Everyone is very busy!* he thought. He got to the boulder and crouched beside it. It was about three feet round, covered in lichen and moss. Long weeds grew around its edge, interspersed with pink campion and cowslips. Art did not know what he was looking for and remembered what William had said 'You'll know it when you see it!' He had never had a need to question William before, but the old guy certainly seemed to have an air of mysticism about him. There had been several times it had seemed William had read his mind and he had confessed to having excellent hearing. William had acted a little strangely too, when they had discussed I Scream's performance on firework night.

Art sat on the boulder, stretching his long legs out in front of him. He could hear in the distance Coco and Rev helping Drayton as they did the final tidy up as the greenhouses were finished. He heard the clattering of metal tools and the occasional brushing sound carried on the breeze as the last bits of building material and dust were swept away. The lorries had long since gone and there was just Drayton's flatbed truck being loaded back up with tools. Nicholson sat next to Art on his boulder and watched the waterbirds glide majestically on the lake. Wild flowers carpeted every clearing in the trees, as butterflies and bees busied themselves collecting pollen. Gnats danced in shafts of sunlight descending from the canopy above. Looking up, he noticed long thin clouds criss-crossing the sky. The tree top canopy that crowned the lake stood out against the blue, checkerboard sky but Art wondered how on earth he could protect his land from whatever they were spraying. Coco and Pod had done a bit of research on these chemtrails, and as they had pointed out, whatever it is can't be good, or it would be all over the news. He stood up to take one last look at the rock he was sat on. He pushed the leaves and blades of grass away from the base, running his hand around the underside of its curved base.

His fingertips caught a collection of bumps and ridges. Kneeling on the ground, Art saw facing east across the lake, the symbol that had been on William's cellar door. It was the same symbol that Coco had witnessed at Temple Bruer a year ago. *What the f...?* he thought. *Something is amiss here!* He sat on the dry ground, looking at the base of the rock. Clearly carved into it, was a small triangle, rectangle and circle, exactly like the cellar door design. Exactly like the thing Coco had described. He sat with a puzzled look on his face. Nicholson tried to get his attention, by shoving his nose into Art's hands. He got a half-hearted stroke for his efforts and so barked to get Art's full attention. His master ruffled his coat and absentmindedly fiddled with his ears, but the little dog felt he was not the focus of his master's attention. Art was trying to piece together all the little abnormalities he'd experienced. William always caught the biggest fish, far bigger than Art could ever catch. He had offered Art some strange advice, 'Watch the birds!' He could even lip-read with his back turned and had a somewhat mysterious background where the tunnel was concerned. He could not quite place his finger on it, but something was not right.

Worthy Farm, Somerset

The site had seen an escalation in activity over the last few months. The little village of Pilton on the outskirts of the farm was perfectly used to the comings and goings as they happened most summers. This year had been billed as a lay year but the council had granted a permit for a licence for the show to go ahead. It had cost the MBHK a lot of money in persuasion, but with the promise of a bigger than usual contribution from the profit of the festival being donated to the council, it was an offer they could not refuse. Therefore, the military-style organisation of the festival got into full swing. It was a tried and tested formula that they all adhered to every year. The local residences did not notice that the security fence had gone up a little earlier this year. Locals did notice that there was a large convoy of all-terrain vehicles that was seen driving onto the farm, but none seemed to leave. Some residents had questioned why there were so many military vehicles turning up at the farm. The MBHK sent out flyers explaining that the festival this year had volunteers from the armed forces helping prepare the site. They were only seen turning up in the morning, as the vehicles left at the end of a long day in the middle of the night. Believing what they were told, none of them suspected that hundreds of the vehicles were in fact being stored on the farm.

Usually the final preparations happened in the last three weeks before the festival, where the site would be fully functioning a fortnight before the festivallers started to arrive. This year everything had to be ready much earlier, so it could all be checked and double-checked. Various members of the MBHK ran mock scenarios at the site, ensuring every eventuality had been considered. Hundreds of portable toilets were put in place, massive flags were erected in colourful groups, 'Celeb Chat' booths were installed and repeatedly run to make sure they worked, and the computer games for festivallers to perform with their favourite bands were wired up to the main computer at the MBHK headquarters. The computerised booths and 'Fans Play with Bands' would only work until 21st June, when the heat would take out the satellites, but by then all of the festivallers would be at the Main Stage. The herbal sleeping agent was tested over and over again, which performed perfectly each time, with no side effects of any sort.

Within the Main Stage's backstage area, which had extra fortification, large marquees had already begun to fill up with bottles of water and nonperishable food. No expense had been spared. The medical tent had been extended and its usual supplies of sun cream, after-sun cream and condoms had been extended to stock medical supplies for burns, cuts and dehydration. Nearer the time, the milk from the dairy cows would also be stored and the cows themselves would be housed in special barns away from the festival, but within the safety of the site. It had been a logistical nightmare trying to work out where to put all of the extra equipment and supplies for 180,000 people, without drawing attention to it. The MBHK had been stockpiling necessary supplies, such as massive quantities of pasta, potatoes and firewood. An articulated lorry turned up with just toilet roll on it, another with army surplus blankets and another with just antiseptic and hygiene wipes. Within the back stage area, the two-storey marquee that had been erected as a warehouse started to fill up. It was hidden from view by trees and the Main Stage itself. Everything was stored in it, protected by the reinforced fence.

'Where's Dylan?' Ed asked Rik, as they walked around the site, checking different parts.

'He'll be playing with Kurt and Dave somewhere!'

'What?'

'If ever you can't find him, he'll be in one of the 'Fans Play with Bands' booths, playing guitar with Nirvana!' laughed Rik. 'He says they each need testing and he has taken it upon himself to try them all. He was playing drums with Dickinson and co yesterday!'

'Seriously? You have to be kidding me?' said Ed, 'How can he be so chilled when it's getting so close to the time?'

'You have to admire him. Rather than griping about it, he's making the most of it. Maybe we should all take a leaf out of his book.'

'Yes, maybe, so long as his department is as ready as it can be!'

'He has a very good team. They like him and work hard for him. Robert on the other hand is having a nightmare. He's having to backtrack as some of his questions and irregularities have been noticed by a few people at the RAF. He's having to lay low at the moment.'

'There's only a few more months, he can keep his head down till then. Most of his responsibilities were over months ago, unlike me and Dylan, and you and Uncle Sam after the event.'

'Yes, but you and Dylan have the hardest jobs to do. Finding the perfect songs, getting the right sound and timing down to the last second, new equipment to test.'

'It's all going alright, on schedule at least. We are as ready as we should be at this stage. Everything has been checked and we have a Main Stage test run this afternoon.'

'Wow, that's going to be exciting!' replied Rik.

'It will be... if it all works.'

By the afternoon, Dylan had been located. All of the technicians from the MBHK who had worked on the sound system for the last few years all stood by, as Dylan and Ed stood behind a massive mixing desk, a few hundred yards in front of the Pyramid Stage. They were on top of a tall tower, where all of the electronics for the main show would be controlled from. Below them, in the shaft of the tower were hundreds of miles of specially modified cables, computer systems and monitoring equipment. While Ed and Dylan would control the show, several geologists, scientists and mathematicians would monitor all of the information that would be recorded as the show went on, advising as to how each aspect of the show was progressing. Uncle Sam and Rik sat on the grass in the sunshine, facing the stage. It was ridiculously hot for the time of year, but they all knew why. The tower behind them stood in readiness until Robert walked onto the giant stage.

'Ya having a good time, Glaston-buryyyyyyy?' he shouted, as no sound came out of the speakers. 'Hellooo, one two... one two three!' Still no sound came out of the speakers. Everyone waited in anticipation, and looked behind them towards the tower. If the system did not work, every plug and lead would need to be checked. That would be a long job.

'Have you switched it on, Dylan?' asked Ed.

''Course I've bloody well swit.... yes, it's on now!' he laughed, totally seeing the funny side to his error, as Ed shook his head in disapproval. Millions of pounds in equipment and hundreds of man hours all rested on the first sound check, and he had forgotten to switch it all on.

Dylan gave Robert a signal with his arm, for him to try again. Concentrating, Dylan checked all of his levels as Robert walked back up to the microphone stand.

'Good afternoon, dick-headdddd!' he shouted, as the whole conversation from the control tower had been heard all around the site. The sound was good, but it would take several weeks to perfect it. They would run checks on the bass frequencies, the reverberations of the sound monitored by the geologists, and the mathematicians would need to calculate the exact balance and levels for their intended maximum impact and the primary interaction of the vibration released. The whole system would have to be run at full strength for about two minutes, which would give everyone enough information to be able to calculate any changes.

Chapter Thirty-five

May 2012, Lincolnshire

By the end of May, the Railway Cottage was blooming and blossoming like it had never done before. The woodland was still carpeted in a rich purple from the tallest bluebells Coco and Art had ever seen, interspersed with a few chickens pecking in the dirt. The hot weather had parched most of the countryside, but life at Railway Cottage was as tranquil as ever. To provide the house with some shade, Art had made some triangular, cream-coloured linen sails, which he strung up and pulled taut at strategic positions, shading the sun off the windows and to give the vegetable patch a break from the sun during midday. This simple process meant each of the open windows to the house was in shade, allowing cooled air to fill the rooms. Mahoney and Nicholson suffered the most and they both found relief from shallow holes the rabbit had dug to lie in. Nicholson took advantage of the rabbit's determined burrowing, and pinched the first hole that was dug. The coolness of the earth below the baked surface offered a degree of comfort, especially as the holes were in the shade of The Brew House.

Willowherb fluff had arrived early too. It collected in corners or snagged on brambles, covering everywhere in fluffy, cotton wool-type candyfloss tufts. Coco had spent ages raking it up, but the task was endless, so she gave up. She maintained the vegetable patch, keeping the fluff collected for the compost bin. The hot weather meant she had to water everything everyday in the greenhouses and plant pots. A hosepipe ban had been imposed, but Art and Coco had rigged a hose from the lake, with a filter fitted at the end, which could pump the lake water for the gardens. Everything was a luscious green, with the trees growing healthy leaves that offered some shade. All the flowers were a vibrant colour, producing larger than normal blooms. It was a little oasis in a parched, flat countryside.

Art had spent all of spring working on his book and he started to edit it and prepare the final copy. He had discussed the symbol on the boulder with Coco, and tried to justify why William was so evasive when he was asked about the symbols. Each time he would answer with a riddle, or reply with something completely different. On a few occasions he had just ignored them altogether, faking a day dream. William eventually just brushed them off, lying that Molay Barn and the lake were originally owned by the same person, who had marked his territory. William was not concerned with the water level of the lake either. He seemed quite confident that in all the time he had owned it, the level had never changed. He was happy for the pump to be used to water the trees and plants. *A little too enthusiastic,* thought Art, still slightly suspicious of the curious old guy. Coco worked at planting seeds for winter crops and maintained growing crops. She had to stake beans and peas which were growing inches a week. There were the sweet peas and jasmine along the south-facing front of the house that needed watering every day and tying back every other day as they rapidly grew. All of the tubs, herb and rock gardens needed watering and she started to wonder if taking so much water from the lake could damage it. Art had been keeping an eye on the water level, but it did not seem to go down. Coco's work had been made a little easier by John who installed an irrigation system. He had simply stabbed a long garden hose with holes that was attached to the hose from the lake. When he wanted to water the greenhouse, he simply turned the valve on the hose joint and water would spray out soaking everything in the greenhouse.

Johns' plants were already showing signs of growth, and it would only be a few weeks until he could do his first aloe vera and spider plant offsets. He already had some pots and compost ready and spent his time reading his plant books to them. He had found a brand new book in a bag in one his greenhouses, which was interestingly about healing plants and herbs. All his memories of his dark past were far behind him, with the nightmares visiting him less frequently. He was excited about the future, could see himself being a success and knew that if it had not been for his first plant, he would not be where he was now. He sat on a tall stool beside one of the greenhouse worktops, looking at his small crop of twenty plants. They each sat in a small pot, neatly spaced apart. In the punishing heat, John watched as a gentle breeze tickled the smaller spider plants. It was over 100 degrees under the glass, but with the doors open at each end and all of the ventilation windows fully open, there was the occasional reprieve from the heat. The smell of warm compost was a smell John loved, as it meant he was at the cottage, at peace, working on his plants.

Looking up the length of the 20-foot long greenhouse and into the next, he could see a heat haze rising in a mystical mirage, hazily distorting the view of the empty greenhouse. Although he was dressed in old combat shorts and a rock band vest, he was clammy and sticky. The discomfort was not an annoyance for him, as he would rather be hot and clammy smelling earthly compost, than being cold and damp in a festering squat.

He looked out of the windows, across the countryside beyond the meadow's fence. It was yellow and dry, with wilting bushes and grasses barely green in colour due to the lack of water. The sky above was the deepest, darkest blue John had seen in a long time. Behind him, the white hot sun injected heat into everything it touched, relentless in its task. He saw Coco tending to her beans, with Mahoney sheltering in the shade of a water butt that collected water from the garage roof. He was stretched out on his side, filling a large shallow hole he had dug. A lilac blue butterfly danced above his head and a ladybird crawled over his front paw. It was as if he had always been there with the insects working around him. His ear twitched as the butterfly tried to land on the tufty hairs on top of his head. Behind Coco and the vegetable patch, John could see the pink shroud of the orchard blossoms and rich greens of the woodland surrounding the property, all beneath a sapphire blue sky. There were no birds in the sky, nor any birdsong. All he could hear was the musical 'ting-ting' sound of wind chimes touching each other, and Coco's trowel hitting stones.

As he sat, he saw Mr Idol's car turn into the drive, whereupon it strangely stopped. John watched as Mr Idol collected the post from the letterbox that stood at the entrance to the drive and then get back in the car. He shuffled about and John saw him add another envelope to the pile, as he moved the car forward till it was parked. John, thinking it was a little odd, put his hand up and called out, which caused William to startle slightly, increasing John's curiosity. The old man waved back with the hand clutching the post and walked over to talk to Coco. After a quick conversation, he handed her the post. As he turned to walk away, she called out to him, showing him one of the letters. Mr Idol took the letter, and walked towards John in the greenhouse.

'This one is for you!' he said.

'How can it be? No one knows I work here. Any post should go to my home!'

'Sometimes things just happen for a reason, son. Open it, you never know what it might be.' He smiled, closely studying the little plants. 'They look good. It won't be long and you will have filled both of these glasshouses!'

'It will be some time yet. But if this sun keeps up and the water level from the lake doesn't go down, I should be okay!'

'What you reading?' Mr Idol asked as he pulled up a stool next to John. The heat was sapping all of his limited energy.

'Just a book about medicines made from plants. I found it in a bag in my greenhouse. If I could get the right natural ingredients, I could make antiseptic cream and all sorts from the aloe plants. I could start my own range!' he laughed, as he fiddled with his letter.

'You going to open that?'

'Yes, I guess. It will only be junk mail,' he said, testing the old man, 'it can't be anything important because I'm not known at this address.'

William sat as he watched the expression in John's eyes change as he read. He started to read some of it out loud, but could not control his excitement. He looked up at Mr Idol, with his mouth wide open and saucer-round eyes staring in disbelief. William got up smiling, patted John on the shoulder and slowly walked away.

'There's something in the boot of my car for you. Two boxes. Go get them when you are ready!'

'Hang on… Mr Idol… Sir…' called John, getting off his stool and rushing to catch up with William. The old man turned round, smiling. 'This letter was delivered by you. I saw you…'

'Knowledge is to know that a tomato is a fruit, but it is wisdom that tells you not to put it in a fruit salad! Don't forget your boxes in my car!'

John stood in shock, re-reading his letter as he watched Mr Idol walk to The Brew House and come out again with two bottles. He raised one bottle as a salute to John and went off down the path to the lake. John could hear Nicholson bark as the little dog would have recognised the old man. He re-read the letter again. After sitting back on his stool for ten minutes, he read the letter out to the plants.

> Due to your outstanding contribution to the Narcotics Anonymous meetings you have shown and your dedication and determination to grow plants and develop your own range of natural creams and lotions, you are formally invited to a celebration festival for people such as yourself. The ticket below will allow you and a friend to free travel and entry to the festival. The headliners include: Ozzie Ozborne, John Lydon, Paul Grey and Dave Grohl, with hologram appearances from John Lennon, James Brown, Jimi Hendrix, Amy Winehouse, Sid Vicious, Joe Strummer and Cliff Barton.

The festival is one-of-a-kind, never to be repeated. Over 100 artists will collaborate and play together covering the greatest rock songs ever written. Some of the main attractions include holograms of playing musicians, the opportunity to play on stage with your favourite bands and have a drink with a celebrity of your choice via a computer link up. The enclosed booklet lists everything. Please read it and return the confirmation slip, with your preferred pick-up location. You have been allocated Nottingham, but this can be changed, or you can drive there.

Please reply by May 30th 2012.

As John sat staring at his letter, then back to the plants, his book and the contents of the two boxes from the boot of Mr Idol's car, John was totally shell-shocked. He could not work out what was happening, nor what the contents of the letter meant. He knew that the festival, if it was real, would be fantastic. He even understood how he had earned himself and Rev a ticket, but no one gets things for free. What he didn't understand was how did the letter know he was going to be a success with his creams when he hadn't even started making them and most importantly, how did Mr Idol happen to have all the ingredients he might need, some of which were quite rare and expensive. He spent the afternoon sat in the orchard under the shade of a large cherry tree, trying to piece together what was going on. He did not want to go down to the lake to talk to the old man in the company of Art. Part of the agreement that he could work in the greenhouses was that he kept himself to himself. He knew Mr Idol was an important man, from the few things that Rev had let slip. What he couldn't work out, was what Mr Idol was doing with two parcels from Lou's N Up, which was Mr Keiffson's tattooist. The two boxes had courier labels addressed to the tattooists in Grantham where he knew Rev had had his tattoo of Jess done.

Coco dropped the rest of the mail as she read her letter. The postmark stamped on the envelope said it had come from Somerset. She stood in the full sun, hardly noticing the heat as she re-read the letter.

Due to your outstanding contribution to the conservation of rare British apples, the introduction and natural use of honey bees and your dedication and determination to grow plants and develop your own range of consumables, you

292

are formally invited to a celebration festival for people such as yourself. The ticket available by registering online will allow you and a friend free travel and entry to the festival. The compère will be Mr Russell Brand and headliners include: Paul Weller, Liam and Noel Gallagher, Dave Grohl, John Lydon and Stevie Nicks, with hologram appearances from Kurt Cobain, Michael Jackson, Amy Winehouse, Sid Vicious, Joe Strummer and Freddie Mercury.

The festival is a one-of-a-kind, never to be repeated. Over 100 artists will collaborate and play together covering the greatest rock songs ever written. Some of the main attractions include holograms of playing musicians, play on stage with your favourite bands and have a drink with a celebrity of your choice via a computer link up. The enclosed booklet lists everything. Please read it and return the confirmation slip, with your preferred pick-up location. You have been allocated Peterborough, but this can be changed or you can drive yourself.

Please reply by May 30th 2012.

Railway Cottage was an excited place that afternoon. The decision by the MBHK to allow Sir William Idol an invite for someone he insisted was to attend the festival had been a tedious, long drawn-out affair, but after he had explained what John had come from and what he was working towards, it had been considered a wise move to include the young horticulturist. The MBHK had insisted that Sir William had to engage the young man in a masterclass to speed his learning up. He only had a short time to perfect his skills. A few weeks back, William had subtly left a specific book in John's greenhouse on how to make natural remedies. The one-off copy had been written and printed by the MBHK medical team with easy instructions to learn, using basic ingredients which were found naturally in the Lincolnshire countryside. The more specialised ingredients would be purchased and stored. William had been pleased to hear from Coco that John had noticed the book and had started reading it out loud to the plants. He had then contacted Mr Keiffson for advice, who then rang Louis Lou, the world famous tattooist and herbalist. Due to his Chinese heritage he had access to ancient natural remedy recipes. On William's request, Louis Lou had ordered ingredients from around the world, with instructions on how to make simple remedies. Once the young horticulturist had mastered some of the basic steps, large quantities of ingredients would be made available, possibly stored in the tunnel rooms at Molay Barn. William had a lot of influence over the MBHK, but as its commander-in-chief he would make crucial decisions once all eventualities had been verified by the Final Decision Committee. As head of the Final Decision Committee, Mr William Idol was the top man.

The MBHK had finally sent out all of the invites, personalising them to each candidate, making each feel like they were special and specifically chosen, which they were. Miriam had received her letter. The letter went on to list some of Miriam's favourite artists. She was beside herself with excitement. Simon had insisted she should take a friend and not him. He would stay at home and look after the kids, cat and house, allowing Miriam a well-deserved break. She rang Sophie and they excitedly discussed what they would need to take. When she came off the phone, she went online and filled out the questionnaire. A confirmation email registered her application, and tickets with a barcode were ready to be printed off.

Coco had run straight down to the lake to tell Art and promptly got told off for making a noise. Art said he couldn't go to the festival, as he had a book publisher coming to the cottage that week about his book. He told her to see if Pod wanted to go. Naturally she was ecstatic and accepted the invite with pleasure, and they texted the evening away discussing the festival, and all the previous years they had been. Coco was so excited she had failed to notice the letterhead symbol at the top of the letter. A pyramid (the Main Stage), a sun, a tower (The Tor)!

The evening was sultry and heavy. Everything was motionless, all energies having been sucked up by the heat of the day. Even though Coco and Art had both showered before going to bed, it was instantly sticky and clammy. Even the white, Egyptian cotton sheets could not keep them cool. All of the windows had been left open upstairs and although there was no breeze, they had still used the homemade doorstops to prop the doors open. As the night continued, the humidity rose keeping the temperature from dropping. The full moon highlighted a purple landscape that still had many days of punishing heat to endure before the apocalyptic show-down. This weather was just the calm before the storm but already people were not coping. Shops had sold out of electric fans, paddling pool sales sky-rocketed and the news on television advised people to check on elderly neighbours as the heat could be just as deadly as the cold. People worried about their pets, schoolchildren were packed off with sun hats on their heads and sun cream on their skin and the media unnecessarily heightened the hype that was developing with the increased temperatures. Hosepipe bans had been enforced as reservoir levels plummeted, small rivers dried to a trickle and the seaside towns relished in increased tourism. Every night, Coco and Art would shower just for a five-minute reprieve from the punishing heat and humidity. They were just grateful they lived in the country, and not cooped up in a block of flats in some inner city complex.

'What the f...!' shouted Coco, as she sat bolt upright in bed. Art had jumped up too, landing more on the floor than on the bed, but he had put his long arm out to stop himself hitting the deck. They had both felt like they had been 'cattle-prodded' out of bed.

'What the f...!' repeated Coco, as she was cut short.

'FU...!' Art was also cut short, as a deafening clap of thunder rattled the window frames. As the sound echoed around the room, strobe lightning flashed at a sickening rate. Coco looked at Art, with the look of a wild animal about to take flight. The thunder clapped again, instantaneously the lightning lit the room. Art went to the window, to look out over the meadow and the open countryside. The storm continued to vent its rage by letting off static electricity that was so powerful he was sure he had heard the static buzz as it struck. A wind had picked up too, which started to whip through the upstairs of Railway Cottage. Art rushed to the front of the house, into the dressing room and closed the windows. Instantly the through-draft subsided.

'Oh my God!' he called out to Coco, who hurriedly rushed to see what he could see.

As the lightning lit the countryside spread out opposite the cottage, a black funnel raced along the ground, connected to the clouds.

'That's a bloody tornado!'

'Don't be daft! Ah!' another clap of thunder made Coco jump and scream. It was deafeningly loud, so much so that Nicholson was barking and yelping. His pitiful noise was accompanied by thumping noises. They felt like they were coming from underground. This upset Nicholson even more as he scratched at the door at the bottom of the stairs. The thumping continued until Coco recognised it.

'Mahoney!'

'I'll go get him and let Nics upstairs too. One night won't hurt. It is bloody scary! What's happening in Tornado Alley?' Art asked, as he put on some baggy, cotton surf shorts, whilst looking out of the window.

'It's still out there. It's not a big one!' Coco called out as Art unlatched the bedroom door and ran downstairs. Nicholson appeared seconds later and ran straight to the bed, diving under the covers.

'Cheeky bugger. You've not been up here before, have you Nics?' Coco said sarcastically.

Art came back upstairs with Mahoney in his arms. The rabbit had wide startled eyes and looked quite distressed. Art put an old towel on the bed and put the rabbit down on it before walking over to the south-facing window. With each flash of lightning, the mini tornado moved across the horizon, until it had blown itself out or had just gone out of sight. As things started to calm down, Coco and Art went back to bed. Coco put the towel in the bottom drawer of her pine bedside table, and sat Mahoney in it. The rabbit would find solitude in the partially confined space and burrowed into the soft fabric, looking over the edge of the drawer as to where his friend Nicholson was. Nicholson assumed he had a right to the end of the bed and so he too turned a few times and settled down to sleep. They had not noticed that the wind had picked up again until the hailstones came. The heavens opened sending hailstones the size of peas racing down to the ground. A natural orchestra struck up, as the ice balls struck metal, glass and tin. One even struck a wind chime, sending the aluminium tubes into a frenzy. Coco and Art knelt on the bed looking out of the north-facing window, with Nicholson in-between them with his paws on the windowsill. As the fading lightning flashed across the sky accompanied by a distant rumbling of thunder, the hail was lit up for a split second. The ground was white and glistening, as stone upon stone piled up on the ground. The wind made them dance and prance, forming patterns in the sky as they fell. Whipping around, swirling and quickly changing direction, out of control as the wind placed them where it wanted them. Some even scurried along the ground, as a gust swept along the surface of a newly formed ice sheet.

It was still unbelievably warm and yet ice was piling up on the ground. The 'ping' and 'tink' sounds continued, as things got peppered by the stones. Art, Nicholson and Coco watched as heavy black clouds raced across the wide view of the sky. The hailstones started to change consistency, until the 'tinkering' sound subsided, only to be replaced by a splashing, sound of heavy rain. Coco wondered how her beans and peas would fare. To lose the plants at this stage of the growing season would mean no crop to freeze. Art thought about all of the glass in the greenhouses, and wondered if they had lost any to the hail. Nicholson thought how great it was, to be allowed upstairs at night for the first time, which was far more exciting than all the times in the mornings when Art had allowed him on the bed when Coco had already got up!

Chapter Thirty-six

June 2012, Somerset

As the sun started to reach its highest point in the sky, the countryside beneath its warming rays basked and baked. An arid dry May had led into a stifling hot June. All records had been broken from all continents, resulting in the world leaders having an emergency meeting about climate change. It had already been recognised that the global warming theory had been thrown out of the window, as scientists had recently discovered that the planet had climate changes every five to ten thousand years, and so the changes could not be attributed to humans and the burning of fossil fuels. The members of the MBHK shook their heads and tutted when they heard this report. They all knew that it was every 5,000 years human kind was wiped out and forced to start again, but each time it seemed lessons were never learnt, and so the problems repeated themselves.

It was the final meeting of the MBHK before the festival, and the commander-in-chief had decided it would be most fitting to visit the site, check everything was in order and to deliver his final speech from the Pyramid Stage.

'Ladies and gentlemen, here's the main man,' shouted Dylan from the stage, 'Give it up for Sirrrr... William Idolllll!'

William walked out onto the stage to a hearty applause from about 1,000 people. He stood and looked around the stage, then out to the sea of faces looking up at him, laying on the hard ground in the full sunshine.

'Well, what can I say?' the emotion was quite apparent in his voice, as he stood leaning on the microphone like an aged rock star. 'I would like to thank you all for everything you have done. Dylan, you've done us all proud. The sound seems perfect. How loud have you had it, son?'

'Well Sir, only up to a third of its potential, but it was pretty serious in the old bass department. Stuff shimmied across the mixing desk and Ed's chair on wheels moved about three foot until he hung onto something!' called out a distant Dylan from the sound tower.

'Okay son. Well, this evening I want a full thirty-minute set. I want to see Hendrix, with Lynott and Bonham and possibly Winehouse on vocals. What do you say everyone? Can you do that, son?' A huge applause went around the crowd as they all turned to look at Dylan for his reply.

'Yes Sir, we can do anything. I need a bit of time to program it. Any particular song?'

'Yes, get Ed on it. He can do a mix and you can have those holograms doing random solos. You've got three hours for a six o'clock showing,' replied William, as the crowd showed its approval. Many of them did not know the true reason for the festival this year, but as part of the annual crew who knew how everything pieced together, they would help set up the site, and man services during the festival. All of the MBHK organisation was there, stretched out on the grass, enjoying a brief spell of calm. 'And make sure you turn it up, son, the villagers have been warned about a firework test run, just in case you give it too much bass. We don't want the old dears having heart attacks. I have paid for all the locals to have a dinner out in Wells, so you'll get no complaints.'

'Okay Sir, six it is. Get ready to be blown away.' Dylan disappeared as he sat back down at his mixing desk.

'Now, as you all know, two weeks today we open the doors to the greatest festival ever staged. There are many reasons for this event, too many to go into. The one thing you all have to remember, is that every single one of the people attending, is to be treated like the most important person in the world. If you're serving food or drink, marshalling or part of the production crew, it is your priority to ensure this festival goes all the way to the end, without a hitch. You never know, someone's life might depend on it!' William tried to joke. None of the MBHK laughed too heartily, but the annual workers just thought the old man was trying to have a laugh with them, and so laughed back without really knowing what was going on. 'Please all be back here for six. Space yourself out around this area,' he used his arms in a fan shape from where he was standing at the centre of the stage. 'We will be asking how you felt and what you could hear from different parts of the field. Please remember, no matter how good the show is, you are *not* to sing, and you're are *not* to dance. It is imperative you remain seated and silent until you are told otherwise. When we hear from Dylan, respond accordingly. Right, have fun and I'll see you all later!'

At six-thirty that evening, 1,000 people sat shell-shocked in front of the giant black pyramid. Ed and Dylan had surpassed themselves, by mixing together songs by Led Zeppelin, Thin Lizzy, Jimmy Hendrix and Amy Winehouse, just as Sir William had asked. As they had mixed each track in, they had put on a light show and slowly introduced each of the holograms, so only one was on stage at a time. This was not a full visual test. That had already been run. It was just a final sound check. The scientists, mathematicians and geologists had instructed Dylan how loud to comfortably take the levels, and the sound quality had been outstanding. As the Amy hologram had stood at the front of the stage singing *Rehab*, Dylan had instructed the audience to shout back the chorus. They had been itching to stand up and dance and sing, but knew it would mess up the run. On command, they sprang to their feet, rushed to the front of the stage and shouted, 'I said, No... No... No...'

Dylan had a choir singing from a raised platform at the back of the stage, and holograms of a brass section and string section appeared then disappeared at the sides of the stage as the few songs they had chosen were mixed together. The more the audience participated, the more data came through to the tower. The scientists liaised with the geologists. It would be catastrophic if the event was triggered early. The planetary alignment was only a few weeks away from perfect alignment and if the pure spring was powered into action, it might reduce the amount of power it had when it was genuinely needed. Ed and Dylan had decided to try the final song, which they had taken six months to pick. Ed started to bleed certain parts into the mix. As soon as some of the audience noticed what song was coming next, they instinctively started singing along, swaying to the music, with their arms around each other's shoulders, singing with all of their hearts. The sun was setting behind the Tor, but the warm evening was humid and still. The crowd swayed together, building up momentum for when they could go crazy, feeling the presence of the music in the air. This was what summer festivals were all about!

'Shut it down. Shut it down. ABORT ABORT ABORT!' Dylan heard in his earpiece. 'ABORT ABORT ABORT!'

Dylan pulled the main power cable and the stage fell silent, while the light show continued to a silent beat. The instant wiring down left a whirring noise buzzing from the speakers. Even though the music had stopped, there was still a rumbling reverberating from the ground. It felt like an underground train passing close to the surface, which might burst out of the earth at any moment. As silent time passed, the rumbling seemed to ebb away, subsiding to become part of the hum from the speakers. Dylan did a full wire down, and switched everything off. From what the statistics had said, their final choice song was definitely the right one.

'We're two weeks early for that one. Slight change in tempo ladies and gentleman, this one's for all you lovers out there, on this hot sweaty night. Let's see your moves people!' said Dylan over the microphone from the tower, as he switched the PA system back on and put on an R Kelly track. A barrage of bottle and cans were thrown towards the tower, as people laughed and screamed 'Noooo'.

'Okay pop pickers, here's a bit of Sabbath for all ya aging rockers!'

As the sun finally disappeared everyone started to make their way to their camping locations. The leading MBHK members had a converted tour bus that they all shared, parked within the safety of the backstage area. This was just a precautionary measure, in case anything went wrong. Everyone else had little camping villages scattered about the empty, luscious site. The long grass remained untrodden, no tent flat patches, no muddy pathways. Just green long grasses, leafy shady trees, and the narrow stream gurgling and rushing as it passed through the valley, dotted with little tent villages. They all felt privileged to be sat looking up at the gigantic stage that stirred so many emotions in so many people. In just two weeks, the fields would be full of tents and gazebos, the fake trading stands would be serving healthy, nutrient-enriched food and music lovers would reach heights of ecstasy as they watched the greatest festival on earth. The foreboding black stage, silent in its slumber, cast an eerie shadow as the moon rose behind it. Various technicians, scientists and labourers remained behind, sipping on cold beers. They sat in little groups in front of the Pyramid in the fading light, discussing their favourite gigs, the advantages of festivals over intimate gigs and vice versa. In just two week's time, the ultimate festival experience would take place on this very spot. But for now, in the distance an owl hooted, and its friend or rival replied. A breeze of warm air skipped through the tall grasses, causing them to woosh and swish. As the darkness fell on the large Somerset farm, the end drew nearer.

Chapter Thirty-seven

Sunday morning, 17th June 2012, Somerset

Early mornings in June were not as they used to be. It was sweltering hot for one thing, but there was a drizzle that was guaranteed to soak all types of clothes, even the ones that were supposed to keep the damp out. Enlightenment came, when it was realised the damp was sweat, from walking and carrying heavy possessions. Uncomfortable is not the word! Damp, clammy and hot. Some had the luxury of travelling by car or coach, but many had walked from the train station.

Many of the travellers were not only struggling with all their possessions, tents, bags and food, they had also chosen the added burden of drink. The smarter ones carried bottles of spirits, after all, a bottle of vodka would lift more spirits than a few crates of beer or cider could, and was considerably easier to carry. In this situation, alcohol was essential. Not only essential, but vital at 7:30 in the morning. It helped those flagging, after hours of tortuous travel. Tired, weary and sometimes slightly delirious from the extremities they were putting upon their bodies, adding sleep deprivation and the exertion of the task, alcohol was essential. To an outsider, they looked like the lowest forms of society, pond scum even. They battled on through the punishing weather, all with one thing on their minds. None wore smart clothes, what was the point? They would only get ruined or trashed. So, with vodka in hand, they migrated together following the signs sporadically placed along the lane.

The country lane was a stark contrast to the bedraggled walkers. Blackberry bushes were fruiting in abundance, heavily laden with branches of developing fruits, knotting the hedgerow foliage together. They were decorated with unnoticed dog rose and pink campion intertwined with yellow ragwort and cowslips. Delicate silver spider's webs clearly visible were festooned with dew; Mother Nature at its best. Summertime festive trees! But these masterpieces were all wasted on the crowds as they trudged on. They kept walking, until the signs pointed towards the entrance to the fenced-in fields stretching out along the valley. There were several fields of cars neatly parked in rows, and as new ones arrived, marshals directed the flow of traffic. These fortunate souls hadn't had the arduous task of walking and carrying all of their possessions, but now it was their turn. The main gates were still a mile or so away, so they prepared for the last stage of their journeys. Streams of buses pulled in at the drop-off point, travelling from all parts of the country. No matter how each traveller arrived at the site, they all did the same walk at the end.

The nearer to the main gates that the travellers got, the busier it became, a bit like a mountain stream heading towards a narrow canyon. The busier it got the tighter and slower the procession got. People were jostled together, though maintaining a reasonable amount of respect, making sure not to invade each other's personal space. That proved awkward on many occasions, as the terrain was treacherous at times. The ground was mainly loose gravel, though there were also rocks and boulders to navigate. Those that had thought themselves clever by packing their belongings onto trolleys were now swearing and cursing, as this certainly was not a Sunday morning stroll around Oxford Street or the local shopping centre. It is quite safe to say, that most of these people had no interests in shopping and wasting money. To these people, though it didn't feel like it at the time, there was more to life. Weaker travellers or those who had packed unwisely made temporary camps. They would re-evaluate their situation, and formulate various plans that would mostly fail. It was a time to top-up the alcohol levels, or have a smoke along the way. Everyone had a different coping mechanism, but to first-timers, nothing could prepare them for this gruelling test of endurance. Passing travellers would look on wistfully, wondering if was better to keep plodding on, or to sit and recoup. This mass exodus all knew one thing, the earlier you got through the main gate, the better chance you had of surviving the week. It was a battle of stamina and determination.

Finally, the walkers came to a stop. The path was steep, with brambles and stinging nettles in abundance along the hedgerows, but still, these went unnoticed. Well, unnoticed until someone sat on one while having a pee in the bushes. This was something they would all have to get used to, being at one with nature. The weather and daily natural cycle would depict what most of them would be doing. Many would not have the need to know what time it was. Those in the know would be wherever they were meant to be, whilst the uninformed few would plan, schedule and organise, eventually leading to being in the wrong place at the wrong time... every time. The crowds shuffled on, putting down heavy bags every few hundred yards as the queue stopped and started. Beaded sweat indiscriminately emerged on men and woman alike, regardless of their fitness levels, as it was so humid and damp. On reaching the final bend, the six-metre metal fence surrounding the compound came into view, just as the morning sun broke through the water-sodden, low clouds. A ripple of applause and cheer could be heard rolling down the hill, infectious in its meaning. This weekend was all about the weather, it mattered. In fact, the weather could seriously break a person out here, with extremities of cold and hot equally troublesome to deal with. The warming sun's rays increased, parting the clouds with vigour, and by the time the travellers were passing through the search turnstiles, it was a proper June morning.

Stepping out into the campsite, the sun bearing down on beautifully coloured flags, rows upon rows of various shapes and complimentary colours, they almost signified the freedom of the following week. Their colours represented all the different walks of life that had converged on this one small part of England, making it the third largest town in southern England... for just one week. Huge marquees hid amongst ancient trees, their bright colours and flag flying domes large splodges of colour like the beginning of a Monet painting. There were already thousands of tents already erected in the valley, though the grassy slopes would be crammed full of campers within a day. This was what it was all about. The summer, the music, the friendships and memories that would stick in the travellers' minds for years to come, if not forever, for this was summer solstice weekend, and this was Glastonbury.

As the festivallers filtered in through the five main entrances to the site, the premium camping locations filled up first. The gentle hill opposite the Pyramid Stage was always the first to fill, so campers could open their tents in the morning, and look down on the iconic Pyramid Field, with its suspended speaker stacks and group of mature trees just to the side behind the tall, black sound tower. Seasoned festivallers knew not to camp too close to the toilets, or too far away that it was a massive trek each time they needed to spend a penny. Landmarks were vital too, with many campers bringing flags on extending poles in order to identify their tent in a sea of blue and green domed homes. The surrounding fields started to fill up, with people wanting a quieter nighttime experience. By Sunday evening, just twelve hours after the gates had opened, 75 per cent of the revellers were settled into their camps. Throughout the night, late arrivals pitched in the dark, trying to beat the following day's rush. Smoke drifted up from the hundreds of little fires that were lit for warmth or light. The valley gradually filled up with a gentle mist of smoke, trapped by the height of the surrounding tree-topped hills. The troops were amassing; let battle commence!

Coco and Pod camped where they always had done. Glastonbury was their favourite festival, along with the mighty Download and anarchic Rebellion, and they had been so surprised and elated when Coco had received her letter and two tickets. Their two tents were in the top back corner of the Pyramid Field, directly under an electricity pylon. A long, thick hedge passed behind their tents acting as a cut-through barrier doubling up as a shelter from the weather, whether it be the hot sun or heavy rain. Their spot was a short walk down 'Muddy Lane', a high-hedged country lane descending to a toilet block and a tea van which did a reasonable breakfast. There was a small hole in the hedge allowing them access a few metres away from their camp. The electricity pylon acted as a brilliant landmark; the view was perfect of the Pyramid Stage from a garden chair and the central location meant everywhere was within staggering distance. From their camp, they could stand and look down the valley, across to the other camps forming on the opposite hills and to where the sun set behind Glastonbury Tor in the west.

Each year they had gone to the festival, they always vowed to pack a lighter bag and for the first time they made the trip in one go. In the past, it had taken till late afternoon to make two trips: the first carrying their tents and bedding; the second for all of their food and drink. However, as a treat they had chosen to buy all their food at the festival, but still bought a couple of litres of vodka and a few breakfast ciders. Making camp was always a slow process, as they would stop every half an hour for a beer. They noticed that none of the usual festivallers were in their corner of the field. These were friends they had met over the years who all camped in the same bit. Coco kept a look out for John and Rev who were travelling by coach, and Miriam and Sophie were due later that day.

By the time the tents were up, it was stifling hot. No matter what the weather did during the festival, anything other than warm and dry became a problem. When it was wet, the ground became a quagmire with anything from sticky heavy mud, to a foot-deep flood. Sitting down would be impossible and all of the marquees would be full of soggy sheltering festivallers. However, when it was hot, shade was a premium commodity. Being exposed in hot sunshine brought all sorts of problems. Sunburn and dehydration could be serious, as people might drink too much alcohol and not enough water. Glastonbury had a brilliant medical tent, and Coco noticed it was much bigger than previous years. The table was still outside with all factors of sun cream, aftersun and condoms, but the tent itself seemed treble its usual size. Coco and Pod applied some factor 15, helped themselves to a complimentary bottle of water, and walked down the hill towards the Pyramid. Pod watched as two security guards rode past on horses. Last year, she had lent her fabric angel wings to a mounted policeman who posed for a photograph. As she looked around, there were no policemen visible, when usually there would be a clear but amicable police presence. There was never any trouble at the festival. The theory that it was a hippy festival spawned from the twilight of the swinging 60s was in part true. There was always a chilled, happy feel to Glastonbury. Besides, everyone worked so hard to save for a ticket and paid so much money to attend, it would be fruitless to start trouble just to get thrown out.

They walked to the right of the Pyramid and onto the main thoroughfare through the festival. The main connection from the Pyramid Stage to the Other Stage was lined with all manner of food stands. At the height of the festival, this three-lane wide grassy walkway would be rammed full of people, all going in different directions to view their next band. There were stands dedicated to roast dinners, fresh fruits and exotic Caribbean, Indian or Chinese choices. They passed the wide track to the Dance Village to their right and continued on to the Other Stage, which pointed at a 130 degree angle to the Pyramid, ensuring the sounds projected in different directions so as not to interfere with each other. This also meant the two main stages could share the same back stage areas. As they walked over a concrete farm bridge, languishing for a moment in the shade of the trees, they continued on their planned route. They looked to their left and saw the Other Stage several hundred feet away looking surprisingly undressed. There were no light riggings or speaker stacks. By Wednesday nights of a normal Glastonbury this whole area would be packed, with music lovers milling about till the stage opened on the Friday lunchtime. It seemed too quiet and unprepared. Fanning out from the stage to define the edges of the arena there were more food and drink outlets. As Coco looked towards the stage she breathed in a huge lungful of air, slowly letting her breathe back out. The first afternoon, before everyone turned up, when everything was clean and fresh, was Coco's favourite pre-music time. Generators whirred in the distance, different radios and stereos blared out from the nearby stands and delicious smells of freshly cooked food were carried through the air, which could be deceitful, as the larger chain-operated vendors rarely tasted as great as they smelt. People staggered past them with their heavy bags, heading for their preferred camping area.

Coco and Pod walked on, crossing over The Old Railway, which was a raised ridge, formerly a train line, now a grassy tracked lane that passed between trees and shrubs further up. They started to climb the hill in front of them, puffing and panting, gasping for heavy, humid air. This trip was something they did every year on the first day of the festival. They would climb the hill that rose behind The Park, a large stage area in the southwestern corner of the site. By the time they were near the top of the tiered hill, a gentle wind lazily wisped past. They sat on the cushioning thick grass, taking their pumps off to feel the grass between their toes. This tradition had become compulsory. They would have a smoke and drink some vodka mixed with orange juice or coke bought from a stand. Depending on the weather, sometimes they climbed the hill, had a look and then walked back down again, to find shelter in one of the bars at The Park. However, when the weather was dry, they would sit there all evening until it was too cold.

From one of the highest points on the site they would look and watch the central area beneath them, which was partially hidden by trees and bushes. The sea of tents would grow by the minute on the opposite slopes as people set up camp, erecting flags and gazebos. Pod looked down the hill into The Park, past the two main stages and over to the corner under the electricity pylon, where their tents were. Something did not seem right. She dropped her eyesight, looking at the back of the Pyramid Stage, the backstage area and then the front of The Other Stage. As she scrunched her toes around the cool blades of grass, she puzzled over what seemed out of place. Tall mature trees partially hid the hospitality of the backstage area serving the two biggest stages on the site. She could see some sort of massive white marquee, with forklifts filling it up with pallets. *We won't run out of booze then!* she thought. Sipping on vodka and orange, she leaned back on her elbows, stretching her legs out in front of her. The hot sun got to work on the parts of her body that did not have sun cream on.

Coco lay in the grass on her side, resting on her right elbow, looking down the hill over the site, as Pod took a catnap. The Park stage lay peacefully just below them, but something again did not look right. Usually from up here, she would see the backstage activity, but there was no one there. No trucks, marquees or people. Nothing. The Park Stage, like The Other Stage, was curiously unprepared.

'You noticed owt odd?' she asked Pod.

'What?'

'You noticed owt odd... look...' she nodded her head towards The

Park Stage. 'There's no one there. And The Other Stage, that hadn't even got any speakers or lights up yet,' replied Coco, but Pod continued with her nap. 'And the medi-tent. It's massive this year.' Still Pod did not reply. It had been a long day. They had set off from Lincolnshire at three in the morning, made the usual stop at the services on the M5 just before turning off into the Somerset 'B' roads. Coco looked into the distance at the opposite side to the valley, where the six-metre high grey fence could be seen in places as the festival perimeter. The countryside beyond the fence looked parched and dry, whereas the trees around and inside the fence were green and healthy. *Just like at Railway Cottage!* she thought.

'And there's no coppers. Those guys on horses were security!' sparked up Pod.

'But there's always police here. Admittedly they are fun-loving, get stuck in, but yeah, you're right. I've not seen any either.'

They sat and watched from their bird's eye view as the sun started to descend in the west. Although it was still very hot, there was a soft, cool breeze licking the contours of the hill. They started to get ready for the walk back to their tents. They would have a 'cup-wash' then go out to the eastern side of the site for the evening.

'Bollocks!' exclaimed Pod. 'I've burnt my feet. Fuck it!'

'Oh boy, are you going to feel those tomorrow!' replied Coco as she lent over to take a look. 'Ouch!'

'I'll put some aftersun on them!'

'Tell you what! I have some of John's aloe cream. It's totally awesome at healing anything. Use that!'

'Thanks. I know it's really hot… just forgot to put cream on them!'

They walked back down the steep hill which was just as difficult as walking up it. As the land flattened out slightly, they passed through The Park, past The Rabbit Hole bar, a 24-carat experience, and the silent disco tent, which also looked empty and neglected. There were a lot more people milling about, some carrying their bags, whilst others started to explore the site. Pod and Coco stopped off at the toilets. They ran their feet under the cold tap, and splashed water over their heads and shoulders. The freezing cold water pumped from underground was shockingly cold and revitalising. When they got back to the tent feeling refreshed, they sat and opened a few beers to watch the sun set behind the Tor. They used cups of water and soap to have a bit of a wash, rinsing off with more water from the 5-litre fold-up container Art had given Coco. As the sun sank lower in the sky. Coco sat bolt upright, making a chilled Pod jump out of her skin.

'Pod… um… Dude… look!' she whispered in a slightly scared voice.

'Look man... Look!' she repeated, pointing at the sun. Pod sat up and putting her hand to shield her eyes from the glare of the sun. 'Look. Pyramid. Rectangle. Circle!'

'Oh my God!' Pod whispered in disbelief. 'Your symbol! Scary!'

'But Pod, it's also the symbol at William's house, and on the boulder by the lake. The one Art was told to look at by William.'

'William has secrets, I'm telling you!' said Pod, 'Lovely, lovely man, but he knows stuff, you know, oh, I don't know. He just knows!'

'Yes, Art and I have said the same! And he's dead evasive when you ask him stuff sometimes! But look at that, the same shapes as the symbol. There's something not right about here either.'

'Don't start conspiracy theorising!'

'I'm not going to, but...'

'Aaa!' Pod stopped her.

'But...'

'Shu!'

'I think...'

'No. Enough!'

Coco sat back in her chair, silenced. Pod laughed and passed her friend another can of cider.

'There is something not quite right!'

'Really, you feel it too?' asked Coco excitedly.

'Yes. Definitely!' replied Pod, as Coco eagerly waited Pod's synopsis. 'We're still sober. Something very wrong there!'

As it turned to dusk, they put everything into their tents and got ready for a night in Arcadia, a part of the festival that opened when the sun went down, and closed when the sun came up. It was a long walk in a southeasterly direction, passing through the central shopping area, then the Avalon and Shangri-La areas. They carried the small water bottles from the medical tent filled with vodka. The lane behind the tents was lit by a string of light bulbs, as were all of the main walkways at the festival. From a view on one of the surrounding hills, the lights looked like droplets of dew on a spider's web, draped around the stages and marquees. After a 20-minute slow amble, Coco and Pod started to notice it was getting busier, as other festivallers had the same idea as them. They climbed a steep slope onto the Old Railway, and turned left towards Shangri-La. The area was covered in trees and large bushes, giving an air of mysticism. It was incredibly humid and the dry dust that was kicked up from the path stuck to sticky legs. Along the sides, trees were decorated with huge googly eyes and giant, brightly painted flower sculptures appeared in-between the trees. Small paths led off the main thoroughfare, lit with tealights in jam jars. Delicious smells of spicy home cooking, apple wood fires and incense hung in the air, as swirls of smoke from fires drifted through the undergrowth. Walking through this realist fantasy world was cleansing. The make-believe world that the festival offered each year; that release from 'normal' life and the realisation you were a free spirit was what Coco and Pod loved most about Glastonbury. They had always said that there was something to do every day, for months, without even having to fit the music in! They had stopped discussing why the festival wasn't the same as previous years. They had read the programme, explaining this year was a bonus year, a special one-off.

Shangri-La was to their right and the entrance to Arcadia was to their left. They decided to go to Arcadia first. The area got very busy later on and numbers had to be controlled by security. The first temporary building they went into was dressed as a three-storey haunted house. It was free entry for anyone with a moustache, and so Pod and Coco purchased fake facial hair, allowing them free entry all week, providing they wore their hair. Beside the fake front door, was a realistic-looking heavy stone and wooden doorway, huge lanterns firing out 30 foot flames randomly, and dry ice cascading down the front of the building from the roof. The smoke-tinged bright orange from the flames illuminated the area, reflecting off the already hot faces of revellers. In stark contrast, once inside the air was cold. The music blasted out from the highest quality speakers, providing a full surround sound, with the bass reverberating from the floor, and high-pitched symbols dancing around the ceiling. Everyone acted quite normally, drinking, laughing and dancing despite everyone, men and woman alike, all having facial hair. The very dark lighting allowed dancers to just about make out each other's facial features with the occasional burst of thousands of fairy lights covering the high ceiling and walls. As they danced to a gypsy punk track, an erotic mixture of folk music and heavy thrash punk, the music came to an end and the room went dark. Then a single, bright yellow spotlight came on in the centre of the room. The fairy lights and yellow spotlights lit up the cavernous ceiling, catching a glitter ball to give the effect of a cosmic night sky as misty dry ice was released. The music had been slowed right down, so all that could be heard was the shrill sharp sound of stringed instruments howling out long painful notes, interrupted by a long, deep drum beat.

Five slim women in floating white gowns glided into the spotlight and using beautifully synchronised hand movements requested the audience to make a space under the light. Five more women joined them each doing the same hypnotic dance. They danced around the circle, following each other with perfect timing. They swayed their arms loosely, then hung their arms above their heads, and then swept them low to the ground, spinning around every now and again. The painful screeching from the stringed instruments that had been used from the gypsy punk track had morphed into beautiful violins and deep throbbing cellos. An acoustic guitar played out the melody as the dancers sped up their routine, keeping in time with the music. They maintained their formation perfectly, with the waves of flowing white fabric causing the audience stood in the dark to squint slightly. Their repetitive, mesmerising movements enchanted the crowd, who marvelled at their beautiful white faces, crowned with bands of large, white daisies. The performance reached a fast, energetic crescendo until the room fell silent and dark. The audience patiently waited for whatever was to come next, wondering whether to clap or not.

'AH!' screamed several women, supported by some male expletives. The music came on as angry violins violated the eardrums of the crowd, and the lights shot on just as the dancers all jumped towards the crowd, pulling scary faces close to the spellbound audience. The effect of 'black light' and clever make-up had made the beautiful dancers turn into ghouls, just as they jumped towards the crowd. A sigh of relief was felt as the lights came on, and the ten women walked hand-in-hand around their circle, like a chain of real, living daisies, their outfits flowing delicately, as they occasionally did a curtsy-step. The crowd applauded and wolf-whistled. It had been a truly mesmerising experience.

Coco and Pod walked out of the haunted house into the relentless heat, totally entranced as a heavy reggae track started to vibrate the haunted house. They chatted and discussed what effects the lights, music and performance had had on them. It had been a moment that would never be forgotten.

'I nearly shit myself!' said Coco.

'So did I, scary bastards. But God, weren't they brilliant!'

They walked around Arcadia, admiring a fake underground train wreck half stuck out of a prefabricated five-storey tower block, with steam and sparks being set off by a pre-programmed pyrotechnic computer. Around the corner, an ice igloo made from glass bricks stood with deafening drum and bass blasting from its huge speaker stacks that pointed into the centre of the igloo. Blue electricity sparks randomly flashed through the clear walls, reaching right over the top occasionally, forming a lightning umbrella. The inside was all white and chrome, with electric-blue lighting and strobes changing sequences rapidly. The

310

whole scene was an assault on their senses, as Coco and Pod wandered over to take a look. The bright lights piecing their vision, the eardrum-rupturing bass line and the added humidity of steam billowing from a machine filled the dome of the igloo, making the whole experience quite uncomfortable. They found a noodle bar and sat on the grass in front of the stand, watching people walk by as they ate. The obvious first timers walked around with their mouths wide open, not believing the fantastic things they were seeing. Glastonbury was not just a music festival, nor a place to experience brilliant performing arts. It was a place of freedom and bewilderment, of make-believe places filled with people being whoever they wanted to be. Free living, free spirited. Experienced festivallers relaxed and socialised with new-found friends in small groups, drinking or smoking with the worries of everyday life forgotten for just a few days.

After eating, Pod and Coco walked up the slope to the raised lane and over to the other side into Shangri-La. The crowds were starting to get busy but Coco led the way to their favourite bar. They passed lots of small, highly decorated garden sheds, each selling just one type of spirit. They stopped outside the tequila shed and ordered four shots. The zombie 1950s diner waitress poured the shots and pulled a bowl of lemon slices and a salt shaker across the narrow counter cut into the side of the shed. Candles dripped wax onto the counter, flickering as the flames danced when disturbed. Some large red and green floodlights shone from high above the trees, spreading faint coloured light, and highlighting eerie shadows as smoke machines puffed out smoke. The area had been decorated with fake crashed aeroplanes, jeeps and broken mechanical robots repeating a malfunctioning default message, with smoke and sparks firing from their short circuits. In the centre of a clearing, The Arcadia Machine was just being switched on. It was similar to a giant insect, with metal legs protruding out from its main body which housed the DJ booth. The two front legs were raised, and two acrobats in cave woman outfits performed a trapeze act, dangling from each of the machine's raised front legs. Flames shot out of fake trees made of hollow metal pipes, which stood in a circle around the beast. The pyrotechnic teams mixed water and flames, steam and smoke to create a blazing orange monster, breathing fire and sweating water as heavy tribal, jungle rhythms were blasted out. The whole crowd which had assembled head-nodded and knee-bobbed in time to the music. It was loud, raw, pulsating and primal. The fast bongo beats and electric synthesizers that were occasionally mixed in were uplifting, electrifying the hairs on the back of the crowd's necks. Playing at a speed to match an average heartbeat, the song cleverly increased tempo and momentum, as did the crowd's movements, reaching such speeds that the beat was lost into one, long repeated note. The crowd stood, with their arms in the air waiting, slightly swaying, either from the alcohol or the entrancing experience. A huge boom exploded as fireworks flew out of the back of the machine, filling the sky with golden stars, as silver fire spurted out around the rim of the DJ booth, just as the music dropped back in, louder and heavier than previously. The crowd at the front of the machine went berserk, jumping up and down. It was chaos as people pogoing bumped into others stood with their eyes closed, feeling each and every beat of the tribal-calling drums, everyone taking something different from the experience.

Pod and Coco downed their shots and headed for their favourite club, The Snakepit. There was a small construction of covered, dark, narrow lanes made from scaffolding and painted plywood shop frontages. There were tiny curiosity shops, some selling real things and others just for show. There was a mad scientist with glass jars of pretend body parts enticing people into his fake shop, a scantily clad woman with a huge lizard on her shoulder, a window full of surgically altered dolls' heads and all manner of other macabre things. The Snakepit was hard to find in the maze of lanes, but Coco knew to head for the bright green cloud being emitted from the top of one of the makeshift buildings. It was only about ten thirty, so there was no queue. They had decided to have a bit of a chill, before heading back to the tent. It had been a busy day, with little sleep and lethargic weather. Tired as they were, The Snakepit had been calling them since they had got the tickets for the festival, so they went through the strict 'checking of skin' before they were allowed in.

The bouncer to the mini club, which held about 100 people, saw Coco and waved her straight in. The tattoo of John Lydon on her leg was more than enough for free entry. Pod was not so lucky, she had to buy a tattoo transfer and have it put on. While she waited, Coco went to the bar and ordered a few bottles of cider. The club was refreshingly cool, draped in green and black velvet, lit with green spotlights. At the end of the short bar was a tiny foot-high stage with a pole in the centre, and in the opposite corner was a two-foot high stage. People stood to watch, as two women played a flute and clarinet. A third woman sang a beautiful song, with the sweetest voice, with the rudest, vilest lyrics Coco had ever heard. The crowd laughed, joined in and clapped as the group went into the chorus again.

Pod joined Coco and they walked up a steep flight of scaffolded stairs to a balcony that overhung the ground floor. Booths had been built with huge cushions scattered on the floor, separated by see-through purple curtains. People sat and lounged as they chatted and got to know each other. Miriam and Sophie were sat waiting for them. They all exchanged pleasantries and settled down to enjoy the cabaret. There was no way of knowing what they would see, anything from acrobats, to musicians and stand-up comedians. Miriam had explained that Art had tried to text, but there were problems with all of the phone networks. Pod's daughters were going to stay in The Den at Railway Cottage with Art, so Logan could look after John's plants for him. She would also look after her little sister Fay, who was quite happy playing with Mahoney and Nicholson. Logan was more than capable of caring for her little sister, but it was a comfort to have Art nearby in the house if he was needed. Pod had been concerned with the weather being so hot. Art had strict instructions to make sure they drank plenty and ate healthily. Pod's daughters had happily settled in, and had been eating strawberries down by the lake with Nicholson.

By two in the morning, everyone was exhausted. As the four girls left The Snakepit, they passed a huge marquee that was still going strong. They looked in through the tied-back sides, and saw on stage a Bhangra group getting the crowd going. In authentic costume, five drummers were hammering out a beat on their handheld drums, accompanied by electric guitars and some unusual Indian instruments. The front man was encouraging people to 'twist in the light-bulbs', 'stamp on the £50 note' and 'bring the clouds down', showing the crowd the dance movements. Coco and Pod made their way to the front closely followed by Miriam and Sophie, and stood waiting for instructions. The twelve guys in the band were counted in, and began beating their drums in perfect time. The movements were easy to remember, as the excellent frontman in his long white tunic, full face of facial hair and a turban demonstrated as he called out the routine. The music was energising, rhythmical and had a very consistent beat. After half an hour, the whole tent was in perfect time with the band, fluent in their moves, and unified by the exhilarating feeling of being part of something so different and unexpected. The musicians were clearly enjoying it, as they smiled and joked with each other. The 500 dancers 'screwed in light bulbs', with both of their arms in the air, pushing their rotating hands up and down in time to the drums. They 'brought down the clouds', by putting both arms in the air on the left, bobbing them up and down, then putting them in the air on the right. The hardest move was to 'stamp on the £50 note', but the crowd maintained their stance, and the song came to an end amidst a rapturous applause. The delighted young men on the stage bowed and waved, surprised by how receptive their audience had been.

The night had been brilliant, with lots of different acts entertaining the clubbers and a beginner's lesson in Bhangra dancing. They all made the long walk back to their campsite, as Miriam and Sophie had managed to camp in the same corner of the Pyramid Field. It was the hottest night there had been during the last five weeks of the heatwave. In their drunken, weary state, it took over an hour to walk up the light-bulb lit 'Muddy Lane' to their tents. Coco stood looking out over the site as mist hung low to the ground, visible by a full moon. She stopped to wonder how it could be so hot with a clear sky. As she looked at the stars, she noticed there seemed to be a heat haze distorting the view of the sky. Stars shimmered rather than twinkled. She thought it was maybe the heat from the parched ground.

She was wrong. It was the start of the destructive radiated heat that was being pulled from the sun by the alignment of the planets.

Chapter Thirty-eight

Early Tuesday morning, 19th June 2012,
MBHK Headquarters, Somerset

Ed and Dylan stood in the control tower in front of the Pyramid stage, looking out over the city that was growing in front of them. It was nearly three in the morning, and they had only just finished running their final checks. Statistics were back from the test run and the mathematicians had conversed with the geologists. The scientists situated at the base of the tower in an underground room that had been specially constructed, were reading through every news item on the weather, trying to monitor how the progress was going. Reports from around the world were displayed on each of their four computer screens as news feeds were sent to them. The approximate time of the event was 11:15 on Thursday night. Events such as the festival at Glastonbury were being held around the world, and some unfortunate revellers would be having their grand finale at seven in the morning. As predicted, there were starting to be electrical failures, poor telephone signals and interference on satellite television. Massive bush fires in northern Australia and California were raging out of control, as very dry shrub caught alight. Rivers in Texas and the great plains of America and European rivers were rapidly drying up. Reporters were claiming it was as if the water on the planet was evaporating. In all of recorded history, there had never been such a catastrophic global drought. Analysts were debating the effects of the weather on the world price of wheat, followed by other foods stuff as farmers struggled to feed and water their animals.

Ed sat in his wheeled swivel chair, looking out over the smouldering campsite, enveloped in an early morning mist and campfire smoke. It was like a sauna, hot, sticky and very, very humid. It was as if the heat was indeed sucking all of the moisture from the earth, slowly drying it like a sun-dried tomato. Dylan had folded the canvas curtains of the control room back, tying them to the scaffolding holding up the platform. The tower had been given some reinforcements from usual years, in case the energy from the event caused ground tremors.

'If this lot are the chosen ones, shouldn't some of them be asking questions by now?' said Ed, watching as stragglers wobbled home to their tents.

'The ones who have been to Glastonbury before will. At the moment they're enjoying a surprise festival, or at least that's what they're all being led to believe. They will notice from the programmes that there is only the Pyramid Stage in use. They will wonder why The Park, Avalon and the Dance Village have been erected, but not in use, but as the programme says, those tents are for the 'Fans Play with Bands'. Besides none of them have had to buy a ticket, so they can't complain.'

'Most of them will work it out when they can only see the main event at the Pyramid stage. We need all of them to be listening to the same tune, hence all the other stages will be closed. Once Thursday night comes, absolutely everything will be closed down except the Pyramid Stage.'

'Mind you, the concert is going to be so mind-blowing, they won't want to be anywhere else.'

'How's it going backstage? Uncle Sam met up with Slash yet?'

'I bumped into Brian May looking for bottled water.'

'Wicked, how's he feeling?'

'There is a strange atmosphere back there. They all know they are doing a mammoth show on Thursday, but quite a few are moaning about having to be here by today. We can't exactly explain "Well Mr Gallagher, your plane might drop from the sky like a Manc footie player dropping down in the penalty box in the ninety-fourth minute, so we thought it best you got here before it gets too dangerous!" You can go tell him if you like?'

'Nooo, I'm fine up here, thank you. Besides, I've rolled this family-sized one, and was wondering if you would like to partake?'

'Why Mr Ed, that would be awfully sporting of you ol' chap!' Dylan replied, as he pulled his chair up next to Ed's, as they faced east waiting for the sun to come up. They each reclined in their leather office chairs, putting their feet up on one of the rails. They were tired, very tired. They each just wore shorts, as were most of the men in the country. They sat and quietly reflected on what they were about to undertake. The most important people in the country were gathering in the fields around them. They were turning up from all over the country, just for the massive event in two day's time. There was the usual electric atmosphere that every Glastonbury festival instilled in its guests, the anticipation, excitement and exclusivity that was felt as the returning family gathered for another year. This year however, the crowds were not just family joining together for the festival, they were also all bonded by the ancient defective DNA.

Chapter Thirty-nine

Tuesday morning, 19th June 2012, Lincolnshire

Art had got up very early. It had been a very uncomfortable night. There was a bucket of water next to the bed, with some small towels soaking in it. Whenever he got too hot, he rung out a towel a little and laid it on his body. It was a brilliant way to cool down. All of the windows were open again upstairs, but there was no breeze at all. He woke at 4:30 and wandered down to the lake. It was just starting to get light and the pink kissed wispy clouds disappeared as quickly as the sun rose. Even in the early morning, the heat that the sun generated was staggering. The thermometers on the outside of the greenhouses had a recorded high of 128 degrees and even though it was very early in the morning, it was already 92 degrees. The weather reports showed no sign to an end of the heatwave and parliament were having emergency meetings about the pending crisis. There had been a media frenzy and public outcry, as a lot of the politicians were sheltering from the heat in cooler countries such as the snowless foothills of towering mountains in Switzerland.

Art sat by the lake, which was covered in a blanket of mist that faded out as it came in contact with the banks, on the trunk bench thinking about Coco, missing her. The four swans glided silently past Art, barely causing a ripple on the water's surface. They quickly disappeared as they became camouflaged by the water vapour. It was very quiet, though the dawn chorus should have been in full song. All you could hear were chickens foraging on the woodland floor, and a few twitters and chirps echoing around the woodland as Nicholson hunted in the undergrowth. Art walked around the edge of the lake and sat on the big boulder with the symbol on it. He sipped from the massive mug of tea he had made. His movements were slow and calculated, trying to blend in with the nature suffering around him. He was wearing just some cream combat shorts and his fishing glasses, which helped him see into the water by reducing the water's surface glare. His bare feet had a few scratches on them, but he had wanted to feel the soil and grasses on his feet. He stood and watched the sun as it rose. For the first time he could not maintain his gaze on the burning star. For some reason the sun caused his eyes to itch and water and as he blinked his eyes stung painfully.

As he watched, the sun rose through the trees, giving him a little shelter from its heat. Bright dapples danced on the lake's surface, and as he watched the sun reflecting off the water, as huge carp passed in front of him. He watched as they swam out of view, hidden by the depths of the water. He took off the yellow-tinted glasses and admired how beautiful everything was. The sky was as deep a blue as he had ever seen but the richness of the leaves on the trees around the lake strikingly stood out. The water reflected all hues of blue and green, as the mist thinned or thickened, hanging over the lake like a puff of icing sugar. Large pink water lilies had opened in one of the little fishing bays, which was the first time Art had seen them open. He studied the level that the water was sat at and could not work out why the level had not dropped. He had put a stick in the edge of the lake, with marks on it. It was so he could monitor what the water did. He couldn't believe that even though they had taken gallons for the plants, the level had not dropped and yet the gentle River Witham in Grantham just a few miles away had dried right up. Even after the massive hailstorm that had caused a mini tornado to pass through Lincolnshire, the level of the water had not risen.

Nicholson stopped in his tracks and cocked his head to one side, as he listened. A few moments later, Art heard the sound of jet planes flying overhead. Three military planes came into view, trailing a white vapour behind them. They travelled 15 miles apart in perfect straight lines, from the east to the west. A few moments later, another three planes could be seen flying parallel to the first set. They too were trailing a white vapour behind them. As Art stood and watched, the sharp white trails started to drift in the wind, spreading out to form the beginnings of a white shield. Nicholson looked up at them, as one flew directly overhead. 'What are you spraying, dudes?' Art said to Nicholson. Art and his dog stayed sat on the boulder basking in the early morning rays. Although it was muggy and humid, it was good to feel the rawness of the sun directly on his face. Its heat complimented the cool stone beneath his legs and the cool grass between his toes. He was at one with nature. He was at one with the earth.

Molay Barn, Lincolnshire

William had been up since five in the morning. He had not slept well, as although the old stone cottage was very cool in the summer, this extensive heat was too much for it. Once the rooms got warm, they stayed warm. His bedroom window was only small nestled under the eve of the thatching but even with a small electric fan on, the heat was unbearable. He even occasionally sprayed water in front of the fan, which was very cooling. He had to get back to Somerset by lunchtime and so had packed a small bag the night before. He had come home to check that the room off the tunnel storing the seeds was secure. He had then sealed the cellar from the tunnel with a hydraulic door that was stored inside the wall. Using a remote control fob, William pushed a button and the door slid out of the wall and then slid back two inches whilst making a hissing and multiple locking sounds. He had been preparing for this moment all of his adult life and now all of his calculations were to be tested. He had been the head of the MBHK for over 35 years. The MBHK was the last remaining strand of The Knight's Templar. It was a worldwide organisation, where each generation ensured the following members were found and initiated. It was the way it was, the way it always was. The symbol that everyone at the MBHK knew and answered to, came from an ancient hieroglyphic, depicting a great pyramid, an obelisk and the setting sun. It had been found in Israel by the Templars in the thirteenth century and rediscovered after years of searching by the MBHK. William's cellar door had come from one of the buildings that once stood at Temple Bruer. While he had been at university with Tarquin, he had utilised all of the journals and documents from around the world that lay at his fingertips. He researched symbols, hieroglyphs and the geological relationship between where the Knights had bought land and where a strange underwater system ran around the earth. He had researched what his parents had told him and what his grandparents had told them.

With the money he had from his magnetic door catches and later the slow-draw mechanism that he designed, he had partly funded the MBHK. Other money makers silently funded the organisation; some were well-known names. They had been approached, and understood that nothing could be done to prevent the pending catastrophe. Like the Templars with the King of France, the MBHK did not mention the correct time of the event. The organisation gave the impression that the donated money would save their children within the next ten years, as the true date of the event could not be disclosed. It had been a priority that the benefactors were given the best chance of survival, as there was not enough room for them at the festival, so the MBHK had organised an exclusive alpine retreat, where they would hopefully be safe. These chosen people could happily live in caves with everything they owned just a few feet away from them. They had to be people whose hearts beat to the sound of tribal drums, igniting an inner spirit that could only be released with a tribal call. They had to be people who had created lives for themselves that were relaxed and stress free, people who didn't need a holiday to get away from the drudgery of their everyday lives. They had to be people who took care of the little things, so the big things would sort themselves out. They had to be people with the defective DNA.

What had to be done was to ensure the ones who were meant to survive... did. This was and always had been William's role.

Glastonbury Festival, Somerset

Miriam unzipped her tent, and recoiled as the bright early morning sunlight stung her eyes and head. The shadow of the hedge behind her had reduced so the sun had started to warm her home. She saw Pod a few feet away, do the same, stretching and yawning, rubbing her eyes. They had managed to make their camps very close together. Miriam crawled on all fours over guide ropes to sit on the grass in-between Pod and Coco, who had been hidden by another tent. She was sat in a garden chair, drinking a can of cider. The perfect festival breakfast. Her bare feet were a bright orange, with two white straps across her toes where her flip flops had been. Pod was sat opposite her, with her back to the Pyramid stage. Her feet were orange too from the scorched dust of farm tracks that had stuck to everyone's bare legs. She had set out the water container and cup for a festival shower. They both wore last night's clothes, and sunglasses. Pod was examining her feet, which had been badly burnt the day before. She had applied John's cream, and miraculously it had stopped the burn.

The morning continued with laughter and drinking. Every now and again the Pyramid would run a five-minute sound check, which became a frequent highlight of the morning. Everyone was getting excited for the show they were going to be part of. Rumours spread as the details were read from the programme. Excited music fans discussed using the 'Fans with Bands' booths, and which celebrities they would like to talk to. They created their own perfect set list, though most could not create a list that would last half an hour, never mind the 11-hour epic the MBHK had had to organise. There was an expectant buzz around the campsites, as late risers had the show described to them by several of their friends all at once. Coco and Pod had decided to walk through The Glades and up to The Stone Circle, to experience the spiritual aspect of the festival. They'd had a thorough wash and put the same clothes back on. Nobody cared what you looked like! Nobody cared what you wore! Although the temperature was already in the mid-eighties, there was a warm, misleading breeze. The heat was unusual for the British Isles. It was the sort of oven heat famed in Egypt, where the atmosphere was so dry and void of moisture, it was possible to endure hotter temperatures.

The Glades was a tranquil place to walk, amongst shading trees and patches of thick undergrowth decorated with wind chimes and ribbons. Handmade sculptures made from recycled metal had moving parts which made a musical sound if touched. Beautifully decorated tents offered everything from head massages, homemade cooking, art classes and tarot readings, lazily nestled between the shrubbery. Long dreadlocked men played flutes and acoustic guitars and sun-creamed, sun hat wearing children played in bare feet. Henna tattoos were expertly applied and crafts were explained. Pod loved this part of the festival. It was somewhere to go when the hustle of the festival became a little too overwhelming. Softly spoken women sat talking to people interested in the knowledge that they had, and men wearing white aprons catered at little al fresco tea tents or coffee shops, selling homemade cakes. Mismatched tables and chairs with enough seating for just eight guests were laid out under the shade of some trees. Coco and Pod decided to have a break and chose two chairs partially hidden in a bushy alcove around a log table. The bushes rose above the chair backs, meeting the lower branches of the nearest trees. They ordered green teas and fruit juices, as a bit of a treat for their bodies after the punishment they had put them through the previous night. The teas came in proper mugs, on a tray with lemon, milk and sugar. None of the crockery or cutlery matched, like the furniture, but the drinks were very good. They spent an hour in the shade sat watching as people ambled by, showing an interest in this strange world that they were being allowed to experience. There were terracotta pots with plants placed around the tea tent, which filled the air with delicate scents of rosemary, thyme and mint as people brushed passed.

The little tea tent did not charge for the teas, just asked for donations. The tea leaves were collected and made by the man who had served them. Pod and Coco got into a conversation with him, and he explained how he did everything himself. He baked the cakes, brewed the teas and waited the three tables. He never charged for the tea, as the farm gave him milk for free, and the water came from the ground, which he did not own. Therefore, 'How could I charge for them?' he would explain. People gave generously, and out of respect would always also buy his cakes. They were wholesome and healthy, but famously tasty. He had been the only tea tent at the first Glastonbury, and had almost become a celebrity. He would talk about all the different things he had witnessed over the years. He would happily talk to people who sought him out and people often found a few hours would fly by unnoticed. Everything he owned was in the 1970s coach that was parked under the nearby trees. The little homestead had a washing line and a shower bag hanging from a tree with a staked canvas screen offering a primitive washing area. It was simple, basic and yet efficient.

'What do you do when it's cold?' asked Pod, admiring the neatness and tasteful way everything had been arranged.

'I have an indoor shower. Come, I shall show you.' Juju opened the side door of the bus and pointed to a large round, cast iron plant pot.

'How does it work?' asked Coco, totally fascinated by what she was about to be shown.

'Well, I put a giant bung in that hole in the bottom of the tub,' he explained, pointing to the base of the cast iron pot. 'I climb into this giant plastic bag that sofas are delivered in. It's sort of like an upside down shower curtain, totally sealed in the tub. The top is reinforced with tape, so I can use hooks to hang it from the ceiling. I stay standing in the bag, turn the water bag on, that hangs on that hook in the middle. After I have showered, there is a foot of water in the bottom of the bag. I carefully get out, get dressed and then pull out the bung in the tub. The bottom of the knotted bag is pushed through the hole, to the outside. When I am next out there, I open the bag, the water runs away, I knot the bag up again, push it through the hole and put the bung back in. It works perfectly, and I can even have a hot shower in winter, as the shower bag is heatproof, used for carrying hot water.'

Pod and Coco stood in awe, how simple and efficient the little shower was, and when it wasn't in use, a lid sat on top of it and it became a coffee table. It sat on locking wheels and could be moved to anywhere on the bus. Everywhere was clean and practical, with heavy, purpose-made curtains and blackout blinds. At the back of the bus was a curtained area accessed by two steps, which was where Juju had a large comfy bed. In the centre of the bus was an oval cast iron wood burner, where a chimney went out through a hole in the roof. An old pan sat on the drum, beside a kettle, and a basket at the side stored neatly piled kindling. There were throws, hanging rugs and various cushions on a built-in semi-circular sofa, which faced the wood burner. It was so rustic and homely, even though the thought of a hot fire was not at the top of the list right now.

Coco and Pod stayed with Juju and had a late lunch with him. He made a stir-fry using vegetables he had grown himself. At the side of the bus there was a large trailer with its roof laid beneath it. There were carrots and potato furrows in the trailer, and the starts of turnips and cabbage.

'I grow some of my own veg,' explained Juju. 'The trailer is quite heavy, but the bus manages quite easily. When I am on the move I stand the plant pots in the bus and put the corrugated plastic roof on the trailer. It acts as a greenhouse too!'

'Your ideas are amazing, and your creativity is limitless!' complimented Pod.

'I just have everything I need on my bus. The tea tent makes a lot of money, but what do I need money for? I have no bills, just the expense of running the bus, which is probably less than some of those modern four-by-fours you see! I don't have water, electric and gas bills. I collect wood and store it under the bus. Everything I need, right here!' he said proudly, patting the bus. 'I like your tattoo of the Punk-father Mr Rotten!' he giggled. 'Go have a look in the bus. Go up the stairs and look at the ceiling above the back window. There's something you might like there!'

Coco walked through the bus to the steps, and kneeling on Juju's neatly made bed, she looked above the opened back window. There, in handwriting she recognised, was 'Johnny Rotten Lydon was 'ere!' The 'W' had been drawn like two boobs, just like the autograph Mr Lydon had drawn on her leg beneath the tattooed portrait. His autograph had also been tattooed, which was nearly identical to the words on the bus's ceiling. *This must have been one of the buses the Sex Pistols had used. It was about the right age!* thought Coco excitedly.

'Wow, is this an old coach that The Pistols used?' she called out to Juju through the open back window, as he fried shredded veg on the stove in the tea tent.

'One of a set of twins, separated after the trauma of ferrying Mr Rotten and his buddies!' he laughed. 'Look down the bus, to the wall on the left, just below the window.' Juju waited for the response he knew Coco would give.

'Oh my God... Bloody hell... Ju-Juuuuu... Oh wow!'

'Coco?' Juju called out in an innocent voice, knowing that what Coco had just seen, was pretty special.

'Mate...'Nancy 4 Sid'... are you kidding me? Nancy... the whore,' she whispered to herself, reading the comments around the heart. '...and

SID... Juju? SID...?' squealed Coco. There, on the wall in a childlike scrawl, was a heart surrounding the words. A long wobbly arrow pointed to the word 'Nancy', with the word 'slut' at the other end. *This is actual Sex Pistol graffiti* she thought.

The Railway Cottage, Lincolnshire

William had finally made it back to Somerset just in time for his short meeting in the sound control tower outside the Pyramid Stage. He had been delayed, as after leaving his home, he called in to see Art. He had sealed the tunnel off from the rest of the house in his cellar and the simple magnetic doors had also securely sealed off the rooms with the seeds in. Once he was happy that his home would not be flooded, he had driven through Sleaford to Railway Cottage. Everywhere was brown or a faded yellow. Dust swirled from the road side as he drove his car through the ghost town and empty lanes. Disturbed bushes and weeds shook a layer of dust off themselves with the passing of any cars, just to be recoated in dust as it settled once again. The usually congested town was quite deserted as the midday temperatures reached over 103 degrees. Patches of the tarmac in the open country had started to become sticky, as the relentless heat caused the tar to melt. Limp trees dropped their branches surrounding fields of dry, lifeless crops. As he turned into the drive of the cottage it was as if someone had cleaned a dirty window. The full range of colourful flowering pots and tubs, healthy climbing white roses and jasmine, luscious mown grass and green, vibrant tree foliage was a total contrast to the surrounding countryside. William smiled to himself. *People will be safe here,* he thought to himself, *just got to convince Art!*

'Art, my good man, how's the heat treating you?' William said, shaking hands and patting Art on the back. 'Good to see you, lad. Any luck?' he asked, nodding his head to the rods extending out into the lake.

'Good to see you, William. How are you in the heat?' replied Art, returning the greeting, just as a little alarm clock beeped. Art turned it off and started to walk back to the house, 'Back in a moment! Drink in the cool box!' he said, pointing behind him. While William waited for Art to return, he analysed the water levels and clarity of the lake. All seemed to be as it should. There were over thirty waterbirds gliding around on the lake and all variety of birds chattered and called, flying around the treetops. William had noticed the increased chicken population and the various bird feeding points that Art had built around the garden, which were attracting more diners. Nicholson jumped up as he saw his master walking back from the house.

'Just had to water the kids!' said Art.

'The kids?'

'Yes, while Pod and John are away, Logan is here looking after the greenhouse. She's looking after her sister too. I must make sure they drink plenty in this heat.'

'And are they? '

'Are they what?' replied Art as he was distracted by fishy movements in the lake.

'Pod's daughters, are they drinking plenty of fluids?'

'Yeah, every hour!' replied Art, nodding his head towards the little alarm clock sat on the cool box, not taking his eyes off the fish.

William was impressed with the way Art did everything to the best of his ability. Art recognised that he sometimes got easily distracted and so to remind himself he had set the alarm when it was time to rehydrate Pod's children.

'Art, do you trust me?' said William in a tone that Art had never heard before.

'Well…' replied Art, wondering if this was a trick question, so he answered it honestly. 'Yes and no. I trust you, but don't understand you. Coco and I have asked you about the symbols quite a few times and you've always been evasive. We would understand if you just said you can't talk about it, but you don't. We just don't understand.'

'If I can do something outstanding right now, will you trust me, trust me with your life?'

'What do you mean?' asked Art curiously.

'I'm asking you to believe, Art, to trust me. Look around you. What do you see?'

'Water, trees, ducks, birds…the birds?' he questioned.

'Yes, remember I told you to watch for the birds. You have been, I know!'

'How do you know?'

'Because they are here. Look around you. They are here because you watched out for them. All those bird tables you have built and supplied with birdseed.'

'I haven't been feeding the bloody ducks and swans, but look at them?' said Art, pointing at the busy lake.

'Have you been fishing much, Art?'

'Yes, lots, it's cool down here, the water seems to be particularly clear, even though there's this drought and we're watering all of the plants. You can see to the bottom in a lot of places it's that clear. I've been seeing more of the huge fish in the deeper water and so have been throwing bait in!'

'So you have been feeding the water birds,' replied William, with a smile on his face. 'Which fish do you want to catch today, son?'

'Anything really, I'm just having a mess around with different rigs as I can see how they act in the water 'cause it's so clear!' Art replied excitedly, but curious about William's smile. 'What's going on William? Enough of the riddles,' said Art, as his smile faded slightly.

'Name your fish!' ignored William, picking up one of the rods and reeling the line in he turned to Art smiling, 'Name your fish!'

Frustrated as he was, Art patiently answered, knowing William would tell him what he was trying to get at, when the time was right. 'Nemo, the biggest fish you have pulled out of this lake. Nemo!'

'Okay, settle in then. I'll catch Nemo, you can make some iced juice.'

'Can you do it in forty minutes, because I have to check on the kids again!' joked Art, knowing it was impossible to catch the same big pike in the middle of summer on demand, as it had not been caught since that first day when John had caught it. He walked back to the house to make some iced juices. Ten minutes later, he walked down to the lake, he heard splashing and shouting. He increased his pace carefully in his bare feet.

'You slippery old bastard, you stay just there!'

'Bloody hell!' shouted Art, as he watched William sit on the giant pike, in the middle of a sweltering summer, using forceps to unhook it. The fish thrashed around for one more attempt at freedom, until William stood up with difficulty with the giant fish to show Art. Art stood rigid to the spot, a jug of juice in one hand and two mugs in the other. His mouth was wide open in disbelief. 'Nemo... in summer... I didn't even have the rods set up for pike. How the hell did you catch a predator on a marmite boily?'

He watched as William stepped into the lake and lowered the fish in, until it had acclimatised. It dropped into the depths and disappeared. William sat on the log bench and looked at Art's shocked face.

'Do you trust me?' he asked once again, wringing lake water out of his socks whilst his trainers dried in a patch of sunlight.

'As I said, yes and no!' replied Art, feeling this was getting too messed up. He didn't like mind games and despite his good friendship with William, he wasn't going to let this old dude head-fuck him.

'The symbols you have asked me about. There is not time to fully explain just now. But I will when I get back. I promise.' The old man said sincerely, staring into Art's eyes. 'The lake... the lake is fed by an underground stream. The water in the corner of the meadow after your mini festival was the stream reacting to the music and vibrations you all made. The water rose to the surface.'

'Are you shitting me? Those greenhouses could collapse if the water floods their foundations, not to mention The Brew House,' Art said angrily, missing the information about the stream. 'You knew, so why let us build. If you knew the stream filled the lake via the meadow, why didn't you say something? Jes…!' said Art, standing up and walking towards the lake edge, with his hands on his hips. He turned and pointed at William, 'Hang on… the water reacts to the music? Am I in Middle Earth or something, or just Cuckoo Land?'

'Art, please son. Remember Nemo? This is why I have not been able to tell you until I could have your hundred per cent trust.' Art seemed to calm down again, and sat back down on the bench. He still had a rarely seen angry look in his eyes, which had gone the palest grey. 'Nemo, I caught the fish you knew I could not catch, as your rods and the time of year is not pike-catching conditions.'

'Yes, you caught Nemo, on carp rods and bait. How? Are you a wizard, William?' he laughed, the anger he had felt completely slipping away. 'Wizard William!' he repeatedly said whilst laughing, 'It suits you!'

'Do you trust me, Art? Please, I need to know.'

Art sat and looked at William. His kind eyes squinted slightly as the sun occasionally broke through the leaves for a second. He could not work out how the old man had caught the fish, or how he had known so definitely that he could perform something incredible. When William had said 'If I do something outstanding right now!' he was making a statement. He knew he would definitely not fail to do whatever he had set out to do, and he had done it. Unquestionable.

'Okay. I trust you,' said Art quietly.

'When I studied at university, I learned "The Law of Attraction". Basically, you think about things differently. If you really want something, and you *feel* how it would be if you got what you were asking for, it will come to you. That's as simple as I can put it. I am a master, having studied the beliefs in it all of my life.'

'Do you have super-human powers?' asked Art seriously.

'No, I don't. I have just learnt to tune my thought frequency into the right channels. The universe controls everything.'

There was a ten minute silence. 'Do you want me to catch Nemo again?' William asked, as he got ready to leave, putting his nearly dry trainers back on. He still had to get to Somerset.

'No. But could you?'

'Yes. Practise at it, you will be able to in time too. If you want something badly enough, feel and think how it would be if you did actually have what you had asked for. I wanted to catch Nemo, so you might trust me and better understand me.'

'Good job Nemo was awake and hungry. You'd have been stuffed if he was having a nap!' laughed Art.

'I wanted him badly, so badly the universe brought him to me! Think about what we have done today. It's important. You'll know why at the right time. Now, I'm off to see my relatives in Somerset. You never know, I might bump into Coco, John or Pod.'

'I don't think John and Rev have got there yet. I've not managed to get a text through to anyone all day. I saw Miriam's partner yesterday, so hopefully he would have passed on a message to Miriam before she left for the festival.'

'Okay, well, I'm off. It's so hot, hopefully it will all be over soon,' said William knowingly. He got into his car, with Art stood beside him. 'The water from the lake… and the stream… stay near it. Keep Pod's children with you here. I've told you about the lake for a reason. Ask yourself why everything here is so green and the countryside is so parched. It's the water. If you truly trust me, stay here for the next few days. I've heard it is going to get hotter. You three will be safer here. If Coco and Pod need me, I will be nearby for them. Coco has my number.'

'The water?' Art said puzzled, but looking at the expression on William's face, he did not question the old man. 'Thanks, but they are veteran festivallers, they'll be fine. Pissed by now I would have thought!' he laughed.

'Okay, just remember, this heat is punishing. If *anything* happens, I will get them home to you, okay?'

'Chill, William, they'll be fine. But thanks, if I get a signal I'll text her you're nearby.'

'Wonderful and if I see them, I will say hello. I drive right by the village the festival is in,' said William, which was only a part lie. He was driving through the village, and into the festival site via a concealed entrance down a remote lane. 'Remember, I will get them back to you son!'

'Thanks, okay, but they will be okay. Have a safe trip, get rest if you're tired and drink plenty!' Art called, as William set off.

William heard the little alarm at the lake beep, and saw Art go to The Brew House. William stopped, *surely he's not giving them homebrew. They will be arseholed!* thought William, surprising himself by his choice of words. Art came out with a pint and a half of coloured juice, with one cube of ice in them each. *Bless him*, thought William, *cool enough to be refreshing, but not so cold that a hot body could go into shock.* William drove off smiling. He was so relieved that he no longer would have to protect his identity from the two people in the world he felt most connected to. Yes, he had his daughters, but they wanted a different world than he did. After showing Art just how much he was capable of, he knew that after the event he would come totally clean with them.

MBHK Headquarters, Somerset

Four hours later, William pulled up in the backstage area of the Pyramid Stage. He was escorted to the sound check tower, smiling at the festivallers as they lazed in the sun. Once inside the tower, he went down a flight of stairs to a large, underground room. Banks of computers and electrical equipment were set up to monitor the event, with an internal energy backup supply.

'Right, gentleman. Ed. Rik. Robert. Sam. Dylan. I'd first like to thank you gentleman. Thank you. Thank you for all of your hard work. So far, we have them all here. There is only about five per cent still to turn up. The Pyramid Stage has been sounding good. The old hairs on the back of my neck stood up when you played a bit of Metallica. Those bins sure kick some arse! Thanks!' They all laughed. The room was hot, but not unbearable. The temperature had to be kept down, but the heat generated from all of the hardware made it difficult to cool such a cramped room. 'How are things? Any problems we need to discuss?' Ed? Dylan?'

'The music is all good. Last night we had a brainwave. We ran the sound system back through itself, recording the levels and got it up to seventy-five per cent. If a plug had come loose you would have heard it three miles away. It was awesome!'

'Err, guys?' interrupted Rik, 'If you can hear it that far away, what about the poor sods stood next to it? You will bust their eardrums surely.'

'Dear Richard,' mocked Dylan, 'that is very true, but the actual sound will come out of different located speakers, so everyone, no matter where they are standing, will get perfect surround sound. All of that sound is not being played in one direction. Each person will only be able to hear up to four speakers at once, because it is being spread out, in different directions. Safe as!'

'Oh, cool. Well, the medi-tent is on full standby, and everything is ready in the storage marquee for when they all start walking up. We have done lots of practise runs covering every scenario. They will all be processed as they wake, and sent to one of the other stage areas.'

'I know it's in our notes, but just simplify it quickly for me, dude. Just a memory jogger please!' said Robert.

'As they wake, the staff who are at present serving them all with food and drink will marshal the campsites. People will be lethargic but totally coherent. They will be asked where they lived. The whole site will be divided geographically. For example, Londoners are to go to The Other Stage area, Leeds, Manchester and Liverpool to The Park and so on. The wake-up process will take about seventy-two hours in total, so it will be a long slow, repetitive process. Once in their geographical areas, they will have an explanation as to what is going on. Once everyone's questions have been answered and it is fully understood as to what had happened, everyone who had a car would be asked to put a magnetic flag on the roof and to leave the keys in the ignition.'

'Flags?' asked Ed.

'Yes, to indicate how much fuel is in each car. We don't want to send a car to Bristol which has enough fuel in it to go to London. Different colours will denote how much fuel there is in the tank. The all-terrain vehicles will be used to reach the longer distances, as they have the solar panels and won't have to rely on fuel.'

'Wow! Who comes up with this stuff. It's brilliant, so long as everyone complies. I would be a bit pissed off if my Merc got swapped with a granny beige Fiesta!' said Dylan.

'You haven't got a Merc!' said Ed.

'No, but if I did...'

'And that is one of the biggest problems we have. People will not fully understand what they are being told. They will be concerned for their families and homes, and rationalising with many of them is going to be problem. We have special bottled water with a gentle sleeping agent in it. For any of the festivallers that become hysterical, we will offer them water, and they will be asleep within a few minutes. When they wake again, it will all be explained again. Please remember that there are over a thousand members of staff on duty organising the processing. With the long period of time by which they will all wake, the system has no other choice but to work. Also remember a lot of these people will be extremely calm and prepared. That is one of the key reasons they are here in the first place.'

They all tried to understand how all these revellers were going to react when they realised what was happening.

'After they have sorted out who has to travel to where, they are then escorted to a car. For example, London may be a blue flag, and so the first travellers for London will be taken to a car with a blue flag. The reg number would be recorded and the names of who was to travel in the car. This had to tally with the records they will have on the main exits. They will then introduce themselves, collect all of their belongings and leave the site together. They will be issued with a survival rucksack on the outer perimeter of the site, and will have another debrief session. After that, they are on their own. We estimate eighty-five will make it home, ten per cent will survive but not make it home, and five per cent will not survive.'

'If all the cars have their keys in them, what's to stop someone taking a different car?' asked Sam.

'Nothing really, except they won't know what all the coloured flags mean. The amount of fuel in the car denotes the length of journey it can make, which corresponds to the flag colours.'

William smiled and nodded as the five researchers discussed the final stages of the event. 'Robert, how about you? I was in Lincolnshire this morning and I noticed they have resumed their spraying. What's going on?'

'Yes, I have had to lay low for a few weeks. They are starting to ask why all of their all-terrain vehicles seem to have been borrowed by a fictional company. The IT guys have done really well covering my tracks, but they are getting very close. Getting my hands on new information has been hard. But I have a friend in Russia. He says that the world government stopped spraying three weeks ago. They decided that it could maybe be the chemicals they were spraying in the skies causing the acceleration of temperatures and so they all stopped spraying. Three weeks later, they have decided to up the spraying, in a hope that the barium will reflect the heat from the sun. Obviously they don't know that the heat is being pulled towards Earth, as all of the planets in our solar system line up to one side of the sun. In approximately nineteen hours Pluto will be the last planet to take up the rear. At that point, the heat will shoot out as a gamma ray. It will only take about eighteen seconds to surround the earth.'

'Now they think the spraying will save them, but it is actually the catalyst that ensures everywhere sprayed will be incinerated?' asked Uncle Sam.

'Yes, the more they spray the more damage they are doing,' replied Robert.

'While we are all here, what will be happening out there, Robert?' asked Rik soberly, thinking of his family.

'Well, the heat will suddenly get hotter very very quickly, over about twenty minutes. The sea, oceans and rivers will start to evaporate. As they start to steam, the final heat blast will send an intense heat that will turn everything man-made, including man, to dust. Everything. Puff!' he gestured a bursting bubble with his hands. After a moment he continued. 'There will then be a backdraft of wind gusts up to two hundred miles per hour as the heat retreats at a phenomenal rate. Huge winds will suck up anything that literally isn't stuck down. The winds will take all the dust back out to space. We have already explained about who has a chance of survival and who does not. The heat will be undamaging on the surface of the ground. The oxygen given off by plants and trees will work in an opposite way to normal. Although the oxygen would normally feed a fire, by the time the heat rays reach the earth, the oxygen will actually protect the plants, keeping them undamaged. So, in short, as the heat shoots down, it is stopped in its tracks just before coming into contact with foliage, then, as it withdraws back into space, huge winds will suck up anything that is not well held down. Plus of course, the underground pure water stream will surface around the world, definitely at all of the Templar sites around Europe and the Middle East. Any vegetation watered by the steam will be extremely strong, with long healthy roots. The pure water is seriously powerful stuff.'

There was a long silence. Some girls screamed and laughed in the faint background above them in the Pyramid field.

'So…' Everyone waited to hear what piece of inappropriate wisdom Dylan was going to come out with. 'The Earth is basically regenerating itself. A bit like a dog shaking off fleas!' William sat and studied all of the faces of the very clever men who had spent so long planning this event. However, out of all the things that had been openly discussed, no one had worded it quite like Dylan. It was so true, the more they all thought about it, the more the sense of importance became deeper instilled into them. This was going to happen no matter what, and their sole purpose was to ensure the event went without a hitch.

'Back stage is going well,' said Uncle Sam. Everyone turned their attention to him. 'If you want to keep one hundred rock stars happy, supply booze, drugs and video games.'

'Drugs?' asked Robert. 'What sort of bloody drugs?'

'Robert, my good man, when you can keep one hundred rockers happy for three days without *any* problems at all, you tell me how you would do it. Until then, Jack Daniels and Playstations are keeping the keys to your door content.' There was an uncomfortable silence. It was an unwritten rule, never question someone else's motives without a suggestion of your own. Robert put his hands up and mouthed 'sorry' as Uncle Sam continued. 'Most of them are happy just chilling and watching Scar Face and talking to one another. The Gentlemen's Club, as we have called it, is a converted tour bus that gets quite rowdy. But, the main thing, everyone is happy. I overheard Paul Weller and John Lydon talking about the seventies club scene. It was fascinating!'

'Oh, and just a quick point,' said Ed, 'We have perfected the text warning. When we press send, and all the texts get sent at once to protect loved ones on the outside...' he paused, looking with raised eyebrows at Dylan.

'What?' he asked, looking indignant.

'Just waiting for your comment!'

'No, I remember this bit. Continue!' smiled Dylan.

'So, the computers here will send a text and loved ones and friends become protected. But what you haven't been told is that at exactly the same time a *fake* text will also be sent directly to the festivallers' phones here, which they will *think* is from their loved ones. Therefore, if they check their phones the following day after the grand finale, they will have a series of texts that they think are from friends and family saying they are okay. If the system works, most of the friends and family will survive, but these "fake reply" texts will reduce panic and stress here.'

'Right. Okay. Make sure you're all ready for tomorrow lunchtime. Sam, make sure Russell Brand knows he's opening the show!'

Chapter Forty

Wednesday morning, Glastonbury Festival 2012

By ten o'clock the next morning, Coco and Pod were up, washed, changed and sat in the Pyramid field with Miriam and Sophie. There was already a group of people stood at the very front. The stage stood fifteen feet off the floor, and its cavernous pyramid shape was imposing. It cast a cold shadow over the revellers at the very front, but as the sun rose, the rays zapped everything and anything's energy. Everyone patiently waited as the arena slowly filled up. Many people brought fishing umbrellas to sit under, as some shade from the sun was mandatory. Many of the waiting audience wore giant sombreros, with wide rims which cast much needed shade. Various pole carriers joined the crowds, with bright, lively flags of all varieties. Nobody really knows when the flags started, but it was so people at home could look out for their friends. There were different nationalities, football clubs, animals and kites attached to various length poles. As each tribe followed their colours to the stage front, the festival family grew.

Revellers had become restless, eager to hear the music and to see what had been billed as The Greatest Show on Earth. There had been plenty to see and do without the music, but the crowds were keen to see their idols. A small crowd had even started to dance to the radio being played by an ice cream van. Coco and Pod had spent the previous day before wandering around The Glade, and spent the evening in Arcadia again. They had hoped to see the White Witch Dancers again in the Haunted House, but instead there was a woman on the stage in a burlesque outfit stapling bits of porn magazine to herself, without feeling any pain. They had come out of the club, removing their fake facial hair, to witness a Mad Max parade. It had been getting dark, and the setting sun cast long shadows over Arcadia. The macabre procession included biomechanically legged machines hissing smoke and spitting fire, massive trikes made into insects, with circular cages on their backs with captured women in them. There were leather-clad men, wearing mad scientist goggles riding massive machines that were reminiscent of something out of Star Wars. Tough-looking women in short, tight, torn leather clothing cracked whips and shouted at the men controlling the machines. The whole performance had been breathtaking.

The mechanical beasts led the procession, which centred around a massive sculpture on wheels, of a metal-plated doll's head, with hideously fiery red eyes. A black, open jeep covered in fake animal skulls pulled the doll's head sculpture. It had a massive, long skull on its grill, and a giant set of horns dangerously pointing forward. Its driver had long, tied back hair and wore leather trousers. His bare torso was muscular and tanned. Beside him sat a slim woman dressed in a white body stocking, and pristine pink cat ears and tail. She had a pink lead and collar on, which the jeep driver held in his hand. The slow procession had warriors on foot, who intimidated the crowd and tried to steal some of the ladies. They all ran to make two rows, as a guard of honour for the procession could pass through. They did a tribal dance, enacting war dances of ancient warriors, warning the people watching to 'back off'. The crowd could smell the diesel fumes and smoke of the beasts and the oil and leather of the actors as they passed.

Coco and Pod watched, wincing at the heat the snorting beasts blew from their biomechanical noses, as their hydraulic legs stepped forward, squeaking and clanging as they proceeded. The power, heat and concept of the machines caused hairs to stand on end, shivers to go down spines, and hot and cold flushes. The crowd clapped and applauded the actors as they made their way through Arcadia and over the raised road into Shangri-La. By the time the parade had passed, it was nearly dark. They went and met Miriam and Sophie again in The Snakepit, and got a wonderful surprise when they bumped into John and Rev too. Rev had insisted on finding the club as the first thing he did at the festival, so he could show off his finished tattoo of Jess.

John and Rev had turned up in the afternoon, and made for the place Coco had said she would try and camp in. They had managed to find a little patch between a few tents, and pitched. They only had tents and a blanket, and planned to stay in the same clothes for the few days they were there. They had clean underwear, but with it being so hot they had not worn shirts for most of the last month. As neither of them were drinking, they did not have to carry much either. The coach had dropped them off in the coach park, and as they had walked to the main gate, they passed marshals recycling beer cans, bottles and discarded trolley parts. Huge piles of rubbish were then collected by a lorry with a grabber on it, and taken to the festival's recycling centre for sorting. All of the rubbish, as with previous years was sorted on-site and recycled. It was part of the rules when traders booked, everything food or drink was served in had to be biodegradable. John thought back to the days when he used to have to survive by rummaging through skips. As they walked to the ticket entrance, they talked about how far they had come, and what they had achieved. As they walked and thought, they started to piece things together. Everything seemed to link together. The plant from the NA meeting that John was given, to Rev drug couriering for someone, who it turned out, owned the lake on the land where John's greenhouses were. Maybe people did have destinies, paths they were meant to follow.

As they had their tickets processed, and a wristband put on their arms, they stepped through the turnstile onto the site. A huge grassy hill sloped down to brightly coloured flags and 'big top' marquees. Smoke from bonfires drifted up, distorted by a heat haze. John was the first to notice how green and colourful everywhere was, just like at Railway Cottage. They set off looking for the spot Coco had talked of. The grassy slope led down to The Dance Village, a cluster of six or seven differently sized marquees, decorated with butterfly shaped sails, and illuminated solar systems of planets suspended on wires. The cool dark depths in the Silent Dance tents offered some shade, as revellers took time to have an afternoon nap and a cool down. There were rows of pink and white flags on long scaffold poles lining the main track through the marquees, joined together by wires of light bulbs. The listless flags hung in the stagnant air, as John and Rev turned left towards the Pyramid Stage, which they had seen from the top of the hill. As they rounded the corner, the front of the gigantic stage came into view, and Rev whistled. The permanent steel frame was covered in a thick black fabric, and as they walked around to look into the stage close-up, its vast size became more obvious. The top point of the pyramid was over 100 feet tall, as was the length of the front. The floor space of the stage was so big, there was a double tier balcony, and rows of raised steps along the back wall.

As John marvelled at the hundreds of spotlight rigs and speaker stacks dotted around the huge triangular field, Rev was staring at one of the crew talking in a group at the back. It was hard to see clearly, as the stage was so tall. The security barrier was about ten feet away from the stage itself, so Rev took a few steps back for a better look. He was about to call John, when the group of men walked off the stage. He was sure he had just seen Mr Idol, *but what the hell is he doing here, backstage too?* he thought.

John was stood with his back to the stage, pointing over to the far corner of the field. Long white clouds criss-crossed the sky, and Rev was lost in a moment of thought as he watched a plane lay another trail crossing over some of the others. Why was Mr Idol here? What were those planes spraying in the sky? John strode off in the direction of where he thought Coco's tent might be, while Rev followed, still watching the sky. As they had no way of knowing which was Coco's tent, they pitched where they could.

Being at a festival was going to be a mixture of emotions for both John and Rev as neither of them was drinking; they had to brave it all sober. It actually turned out easier than they had thought it might be. They took in the sights and smells and appreciated all the hard work they had gone through for such a fantastic reward. They had talked with some celebrities in the video game booths, and were far too sober to try and play with one of the 'Fans Play with Bands'. They took in the colours of decorative sculptures, bunting, and all the different eating places. Everywhere was so vibrant and fantastic, carefully thought out, so flags complimented each other and their bright contrasts stood out against the bright blue sky, which as the day went on, turned into a thick white layer of cloud. Towards the late afternoon, the humidity was unbearable, and weary campers took shelter wherever they could. The site was peaceful, as people dozed in the shade or simply admired the views whilst sipping on cold water and beers, grateful for the opportunity they had been given.

Most people sat outside their tents, having a few naps, and talking about the festival site until the sun started to set behind the Tor. The sunset was spectacular. The watery green sky faded into blue and the darkness of the coming night. Bright orange clouds that looked like they were on fire passed in front of the sun, causing huge sunrays to shoot into the sky from behind the cloud. The celestial sight caught the attention of other campers, as people stood up to get a better view. As the sun sank further, it grew bigger, a burning bright orange ball softened by pollution in the atmosphere. As it grew darker, the romantic colours of the sun set were gradually replaced with the dark purple cloak of night. Stars started to shine over to the east, and the campsite once again had orange pimples of smouldering fires dotted about, as people cooked for the evening, or needed some light.

During the last half hour of dusk, John and Rev went to find The Snakepit. It was the one thing that Rev had wanted to do. Use his tattoo of Jess, show people the fantastic design and put a full stop at the end of a very desperate, lonely path. They thought it would be a good idea to try and find the club while there was still a bit of light, rather than struggling in the dark. As it was, Shangri-La had been very easy to find. Long wide grassy pathways were lit with strung-up light bulbs and frequent hand-painted signposts helped them find their way. They were some of the first few people to arrive in the night-time hotspot, and walked around looking at the crashed aeroplane, and malfunctioning robots. They spent an hour looking at everything, stopping for a can of pop, constantly talking about what they could see, hear and smell. The Snakepit club had just opened when they found it, and Rev proudly showed his tattoo for free entry. As it was not busy, the doorman took time to admire the artwork, marvelling at the delicate roses that framed the portrait of a young girl. He had seen all sorts of tattoos working at this little club, and this young man's had one of the best he had ever seen, and told him so.

The Pyramid Stage

As midday approached the following afternoon, the Pyramid Field was full of people either stood near the front of the stage, or sat on the grass at the back. The Russell Brand set had been a resounding success with many of the musicians backstage joining him backstage for interviews. Giant hoses sprayed water over people from the edges of the stage enclosure. The water jets were so powerful they reached the people half way up the arena with a cooling mist. The giant television screens on either side of the stage flashed up music videos, a giant thermometer showing how hot it was and an info-ad advising people to drink plenty of water. The marshals had added massive florescent orange flags to identify the freestanding water taps around the edge of the arena, and a tiny little truck drove around handing out bottles of water. Faint music played through the fifty feet stack of speakers, as the buzz and anticipation levels of the crowd rose.

Hundreds of tall poles with flags on waved in front of the stage and beach balls were bounced through the air, covering the whole area of the crowd. Gradually, the anticipating crowd started to fall silent, as movement on the stage was seen as a start to the show. The sun beat down on 180,000 protected heads, covered by everything from sombreros, hats and T-shirts, as Coco, Pod, Miriam, Sophie, John and Rev stood together waiting.

The speakers suddenly came alive, with the pulsating sound of a slow heartbeat and the audience burst into applause, shouting and whistling their approval. After a few minutes, the blinding white lights on top of the stage flashed with the increased heartbeat and stringed instruments that enhanced the beating heart until suddenly the stage was silent. People could not contain their excitement, with not knowing what to expect and so started to call out and applaud, raising their arms into the air. The whole thing started over again from the beginning, a slow heartbeat eventually accompanied by the lights and strings, and again, the stage fell silent. The audience was beside itself as whispers started that there might be a malfunction with the equipment.

'Right people, we ready?' said Dylan over the walkie talkies to security and the headphones of organisers around the stage. 'Let's do this. Get set to record the results as we crank it up. This is the final practise for tonight's main event.' The heart started to beat again, but this time a heavy bass drum joined in. Curtains on the stage dropped, just as the stringed instruments started to play, and revealed a full choir stood at the back of the stage on tiers and the orchestra set out around the balcony above the stage. The crowd went berserk, shouting and cheering. Goosebumps stood up on end as Dylan slowly turned up the volume as the beat got faster and more intense. 'On my mark people. Standby stage right.' Everyone heard Dylan, and waited for the all-go. 'Ed, we good dude?' Dylan asked as the two of them stood in the sound tower, looking out over the crowd. The sea of heads went as far as they could see, thousands of different hats and headdresses. The flags energetically waved as every single person faced the stage.

'Dylan mate, we've teased them all enough. Some of them are close to bursting. Give it all you got buddy. Let's do this!' Ed replied, as they high-fived each other with the choir, strings and heartbeat pulsating menacingly, as the lights flashed.

'See you on the dark side, flower,' Dylan said, as he flipped two switches.

Powerful wind machines started a vortex of swirling, iridescent smoke, circling around the outer edges of the audience, causing people with unsecured hats to quickly put a hand on their escaping headdresses. The increase in volume as the wind moved faster was subtly accompanied by the string section of the orchestra, followed by the choir and then a mash up of various emergency vehicle sirens as the sound drilled through each member of the crowd. Strobe lights flashed amidst the smoke, and blue spotlights darted over the crowd as dry ice waterfalled off the top of the stage, creating a menacing, alternative world. The noise was deafeningly loud, even though it wasn't being played at its top volume. Slash appeared on the right hand side of the stage, playing one of his world famous intros. The echoing, solo guitar lay the foundation to what would indeed, be the greatest show on earth, as two sets of rock drums joined in. Collectively, the musicians, singers and special effects reached such a crescendo, that when the drummers finally dropped the beat to launch the song, people nearest the speakers could actually feel the sound waves pass through their clothes. As *Welcome to the Jungle* by Guns N' Roses started the show, hundreds of fireworks shot into the sky, as the front of the stage exploded in a shower of silver and gold sparks. Rockets flew out from the pyramid point on wires, guaranteeing to meet their target of huge balloons filled with metallic confetti. The sky, stage and spectators merged as one, mimicking a newly born universe. The crowd surged forward a little, as everyone took a few steps closer to the stage. Session musicians started to play the rest of the song, as Slash, in his signature clothing, tall steam punk top hat and big curly hair, stylishly led the final battle cry. Axel Rose appeared to walk onto the stage from the left, but only the people close up could see he was a hologram. The audience screamed and shouted, clapped and whistled as the singer wailed into the first line of the first song of the last festival.

Coco and Pod screamed the lyrics back to the stage, jumping up and down. From the sound tower, Dylan looked down as the whole arena bounced and sang together. Slash's guitar levels were turned up during his solo parts, which he had rewritten and extended, sending the crowd wild. *Fucking hell,* thought Dylan, *If they're this mad with this song, we'll sure have enough oomph to kick-start the main event.* After the test run, the scientists had been concerned and aborted the test. They had all sat down and formulated a plan, so they could crank it right up for the Wednesday day, but not so it could trigger the event that needed to be saved for the Wednesday night. They had disconnected the copper stakes running from the fence into the ground, and so the energy of the crowd and music vibration was only a fraction of its strength.

All 180,000 people sang along, shouting the chorus as loud as they could. Rev was quite overcome as he sang the words, thinking of Jess's memory in a totally different way. In a way he knew he didn't need alcohol. The unified crowd, controlled by one man with a guitar and a singer, waved their arms in the air, played air guitar and jumped around. As the song came to an end, the backing choir and strings fell silent, and Axel walked off the stage so it was just Slash and his guitar again. A second guitarist had subtly joined him, playing parts of the intro to *Living on a Prayer* by Bon Jovi, and as Slash and the session musician mixed the two songs together with impeccable timing, watching each other's hand movements and timings. The crowd was held with baited anticipation. The full guitar intro for the next song started, as Slash gave a small bow before leaving the stage, saluting the new guitarist on stage. The choir stated to sing the backing tracks, and as the other instruments joined in, three drummers played in perfect time together, the beat of the bass drums turned so deep, that the vibration could be seen in the air.

'Ed, is this going to work?' Dylan asked his friend when his microphone was switched off. 'Stage right, get ready for *Boys are Back in Town*. Lynott hologram enter stage right!'

'Look at them, we've only played two songs. They are beside themselves!'

'I know, but they can't keep this up all day!'

'They don't have to stay here all day. We just have to make sure they all turn up tonight with the same enthusiasm.'

'The songs are good Dylan. We chose well!'

'Yes, we did. After *Boys are back in Town*, we have Hendrix doing *Watchtower*. This lot don't stand a chance, they don't know what's going to hit them!'

'We did good, mate. We did good. Man hug, dude?' Ed and Dylan had a back slapping hug, and stood looking all around them. They had created this euphoria, the uncontrolled freedom that good, live music releases in people. They watched as 180,000 carefree campers jumped in time to the song, pointed raised arms in the air for the chorus, singing along.

The day continued with hour-long sets with twenty-minute breaks in-between. Different musicians played together. Paul Weller and John Lydon played The Pistols, The Jam and The Clash songs, Noel and Liam Gallagher did an acoustic version of *Wonderwall*, backed by a full choir. The brothers even 'play-boxed' at the end as they took a bow, waving as they left the stage together. Damian Marley sang some of his father's greatest hits, with African and kettle drums, led by four bassists. Gary 'Manni' Mainfield, of Primal Scream and Stone Roses fame, performed a spectacular solo, along with holograms of Sid Vicious and Cliff Burton from Metallica. It really shouldn't have worked, but it did. Every song was a delight to watch. The composition might have been changed, the instruments played differently or big tunes were mixed together. The artists excelled with their fluent, note perfect music. Uncle Sam had done really well. By having all the musicians staying together for a few days before the show started, they had all bonded and got to know each other well enough to be able to play together with a professional excellence that made their names big in the first place.

Chapter Forty-one

22:00 Thursday night, Glastonbury Festival, 2012

The stage had been lifeless for half an hour, as the crew invisibly prepared the stage for the final set behind huge black curtains, which were used as a screen to show photographs that had been taken of the campers over the last few days. Various pieces of famous music from film soundtracks were played at a moderate volume, including the Star Wars, Indiana Jones and Superman themes seemlessly mixed together. Hour-long sets had played throughout the day covering different genres of music played by different musicians. In the heat, the reggae and blues tracks had gone down very well, with the relaxing beats under a relentless sun slowing things down a bit. But it was of little relief as although the humidity had gone the heat was a very dry, oven heat. Robert had sent a memo round to everyone, explaining how it could be so humid with clear blue skies. The chemicals that the military had been spraying had trapped moisture trying to escape from the earth, as the sun literally baked it dry. The clear blue skies meant the sun was at full strength all day, and dried up the land to dust.

The show through the day had been totally spectacular, with more hoses used to cool the crowds. The festivallers had responded with renewed energy each time the next set started. They felt there was something special happening, the clarity of the music surrounding each and every one of them, had never been heard before. The heavy bass rumbled from the ground, and high-pitched notes seemed to shoot around above their heads. All of the choir's backing vocals seemed to be on the outer edge of the arena, behind the audience, and the main vocalist could be heard in the dead centre. The music had swept the crowd to their feet, stirring a shared, deep-down emotion that can only be called into being, by infectious, invigorating music.

The band had already played *Firestarter* by The Prodigy, *Apocalypse*

Now by Transplants and *Alive* by P.O.D. in the same set, and as the sun disappeared in the west, the whole arena turned a bright pink. The coloured stage lights had been turned off so the sunlight slithered across the ground as it was chased by darkness, taking the pink hues with it. The sun glistened as a huge, fiery orange ball, as it passed behind the Tor, majestically crowning the man-made hill in the distance. As the stage stood dormant, a mighty beast catching its breath before a final battle, the whole audience stood and watched the sun as it disappeared behind the horizon. As it disappeared, it took with it the hot shimmering colours of the day, dragging dusky pink and purple tones with it as the darkness followed. The crowd to the left of the stage gasped and shouted, pointing to the stage and sunset. Half of the audience did not know what the other half were looking at, but word soon spread. The landscape they were looking at; the pyramid, sun and Tor, were exactly the same as the symbols that had been noticed by most of the festivallers. The huge television screens on either side of the stage showed the sunset so everyone understood what had been seen. The pale blue and green skies scattered with bright orange chemtrails lit up as the sun sank lower. The stage had called all of the shots throughout the day, as the crowd dutifully responded to the rhythms, melodies and beats. The time had come. Everyone waited for the final set to be prepared.

Holy Island, Cumbria

The heat had built up to such a degree over the last few days that Elizabeth and Victoria had made rooms in the cellars to live in, which were much cooler. The castle sweltered on a bed of smouldering sand. Once the tide had gone out, the heat of the sun caused steam to rise and dried the surface sand within a few hours. Elizabeth had spoken with her father, who had told her to go down into the cellar and to stay down there. He had sounded distressed, but tried not to convey his worries to his daughter. Ivan Claudius told his daughter not to worry and everything would be alright. He had rung William Idol for a catch-up and his old friend said he had heard from his military source that the heat was going to peak and that if Ivan and his family could take cover somewhere underground, preferably at the castle, they could ride it out. William could not say anymore, just repeated what he had said to the benefactors of MBHK who had been supplied with well-appointed survival shelters, but he had to advise his old friend with a young family. Besides, William knew that Holy Island would offer enough protection for the entire village of the mainland, with its ancient monastery and abbey when the pure water stream reacted with the Event. Ivan and his wife were skiing in Austria, staying with their friends again, and had planned to go cave walking. William was satisfied that they would all be safe.

The Railway Cottage, Lincolnshire

Before Coco had gone to the festival with Pod, she had organised with Art for friends to come over. CT picked up Deano who brought his television round, (as Art and Coco did not have a television, or 'Brainwasher' as Art called it). They sat on the patio in the shade of the trees, surrounded by strong smelling herbs watching the festival. Kay turned up too, with her young daughter, who played with Mahoney and Nicholson. Logan watched as her younger sister played too and took the unofficial role of nanny, while the group of friends looked out for anyone they knew on the television. The picture kept cutting out as static bands of snow passed the screen. The sound kept cutting out and distorting until it got to the point where the image was lost, and the sound was a few random notes amongst hissing static. They turned the television off and CT put it back in his car. Annie and Charlie turned up too, bringing lavish ice cream and various sauces, marshmallows and chocolate flakes. Annie was still bitter that she had thought the ticket for the festival was a scam and so she had not gone. On realising her mistake she had been in a bad mood for several days.

They spent a lazy day drinking chilled apple juice, making ice cream sundaes and checking on the greenhouses, orchard and lake. Everyone found a little place to relax and have a snooze or read of a book. Art sat by his lake, watching for all the fish. It was so hot and there was no movement at all, which he had expected. There was no birdsong from the trees as he looked out for the kingfisher or robin. Although there was no vocal evidence of the birds, he saw the branches full of them, all hopping and scrapping with one another, *Watch the birds* he remembered William saying. *Why have they all come here? There are thousands of them all living close together... strange... they're all in total silence...* he thought as he watched them. He eventually realised that every bush, tree and hedge was full of birds. He sat on the edge of the lake and for the first time he put his feet in the water. It was cooling and instantly lowered his body temperature. He had carefully calculated what effects putting his feet in the water would have on the fish in the lake. The fish were hard enough to catch, except for William. He had no problem getting Nemo whenever he wanted to. *What's that all about?* Art thought and not for the first time.

He lay back on the bank on the soft grass with his calves in water. As he shuffled to get comfy by removing one of Nicholson's throwing sticks, he noticed the lake from just above the level of the water. He stopped in his 'bed-fluffing' and stared, looking around the lake to see if what he saw was an isolated thing. The whole of the surface had a film of steam over it with a silver sheen.

'Bloody hell... it's evaporating!' he whispered to himself. He looked over to his measuring stick in the water. It was at the same depth it always was. 'It's the water, stay near it!' William had told him. 'It should all be over soon!' and what was all that about bringing Coco back to him? 'Old man is barmy!' he laughed, with a renewed admiration for William. He lay back again, wondering about the lake vapour, thinking about Coco as he missed her a lot, hoping she was having a great time. He thought about the lake, the boulder with the symbol, the flood in the meadow and Nemo. The perfectly still water gently steamed away discreetly, as the day got hotter. The more it evaporated, the more birds seemed to turn up at the little lakeside oasis.

He went back to The Brew House and got some cold ciders. The others may as well stay if they liked, while it was too hot to drive and it was so much cooler in the orchard or by the lake. Kay said she ought to go home, but her car would not start. CT and Annie tried theirs and they would not start either. Art could not get his car to even turn over. They all stood discussing what might be the problem with them all. Kay and CT tried to connect to the internet to call out the RAC, but there was no signal. CT explained that the heat can do strange things to electrical things, so they all had to accept they would have to wait till the cooler morning to drive home. Art made a green leaf and bean salad, garlic mushroom pasta from the fridge and cold new potatoes with mixed herbs from the garden. He also cooked Mexican chicken on the stone barbecue he had made, which still stood on the patio. They tried the television again, but like the cars, it was not interested in firing up. They discussed the part of the festival they had managed to see. It had looked and sounded fantastic. Thousands of people jumping and singing. The aerial view had shown the true extent of the whole crowd and it was immense. Double the amount of people that could be seated in Wembley stadium, all united by the musician in charge on the stage. All united in their love of the loud, outdoor festivalling. All united as one tribe, one family. For the love of the music.

Dylan and Ed cut the lights on the whole arena and darkness fell. The sun had set and a hushed silence hung over the pumped-up crowd. This is what they had waited for, and the time had come.

'Right guys, here we go. We're still expecting to peak at 11:15, but be ready to extend or cut short that time. Ready stage left? You ready with the drummers? Okay, here we go. 'Sweeeeeet Home Alabama yowwwwwww,' sang Dylan into his headphone's microphone. He checked his levels while he queued the next pyrotechnic and lighting sequences and got the green lights from the geologists, mathematicians and scientists below him in the tower.

'Ed?' Dylan said softly, turning to his friend.

'Dylan?'

'I love you, brother!'

'Dickhead!' Ed replied laughing. They looked at each other until Ed put a hand out to Dylan. They shook heartily. 'I love you right back brother!' They had another man hug, toasted themselves and chinked cider bottles together. 'If you're ready, Sir. The fat lady is about to sing!'

'The queen you mean?'

'What?'

'The queen... Mercury... from Queen. 'It's not all over till the old Queen sings!" said Dylan, knowing he had pushed one of his comments just a little too far. But after all, there was no one to hear him. He had checked his microphone was off this time!

The final set started in darkness, except for over ten drummers drumming together. There were some African drums, orchestral drums and three sets of rock drums. As the beat increased in tempo and volume, Ed and Dylan checked the levels. The full system was now all primed and ready to go. The bass speakers had been turned up, the copper stakes around the fence were connected again and over 50 musicians were ready to perform the show of their lives. Uncle Sam had kept them all happy and they had all complimented him on their comfortable quarters and entertainment. They were impressed with how efficiently everything had run and had thoroughly enjoyed themselves. The viewing gallery at the side of the stage had been full for every performance, as artists watched their friends and idols.

The drummers reached a heart-bursting crescendo as the crowd were jumping in time to the rhythm, each with either an arm in the air or over the shoulder of their neighbour, whether they knew them or not. The drummers came to a culmination, all the while just a few spotlights lighting the stage. The bass drums reverberated from the ground, like a sleeping grumbling animal. The higher pitched African drums danced and played at head height, and the symbols and high pitched sounds dashed and clashed above in the air. As the last drum beat was played, a very distinctive guitar rift twanged out over the dying drums. The stage lit up with fireworks that showered down from along the top, and thousands of white sparks cascaded down the front of the stage, enhanced by strobe lights that were so powerful the whole arena was lit up. Green, red and blue lasers shot out from the very top of the pyramid, dancing around the surrounding campsites, hills and sky as *Sweet Home Alabama* started to play. Lynyrd Skynyrd led the intro to the old time classic, as once again the crowd sang along.

The final set continued with Nirvana's *Smells Like Teen Spirit,* Faithless' *Insomnia,* The Verve's *Bittersweet Symphony* and a selection of other tracks by The Stone Roses, Arctic Monkeys, Foofighters and Deep Purple.

'Okay, we are good for go. Phone communications have been activated, just need the oomph from the crowd to power it. I repeat. All teams, all crews, we are good for go!' said Dylan, as Ed passed him the latest statistics from the scientists in the underground room. 'And people, let's not fuck this one up, ay? Good luck brothers. This is your fifteen-minute countdown, prepare the extra boosters. Love you, peace out!'

'Peace out?' quizzed Ed.

'Yeah, why not?'

''Cause we can, I guess!'

Dylan and Ed checked the statistics they had been passed by the geologists and mathematicians, and compared them to their sound level records.

'The show must go on!' Dylan joked, holding out a pretend sword pointed towards the stage.

'How do you do it, dude?' Ed asked sincerely, 'all that is about to happen, you are so spirited. We might all die in fifteen minutes!'

'Yeah, we might, so why be dump-arse miserable for your last moments on earth? Fuck all we can do about it, so why worry about it!'

'You're a fucking genius!'

'Thanks, you're not so bad yourself. Stage right, prepare. Starting final intro. Make sure Brian is ready for front central. Choir. Orchestra. Check for go. Fourteen minutes people. Ed, have faith in us. This is a good thing. It can't fail,' said Dylan, holding two conversations at once.

Chapter Forty-two

23:07 Thursday night, Glastonbury Festival, 2012

The looming shape of the Pyramid Stage stood silent and black as the fireworks and lasers entertained the crowd. The speakers around the edge of the arena played whooshing, wind noises, and such was the perfection of each speaker's location, the sound echoed around the festivallers, bouncing from speaker to speaker. In the sound tower, Dylan and Ed checked all departments for a 'clear'. White lasers danced above the heads of the crowd and high pressured jets of smoke were jettisoned from the top of the stage as dry ice smoke slithered off the stage and into the front of the crowd. A solitary spotlight shone onto a world-famous guitarist, who played the first few bars of a very well known song. The crowd went wild, cheering and clapping. The spotlight faded out as another guitarist was illuminated on a different part of the stage. Again, the crowd cheered its approval at the intro he was playing. In total, six different guitarists played a popular intro, as the white laser danced over their heads. The choir had started singing long harmonies, lifting the excitement and anticipation with the power of their voices. As the crowd watched, they experienced adrenalin rushes, hearts skipped a beat and emotions started to grow. All of their senses were at a peak of exhilaration. The darkness was mystical as each spotlight went off and on, teasing the crowd as to what the last song would be.

Around the balcony of the stage twenty white spotlights lit up the faces of some of the choir, as they broke into song, with a bright, narrow spotlight shining onto a white grand piano, with Ray Manzarek behind the keys.

> Is this the real life?
> Is this just fantasy?
> Caught in a landslide,

No escape from reality.
Open your eyes,
Look up to the skies and see.

Coco and about twenty per cent of the audience just realised that there was something going on. Something big. Those words, written all the way back in 1975 could quite easily describe how she felt right now. She looked up at the night sky above her. There was a heat haze shimmering above the site. The singers' voices echoed around the speakers, all of which were now in use.

Anyway the wind blows doesn't really matter to me, to me.

As the voices of the choir rose and the tempo of the piano increased everyone was singing along. Although it was stifling hot, cold shivers ran up people's arms, causing goosebumps. Their hands became cold and sweaty as their minds raced to try and take in all of the spectacle. The song built up and faded away again, as the whole crowd swayed together. Most of them didn't even realise they were doing it; it was the emotion of the performance taking over their ears and eyes. Every nerve ending tingled and prickled. The song built, until the crashing symbols introduced the rest of the choir and the strings of the orchestra joined in. The whole crowd sang with all of their hearts, some with tears splashing down their cheeks.

Mama, ooh,
Didn't mean to make you cry,
If I'm not back this time tomorrow,
Carry on, carry on, as if nothing really matters.

On the stage over 50 musicians both in the flesh and holograms began to be lit up, as the song built, playing guitars, drums and John Lydon holding a triangle.

Too late, my time has come,
Sent shivers down my spine,
Body's aching all the time.
Goodbye, everybody, I've got to go
Gotta leave you all behind and face the truth.

Seven of the best guitarists in the world got ready to play, standing quietly and patiently as the rest of the stage got ready. The same three drummers sat in a pyramid formation, with the orchestra behind them and the choir around the sides above them. Bassists stood in a row opposite the guitarists.

The most respected vocalists in the world stood amidst the choir, lit up by coloured spotlight. As the song got to the first distinguishable guitar solo, Brian May appeared in the centre of the stage to play his solo.

'Here we go. Thirty seconds and counting. On the 4:20 mark. Love you guys. Good Luck!' Dylan told everyone.

> Mama, ooh,
> I don't wanna die
> I sometimes wish I'd never been born at all

Slash and Paul Weller walked up to either side of Brian, and joined in as they had practised. The sound zapped around the arena, the high-pitched guitar screaming as loud as it could, as the choir sang for their lives, helped by the audience.

> I see a little silhouetto of a man,
> Scaramouche, Scaramouche, will you do the Fandango?
> Thunderbolt and lightning,
> Very very frightening me
> Galileo... Galileo

And then the note dropped and the whole crowd was beside themselves.

> Easy come, easy go, will you let me go
> Bismillah! No, we will not let you go.

Each line was then sung by just a few singers, but they were fed through the sound system at different places, so they bounced all around the arena. The effect was mind-blowing, as if the whole crowd had become part of the song. They were the energy propelling the vocalists to sound from different speakers, the energy that projected the fireworks into the illuminated sky. But most of all, they came through, and provided the energy to keep the site safe. They were indeed, The Chosen Ones. They felt the piano notes in their veins, the drum beats in their hearts and the guitars exploding in their muscles.

> Beelzebub has a devil put aside for me...

'Count you in guys...Three. Two. One. Go!'

> FOR ME, FOR ME
> FOR ME...

Exactly on queue seven guitarists, three drummers and five bassists hammered the notes out, along with all of the choir and orchestra.

A huge blast of fireworks and lasers shot from the top of the pyramid. Fountains of fireworks encrusted the front of the stage until it sparkled like it was diamond-studded. The volume of the music was unbelievably phenomenal. The ground rumbled and shuddered as the air pressure changed. A 200 foot spout of water shot out from behind the Pyramid, sending a plumb of water shooting up into the sky forming a protective umbrella of energy. As people sang along, swaying and watching, they saw a dome of fireworks curved above their heads. Millions of orange balls of fire with bright blue sparkling tails buzzed about, whizzing and exploding into tiny white stars. The spectacle was outstanding. The full choir and orchestra accompanied the musicians as fireworks exploded filling the sky for as far as the eye could see, with tiny balls of fire.

The choir rose in volume and determination, as the following lead vocals echoed from different parts of the arena. The crowd shouted back the lyrics, with the girls automatically singing the high notes and the guys singing the lower ones. As the song increased in momentum, the energy from the crowd sent sound and energy waves deep into the ground. The pure water spring gushed out of the uncovered well situated behind the Pyramid Stage with such force, the surrounding four miles radius from the farm became protected from the heat incineration. The sky looked like a space invader war, as electricity and heat was repelled from above the site. The purity of the water filled with oxygen of the purest form provided a protective shield, as radioactive rays scolded the Earth. The festivallers saw the greatest light show on earth, with water mixing with heat to cause plumes of steam and smoke. The clouds became multicoloured, as lasers and fireworks passed through them. It was a cosmic experience, as if the universe had exploded above them.

The sound control tower tweaked a few knobs and adjusted the levels, making sure every musician could be heard separately from the whole group. The energy Dylan saw as he concentrated on the timing of the event was breathtaking; 180,000 people singing word perfect as the emotional composition, choirs and orchestra created the most powerful sound any group of humans had ever heard. The musicians gave it their all, keeping in perfect time, making their instruments scream and plead for mercy, as the sounds were torn from their guts. The passion in the playing carried the emotions of the crowd. The lighting moved from singer to singer, as different artists sang different lines.

Just gotta get out, just gotta get right outta here,

As the song started to slow down, huge gusts of wind swept down the valley. Loose rubbish was sucked from the ground as storm force winds could be heard whistling around the site, as if they were in the eye of a hurricane. The air pressure dropped again, and some people's ears popped. With the wind came cool mist, falling from the sky as the aftermath of a cup-match between the heat and the pure water.

Anyway the wind blows...

The music faded out softly, lights gradually went out and the stage once again became silent and asleep. The effects continued for a few more minutes, as the song ended quicker than the solar storm and winds did. The protected dome sky still flashed with orange balls of fire and the electric blue trails continued to zap around above their heads. All of the effects they were watching after the song had ended were nature cleansing itself with a bit of cosmic help. Static sparks randomly shot from the top of the pyramid and descended back to earth following the contours of the dome as the power of the energy from the crowd continued to gush water into the air.

Chapter Forty-three

Thursday night, 21st June 2012, The Earth

As the heat fuelled by gamma rays hurtled to earth, any space debris was immediately incinerated. Huge, spent space rocket fuel tanks disintegrated quicker than ice in boiling water. The rays slowed down slightly as they entered the earth's atmosphere, but ripped through planes that had managed to stay in the air after their flight circuits had shorted. Drawn to cities and anywhere where there was a large electrical current, the rays descended. Cars, buses and trains slowed to a halt, causing numerous traffic accidents. The tops of tall buildings seemed to disappear, as they were incinerated before the lower levels crumbled in on themselves before disappearing into dust. Electricity cables carried a deadly current through every electrical appliance, even those in basements, the underground train systems and power lines. There was not enough time for panic. People saw the burst of heat distort glass and bend steel before they could realised what was happening. It was all over for them.

Huge thriving cities were reduced to broken tarmac roads, with incomplete bridges and flyovers totally destroyed except for a few random pillars. Nothing else was left. After the fierce winds picked up anything that was not strongly rooted to the ground, what was left looked clean and fresh. The winds took the heat with it, leaving clean air totally devoid of pollution. Once the howling whip-lashing winds had subsided, cool breezes swam through grassy parklands, travelling freely whereas before huge buildings had scarred the landscape. And there was silence. There was total silence with the exception of a gentle whooshing of the subsiding breeze. But there was no one around to hear the silence. There was no rubbish, dead leaves or even dust, just footprints of buildings standing a few inches off the ground.

In remote areas, citizens watched across familiar views as an oven-hot gust of wind barraged across the countryside, with electrical pylons exploding before disappearing. Planes that nearly made emergency landings exploded as they were attacked by the heat rays before disintegrating and disappearing. The heat caused vast amounts of snow to melt and great ice shelves broke away from frozen landscapes. Isolated alpine residents watched as hundreds of tonnes of snow rocketed down mountainsides with a deafening roar, flattening anything in its path. The whole planet was enveloped in the deadly heat and virtually no one was spared.

Animals that survived falling masonry and carnage, in most, showed no fear. Flight animals ran in hap-hazard directions, until they stopped, observed and listened, before darting off again. Horses spooked as the winds wrapped around their legs, tails held high with pricked ears and alert eyes; cats smugly took refuge in the tops of trees just out of reach of branches full of birds. Although their new found freedom would be liberating, there was the issue of having to learn to fend for themselves. Without domestication they would have to deal with escaped zoo animals that would have to hunt, and those that hunted for food not native to the British Isles would soon perish, or would have to learn to adapt. As the water in the underground stream was brought to life by the energy of the crowd at the festival, it broke free of the ground and formed anything from a small puddle to gushing fountains. It flooded down the tunnel at Molay Barn, collecting in huge water tanks under the tunnel, as it gushed over the metal grill that ran its length, not stealing the seeds stored in the secure room as it passed. Four fountains of water penetrated the ground in the meadow, the lake and two in the orchard at Railway Cottage. The floodwaters, caused by the heat melting snow and ice instantaneously, caused sea levels to rise by various degrees around the world. The pure water ice released was a diluted version of the water in the underground stream. The ice formed thousands of years ago, was from water nearly as pure and clean as the spring water. It eventually made its way to the seas, gradually integrating with the salt waters of the world's oceans, cleansing it.

On Lincolnshire Sands, after a short, sudden howling wind had skimmed over the flat countryside, the tide suddenly started to rise. Drayton stood and watched as the sands, still wet from the tide going out, suddenly started to disappear as the sea rose. There had been a few kitchen items that had been in use which blew up, and a few water pipes had burst, sending plumes of cooling mist high into the air. Luckily no one got hurt as no one was sleeping in the house. Drayton had made some bed hammocks and hung them from the trees at the edge of the lodge, overlooking the sea for the women and children while it was still so hot. They had all been woken by the kitchen explosions and watched as a heat-haze distorted moon had lit the sands as the waters returned.

At Cauldy Island on the south coast of Wales, the monks watched as water flowed over the old well in the Monastery garden. They had been woken by a massive explosion as a power station ten miles away on the coast exploded. Huge flames lit the sky with an angry orange but quickly disappeared as a strong wind wrapped itself around the little island. There was a little fire just outside their compound as an electrical fire started in a junction box. The wooden fence had started to smoulder, so they went to the well to get water to dowse it. However, they could not believe what they saw, as water bubbled and spilled over the top of the well like an overflowing bath tub. It was the same at Holy Island. Elizabeth and Victoria were woken as the island rumbled and vibrated. Pottery fell off tables and they heard a few pictures fall off the walls, above a distant roaring sound. They were asleep in their makeshift cellar bedrooms, soundly asleep as the rest of the planet roasted. As the vibrations increased, a high-pitched whirring sound grew to deafening levels, until there was the sound of giant pipes clanging together. Thinking it was an earthquake, they ran upstairs with Baby Adrian and out of the stone front door. As they did, a massive plume of water gushed out from the weathervane, shooting high into the sky. The air pressure changed, and they noticed a strong wind started to batter the little castle. They had trouble closing the heavy front door, as they went back into the house. They could hear the wind howling, as it came undeterred from the sea gathering force, and the rushing water powerfully surged up the metal pipe in the cellar by the seed draws, from the underground stream.

Epilogue

The sun slowly rose, as it had done for millions of years. The beautiful, clear, bright skies displayed a changing array of rainbow colours, as the dark blues and purples were pushed away by the brightness of the new day. Every bird was singing in the hedgerows, woodlands and former gardens. Rabbits nibbled on grass, and farm animals roamed freely where all man-made fences had been destroyed. The fresh new morning was cool and the air was scented with the smell of fresh rain. Unpolluted rivers and streams carried on doing what they had always done, shaping the countryside and offering food and drink for wildlife. There were fewer shadows than previous sunrises, with nothing to block the life-giving light.

Dylan and Ed sat in the Stone Circle at Glastonbury and watched the sun come up. It was one of the 'must see' things to do at the festival. Peter rabbit hopped around the luscious wildflowers. The whole hill had been closed off, as no one was sure if the stones would be part of the event, and they did not want them disturbed. Peter started to dig a little hole, the first time Dylan had seen the rabbit dig a proper hole. He kicked up dry earth as his little feet quickly worked. It was good to be out of the pet carrier he had been in for the last few days.

The valley full of sleeping revellers had a thick mist shrouding it. Hours would pass before the first few started to wake. *Then the shit is really going to hit the fan!* thought Dylan. In the preparations for the event, no one had properly stopped to think about the second stage, relocating everyone, the chaos, stress, drama and anguish that they were going to have to help with over the next few days was going to be harrowing. Everyone had been focused on making sure the event was a success, but no one had really stopped to consider what would happen next. Rik was now in charge with the massive task of helping everyone. Dylan got his phone out of his fleece pocket. It felt strange to be wearing a jumper again. There was no signal, and his battery was nearly dead. There was an unopened text message, sent at 11:07 last night. He read the message, and a single tear trickled down his suntanned cheek.

'The text system worked. Robert will be pleased, dude!' he sniffed, looking at Ed, knowing he would feel exactly the same in a moment or two, as they both stared at two of the few LED screens left in the world.

The valley turned a golden yellow as the sun broke over the horizon. The air was so clean, Dylan and Ed could actually watch the nighttime shadow shrink away, to be replaced by a warm golden glow greeted by hundreds of birds singing a welcome to it. It was as if they had put on their first pair of glasses, increasing their eyesight so everything became sharp and clear. From their viewpoint, everything looked as it always had done, except for the first time in months a cool gentle wind made all of the flags dance and ripple as they towered above the early morning mist. The power of the stream at the event had been immense. There were no signs of destruction, which got them to wonder if anything had actually happened beyond the boundaries of the event. *Fuck paying all those bills off!* thought Ed, as he too wondered what the outside world was like.

Rev and John woke when the sun touched their tents and instantly the change in temperature woke them. It had been cool for a few hours and they had not packed for cold weather. They lay in a broken sleep, not wanting to get up yet. The only sound they could hear was the sound of the gentle wind catching flags and saggy tents that flapped and tugged at their restraints. They had attended a massive music festival without any alcohol or drugs, both their worst best friends. Everyone else had been drunk-as-skunks, but they had battled their demons and won, by just drinking juice they had brought with them, and buying the occasional can of pop. It was amazing what fun they'd had, and the emotions they had felt. They would be the first to wake at the festival whilst everyone else slept off their herbal sleeping agents.

William stood on the Tor looking east as the sun rose. They had done it. Everything that the Templars, Hopi, the Chinese and Mayans had started all those centuries ago, he, Sir William George Arthur Idol had accomplished what he had been destined to finish. He knew his seeds would be safe, which would be needed to grow for building materials and fabrics. Hemp would now be the staple crop grown everywhere by everyone and cutting down trees would be controlled. The seed collection from Holy Island would be essential to make herbal remedies and for cooking. A cool gust of wind flapped the bottom of his long trench coat and bare legs in shorts. He clutched his phone in his hand, having just read the fake texts from his daughters' phones, watching as smoke billowed from spent campfires and the swirling mist thinned in the valley. The tranquillity of the site was reminiscent of an Bronze Age village, little huts congregating around a source of water. There were no man-made sounds. No vehicle noises, sirens, or any artificial sound. *The third biggest city in Southern England is now the only city in England,* he thought.

He turned and started to walk down the path that ran around the mound. There was much to do. The earth had cleansed itself. It was now his job to make sure the same mistakes were not made again. *You can do anything if you put your mind to it!* he thought. *Bet my daughters would have been pissed when I told them I've sold the lake,* he thought sadly, throwing his phone over his shoulder as he started the long walk back to the festival.

Five minutes later, he retraced his steps and picked it up again. *Bloody litter louts!* he thought, putting it back in his pocket, looking down the valley away from the encampment of sleeping survivors. There were no signs of civilization; no pylons scarring the landscape, no church spires opulently standing erect amidst a little village or town, and most significantly of all, there were no vehicles polluting the atmosphere. As he walked back to the site to find Dylan and Ed, he chuckled to himself as he thought about the success of the event, *of course it was going to work. It's elementary!*